America the Last Stand

By Andrew Gouriet

Chapter 1

"Father, wake up". Arthur said in a concerned voice.

Charles was holding Rebecca tight, and the warmth of her body kept him asleep. He didn't stir when Arthur spoke to him.
Arthur then began to rock him by putting his hand on his shoulder and moving it backwards and forwards.

"There's something outside my window".

Charles reluctantly began to open his right eye. "Arthur, it's probably just a wild animal."

Arthur just stood there with a determined look. Charles begrudgingly forced himself out of his warm bed, trying not to wake Rebecca as he did so. He put his hand on Arthur's shoulder. He had grown so much since they had landed in America. He would soon be fourteen and wanted to explore more of the country they now lived in.

Charles bent down and pulled a small wooden box from under the bed. It had two engraved letters on the top, which read 'CH'. He turned the catch and slowly opened it. Their sitting snug inside was his Enfield revolver. Alongside it were several bullets. He took out the revolver, which was cold to the touch, and carefully loaded the bullets into the cylinder. Arthur watched with keen eyes. He had started to learn how to shoot over the past year and was keen on getting his own revolver, which had not been allowed yet by his mother or father.

Charles slowly stood up and whispered to Arthur to follow him. They moved down the corridor and stopped by Emily's room; she was curled up into a small ball on her bed. Charles walked in and looked out of her window. He saw nothing; as he left her room, he pulled up her rose-embroidered sheets to cover her torso. Arthur followed him further down the corridor towards his room.

Charles waited outside the door momentarily and put his index finger to his lips. His nostrils hadn't quite gotten used to the wood cabin's different aromas and sweet smells. He paused a second to breathe in, slowly pushed the door open and raised his revolver.

Arthur's room was sparse; his bed was tucked against the wall on the right-hand side, and a wardrobe and a small chair were beside it. He had some unused toys poking out of a wooden chest, Arthur was young, but his innocence had been lost over the past few years.

Charles moved towards the window, pulling back the sheet used to help keep out the chill on cool evenings. He slowly leaned against the glass of the cabin window, his forehead embracing the coldness as he did so. Charles's eyes danced side to side to look for movement in the darkness; the moon poked out between intermittent clouds and gave him just enough light to survey the landscape. Sure enough, there was something out there.

"Arthur, follow me." He led him out of the room and into the living quarters of the cabin. The embers in the fireplace had long since gone out, and it felt colder than Arthur remembered from earlier in the evening. Charles went to a cabinet in the room's far left-hand corner. He searched around for a small box which had been kept on a side table parallel to the cabinet. When he found it, he opened it and took out a solid brass key to unlock the cabinet. Inside were several rifles and ammunition boxes. Charles went straight for a Winchester rifle and brought out the ammunition box. The sound of the bullets going into the rifle echoed around the room; once it was loaded with ten rounds, he then handed the rifle to Arthur, "Stay close, son, and do not fire unless I say so."

They made their way to the front porch. Charles looked at his son; he was proud of him, but scared of what lay ahead for them in this changing world. He put a hand on his shoulder and nodded towards the door. As quietly as he could, the bolts were slowly drawn back. Charles brought his revolver up to shoulder height and leaned on the door, which caused it to creak a little as the heavy wooden frame began to move on its joints.

A rustling noise could be heard from one of the paddocks to the side of the barn. An old sound familiar to Arthur and his father crept towards them; its breathless groans and gnashing of teeth hung in the air. Charles looked at Arthur as the clouds moved through the sky and told him to stay close.

They both took light strides over the veranda and down the steps leading to the front of the cabin.

There was an open space of trodden soil, which ventured into a track away from the cabin. You would have to navigate that before getting to the paddocks. All around the farm were Colorado blue spruce trees mixed in with quaking aspen and a large old Elm tree standing proudly beside the barn. Arthur brought the rifle up with the barrel pointing upwards. He got a glance over from his father, who made sure the rifle was not pointing at him.

The crunching and tearing noises grew louder the closer they got to the paddocks. Soon, their eyes fell upon a fallen horse. It was trying in vain to raise itself, but to little avail. Its body was covered in flesh-eaters. These creatures were now drawn to this distressed animal. Some of them had emancipated bodies with rotting flesh hanging from their bones; others almost seemed normal and probably had only recently turned.

Their appearances were softer, but they had one thing in common: the same unquenchable hunger. Charles carefully opened the gate to the paddock and looked at Arthur.

He brought his left hand and index finger to his lips again. Six flesh eaters were feeding on the horse, possibly two or three emerging from the darkness. Charles was going to shoot the flesh-eaters clamped on the horse and then target the others.

Arthur followed his father as he raised his pistol. They both picked their targets and slowly squeezed the triggers. Charles hit a flesh-eater directly in front of him. Its scraggy grey hair stuck to each side of his cheeks, hiding what was left of his features since he became infected. The bullet penetrated through the head and was enough to end its cruel existence. Arthur hit a woman in the shoulder; she turned, showing the skin around her eyes and nose and peeled away; she shuddered back from the bullet hitting her but then began to rise from the horse and make her way towards Arthur. Charles started to open fire on the other flesh-eaters around the horse.

The woman whom Arthur shot was now stumbling towards him. He cautiously looked at his father to check if he had seen his missed shot and whether he would finish off the flesh-eater now bearing down on them. Charles was conscious of only having six bullets in the revolver. He had killed five around the horse and was aware of the women closing in.

"Arthur, aim again", Charles spoke calmly but authoritatively about what he should do.

Arthur raised his Winchester rifle and cocked it, expelling the previous round and loading another bullet into the chamber. As the female flesh-eater got closer and closer to him, Charles raised his revolver to shoot her. His son stood still for a second, almost caught in this creature's gaze as it slowly made its way to its intended victim. He did not miss this time; the bullet smacked into the flesh-eater's head, shattering bone and flesh as it mercilessly tore through her skull.

The gunshots had awoken Rebecca. She could see that Charles was no longer lying beside her in the bed, making her heart skip a little quicker. Without thinking, she quickly went to check on Emily and Arthur. Arthur was also missing from his bed, but Emily was fast asleep in her room. She gently woke her up and asked Emily to follow her to the rifle cabinet. The key was sitting snugly in the cabinet door, so she turned it and pulled it open. Rebecca went straight for a Winchester rifle. Emily was told to stay behind her as they made their way to the entrance to the log cabin.

"Arthur, we must get back to the log cabin." Charles could see that the flesh-eater's numbers were more significant than he first thought.

Arthur had given his rifle to his father and was holding the Enfield revolver with one bullet in it. They started to back out of the paddock. The groans and gnashing of teeth filled the airwaves around them. The shadows were moving; Charles thought they could now face thirty to forty flesh-eaters. He tried to think of a quick plan as the dead moved closer to them.

"Arthur, I will lure them away; you must get to the cabin and help your mother and sister."
"I will not leave you," Arthur said, looking concerned.
"We have no choice."

Charles then approached the Elm tree, which caused several flesh-eaters to change direction and follow him. "Come on, you fools", Charles shouted to entice more. Arthur shook his head but saw his father's defiant expression urging him to run.

Rebecca came onto the veranda to see what was happening and told Emily to stay by the door until she was told to come out. Arthur had begun running back to the log cabin; he had two flesh-eaters following him. Rebecca could see Charles was starting to be surrounded by the old Elm tree, and she raised her rifle.

Her first shot was accurate, and a flesh-eater fell about six metres from Charles. He looked across in her direction, concerned about how many flesh-eaters there were and whether his family could escape this attack. He then shot a younger-looking flesh-eater boy who was missing his arms.

Rebecca's second shot hit a female flesh-eater in the throat; blood ran out from the wound, but she kept on coming. Half her scalp was missing, possibly from being attacked by the dead before. Then, only to die later on from the infection, which is followed by a bite.

Charles knew he was running out of bullets, but he could see Arthur following his instructions and going to the cabin. The first part of his plan was working, and the second part was to stay alive and try to help his family.

Arthur stumbled a couple of times onto the dirt before reaching the steps to the cabin. His mother was reloading her rifle as the two flesh-eaters that were following him began to close in. "We must help Father," Arthur said with a strong, confident voice.

"I know, we will do everything we can." With that, Rebecca shot twice, killing the two creatures that were coming their way.

Emily was allowed to bring bullets to her mother and then return to stand behind the log cabin door, which was left slightly ajar so she could see what was happening. Her heart was racing, and she was concerned for all of them.

Charles unloaded his last bullet into a badly decomposing flesh-eater who was closest to him. He then used his rifle to help push back the oncoming creatures. He could hear Rebecca telling him to keep moving back to them.

Arthur had taken bullets from the cabinet and was frantically loading his revolver before shooting at the flesh-eaters with his mother.

There were another fifteen to twenty behind Charles; he tried to swing at three in front of him.

Their numbers were too great, and he faced a battle not to be surrounded. A flesh-eater grabbed his shoulder, but before he could react, a whoosh of air passed his head, and an arrow stuck in this foul creature's skull.

The groans and gnashing of teeth stopped abruptly; there were now yelps and war cries. Emerging out of the trees and darkness were Native American Indians. Some were on horseback, firing arrows as they rode; others were on foot. Their impact was pivotal; the flesh-eaters began moving towards different targets, removing their effectiveness en masse.

There were maybe twenty Indians in this attack, and their effectiveness was brutal. They soon managed to finish off the attacking herd of fresh-eaters, and with the help of Rebecca and Arthur, Charles was helped back into safety. He hugged both of them and watched the Indians swoop around and check the paddocks and surrounding woods. Rebecca went back to the Cabin and collected Emily to take her to join them. She had closed the cabin door when Rebecca and Arthur moved on from the cabin and waited for instructions to open it again when it was safe.

Whilst this unfolded, a small group of riders slowly approached them. Their horses were in good condition and had painted symbols on their necks and hind legs.

Charles stood there and lowered his rifle, as did Rebecca and Arthur. The three riders stopped short of them, and the middle rider came forward. He looked young, with long, flowing black hair and a muscular figure.

"My name is Hosah" His English was quite clear.
"In your language, it means 'Young Crow.'"
Charles stepped forward, introduced himself and his family, and expressed his gratitude for their help.

Young Crow moved his horse a little closer. "We are part of the Arapaho tribe." He looked to the ground as if bitter and angry. We are being moved to a new reservation." He paused again. "We saw these demons approaching your farm. We followed them, then attacked."

Charles asked if they had enough food and clothing. He knew they had some supplies they could give as small offerings of thanks for the help the Arapaho gave. Hosah nodded and said they could do with some supplies and would return in a week or so. He turned his horse and led the other warriors back into the darkness.

The British army was now spread out over America. Like many of the European forces, they were falling under the control of the United States of America government. It was struggling to cope with the amount of new arrivals, and the arguments about who would feed them and how it would all work were ongoing. The other major problem was the arrival of the flesh-eaters. Some came over with the refugees that had been bitten; others had been transported by Nazar's priests and landed on American shores. Sightings of long limbs were also reported.

Captain Hayward's Engineers had been stationed with their families not far from the farm. The Engineers were awaiting a new commander, and there were rumours that it was only a matter of time before Captain Hayward would be commissioned to a Major. The official line of command had been affected since Great Britain had fallen. Naturally, they were all under the laws of the United States of America. Some of the British high command were allowed to operate with the American forces, as were the other nations, but this was still tightly controlled by the American government. The plans were being laid to invade Great Britain and Europe and then repatriate its citizens to their natural homes. Still, there were grave concerns that Nazar was coming for America now, and whilst the talk was of bringing the war back to him, the reality was that he was readily planning his own invasion.

Charles took his family back inside. They shut the door behind them, leaving the clearing up of the flesh-eaters' bodies until the morning. He would visit the Engineers in the morning and inform the chain of command about this latest attack. Emily went to sleep between Rebecca and Charles, and Arthur returned to his room and made sure the window was shut.

Charles laid his head on his pillow and tried to get some sleep.

Chapter 2

The next morning was a glorious one. Spring was taking hold, and freshness crept in once the windows were open. Charles had walked around the farm to check that no more flesh-eaters were lurking in the shadows. Rebecca had asked him to put a fence around the side of the cabin so the children could at least play outside and be safe from a flesh-eater walking up on them. He agreed and said he would bring help from the camp where the other Engineers were stationed. They had plans to build a good number of cabins around the farm. The Engineers knew that safety in numbers was a crucial part of their survival.

Rebecca came with a coffee to where Charles was kneeling while loading his kitbag. She had been thinking about her brother and was concerned for her husband and children. "I miss him, my love." Tears ran down her cheeks.

"I know you do; we all do." He got up and slowly took her into his arms. James died fighting for his country. He would have given everything until the end. He wanted his family and you to be safe, and that is what he gave his life for." Charles held Rebecca in his arms. He felt her heart beating a little faster. She knew they would have to continue in this new world, but she worried for her family. "Promise me you will stay safe."

Charles knew the attack had brought back the reality of what was lurking out there. He also knew Rebecca was a strong woman and a good fighter, but the fear ate away at them all.

"I will do my best, my love."

Charles's and Rebecca's parents were with his brother near the Canadian border in Oregon. He had asked if she wanted to take the children there to be closer to them, but she had rebuffed that and said she would help him and the other engineer families here in Colorado.

Before Charles set off, he told Arthur to look out for Emily and his mother, kissing each of them on the head. Rebecca came over to him as he saddled his horse. She gently rubbed his arm. "Take care," she said, resting her head against his back and holding him. He slowly turned around, taking her into his arms. He looked at her face, her blue eyes glowing more in the spring sunshine and the softness of her skin. Her lips came closer to his, and he began to kiss her. A cough broke their embrace after thirty seconds or more. Arthur was shaking his head, and Emily was giggling. Charles smiled at them, "If I can't kiss your mother, who can I kiss?" Emily lifted her dirty teddy bear with a big grin on her face.

He smiled and hoisted himself into his saddle. "Stay safe, children; I love you all." His eyes looked at Rebecca's as he turned his horse

.

"God's speed, Charles." She said this, trying to stay strong in front of the children.

He nodded his head and kicked the horse on. Charles knew that having more people around his family would help them feel safer. The feeling in his heart was one of worry. There was nowhere left for them to run to. America was their last stand. He was one of the unfortunate few who had met Nazar face to face and realised this demon would take some stopping on a battlefield; the trouble was, how would they stop an army as large as his?

The hours passed as he gently moved along the meandering dirt tracks. The sun's warmth was pleasant, and he stroked the horse's mane as they both moved towards Golds Hill. The dust kicked up from the track as the occasional gust of wind whooshed around them. All along their route, the wind lifted the prairie grass up and down, making it look like someone was walking through it, even though no one was there. Charles's eyes scanned the horizon, taking in the odd, lonely figure going about their business. He also started to look at the way they walked. Did the figure in the distance have a purpose? Was it going at an average speed, or did it carry the hallmarks of something more sinister?

He kept riding, passing the odd farm on the way. He was looking forward to seeing some familiar faces and telling them it was time for them to move closer to the cabin and farm.

On the outskirts of the town, a lone rider approached him at a steady pace. He had a rifle drawn across his legs and looked agitated. The closer he came, Charles could see he was from Golds Hill town.

The cowboy was called Texas; he was almost as large as the state, not in an overweight way but in sheer muscle. He was nearly six feet five inches and had shoulders that could carry

a calf. This rancher and prospector had spent many years herding cattle and digging for gold. He was also working for the American army as a scout.

"Captain Hayward". A smile came over his face as he said this. He brought his horse alongside Charles's horse. "Everything all right?"

"Good to see you, Texas; we've encountered a small herd of flesh-eaters."

"Was anyone bitten?"

"By the luck of God, no," Charles said, shaking his head.

Texas started to turn his horse and led the captain along the track towards the town. As they trundled along, Charles gazed over the terrain; dry prairie grass covered most of the ground around them, spread over rocky hills and under the pine trees. With the mountains in the background, he enjoyed this new world but also yearned for the green fields of England.

Outside the town, they had erected watch towers. Captain Hayward could see figures moving from side to side. Their rifles were raised, but not in an aggressive way. The British forces had been camped with a small detachment of American soldiers. Their government was in consent discussions on how to utilise the soldiers who were now living in their country. They did not want to arm all the foreign forces due to the fear of a civil war or a grab for power. The European and British troops insisted on preparing for Nazar, but many felt the American government did not see the danger; it was not pressing at the forefront of their political agenda. The arrival of flesh-eaters and long limbs had made them question their judgement, but also confused the issue regarding tackling this abomination.

The focus had switched to dealing with this sickness and its creatures. Some had even questioned whether the Europeans had caused the disease. They had brought it over, as many originally came with concealed bites. When they died, they changed. Nazar's tactics of landing flesh-eaters and long limbs had also been working.

Captain Hayward rode past the watch towers and into the town. Texas led the way. They dismounted their horses by the staff quarters and tethered them to fence posts outside. Charles noticed children playing in the fields to the side of the fort. There were soldiers mounted and stationed around them on foot. Women were washing clothes at a nearby well. He looked to see if he could see any of his Engineers, but none came into sight.

"Follow me, Captain". Texas led them inside.

The cabin smelled of freshly cut timber. Two American soldiers, both corporals, sat at two desks. They were busy scribbling away and did not notice Texas standing there with Captain Hayward.

"Gentlemen", Texas was to the point.

One of the officers stood up and offered his hand. "Corporal Collins". He looked very young and had grown a beard, probably to disguise this. The problem was that his beard was too wispy and did not help hide his youthful appearance. His brown hair was well-kept and uniform smartly pressed.

"It's nice to meet you, Captain Hayward." Before the Captain could update them about the attack at his cabin and ranch, the door adjacent to where the corporal was sitting began to open. Standing there was Captain Steinberg; he smiled at Captain Hayward. Come in, my old friend, and update me." Texas nodded to the captain and shook Charles's hand before leaving the cabin.

As Captain Steinberg closed the door behind them, he commented that he had not seen Charles for several weeks. A strong smell of coffee filled the room; sitting in the left-hand corner was a small agar with a pot cooking away. "Would you like a cup of coffee?"

"Yes, thank you." Charles then sat in a chair opposite his desk.

A picture on the side of the desk depicted George Washington's victory over the British. Charles looked at it momentarily before refocusing on Captain Steinberg pouring a cup of coffee in front of him. The American Captain looked at the picture and smiled, "I guess it's time to take that down now; we're going to need to work together if we're going to defeat Nazar."

Charles leaned forward and accepted the cup of coffee in front of him. "You'll be right about needing numbers against Nazar. His armies are beyond the imagination; they move like African soldier ants, destroying anything in their path." Charles sipped the coffee and breathed the aroma from the steaming cup. He spoke about the European forces using the most up-to-date weapons against this force, but even machine guns could not stop the masses.

"How do you think we can stop him?"

Charles leaned forward and scratched his beard whilst thinking. "We have hit him at the source, but I'm not sure that will be enough." He took a longer sip of coffee and focused his eyes on Captain Steinberg. "We will need mobility and the willingness to meet our maker on the battlefield. I would also add a bit of luck and hopefully God on our side."

Both men smiled.

Captain Steinberg sat down in his chair behind his desk. The cabin had only recently been built, so there was still a sweet smell of freshly chopped wood. The American reached down into a drawer on his left-hand side. He then pulled out an envelope and put it on the table. Captain Hayward looked puzzled momentarily before the American Captain told them the letter was for him. Charles reached across and picked up the letter. He slowly tore open the top of the envelope and pulled out the paper within it.

The letter was from the acting British high command. It congratulated Captain Hayward for his sterling efforts in fighting Nazar and his army. He was now being rewarded with this by being commissioned to the rank of Major. The letter did not just contain information about his commission; it also carried another message. The British, American and allied forces would now start preparing for the invasion of Great Britain.

Charles sat back in his chair and brought his coffee to his lips; he took several sips. Captain Steinberg let Charles take it in for a moment and then said he knew about the impending invasion. The armies around the country were to start training and preparing for it.

The two men spoke about what this meant for them. Charles was thinking about having to leave Rebecca and the children. They had been in America for nearly two years, and it had not crossed his mind to leave them again. He had thought about Nazar invading America, but taking the battle to him was another thing.

Charles spoke about the flesh-eater attacks and how a herd had recently come through their ranch. He spoke highly about the Arapaho Indians who had helped them, and his promise of food and clothing. Captain Steinberg nodded; his stance differed from the official government line on the Native American Indians. They both agreed they would be a valuable asset for what lay ahead. Still, they realised the past actions of former governments against the indigenous Indians had possibly damaged the chances of that ever happening.

Nazar was planning, but Charles wanted to avoid the feeling of uncertainty. He had met him face to face and looked into the eyes of darkness. This would be Emperor was swallowing up the civilised world and would soon be coming for America.

They spoke for an hour before Corporal Collins brought in soup and bread. After they had eaten, Charles politely asked if he could go and see his Engineers; he thanked the captain and said they would have a lot to talk about soon regarding the invasion. The American officer asked one of his junior officers to help take Major Hayward to the British quarters. The walk was not far, and he could see Corporal Heinz chatting with Sergeant Butcher. Both men saw Charles coming and smiled, then began walking towards him—a hearty handshake followed by a pat on the shoulder.

"Good to see you, Charles."

"Good to see you too." A young girl ran up as Charles spoke and attached herself to Sergeant Butcher's large frame.

Charles smiled, "How is young Anna, Thomas?" "She is doing very well, thank you, Charles."

Charles bent down, reached into his tunic pocket, and slowly pulled out a bar of chocolate. Her face lit up with delight, but she waited patiently to be offered the bar of chocolate. Charles said she could share it with her brother James as she put her hand out to take the bar. She said thank you and said she would do that before running off into the camp. "She's grown since I last saw her, Thomas" "She has Charles; time is just flying by." They walked briefly and began talking about the engineers moving to the ranch.

The plans were being laid for the engineers to help prepare for the invasion of Great Britain. The grand idea was to hit them first before they could invade America. Landing crafts had been designed to take more soldiers, and ships were being altered to allow them to carry such vessels. The work on these ships and crafts had begun a year and a half earlier. The European forces had been kept a lot in the dark. The Americans knew they would need ample supplies, but also wanted to utilise the broken armies now residing in their country. A large American force would accompany this invasion, and an American command would lead it.

Charles spent several more hours meeting some of his soldiers and talking to their families. He was conscious of not spending too much time at Golds Hilltown. He wanted to return to his family, especially after the flesh-eater attack. Texas would ride with him out of the town and back to his ranch. He would then help coordinate the movement of British soldiers and their families. As they passed the last guards on the lookout towers, both men glanced back at the town.

The journey was smooth; a deer with its young foal passed before them. The mother briefly looked up at the men before leading her young foal into deeper woodland.

"Major, is it now?" Texas said with a smile.

"I guess I'll need to get used to that." Charles smiled.

"You've proven to me that you have the support of your men and come across as a good man."

"Thank you, Texas. We'll need everyone's support if we're going to stop Nazar."

The sun was slowly starting to go down as they approached the ranch.

As they drew closer, they could smell a log fire burning away. Another aroma was carried on the wind. Texas sat up in his saddle, saying, "That smells like a stew to me."

Charles smiled, "I hope there's enough for you?" Texas gave a scornful look his way.

Charles brought his horse to a standstill outside the ranch. He then called out to make sure Rebecca knew it was him outside. Texas sat in his saddle and looked at Charles to make the first move. The cabin door slowly began to open, and Rebecca walked out into the fading light. She looked more beautiful than ever, and a spontaneous smile erupted as she gazed upon Charles. She came over to him, and he leaned down to kiss her on the lips.

Texas looked on and felt a little envious of this love, not maliciously, but in a profoundly human desire to meet a partner with whom he could share his life. He had had many lovers over the years, but he had also chased the gold in the mountains. With the changing world, his focus shifted from money to true happiness.

Rebecca said hello to Texas; she had met him before when they arrived in Colorado. The men tethered their horses and followed Rebecca into the cabin. Standing by the door was Emily; she was giggling with happiness. Arthur was putting a rifle back into the gun cabinet; his aura had changed since the attack by the flesh-eaters. He looked different, even if he was the same boy.

Chairs were pulled to the dining table, and extra places were set for Charles and Texas. A large steaming pot was brought to the table, accompanied by fresh bread; Texas's eyes lit up, and he said under his breath about loving stews. The meal was enjoyed with conversations of old times and new discoveries. Texas looked around the table, smiling to himself at this family life, but he also felt slightly worried. If Charles were right about Nazar, he would be planning to invade. Captain Hayward's family would just be one of many that would suffer.

He thought of how many were suffering in Europe under this monster. Only a question from Rebecca broke him out of his thoughts; Arthur and Emily wanted to take on Texas with a game of indoor Skittles after the meal. He gladly accepted.

Chapter 3

"Spring is upon my lord, "Lev said as he emerged from the shadows.

"Be patient, my brother, "Nazar spoke softly as he looked over the bay at St Ives.

"America lies to the West. You know the plan. I have made you King of this Island".

His brother twitched a little. "How can you be sure it will work?"

"Mankind will always want to take back what it has lost. Our armies have grown stronger over the years. Many of the conquered lands have given us fresh drone soldiers. We have millions of dead walkers; our numbers are ready. The ships are ready." He said this, allowing his teeth to show as he smiled. They walked to an open canopy; the wind picked up around them, causing the sides of the canopy to flutter. Inside was a table with a large map nailed onto it.

Lev pondered over the large map of America.

"They will attack towards the end of the summer; my spies are certain of this." He rubbed his chin and looked at his brother. "You will fight them and slow them down."

"My brother, what if they win?" Lev looked into the eyes of his sibling.

Then, Nazar let out a deep, raucous laugh.

"What is there to win here?"

Both brothers laughed.

The destroyer drones guarding outside the tent felt uneasy.

Nazar went on to point out that most cities and towns were burnt down. Those who cooperated with him now saw themselves as servants under his control. Some of the influential figures who stayed behind from the fallen British Empire wanted to have land and run towns and cities for their own interests. The politicians had sworn an oath to their new king. There were also mass slave camps to remind the remaining civilians not to stray too far from their newly chosen paths.

Many worked in mass work camps, building ships or weapons for Nazar's army. This was also happening across Europe.

Those who tried to escape or fight back were hanged or beheaded in villages and towns. Mass public trials happened in the remaining cities, and justice was corrupt and benefitted those with money.

Oksana had been tasked to gather the generals and high Priests for a war council. She had selected a hill overlooking rolling fields which undulated down to the sea. General Georgiy entered the tent, which had one open side, followed by General Eltsina. The map of America was laid out on a giant table. Small miniature figures marked the Nazar's, American and European forces on the map. He looked at it and seemed to nod his head. Oksana had hoped Eltsina would have been killed in the battle for Great Britain, but for now, she tolerated her; her king had an eye for women but took a particular interest in Eltsina. Younger officers entered the room, both male and female. The last General to enter was an English officer. He had defected to Nazar's army; he felt the power in the world had shifted irreversibly to Europe's new leader and soon-to-be world conqueror.

Nazar had previously stuck to a hard-line rule of mainly Russian priests in his higher council. This had given way to the infected Generals and now to some Generals who were deemed useful. General Richard Conway was an asset to Nazar. He was well-versed in the battle tactics of the British army. He was a physical man, broad and burly, and had never been liked by his soldiers under his command, as they saw him as self-serving. Having missed out on promotion in the regular British army, he had seen this as a chance to serve a new empire. He was not married and was promised several brides, and he took pleasure in choosing the unfortunate women. He let his neat and trim black hair grow long and dressed the same as the priests.

General Conway was tasked with hunting out the last drops of resistance in Great Britain. He had carried this out so well that the promotion he had dreamed of followed. His sadistic side was allowed to fester, with mass executions and torture of those who stood in his way.

His broader role in the invasion of America was to lead the converted European forces of Nazar. The priests would still be present in this army, but they wanted a European general to help lead this force. He would be allowed to select officers to make up his battle command.

Oksana waited for the generals to settle in the tent and then began to deliver the plan for the invasion. There was an air of excitement within the tent. The generals looked at each other and the map, nodding in approval.

Chapter 4

The relocation of the Engineers had gone well. It had taken several weeks, but cabins had been built, and a defensive fence had been put around the ranch. A detachment of American soldiers had also been stationed there. Corporal Collins from Gold's Hill Fort was in charge of this unit. They were there to assist Major Hayward with his preparation for the invasion of Great Britain. Wood was being cut, and the logistics corps was notified of where they should store it.

Many factories along the coast were building the remaining landing ships, and provisions were stored in warehouses at the key ports.

Charles had been notified that his regiment would not land in the first wave, and the engineers would be needed after securing the beaches. April would soon be approaching, and the brighter weather was good for preparations.

Arthur had been allowed to practice firing a rifle daily and improved with each session. A reasonably sized gully was designated for shooting practice, and he would take some handmade targets and go there daily after lunch.

The spring air was fresh, and the sun was warmer as Arthur held the rifle over his shoulder. He took around ten bullets. He was to be moderate with his ammunition.

He set his target at the gully, and the soil was covered in new plant growth, with deciduous trees coming into life. He ran his hand along the ponderosa pine bark and onto the soil beneath it. The sun's rays pierced the pine trees and onto the ground below. He aimed with his rifle, loading the bullet into the chamber with the bolt, and then tucked the rifle butt into his shoulder. He slowly began to squeeze the trigger. Boom! The bullet fizzed out of the barrel and into the target down the gully. Arthur lowered his rifle, and he sensed he was not standing there alone. The breeze had picked up, and he could smell the freshness of spring being carried on it. His mind returned to the children's camp in Denmark; he thought of Anna and Samuel and how Philippe had killed Samuel. The thought of this made him load another bullet into the chamber, and without thinking, he took aim and shot at the target again. A tear fell from his cheek; it may have been two years or more, but he could never forget the events of the camp. He had seen Anna briefly when they travelled to America, but she would stay in a European camp near New York.

He imagined her beautiful face and hoped to see her again soon. Emily said he fancied her, and in a way, it was true.

Inside his right-hand side pocket was a biscuit. Arthur went and sat by the pine tree he had felt earlier. He leaned the rifle against the tree and let the sun rays fall on his face as he sat down. Reaching inside his pocket, he took out the biscuit and ate it slowly; a few crumbs fell onto his lap, which he picked up with his fingers. The taste lit up in his mouth; treats were rationed now, and sometimes, chocolate was brought in on the supply wagons, but generally, it was everyday supplies.

As Arthur sat there, he felt the sun's warmth instantly disappear from his face. Without thinking, he reached for his rifle. Opening his eyes, he saw an American Indian sitting on his horse. The Indian had long black hair and was dressed in breechcloths and leggings. He had a bow and arrows strapped across his back.

"My name is Hosah, 'Little Crow' I have come to speak with your father."

Arthur recognised him now. He was the leader of the Arapaho attack party who saved their lives several weeks ago when the herd of flesh-eaters attacked them. He got to his feet and smiled at Little Crow. He reached down, gripped his rifle strap, and put the rifle over his shoulder. "Come with me, and I'll take you to him."

Arthur looked at his feet as he walked over the fallen pine needles; he liked how they compressed into the soil with each step. Little Crow manoeuvred his horse slowly behind the boy. His horse's tail swished side to side as they moved along.

The ranch now had a perimeter fence and several watch towers looking out over the surrounding forests and farmland. A call went out that a rider was approaching, followed by a creaking gate opening. Two engineers, Sergeant Butcher and Private Green, rode out to meet the rider. Sergeant Butcher instantly recognised young Arthur and asked him who his friend was.

Arthur felt empowered to be talking with the soldiers and a native Indian.

"The gentleman with me is a warrior by the name of 'Little Crow'."

Little Crow looked at the young lad, almost nodding with respect. His long black hair was tied back, with a bow poking out over his left shoulder, with the rest of it obscured by a large buffalo hide resting on his shoulders. Arthur looked at the beads hanging off Little Crow's fringed top and the tassels hanging off the leggings. He instantly wanted to be an Arapaho warrior.

Sergeant Butcher led them into the fortified ranch. Arthur watched the soldiers take Little Crow to see his father. He liked how the horse moved quickly with its rider and watched them until they disappeared around a storage shed.

Arthur improved his riding skills and would go on horseback with the other children on the ranch. His mother would take them out to collect wood and other supplies, and he would use this opportunity to take a horse and patrol on it. He loved the way he could see so much more riding up in a saddle. The world looked different; the trees felt different when he ran his hand up against the bark. He watched the squirrels dance in the sunlight and the birds looking at him as he moved through the woods.

Sergeant Butcher showed Little Crow where to tie his horse and watched him slide off his horse in one motion. He admired this man's presence. They would need warriors like this to stop this force of evil that was coming like a black tide of hate.

"Follow me to Major Hayward."

Two British soldiers looked at Little Crow as he walked towards Major Hayward's office. They had not seen too many native Indians before and were unsure of what to make of this young Indian. Little Crow looked at the ranch buildings, taking in how much had changed since the attack by the flesh-eaters. He had seen many changes in his short spell on these lands. The influx of Europeans had put more pressure on the natural resources around Colorado. There had been fewer animals to hunt on the reservations, and they had also brought the dead with them. Little Crow was shown past a sentry guard outside Charles' office. As soon as he walked in, Charles got up and approached him.

"It's been longer than I thought it would be." Charles smiled as he said this and showed Little Crow a chair.

Little Crow looked at it but then went and stood by a window at the side of Charles's desk. He studied the people outside, who were moving about like ants.

"My people have seen great changes to our lands. We now live on reservations, where once we were free." Little Crow turned and looked at Charles. "I was taught English by a missionary trying to make us more like the people who took our lands. Charles said nothing and just listened.

"Now the white man has brought the dead with them, and our medicine men hear whispers in the wind that a king of darkness is hunting them."

Charles was surprised to hear Nazar's presence was felt even here in America "I cannot say what has happened to your people is not wrong. The British Empire has controlled most of the world, and we have done it by force. He sat back on his desk." He rubbed the stubble on his beard. "I apologise for what part the British played in first conquering America and for the future destruction that occurred from that many years later. I now know how it feels to lose the lands you were born in and to see your people suffer".

Little Crow listened. Charles did not know if he believed his apology or accepted it.

"The king of darkness is true, and he is coming to these lands. He will destroy everything in his path."

Little Crow looked out of the window again. "This is not a war for my tribe or the Arapaho."

"The flesh-eaters and the creatures with long legs and arms have attacked us." He paused. "All of these arrived when more of the Europeans came. We shall let the white man fight his demons; if you lose, we shall re-take our lands."

Charles felt the distrust but knew Little Crow and his braves had saved them before. "Why did you help us before?"

"It was not your time." Little Crow turned as if to leave. "I have come for supplies for my people."

Charles nodded his head. "I have a wagon for you. It has clothes and food and even some rifles." Little Crow looked a little puzzled.

"Rifles?" Why would you give us weapons?"

"To help protect you from what's coming."

Little Crow looked at the Major. "How do you know we will not decide to fight with this Nazar?"

Charles stood momentarily looking out the window and then at a picture of his family.

"I have met the enemy face to face, and he will not care about the living or the dead in this country."

"When the time is right, Little Crow, you and your tribe will have to choose for yourselves what path you take."

Little Crow acknowledged his words and thanked him for the supplies.

"We will meet again, Major Hayward." He then turned and left the cabin.

Charles had instructed several of his men to escort the wagon to the Arapaho reservation and then return to the ranch.

Chapter 5

"My lord, the destroyer drones are training hard." General Georgiy could not hide his excitement.

"Good, double their training, get the European forces working faster." Nazar paused and looked down at the ground beneath his feet. "I will be returning to Serbia to the Monastery with Oksana."

"Sire, have they recovered the rock?" His voice wavered a little, and in his anxious state, he bit his lip, drawing a small amount of blood in his mouth.

"The rock is no more at the Monastery." Nazar's teeth began to show, and his nostrils flared a little. "My brother has news for me about something they have found in China." Upon saying this, his demeanour began to relax a little.

"Send more of the dead to America, send more long limbs, more spies. I want to rule the world, General Georgiy."

He turned and began to leave the tent.

"Have the generals meet me in Russia as the days draw longer. The time is closer for the war to be won."

Lowering his head, General Georgiy nodded in agreement.

Chapter 6

Rebecca leaned in on the porch and kissed Charles on the lips. "I know you will be leaving soon again". She gently rested her head on his shoulder. She could hear his heart softly beating, and the skin on her face sunk into the soft fibres of his shirt.

"I will be part of the invasion force; we can only hope most of Nazar's armies are in Europe and we weaken him." He looked into her eyes. "I love Rebecca."

"He's coming, though; you know an invasion of Great Britain will only bide us time." Rebecca looked back into his eyes. She had lost family and friends in this war, and she did not want to lose the man she had fallen in love with all those years ago, but she also knew the war was coming to America, and they needed more time.

"Arthur will want to come and fight with you; the closer he gets to fifteen, the more he wants to be like his father."

Charles sat up a little. "He may yet have to fight, but it will not be on the shores of Great Britain." He must stay and help protect his family." Charles said with a half-smile. He knew Rebecca would do everything to keep them alive and was a leading light for the children.

They leaned into each other and kissed on the lips; before it could become more passionate, a little giggle broke the moment.

"Where is Arthur, mummy?"

"He's probably out training with the Americans." She smiled at Emily as she said this, but inside, she knew he had survived the horrors of Nazar children's camp, and he would never really be the Arthur he was before the war.

He also had an eye on a girl who had come with a family across the plains. He had written to Anna and wanted to see her after what they had been through together.

Emily came and sat next to her parents and looked at the pine trees from the front porch. Then, she watched the soldiers and civilians going about their work; some gathered water, others hay for the livestock. She had met some girls from the prairies and some British girls who were daughters of the Royal Engineers. They would play with dolls and pretend to be grown-ups. Emily especially loved going with them to feed the animals and the horses. She had complained that Arthur could travel out of the fort with the soldiers, but she couldn't. The rules seemed unfair, and she did not like being told it was because she was too young.

Today was a day she wanted to do something different. She knew the rules were in place since the flesh eaters walked into the ranch, but she wanted more.

Taking deep breaths, she moved and stood before her parents.

"I want to go with Charlotte on a horse ride."

Rebecca looked at Charles, and they smiled.

"I'll take you out on the horses," Rebecca said with an understanding smile. She walked over and brushed Emily's hair.

"I'll take her now, my love. "Rebecca leaned forward and kissed Charles on his lips.

"Rebecca, take a revolver and go with several of the soldiers. Do not stray too far from the fort, as there have been sightings of long limbs."

She agreed she would gather the girls who wanted to go for a horse ride and ask some of the Engineers going out foraging to go with them. The girls would be accompanied by their mothers, and there would not be too many for safety reasons. Rebecca remembered the attack in Denmark and how the Riders of the North had stolen Arthur. The years had rolled past, but the memory was still vivid.

Whilst the civilians were allowed to come and go from the fort, it was recommended to be wary of what was lurking on the planes. The horses were lined up and had tackle fixed over their heads. Each girl was allowed to groom their horse before it was saddled. They took pride in making the coats clean and shiny. Most had seen horses as working farm animals or means of transport to pull wagons and carts, but this was different. They had come to America fleeing Nazar and his army; they had lost friends and family. Most accepted, they may never go home.

Major Hayward had asked the Engineers to pick the most docile animals they had. The odd pink ribbon was starting to appear in the horses' manes, which brought a smile from the soldiers helping them get ready.

Fifteen soldiers, a mixture of engineers and American cavalrymen, were going out with the girls and their mothers. Six wagons were coming with them for logs and fresh water. The fort had two wells, but collecting extra water in barrels for the livestock was also helpful.

Extra Martini-Henry rifles and Spencer repeating rifles were loaded into the wagons. The civilians had been having shooting practice, which was considered an asset if needed.

Rebecca spoke to her close friend at the fort, Eleanor, as they started to prepare the horses. She commented on how each day was growing warmer and how the flowers and grasses were coming to life. Eleanor spoke about growing up on a farm in Wales and her love for the countryside; she was a hardy woman with robust, beautiful features and long brown hair. She said she marvelled at the great planes and their vastness, but missed the valleys of home.

Soon, they were ready; scouts led the wagons out of the south fort gate. Charles went to stand by the gate and spoke to Sergeant Thatcher. He was an experienced soldier who had fought on the beaches at Portsmouth and the South Downs. He wore a sword and had bought two Colt 45 peacemakers. The British army had tried to maintain its rules with uniforms and weaponry, but since the evacuation to America, many who had faced the enemy wanted extra weapons.

Rebecca let Emily ride with Eleanor, whilst she steered her horse towards Charles. She had a Winchester across her back and a Colt Cavalry in a gun holster at her side. She dismounted and came close to Charles. The two American cavalrymen, who were bringing up the rear, rode past, both looking at Rebecca standing close to the Major. Once they were out of sight, she looked around and kissed him quickly.

"When the children are in bed, we can continue this." Her infectious smile made Charles smile.

"Stay safe out there." He looked at her as she remounted and then watched her join the others as they slowly went out of sight. The fort gates creaked as they closed, and Charles turned and looked up at the sky; the trees around the fort were starting to sway more, and clouds appeared in the blue sky. He began to walk back towards the barn to check on the supplies.

"Father, look what I caught with Tom," the voice came out of the storage hut attached to the barn; emerging out of the darkness was Arthur holding two rabbits over his left arm.

"Where have Mother and Emily gone?" He looked intrigued.

"They have gone for a horse ride to get supplies with a small detachment."

Arthur nodded and said he would take the rabbits to the cabin with Tom. Tom was Eleanor's son, a year older than Arthur, but shared his thirst for adventure. He hadn't seen the world in the same light as Arthur had; he also hadn't seen the child camps and endured their hardships, but he had seen Nazar's army sweep through his town and villages around it. He knew the flesh eaters would spare no one, and the long limbs were fast and ferocious. Nazar's drone soldiers had killed members of his family, and his uncle had sacrificed his life to help them escape. They had taken different paths in this war, but were bound by it.

Charles looked up again as the weather started to change. A warmer breeze blew around them, and the light colour also changed.

A couple of hours had passed when Charles looked out of his cabin window. Tumbleweed danced its way along the dirt track by the wooden panels. A strange orange light filled the skies outside, giving all objects an unnatural look. His eyes returned to the room and focused on the letters strewn on the desk in front of him. Some were regarding British civilians being relocated to Canada, others about the pending invasion of Great Britain.

Charles had heard first-hand accounts of how his country fell to Nazar's army. He had seen their might on the battlefield and knew they were coming to America; this enemy did not care about the massive loss of life taking any country. This prompted calls within America for dialogue with Nazar. Should they not negotiate with the new King of Europe? Maybe he would not invade them if a deal were offered. Fortunately, for now, those requests had been brushed aside.

The Great British Parliament, which had fled the invasion, slowly reestablished itself in Canada and was now planning how to rule Great Britain again. Queen Victoria may have perished in her beloved country, but the monarchy had survived. Edward the 7th pleaded to stay in Windsor to the end with his mother, but she ordered him to retreat with the other family members. Queen Victoria wanted him to lead the British back to their homeland, and he knew he should follow her wishes.

They had drafted in more soldiers from the Commonwealth, and they were amassing in Canada. The European forces had been gathered to help bolster the American troops. The British armies' losses had been heavy during the defence of their country, but due to some heroic sacrifices, many escaped. The plan was to boost the invasion force with some American regiments. Reports had circulated that a lot of Nazar's army had moved back to mainland Europe.

A knock on the door broke his train of thought. "Come in."

Standing there with a rifle over his back was Texas.

"Charles, we should ride out to collect the mothers and daughters." His concerned look was noticeable.

Charles looked outside his window again. The trees swayed from side to side more violently, and the orange light created a horrific backdrop.

"Texas, can you speak to Captain Steinberg and ask for a small detachment of cavalry to accompany us?"

"I will." He left in haste.

Charles went to Sergeant Butcher and asked him to gather thirty Engineers.

Arthur let the log in his hand roll onto the fire below. The wooden walls carried the boys' silhouettes as the flames licked around the fresh piece of wood, which now sat snuggly in the fire. He reached down and grabbed a cloth which had been placed close to the log basket. He then used it to take an old black rusty pot held by a hook over the fire. The steam rose from the sprout as he poured hot water into the China teapot on the table between two chairs. Tom moved his chair a little closer to the fire and watched Arthur add milk to the tea.

"The storm is strange with this orange light." Tom looked out of a cabin window as he said this.

Arthur nodded his head. "I'm sure our mothers will return soon."

Tom sat back in his chair as Arthur handed him his teacup. "Thank you."

He looked concerned and anxious, his eyes not making contact with Arthur's.

"Are you alright, Tom?"

"I am. It's just this war and my thoughts."

Arthur let Tom sit and drink his tea for a moment or two.

He then began to open up about what was troubling him. Tom explained how his two older brothers were in the British army, and one of them was now missing, presumed dead. His father had travelled along the American coast, hoping for news on survivors.

Arthur took his teacup and brought it closer to his lips; as he sipped, he listened to the story of what happened.

Chapter 7

The weather was changing in the Carpathian Mountains. Winter was coming. Sergeant James Smith and his brother, Private Isac Smith, were resting their horses by a small brook flowing into a wider channel. The men were taking time to wash and clean as the clouds gathered above. The water was cold, and a slight breeze added to the uncomfortable feeling on the skin, causing goosebumps everywhere. James was the first to come out and stand by a fire they had made. The smell of cooking meat made Isac grin with excitement.

"How long do you think we have?" His voice wavered a little.

"Come and stand next to the fire, Isac, or you won't have long." James looked at his brother; he had lost weight over the past month, his beard was unkempt, and his hair was not military length. They had fought hard to make it this far and knew what was coming from the forests to the North.

Isac took the blanket his brother had handed him as they stood by the fire. The heat radiated around his legs, and he crept underneath the blanket, drying his skin as the hot air travelled upwards.

James dried off and began to change. He suggested his brother stop daydreaming and dress before the food was ready. Two rabbits had been skinned, and their stripped bodies were cooking over the fire; they had some dry biscuits and vegetables cooking in a pot. Isac finished getting ready, as the cold wind took him out of his dream world.

James served up the rabbits and vegetables in two army mess tins. Steam rose from the freshly cooked rabbit meat. Isac didn't even wait for it to cool as he wolfed it down. The warm food sat in their bellies as they sat by the fire.

"We're going to have to turn the fire in soon." James looked to the distant forests and the ridge that hid the river below. A heavy storm from several nights ago had swollen its waters and meant the brothers would have to ride downriver and cross a small bridge there. They were trying to reach the lookout fort in the Carpathian Mountains and warn the British and Austrian Engineers there.

Isac held his hands out to soak up every last drop of heat, then used a water canister to put out the flames. The fire hissed and popped as the water went to work, cooling the ambers below. The late afternoon sky was reddish, as if it carried snow in its clouds. James ensured he had packed his kit before taking his blanket out, and he told Isac to do the same.

Without the fire, the cold wind attacked areas of the skin that weren't covered. James took out his Martini-Henry rifle and his sword in its scabbard.

He sat next to Isac, who had perched himself against two pines. They had built a small shelter as a temporary camp for that night.

They spoke briefly before James said he had to take a light relief. Whilst his brother left for a short walk to the woods, Isac pulled up the blanket and covered himself. He closed his eyes and thought about summer.

"Isac, don't move." James knelt beside him.

Isac opened his eyes and stared at his brother. "What's wrong?"

"They're here."

Isac moved to get his rifle, but his brother put his hand on his arm.

"Ride to the fort and warn them of what's coming." He said in a soft voice.

James then went to get his brother's horse.

"I'm not leaving you, James." Isac's voice was stern and resolute.

His brother took the horse over to him.

"You have to get there before they do."

Isac looked at the soil beneath his boots. "I couldn't save Abbey that day, but I can help you."

James put his arms across his brother's shoulders. "No one could have saved Abbey, our daring little sister. You did everything you could."

James had flashes of them playing by the canal lock and his sister accidentally falling in. It happened so fast that the lock keeper and their father raced to help, but Isac dived in to save her. He fought with every last breath he had to reach her and held her as long as he could, but it was not enough; the feeling haunted him; he was only a young boy and was lucky to be pulled out himself by his father. The years had softened some of the pain, but it still lived in both of their memories.

"You should go now, my brother," James said whilst doing up his tunic.

Isac could see in James' eyes that he only wanted the best for him and knew his brother would give his life for him to escape.

A shrill pierced the space around them, followed by cackles and growls. Isac fastened his helmet and slid his rifle into the scabbard alongside his saddle.

"James, you were the brother I wanted." Isac wiped the side of his face and turned his horse so he could look at his brother straight on one last time.

James smiled; he felt the emotion coming over him, but knew he had to keep it within for his brother's sake. "Ride to the fort, my little brother, and never look back."

Isac let out a roar, kicked his heels in, and drove the horse on.

The sun slowly sank into the sky, giving off a deep red backdrop. James took his horse and led it around; its hoofs scuffed the soil beneath as it turned. The horse started to get anxious and stir; its nostrils flared as it jostled on its reins. James steadied the animal, stroking its neck; once it had calmed down, he loaded his rifle and put it into the sheaf to the side of his saddle.

Emerging out of the darkness were several riders. In the dense woodland, figures moved side to side. There were thousands of eyes looking at him, but these creatures stayed

out of the fading light. They seemed to be controlled by the riders now coming towards James. He mounted his horse and relaxed into the saddle whilst patting the side of its neck. The animal stirred, sensing the danger in the air.

Eight riders, all dressed in black, slowly came forward in a single line. None of them carried a weapon, but all had swords strapped across their backs or around their waists.

The middle rider of the eight raised his hand, bringing all of them to a stop; he then moved his horse forward, smiling as he did so, showing off his yellow teeth.

"You have come a long way to die, soldier."

James looked at this man, his black clothes covering him from top to toe. His face was pale, his eyes sunken, his beard was unkempt, and an upside-down cross on a chain hung around his chest.

"For a former man of god, you've fallen far from the heavens."

This drew a snarl from the rider as he moved closer.

"I was a man of god for sure, but I have found a different path now, and that path is my enlightenment."

"You are no different to any barbarian army; you're killing men, women and children en masse, and you will pay for your sins." James began to lower his hand towards his sword.

The Priest shook his head, "If you give up now, I'll make sure it's a quick death." He said this with a dirty smile on his face.

James looked over his shoulder to his left and right. The creatures had moved to both sides of the dense woodlands. This left him with a backdrop of the swollen river from a small ridge. His horse backed up a little as the prominent Priest sat there for a second or two.

"So be it." He paused for a second. "Kill him."

Four riders started to move forward, and a younger rider behind the Priest began to go but was stopped by him. "Nazar has ordered not to let his cousin fight."

The look from the young rider was one of impatience.

The three riders moved towards James.

James withdrew his sword, and the riders did the same. He turned his horse and moved it towards the ridge. The first rider of the three came at him with purpose. His eyes were wide open, revealing an almost psychotic stare. This rider raised his sword in the air and let out a roar as he charged down at James. The soil was flung up from the hooves as the horse gathered speed towards the British soldier; the other two held back as they watched the attack unfold. Both priests were grinning at the pending death, hoping to bring down their prey like a pack of wolves on a buffalo.

James was not a cavalryman, but his grandfather had taught him how to ride. He spent hours training with him in the saddle, mostly passing the time, but he had picked up valuable tips.

As the rider came in close, he spun his horse around, blocking the priest's downward swing with his sword, forcing the rider to lean to the left, putting him slightly off balance. As he passed, James ran his sword down his back, causing the rider to fall from his horse; before he could finish him off, the other two priests were upon him. The impact sent him and his horse juddering backwards. The priest on the floor was still trying to rise to his feet. The dying light of day lit up the two mounted priests as they closed in for the kill. The rider on the left had an axe, and the one on the right had a Sabre. They came forward with purpose; their eyes fixated on James; he regained his composure and came at them; his movement was swift and elegant, leaning left, then right, as he unleashed two quick, savage blows, taking the axing-wielding priest's head clean off and opening a deep chest wound on the other. He then caught the eye of the prominent priest, his anger seething beneath his robe.

James moved forward and dismounted for a moment. The third priest, who had been dismounted, was holding himself up by his arms. His death was quick as James brought his sword down through his neck.

Several more riders came forward out of the shadows.

"You have fought well, but it changes nothing." The prominent priest nodded to the other riders. "End this."

They charged forward together, and as they did so, the young priest also came with them. The prominent Priest screamed at him to stop. He had no intention; pouring forward, they came at James; he had remounted and turned his horse to face them.

From a distance, Isac looked on. He knew he had to leave, but could not turn his eyes away from his brother. He felt his heart racing and sweat running down his forehead; his anger and fear swept across his body equally.

James blocked the first Priest's sword as he came in, but was caught on the shoulder by another; the pain forced him to lower himself onto his horse's neck. The other riders battled for space as they rained down blows upon him. He sat firm, blocking and countering where he could. His horse reared up as it was hit and spun around. One rider lost his direction for a second, and James could run his sword through his back and out of his stomach.

This was a moment for the other riders to close in and try to finish the British soldier off. Soil was flung in the air as the horses churned the ground around them. James' eyes looked from side to side, keeping himself in the fight. A sword took a piece of flesh from his left thigh; the pain was excruciating, but a spear swiftly followed this to his right shoulder.

The prominent Priest pushed himself up in his saddle as he enjoyed the pulsating end to this fight. Nazar's cousin was on the outskirts of the fight, which suited the prominent Priest. This changed quickly as he pushed his way in, wanting to deliver the killer blow. It momentarily disrupted their advantage; the horses were backing towards the ridge, which fell away to the swollen river. James knocked a rider back he had on his right, allowing the young Priest to come in close. His young eyes lit up at the chance to claim his first kill and the glory he perceived it would give him.

He lunged at James, who was expecting it. James had blood flowing from his shoulder and leg; the Priest shouted something in Russian as their swords tangled. James looked over at the prominent Priest, who was eager to see the cousin kill him. His eyes turned from excitement to sheer panic, and he saw the British soldier's plan in that split second. He screamed at the young Priest to break off the attack, but it was in vain. James leaned into the attack, seizing the opportunity by grabbing the young priest's cloak and sword arm. Their horses were side by side as they veered towards the edge; James dropped his sword and punched the young Priest to the side of his jaw, causing him to look at him with a shocked and confused expression. He tried to hold his sword with his right arm, but James had it too tightly. His other arm firmly gripped his cloak.

The other Priests tried to get in close, but just compounded the situation. The horses began to lose their grip on the edge of the ridge. He let out a worried yell, but it was his last.

Both horses and riders fell into the river below. Another Priest tried to reach out and follow them into the icy waters, but the current swept them along and out of sight within seconds.

Isac turned to follow the river downstream. He hoped and prayed his brother would make it, or he could pull him from the water. As he steered his horse's head around, he could see Priests coming through the woodlands down from the ridge. He watched other riders galloping off in the other direction. The ones now coming his way were trying to find him. The decision was heartbreaking. Should he fight, try to out-ride them down the river, or turn and ride to the fort to warn the others? With a heavy heart, he followed his brother's orders and set off at speed to the fort.

Chapter 8

Tom looked at Arthur; he wiped away a tear from his eye. "I hope James made it, but we'll never know." He explained that Isac was stationed near New York with a brigade of British riflemen and came to visit them when he could.

Arthur sympathetically nodded his head, explaining about his uncle dying at Windsor Castle in the final defence of the Empire and about other members of his family who didn't make it in the evacuation. He said it had deeply affected his mother and father and made him question the future.

They both moved towards the window and looked at the orange light filling the sky. The dust cloud had grown more robust; as the boys looked out and wondered over this strange weather phenomenon, the cabin door slowly opened. Charles called Arthur through the ajar door.

Arthur turned and went towards his father's voice.

"Are Mother and Emily ok?" He felt a slight tightness in the pit of his stomach.

"I'm sure they are, but with this storm, I'm taking some soldiers out to help bring them back safe and well." He looked around and signalled to his men to mount up.

"Arthur, stay here and keep safe." He leaned in and ruffled his hair, which brought a disgruntled teenager look from his son, but a look of anxiety followed it. "Take care, father."

Corporal Heinz led the Major's horse to him. Texas, Corporal Collins, and fifteen cavalrymen were joining them. The storm was picking up, and the orange light was clouded by the sandstorm tearing through the fort.

Major Hayward led from the front as he rode out of the fort gates. Arthur watched them disappear one by one and prayed that they all returned safe and well.

Rebecca spoke to one of the cavalrymen regarding the worsening storm. Sergeant Longway had grown up in New York. He was a stocky man with a large moustache and dark brown, wispy hair. He had worked on the railways before joining the army and, for a time, made good money that way, but he had joined the army for adventure. He was concerned about the deteriorating weather and the safety of the women and children with him.

A scout returned to the group, informing them about a safe place to wait out the worst of the storm, but he also reported seeing a small group of flesh-eaters coming their way. It was hard going riding through the sand; it swirled around, scratching against any bare skin it found. Sergeant Longway led the group to a small clump of trees. He then circled the wagons around in an arc, leaving the trees behind them to help protect the rear. The fifteen soldiers helped gather the horses. The children and their mothers were asked to move into the thicket of trees. The women who had fired a gun before were given rifles and were asked to be vigilant of what could come through the trees.

At first, there was nothing, just the storm shaking the trees around them and causing the canvas on the wagons to flap in the strong winds. The cavalrymen had their bandanas high over their faces, exposing their eyes. They scanned the horizon for signs of movement. Slowly, shadowy silhouettes begin to move towards them. Due to the sand and orange light, they were in and out of focus.

What was hidden by this freakish weather was a herd of long limbs coming directly towards the wagons. Picking up speed as their long claws extended out and tore into the soil below them, each movement brought them ever closer to the unexpected women and children.

The first cavalryman to spot this shocking sight tried to raise the alarm, but the constant noise of the wind and storm drowned out his shouts.

He began firing his Winchester rifle in the direction of a creature as his eyes locked on this abomination hurtling directly at him. The long limb opened its mouth, showing its teeth as it flung itself into the wagon.

The wagon frame jutted back into the soil beneath it as several long limbs ploughed into its side. The other soldiers began to fire at the creatures on the other side. The first long limb to breech the circle lunged at the nearest soldier to it. The bullets pierced its skin, splitting bone and flesh, causing it to wince as it fell to the ground. It was only the start; more of these beasts, with their overstretched limbs, long necks and sharp teeth, piled into any gaps that emerged as the wagons began to turn under the sheer weight of the bodies pushed against them.

Rebecca let out a cry as she saw flesh eaters coming through the thicket where the mums and daughters were sheltering. She took her Burgess rifle and pushed the butt into her shoulder; looking down the sights, she focused on a rotting older man, his clothes dishevelled and left arm hanging at an awkward angle. Rebecca pulled the trigger back, hitting the man in the head; he fell forward into the scrub bushes around him.

The flesh-eaters' numbers swelled as they pressed hard through the small bushes and trees. The mothers gathered their daughters behind them. Those with rifles followed Rebecca's example, firing into the oncoming dead. The others broke off branches and used what they could to beat the flesh eaters back as they came closer.

Conversely, the cavalrymen started to fall back, the wagons buckling under the overwhelming pressure. The long limbs were pushing together, their jaws moving up and down, hissing and squealing as they did so. This added to the surrounding storm sound, blending into a terrifying white noise.

Rebecca looked at Emily; she looked back fearfully at her mother, but gritted her teeth and picked up a stone to throw at the flesh eaters. The mothers began to back themselves towards the soldiers, and the soldiers did likewise. Ammunition was starting to run low. Swords had been drawn by the soldiers who had run out. They picked their targets as the long limbs came at them, aiming for the head to maximise the chance of stopping them. The flesh-eaters were now meters from the mothers; one tried to grab a child as she fell back, and the two women close by kicked and punched at it; its skin had fallen off, but it dug its hands into the child's legs, then started to bring its mouth closer. Rebecca took aim and shot it in the jaw; it was just enough for the others to pull the girl further away as more sensed fresh blood.

As the situation became more desperate, a bugle call pierced the mayhem; it was music to their ears. Fighting erupted from the other side of the wagons; the long limbs seemed to turn and move towards this distraction. The detachment fighting these creatures had come from the 10th Cavalry, an African American regiment nicknamed the Buffalo Soldiers by the Native American Indians. There were enough of them to turn the tide of the fight; they had swooped around the thicket of trees and engaged with the flesh-eaters. The unorganised creatures were also splitting off to chase the horses and riders, but were getting picked off by the 10th Cavalrymen.

Their speed and mobility were too much for these beasts, who succumbed to this attack. The 10th Cavalry was soon reinforced with the arrival of Major Hayward and the soldiers from the fort. He wasted no time bringing his soldiers into a line and charging the long limbs and flesh-eaters. Corporal Heinz took several Engineers and charged around the back of the thicket to help out the 10th Cavalrymen, and Corporal Collins joined Major Hayward and Texas in the front assault. The creatures with no leadership from a Priest broke in different directions; Major Hayward brought his sword forward, the light from the sun rays breaking through the diminishing storm; when he swung it down, it was to slice open a flesh-eater staggering from side to side, trying in vain to grab at the nearest horse that shot past.

The Major was thinking about Rebecca and Emily; he controlled his fears and anger to help control his thoughts.

Corporal Heinz started to break through to the mothers and daughters on the other side of the thicket. Their faces were ecstatic to see the soldiers coming their way.

The 10th Cavalry picked off the remaining stragglers around the wagons, which coincided with the orange storm fading away. The only creatures to escape with their lives were several long-limbs. The remaining few bounded away into the surrounding forests.

Major Hayward re-sheathed his sword whilst dismounting and quickly moved into the circled wagons, stepping over the dead and dying long limbs. His eyes frantically searched the faces of the women and children for Rebecca and Emily. When he saw them both, he felt he could breathe again inside. Rebecca grabbed Emily, and they both rushed over to Charles; he fell to his knees. Rebecca took him in her arms and pulled him up close; Emily's face was covered in dirt, her smile showed off her white teeth, and the tears rolling down her cheeks left streaks on her skin where the teardrops cleaned off the soil.

"How can we live in a world like this?" Charles said this, looking into her blue eyes.

Rebecca leaned down and kissed him on the lips. "This is the new world." Her left hand caressed the back of his head.

Emily hugged her mother and father. She was only starting to know the new world, where monsters were real and darkness brought danger. The world of before seemed a long time ago. Charles slowly got to his feet but continued to hug his wife and daughter.

The captain of the 10th Cavalry detachment interrupted their embrace. He introduced himself as Captain Mason Somersett. He was a towering figure, 6ft 5 in and with a heavy build. Charles would later find out he had grown up on the slave plantations in the South and then later joined the Union soldiers to fight against the Confederates. He was a well-spoken man with a calm aura around him. Captain Somersett apologised for interrupting the moment and said he would speak to the major soon.

Charles said it was no problem and would speak to the officers in several minutes. Corporal Heinz came over with Texas. "Rebecca, good to see you and Emily."

She smiled at the Corporal; Texas lowered his cowboy hat and said, "Ma'am."

Emily tugged at Charles's hand, "Are we returning home soon, Daddy? I want to check on Arthur."

"We are my little, my little sweet pea." He leaned down and kissed her on the forehead and then returned to kiss Rebecca on the lips.

Charles turned to face both men.

"Corporal, gather the officers; we need a quick briefing."

The wagons started to be turned around, and the mothers and daughters gladly accepted the invitation to board them.

Charles spoke to the officers and Texas. He asked for an update on the soldiers and their welfare, and he had to double-check that no one had been bitten. The reports were excellent; no one had been lost or bitten. This made Charles look to the heavens; he thanked God for any small mercies that came their way.

Major Hayward mounted his horse and ensured all the soldiers, women, and children were on wagons or mounted on their horses. He then rode to the front to lead them forward. He had asked Sergeant Butcher and Corporal Heinz to hang back and bring up the rear. Everyone was a little on edge.

Captain Somersett was riding alongside Major Hayward. It was a good time for them to discuss his instructions regarding the invasion of Great Britain. He explained he had received orders from Washington that the President of America, Grover Cleveland, wanted to help the British take back their country. Some pointed to the fact that America was struggling with the influx of refugees and was only one bad harvest away from mass starvation. Charles tried to gauge his newfound ally; he was well-spoken, courteous, and had an air of confidence about him.

Captain Somersett spoke about fighting in the American Civil War and how this conflict had helped forge the abolition of slavery in his country.

He spoke about his past and how he grew up on the plantations in the South, how he had seen his father whipped daily, and his mother separated from them. He said he would never forget what happened or forgive the men who did it, but he wanted to help build a better world after what had happened to him and his family.

They spoke of this new enemy; it was something darker than humanity, more sinister than humans, and now swallowing up the world. There were rumours that the planned invasion was more of a delaying tactic by the Americans; some had been advising the President to try to negotiate with Nazar and stop the invasion of America altogether. They saw this as an opportunity to save America from the same fate as the rest of the world. The influential businessmen wanted negotiations to start, not this foolish plan to invade Great Britain.

The wheels were in motion, though. Different regiments were gathering in Boston, and training was taking place with beach landings. Private John Brown had written to Major Hayward to say he was coming with a small detachment to join his command. The British had mobilised a strong force mixed in with European forces. It was hoped that Great Britain would be a staging post for the invasion of Europe. The recruitment had focused on many younger soldiers who had not fought too much against this new enemy. The theory was that they would be full of hope and naivety and not think about the enormous task in front of them.

Major Hayward let Captain Somersett take the lead from the front while he fell back to speak to Rebecca and Emily. He felt his heart flutter, knowing they were safe and sitting on the wagon together. As he brought his horse level with the back of the wagon, Rebecca smiled. Emily waved.

"We're going to be back in the Camp soon; it's been quite an adventure for Emily," Charles said with a smile. He couldn't hide how the world had changed, but he still wanted some air of hope to remain. Rebecca smiled back as he trailed the wagon for a while.

Chapter 9

General Richard Conway let wine spill out of his mouth. His left arm reached out to a naked woman, whilst his right hand held a goblet. His eyes were fixed on the woman dancing in front of him.

"Dance faster, dance I said, you bitch." He then threw the goblet at her.

"Leave me, you disgust me." He pushed the woman off his arm and watched her dress quickly before leaving.

He began to laugh, a nervous, unsure laugh that turned into a squeal that turned into a growl. He slowly moved from his bed, swinging his legs around, dangling them over the side; the sensation in his bones was that of weight; the legs were heavier. The general struggled to stand before falling to the floor. He lay there motionless. Time passed, as night turned to day.

The cold morning air swept in around the General, and he began to open his eyes. A goblet lay next to his head, and bottles of wine lay strewn around him. He tried to remember the evening before, but most of it was a blur. The bits that were coming back were hazy and made him feel uncomfortable. He had read about demons being able to change their body shape, but he believed those stories to be only fables. This, of course, had changed with the arrival of Nazar. His army of darkness was vast, the creatures unearthly. Richard now pondered if he had the ability to shape change to a degree; he wasn't sure if he should laugh or cry. He moved his legs and started to raise his body by pushing his feet into the ground, allowing him to sit up. He still felt a little giddy and moved the arch of his back against a trunk that sat next to the bed.

He shut his eyes and opened them quickly. They were drawn underneath the wooden bed frame. Nestling in the middle lay a case made from dark brown leather. This case had come with him when he evacuated the north. It was shut, but he was attracted to it. Extending out his sore hand, he reached for the handle on the case. His fingers pressed against it until his index finger could get a firm grip. Pulling it from under the bed, he rested the case on the bottom of his feet. Richard now let his hands feel over the case; he saw the flames and the desperation in the eyes of the ones he loved. He heard their screams and panic; he saw himself begging with the European generals to make a last stand to help the women and children escape. It fell on deaf ears, and the army of the dead swept through the camps, tearing and killing in an unrelenting way.

Richard did all he could as he moved his family to the wagons. He fought hard with the remaining soldiers and women to protect the children, but there was only going to be one winner. He slowly opened the case, revealing family pictures and belongings. He felt the anger grow within him; he noticed his body changing. This was only stopped by the sadness inside his heart; tears dropped off his cheeks and onto the case below. He held the picture of his family tight to his chest and sobbed. He hated the creatures that did this to his family, but he despised the British and European forces that failed his family.

Fuelled by rage, he had sworn to have his revenge.

Nazar had given command of Great Britain to his brother Lev, who had appointed General Richard Conway as his second-in-command. Lev wanted a General who knew the lay of the land. Richard was trusted to help with the defence of Nazar's lands. Richard spent time looking over the maps of the new empire.

With thick mud on her boots and her gown dragging behind her, General Eltsina stomped to the sizeable round tent with burning lanterns outside. Two burly Destroyer drones stopped her.

"General Conway isn't expecting anyone."

"Do I look like anyone to you?" She smiled, showing two sharpened front canine teeth.

"I'm Sorry, General. I didn't realise it was you." The two drones lowered their heads.

"No need to worry; it's late, and I'm tired." She paused. "Tell him I'm coming in."

As the drones turned to let Richard know, she began to walk behind them, allowing her gown to slip off her shoulders, revealing her naked body, apart from a belt around her waist with a dagger tucked into it.

"Richard." She said without a care in the world as she walked naked towards his bed.

He looked at her, a bit bemused and yet a bit curious.

"General Eltsina, I was not expecting you until tomorrow." He tried to be sincere about the situation as she slowly approached him. "He was in his evening gown, with only long johns underneath. He got up from the bed to stand in front of it.

The destroyer drones closed the tent curtains from behind her and continued to guard the front of the tent.

She slowly continued to advance until she was only a metre away from him. Her long brown hair swept over her breasts as she began to undo her belt, which was wrapped around her waist. The clunk hitting the ground made the guards look at each other, but they had learnt not to move unless called. Nazar and Oksana had killed two guards for coming in when not wanted, so it was a task not to be undertaken lightly; if you were summoned to guard duty, most did it with a heavy heart. Dammed if you do, dammed if you don't.

She pushed her body into his, making him feel the curves of her figure against his clothes. Richard stood there wondering why this was happening now. She had never chosen to make any advances towards him before. They had met numerous times at the war council and even in the officers' mess, but she had only ever been civil to him. Her provocativeness aroused him, but he was wary of her intentions.

She began to take his hands and lower them.

"This is a surprise and something I'm not sure of."

She pulled him in close and kissed him passionately on the lips; she kissed him with venom and more wildly the longer they embraced. Richard began to step back, and the motion meant they both fell backwards onto the bed behind them. She aggressively pulled off his gown and started to bite him all over his body. He thought about whether she could change like he could, but only let that be a fleeting thought. She had blood dripping from her mouth, and he looked down at the bite marks on his torso. He then lifted her; for a short moment, she had fear in her eyes, but he brought her in closer and whispered in her left ear before flipping her over and kissing her all over.

The breeze picked up, blowing into the tent's opening, and the lanterns inside flicked from side to side until the breeze settled down. This only added to the sexually fuelled situation, which carried on into the night.

In the morning, Richard awoke to find a naked female body next to him; he gave her a quick prod to make sure she was alive and got a remark in Russian that sounded hostile. He did remember General Eltsina coming into the tent and then her undressing; he also remembered them drinking heavily throughout the night, but then his memory started to go a little hazy.

"Yes, it happened last night, Richard." She said, half-burying her head into a pillow.

"My first name is Veronika." Her voice was a bit hoarse and dry.

Richard looked for his pocket watch by the side of the bed.

"Well Veronika, its 10am. We need to meet Lev soon."

"Come back to bed, Richard; there is plenty of time to meet Lev."

With that, he looked around and slid back under the sheets beside her.

She turned over and looked at him; her beauty was more apparent in the light of the morning. She caressed his cheek. "I have plans for us, Richard, great plans."

Chapter 10

Heidi pulled John in close.

"Let's stay in bed all day."

John looked her in the eyes. "We're leaving soon for Boston. Major Hayward is gathering the Engineers there."

"I like New York." Her dimples showed as she said this. "I love it here with you."

This brought a smile to John's face. "I know; I love it here with you, too." He paused. "But Nazar will return; you know that. At some point, we will face him again."

Heidi lowered her face into the soft pillow on her side of the bed, causing her blonde hair to fall effortlessly on either side. John softly stroked it back from her right cheek. He then brought his lips to her ear and kissed her.

"Come on, we can have a pint and food at the Landmark Tavern." John felt his stomach rumble as he said this.

Heidi turned over and undid her blouse. "Before we go, maybe you can warm me up one last time." John looked at her naked body and undid his shirt.

"I guess the Traven can wait."

John held Heidi tight as they passed through the narrow alleys. He smelt her hair and thought about their morning together. He looked at his shoes as they walked through puddles, causing the water to splash up against them. A young boy stood beside a corner, shouting out 'papers for sale'. He added the 'read all about the rise of the dead'.

Heidi looked at John. His eyes betrayed his thoughts, and she could see the army of flesh-eaters wandering across open fields in their thousands—an army that never stopped marching and never stopped wanting flesh.

Heidi squeezed John's right hand and nuzzled her head into his shoulder. She knew that until Nazar was defeated, the darkness around the world would not be stopped. It was spreading, and it was only a matter of time before he arrived on the shores of America.

The day passed peacefully, and soon, the lanterns were being lit.

The next morning, Heidi and John mounted their horses and joined a small group of soldiers and nurses heading for Boston. She looked at him sitting on his horse, smiled, and then kicked on.

Wooden struts creaked as the camp doors began to open. Calls rang out that the soldiers, women, and children were returning.

Arthur was there with Tom, standing inside the camp by the large wooden gates; both had anxious faces at first, but this soon turned into oversized smiles. The feeling amongst the gathering families and soldiers was one of relief. They were happy they had all survived the storm. They didn't know about the flesh-eater attack. Raucous cheers broke out once the wagons and soldiers passed the gates, and then they were promptly shut. The jubilation was infectious. Charles dismounted and went to hug Rebecca and Emily. He helped Rebecca and Emily down from the Wagon. Then, he gathered them in his arms and held them there. Other families were being embraced around them.

Holding Rebecca and Emily close brought deep happiness from within; Arthur soon joined them. Charles embraced his family. He looked around at others doing so, making him feel emotional. On one hand, there was relief, and on the other, dread and fear; this was because he knew what was out there. Charles understood that the things he held on to tightly in his arms could be ripped away from him. All he loved in the world was a moment's breath away from disappearing.

After a few minutes, Sergeant Butcher approached the Major. "Excuse me, sir. The officers are with Captain Steinberg.

"Thank you, Sergeant; tell them I'll be with them in two minutes".

He slowly released his grip but continued to look at Rebecca in the eyes, and she looked back. It was a reaffirming glance that they must face what was coming, knowing whatever happened, there would always be an unbreakable family bond, in life or death.

The Major looked at the damp orange soil sticking to the underside of his boots as he walked over to the American officer's cabin. He was pondering the mission to invade Great Britain and the implications behind such a move. This latest attack played on his mind. His family would be left with many others, open to whatever was roaming the American plains. Nazar's tactics were simple and effective, creating fear amongst the civilian population and splitting the country's resources.

The Cavalry was deployed around America looking for flesh-eaters and long limbs, but some of the herds of these creatures had become too large to handle with just a detachment and needed a more significant force. This would take time to assemble; half the problem was that the flesh-eaters and long limbs were constantly moving. Their herds grew more sizeable by the day.

There was friction in the Senate over the costs of the planned invasion and the worry about American civilians and what was happening at home.

Charles walked into the office and sat across from Captain Steinberg. The other officers gathered around his desk, reviewing a map of Great Britain. Captain Steinberg started the meeting off by saying the orders had come through from the President regarding the invasion of Great Britain. The European and American forces would be split into different groups and land in various parts of the British Isles. Major Hayward would be part of the beach operations in Wales. The Pembrokeshire coastline had been earmarked as a suitable access point for the Engineers to establish a base camp. They would land at New Gale Beach and help with preparations for further encroachments into Great Britain. Other landing points had been selected along the West Coast.

The date had been set to July 15th. They were praying for good weather, which would give them time to advance quickly around the country. This could slow down the whole plan if it turned out to be a wet summer. Spies had reported that Nazar's main forces were still in Europe, and it was assumed he would be reluctant to re-invade. The American Senate saw this as an opportunity to try and negotiate a peace treaty with Nazar. He may not want to invade America if he were preoccupied with Great Britain. Many thought this could be wishful thinking, but all avenues were being urged to be explored before accepting the inevitable.

The regiment would set out for Boston within the next few days. The remaining civilians and a small force of soldiers would move to a larger camp near Seattle.

The officers looked at the map and then at each other; now that the landing date had been set, it felt more imminent. The British and European forces had been fighting this enemy for much longer than the Americans, but both parties had a vested interest in making this work.

The build-up of ammunition and weapon-making had begun a year and a half earlier. Supplies for the invasion were good, and the ships taking the men were ready. The landing crafts were the only vessels, a couple of months behind schedule. There had to be enough to get the main force to land quickly. Intelligence had indicated minimal artillery emplacements along the West Coast, another reason it had been selected.

The conversation lasted another thirty minutes before it was decided to reconvene the following day.

Charles left the cabin, thinking about what lay ahead. His position meant he had no choice in what he had to do. As a Major, he would be expected to help with this invasion; it was his duty.

The evening passed quietly. Rebecca read stories to Emily by the fire, and Arthur spoke about his hunting trips and chatted with Tom's father. It felt normal and serene.

Rebecca and Charles tucked Emily into bed and told Arthur not to stay up too late. They then went to sit by the log fire.

"They are growing up fast."

"They are changing; I pray we make it through this." Charles let his eyes sink to the floor. Rebecca came a little closer to him on the chair. She leaned into him and kissed him on the neck and then the cheek. "I'll keep them safe."

Chapter 11

Charles moved out onto the veranda. He sipped at his morning coffee and looked across the camp. The hustle and bustle of the day had not started; there was the odd person gathering wood or water, but there was a calmness in the air. He thought back to the evening before and smiled to himself. Those moments of family life had to be stored deep within his soul and cherished.

Charles sensed something behind him. He didn't have a weapon and looked around quickly at the floor for something to grab.

"Major, it's me, Hosah.

Charles breathed out a sigh of relief and turned around.

"It's a bit early to creep up on me like that." He said with an anxious half-smile.

"We have our tepees outside the fort." Hosah stood there looking serious.

"That's ok. Would you not like to set up inside the fort?"

Hosah nodded his head. "The wind carries another smell on it; it carries death."

Charles's facial expression was one of sadness. He spoke of what had recently happened with the flesh-eaters & long limb attacks on the women and children.

He then moved closer to Charles.

"I want to come to Great Britain with you."

"Hosah, we do not know what to expect when we arrive. The armies of Nazar control most of the world, and nothing has stopped his quest to become ruler of it."

The young brave looked out across the camp.

"My world has changed from my forefathers; the white man has brought with him war and disease, but I know what is coming will be worse than what is already here."

Charles rubbed the stubble on his chin.

"What would you gain by coming with us? you have helped us more than we have helped you?"

"Some tribes will side with Nazar when he lands in our lands. Some will move to the winter hunting lands and hope white-man and this foreign army kill each other." Hosah started to turn and walk towards the wooden steps leading down from the veranda.
   He looked back briefly." The chief in my tribe has said things will never return to how they were." He walked down the steps, "I want to fight them along with many other young braves from the Arapaho."

Charles watched him as he started to walk away. "We will need everyone we can get," he called out.

Hosah did not look back.

Chapter 12

"My Lord."

The trees are ready.

General Georgiy moved along with Nazar to a small pine woodland.

"Holland is looking like it's coming to life, and this is why we must take some"

Various generals and priests were gathered around the small woodlands. Oksana came to Nazar's side with their two boys. Thirty or more blindfolded people huddled together in silence amongst the pine trees. The grandmaster priest came forward with a scroll. His hands were bony and jagged, his eyes sunken into his dull skin, and his long grey hair moved slightly in the gentle spring breeze.

"These citizens of Nazar's realm have spoken out against our gracious leader."

There was a slight pause.

"The punishment is death."

Nazar looked over to a group of riders of the North. These men and women carried axes into the allotted area.

The grandmaster priest looked up.

"There is one caveat: if you survive this, you will be pardoned" With that, he rolled up the scroll and shuffled to join the crowds further back.

A woman within the blindfolded group shouted out that she was innocent. This action was met with an archer shooting an arrow into her chest. She let out a groan and fell to the ground, her blindfold still tightly wrapped around her head. There was a moment of silence before the crowd clapped and roared.

Nazar raised his left hand, and it fell silent again.

There was the odd whimper as the group sensed the change in the crowd. The noise coming from the onlookers was of excitement and expectation. It carried on the wind as this imminent event was about to unfold.

The trees around the blindfolded group had been pre-cut with bird-mouth openings, meaning it would not take long for the Riders of the North with their axes to cut through the trees, allowing them to fall on the unsuspecting victims. A small clearing in the middle of the woodland would allow the accused a starting point. It was then up to the Riders of the North to fell the pre-cut trees in their direction as they tried to make their way out. An added incentive to move was in the form of five long limbs. These creatures would be chained to the stumps in the middle of the woodlands, and as time went by, they would slowly be released from the stumps. If you tried to stay in one spot, you would eventually be caught by the long limbs.

Nazar raised his hand to bring a complete stop to the rumblings. The thirty Riders of the North were in place, their axes paused.

"Let the judgement begin."

The Riders of the North were big men and women; their average size was 6ft 5, and they carried a heavy build with that. Hearing Nazar's words, they raised their axes and began cutting away at the trees around the accused.

The first tree fell in the direction of the group. A gasp went out from the crowd, watching as it missed them all. This triggered panicked movement, sending them in different directions. The long limbs were then allowed more slack on the rope, keeping them from feeding on the blindfolded group; they began to get closer to any stragglers but were kept at a safe enough distance not to get crushed.

This triggered ten more Riders of the North to begin chopping. The sound of metal splitting wood reverberated around the woodlands; the crowd started to get excited again as the trees began to creak and edge towards the direction of the cuts.

The sound of axes striking wood unnerved the blindfolded group, and they began to break from their tight-knit circle.

A former French regional governor began to lead his wife up an embankment. Their crime had been not to supply Nazar's army with enough food during the previous winter. They had given all their town's supplies, but this was neither here nor there with Nazar.

The trees were creaking around them. The governor pulled his wife up, but they both stumbled on the slippery soil below. They never got up; a tree came down on top of them both, crushing them into the ground. The crowd roared with delight; it was the first victim of this new style of punishment.

Nazar nodded in approval to Melania, one of the officers in the Riders of the North. She had come up with the idea for this form of retribution.

This triggered ten more Riders of the North to begin chopping at the trees around the stricken group. The onlookers cheered and laughed, sensing that more action would surely follow.

As more trees began to fall in different directions, the blindfolded group split and headed everywhere. Three governors from Lyon fell victim to a falling pine tree. The weight of the tree crushed through their skin and bones and smashed them into the ground below. Their screams and yelps were lost in the noise of branches and splitting wood.

A clerk from Brittany broke free from her tied hands and lifted her blindfold. Oksana took a bow and arrow held by a destroyer drone standing next to them. She skillfully pulled back the bow and let the arrow fly effortlessly past the falling trees and into the woman as she looked around at what was unfolding. It struck her in the chest, forcing her to stagger backwards into a descending tree. She was buried within seconds.

Nazar was starting to get bored; even though the spectators were jumping with joy every time a tree landed on one of the blindfolded victims, his mind was focused on America. Oksana could sense his growing dissatisfaction that the vessels he needed for landing in America were not fully ready yet. This was partly the reason for the executions. He was letting his growing Empire know that failure was not an option.

His armies were training hard around Europe and Russia. His Brother Lev had his instructions for Great Britain, and fear and force kept the population there downtrodden. The infected walked in America, and this caused havoc amongst the communities across the country. Pavel Grengo was an officer who had helped bring the long limbs to the United States of America; his continued mission was to take over Europeans who had been recently bitten. Nazar knew the numbers in America would continue to grow as they infected more people in the towns and cities, but he wanted to add to this mayhem and keep the numbers high.

With a wave of his hand, he signalled to the long-limb handlers to release them. A handful of blindfolded people were closing in on escaping the woodland. This was an opportunity they would never get. The long limbs scrambled through the mud and leafy floor matter towards the fleeing few. The trees were still falling, but it did not mask the long limbs' chattering, groaning, snapping jaws.

They ferociously tore into the last surviving victims, who screamed and pleaded to be shown compassion. Nazar turned to his advisers and ushered them to his tents. He wanted to know more about how the Americans and British planned to take their homeland. This was crucial to his American invasion. He knew the remaining forces within America would be strong, but if they did not attack Great Britain, the quest for world domination would be more problematic.

Once his immediate council had gathered in his tent, an envoy came forward and told Nazar the British and American forces were massing near Boston. His response was to smile, and his sharpened teeth briefly showed to those in the tent.

"I have not ordered my officers here for a reason, but I will now act on this information given. I would hate for it to be miscalculated in any way."

Nazar called for his servants to fill the goblets. Once full, they raised them to eye level with everyone in the tent. They then tipped the goblets back swiftly, letting wine spill from the sides as they all drank at a forced pace. Nazar finished his first and let the goblet fall to the ground.

"Oksana, fetch the generals."
She returned with General Robert Conway and General Georgiy, Eltsina, and Pavel.

Two newly promoted officers accompanied them as they entered the tent. A 6ft 4 woman with dirty, long black hair and a thin, gangly young man stood behind the Generals. Robert Conway introduced them as Captain Turner and Captain Ward.

They stood there looking at Nazar, looking at them. The High Priest and a new Priestess soon joined him. She was promoted after Isabella Dupont's loss at the children's drone camp.

"It is nearly time to launch the greatest invasion of all time."

"Drink to success, and death for failure."

Chapter 13

Hagen, the Danish Viking, would be joining Major Hayward. He had sent him a letter stating his wish to join the fight for Europe. Rebecca had told Charles of his fighting prowess, and having someone who had fought in Europe would add value to their quest.

Charles had also heard that the Indian Lancers would accompany the Engineers. This would mean his command would consist of the American forces, Engineers, Indian Lancers, and a small collection of Europeans. Their role would be, as ever, to help support the invasion of Great Britain by building temporary bridges or helping maintain the camps and resources to aid a rapid advance inland.

There was a steady noise in the fort as preparations were made for the journey to Boston. Many British families would go to Montreal after the soldiers settled into the camp in Boston. The Native American Indians would stay within the fort; some had requested to join the land invasion, and Charles had agreed. Hosah wanted to explore the world. His elders have said he should stay with his people, but he said the world was changing, and it was the only way to see what lay ahead.

The planned trip would take around four weeks by steam train, meaning it would be mid-May by the time they arrived. Once in Boston, they would go over landing drills before settling off to sail around early June. The weather had to be considered, and a summer crossing was considered a safer and more suitable option for success. The spies had brought back news that Nazar and his forces were still not stationed in Great Britain. This was still being monitored, as they wanted to avoid landing against his entire force.

The long-term plan was distraction and divide and conquer. Some Senators wanted to work to cut a deal with Nazar, saving America from war. They even thought they could offer key British & European dignitaries as a bargaining tool. This, fortunately, was not a wholly shared view. Most thought it would only be a matter of time before he invaded anyway, and the President was of the same persuasion. If he fought on several fronts, his forces would be weakened. The British and the Americans thought that if he were to reinforce his armies in England, this would delay any American assault. There was a lot of speculation going around, and no one knew his next move, but the combined allied invasion was happening.

Charles and Rebecca had a family meal with their children. He cooked roast chicken and served it with seasonal vegetables. Rebecca had been given a bottle of wine from one of the French wives who had arrived at the fort, and this was thoroughly enjoyed with the meal. The evening passed with the children talking and sitting by the fire. Arthur told Emily how he and Hosah had encountered a brown bear, although only Arthur knew how true the story was. Rebecca gave him a look, as if to say,' Do not scare Emily too much, ' and then continued to read a book while sitting on a settee near the fire. Charles was seated in a large armchair, which had seen better days, directly across from them. He looked at the flames licking around the wood and saw how a newly placed log slowly ignited and burned. He listened as the fire popped and wheezed; it seemed alive, craving more fuel, always hungry and never satisfied. It was essentially the same as a flesh-eater, always looking for new food, never satisfied. His mind raced through the creatures now wandering the planet and how everything had changed.

Rebecca broke his gaze by stroking his cheek softly. He looked up at her loving face; he did not want to leave his family again; there was every chance he would not make it back, and he did not know how safe America or Canada would be for his family, but sadly, there was no natural choice. Rebecca said it was time to get them all to bed as the journey to Boston was long. That evening would represent the last quality time together as a family. Yes, they would have moments on the journey, but Charles would spend much of his time with his soldiers. Rebecca and Charles looked at each other as they said goodnight to Emily and Arthur. Arthur was growing daily; his hunting trips and newfound friend Tom had changed his mindset on the new world.

The shutters on the log cabins rattled, and the structure creaked a little as the wind blew in from the East. This made Charles stir; he looked over at his wife sleeping, her head nuzzled into her pillow, which brought a smile to his face. He got up quietly and did a quick check on the children. He checked that the windows and doors were secure and, on his way back to the bedroom, took a moment to sit in the old armchair for a few minutes, contemplating what lay ahead.

Chapter 14

The wagons were loaded and ready to roll out by mid-morning; there would be a detachment of American soldiers staying at the fort alongside the Native American Indians who would be camped inside it for safety.

The plan was to travel to Boulder and then on to Denver to get the steam trains to Boston. Sergeant Butcher mopped his brow with a handkerchief he had in the top pocket of his tunic. It had been heavy work getting supplies ready for the long journey ahead. His wife, Christina and their son and daughter would travel to Canada with Rebecca and the other wives and children.

The buzz of expectation grew around the fort. The younger soldiers wanted to meet the enemy face to face, and the older ones wanted the war to be won. Charles met with the officers briefly to have coffee before they set out. The spirits were high, and Captain Steinberg spoke about his replacement, who would be coming in a week or two; in the meantime, Corporal Collins would man the small unit that was staying behind.

The wagons would be in blocks of ten and have cavalry between them in case of a long-limb attack. Scouts had been sent out a week earlier, and the route had been given the all-clear.

Charles called over his officers and scouts, and Texas was allowed to join them. He was an experienced frontiersman and would join them in the invasion of Britain. Hosah also came over to listen to the debriefing. Once the officers and scouts were gathered around, he went over the route again. He talked about the recent attack by long limbs and flesh-eaters. They would not have the mounted machine guns or artillery they had if it hadn't been for the experience of fleeing Europe all those years ago. There would be points along the Train to have lookouts posted, and at the back of each train, there would be a guard's carriage with soldiers armed with Winchester rifles. It was hoped the journey would be uneventful, and no military deployment would be needed.

There were enough food supplies for the whole journey, and there would be stations along the route for the trains to gather coal and water. It had been envisaged that they would stop along the route to get out and stretch, maybe staying a night or two in certain towns. The officers put forward questions or ideas, including using flags to signal codes to the different trains. This was seen as the quickest form of communication they could use. After the debrief, Charles smiled at them and shook their hands, "Here's to a safe journey."

The dust kicked up as the wagons started to roll. Bandanas were raised over the faces of the horseback riders and those sitting at the front of the wagons. The Buffalo soldiers were riding at the back of the convoy until they reached the station. This way, there would be protection from the rear and the front.

The sun shone brightly in the sky, and birds flew from tree to tree, gathering twigs for their nests. Spring was erupting everywhere around them. The children in the wagons looked out the back, watching this unfold.

Charles rode behind Rebecca and the children's wagon. He watched them interact; he liked seeing his family safe in one place as they moved. He thought about the soldiers under his command and the journey ahead to Great Britain.

The responsibility weighed heavily on his shoulders. There was no real place to run to; Nazar's creatures were spreading throughout America and were probably in Canada now; it all had a sense of pending inevitability.

The group camped out on a ridge just a short distance from Boulder. The wagons were circled together, and guards were posted around the perimeter. They would move on to Boulder and take the steam train to Boston the following day.

An owl landed on a wagon and kept hooting until a cavalryman took a wooden pole and scared it off. The night passed without incident.

They left early the next morning. As they approached Boulder, a small band of American soldiers came out to meet them. The spring weather brought everything around the town to life, and the craggy foothills overlooking Boulder gave it an impressive backdrop.

They entered the town at a steady pace. The hustle and bustle around them felt good; people did not pay too much attention as the wagons rolled towards the station. Markets were selling various foods and other items. The local population seemed unconcerned with what was happening in the outside world.

Arthur watched the children playing in the streets and women washing clothes in long water troughs. It was how he remembered England used to be and the life they once had there. The thought of the terror coming to this town when Nazar's armies landed made goosebumps erupt across his arms. It was something he wished on nobody.

Boulder had watchtowers already looking for flesh-eaters, but he would bring fear and destruction across the lands if Nazar came.

When they finally arrived at the station, three steam engines with carriages were waiting for them. They had guard carriages along each train, at the front of the train, behind the tender and at the back behind the last carriage. The plan was for them to travel at a safe distance from each other so that, should they have to stop, the other trains would not smash into one another. They all had horse carriages and carts to load the wagons onto. Moving the provisions and supplies onto the trains would take a while. This meant the soldiers and families could walk around the town while waiting. Money had been issued to European soldiers, and small wages were being sent down to the major camps, but it was hard to administrate this. Great Britain was using Canada to help facilitate payments. The main focus was ensuring the refugees had food and a roof over their heads. It was a moot point, of course, being argued in the Senate about the cost and support for Europe.

Charles held Rebecca's hand as they strolled along with Emily. She was walking just in front of them, swinging a doll around. A warm, soft breeze carried the smell of freshly baked bread. This drew them all towards a baker's shop tucked just off a main street across from them. They could almost taste the air, fresh flour and yeast enticing them in. They bought several fresh loaves and butter to go with it. After a short walk, they took them to a bench where they sat down to devour the warm bread. Emily rolled her eyes as she enjoyed each mouthful. "We best save some for Arthur". Rebecca shook her head, drawing a look from Charles.

"I'm just kidding, Emily; we'll save him a loaf." This drew another look from Charles.

"He's a teenage boy and will need the food." They all smiled at this. Arthur was with Tom near the trains. They had stayed to help load supplies with the soldiers based at Boulder.

Whilst Charles finished the last bit of his bread, something caught his eye. To the side of the bakery, he saw a tall, thin man speaking to a police officer. Both looked dishevelled and out of place in the town. The thin man was chewing tobacco and spitting it out every few minutes. He was showing the policeman a piece of paper, and almost simultaneously, they turned to look over at Charles. The policeman then nodded his head. With that, they both turned and left in different directions. Charles told Rebecca to meet him at the train station as he had to grab one more thing from a nearby store.

The tall, thin man moved at speed down different interconnecting streets; Charles kept a safe distance as he followed him through various alleys. He stopped at a barbershop—Mr Miggins Clean Cuts. He then looked around once before entering.

The tall, thin man sat in a barber's chair near the window. One barber was busy cutting the hair of a slightly round man; his hair was wet and flopped over the side of his face. The other barber came forward and brought a towel with him. Within a flick, he had placed it across the gentleman's lap and upper body, wrapping it around his neck. He muttered that he wanted a shave.

The barber quickly removed his razor and shaving foam from a bowl beside a grubby mirror. He had a small brush to apply the foam to the thin man's face. Charles sat behind him, trying to gauge what was happening with the paper and why they looked at him. The uniform Charles was wearing was khaki. He wasn't wearing his tunic, so he had army trousers and a thick jumper. The thin man had not clocked; he was sitting behind him and lowered himself back in the chair.

Charles looked around outside and then noticed another man with a scruffy long beard and dark clothes hanging around the barbers. After a few minutes, he came into the shop. He went straight to the thin man sitting in the chair. "Do you have the map?"

The thin man raised his hand to get the barber to stop cutting. "Why are you here now? I've shown the officer; he knows where they're going."

Charles stood up, causing the thin man and the other man to turn around. The scruffy, bearded man placed his hand across his coat, exposing the tip of a revolver.

"What are you after, stranger?"

"I saw your friend looking at me and my family, then showing a policeman a map."
The thin man stood up. "What's it to do with you?"

"Maybe nothing, maybe everything."

The thin man laughed. "The British have already been beaten from here a long time ago; you should never have been allowed back in." The scruffy-bearded man let out a fake laugh to accompany the thin man's laugh.

The thin man stood up from his chair. Reaching inside the shaving poncho that covered his body, he pulled out a knife. The scruffy man smiled.

"You better start talking English. Otherwise, I'll make you."

Charles reached under his coat, revealing the Enfield revolver. In one instance, the scruffy man pulled out his pistol, which Charles matched. "We have the upper hand, English. Throw down the gun."

Charles looked at them. The tension was suddenly broken by the barber's door being flung open. An arm was extended, and a revolver was grasped firmly in their hand. A sharp, aggressive voice shouted, "Put the gun down" Charles knew the voice; it was Rebecca. She was edging her way into the store and had the gun pointed at the head of the thin man. They were now facing two guns; the scruffy-bearded man started to twitch and shake a little; he then spoke up. "We don't want no trouble."

Charles replied. "Show me the map".

The thin man answered.

"We don't have it, the policemen took it."

"What was on the map?" Charles pulled the hammer back on the revolver.

"Nothing, just names of stores and monies owed."

Charles shook his head.

"You know, we are part of the invasion force. You're lying to me."

A crowd had gathered outside; several policemen soon joined them. They had their guns drawn on Rebecca and pointed at the shop. A police sergeant with a large moustache slowly moved past Rebecca. He didn't stand in front of her gun, but to the side. He looked at Charles standing there with his revolver.

"Someone not happy with their haircut." He said in a calm voice. It got Charles and the two other men to look at him. The two barbers stayed still.

"This looks like a difficult situation, but let's calm down."

Charles looked again at the men. "It's not difficult. I'm heading to Boston with the British Engineers. These gentlemen have something on a map, and I believe it could be relevant to a future mission."
The sergeant looked at everyone in the room.

"Do you have a map?"

The thin man shrugged his shoulders. "What, map?" Search my coat?"

The scruffy man nodded, feeling this conversation was moving in the right direction. The sergeant searched the man's coat and found nothing, which brought a massive smile to the thin man's face. "Lower your weapons, everyone."

Charles did this reluctantly, and Rebecca followed suit, along with the others. The sergeant pointed out that there was no map. He asked Charles to step out of the barbershop. Outside, a Police Captain stood by a street lamp. It was the same officer the thin man had been talking to. He smiled and told everyone to move along.

"Go to Boston, Englishmen." He waved his officers to move everyone on.

Charles glanced at Rebecca; he knew he didn't like this, but it wasn't his country to make any bold moves. "We should go, Charles."

"Is Emily ok? Yes, she's with Sergeant Butcher."

Charles stared at the police officer. "Nazar won't win, you know."

This just brought back a crude smile.

"Maybe we'll meet again, Charles, or should I say Major?"

Charles just looked at him and then at the barbers.

The thin man had sat back in a barber's chair alongside the scruffy, bearded man. Both of them smiled as Charles and Rebecca walked away.

"What was that about, Charles? Why didn't you say anything earlier?"

She was cross with him for going off on a whim.

"I know, I'm sorry. They were looking at us; they must be in alliance with Nazar."

He rubbed his stubble. Rebecca brushed the side of his face. "It's not safe to stay here. We must move." He agreed and took her hand to walk back to the station.

The station was busy with soldiers helping load supplies. Arthur was standing next to Emily, both of them giggling. Tom was also there, laughing away.

Seeing the children safe and well helped Charles relax more.

"Thank you, my love, for helping me back there; you turned up in the nick of time."

Rebecca smiled at him, "Just promise me you will keep your wits about you in Great Britain." A stern look followed.

"I will; no rushing in, I promise."

Rebecca nodded and then went over to Emily, Arthur and Tom.

Charles thanked Sergeant Butcher for looking after his children and asked if he could quickly gather the officers. The debrief was to the point; they wanted to keep to the journey time. He explained that they needed to be extra vigilant, as the men with whom he had had an altercation with were seen discussing something over a map. What was on that map, they would never know. They would now double the watch on the guard carriages and have spotters along some of the train rooftops when pulling into towns.

They continued to load the horse carts and reinforce the back carriages with sandbags and wood. Glass was taken out of some of the carriage windows. Charles pushed for the back carriage to have a Gatling gun fitted. There would not be time to add one to each guard carriage. There had been requests and timetables sent from Washington to not clog up the supply routes. They were instructed to stick to the correct time slots so that things would work more efficiently. There was a lot of land between Boulder and Boston. Once the supplies and ammunition had been loaded. The civilians and soldiers boarded the trains in earnest. The warmth reflecting off the glass struck Rebecca as she walked towards the front train. Charles and the Engineers would travel on the front train, along with the Arapaho Indians and the British civilians. The American soldiers would be in the other two trains. There would be some American civilians travelling with them.

Arthur was larking around with Tom; both had taken a fancy to some American girls. They had caught the eye of two girls in particular who were travelling on the second train. Their teenage hormones were kicking in and driving them on. They didn't know their names but were grateful they were travelling to Boston. Tom had a crush on one of the girls with long black hair and big green eyes; Arthur's crush was slightly different; she had blonde hair with blue eyes, and she was nearly as tall as him and had particularly strong cheekbones. The boys hadn't spoken to their newly found love interests, but they were trying to build up the courage to do so. Tom was egging Arthur to break the ice and said if he didn't do it soon, they would have to wait until the next station, where it was planned for them to stay a night.

Arthur saw some of the American and British officers checking sheets for names and orderlies, asking the families and civilians if everyone was accounted for. Tom said he understood if it wasn't the time to find their names, as he was too nervous to ask. Arthur thought of Sophie and their short time together; a lot had changed, and he hoped to see more of her in the future, but now he was facing a challenge. He knew he could not travel on their train, as it would separate him from his mother and fathers. They would not allow him to leave their sight at any station afterwards if he did something that caused a delay.

On impulse, he ran and banged the window of the girls' carriage. Tom had left to stand on the end guard carriage. "Come on, Arthur, quick, before we go."
The girl with the black hair pointed to the carriage door. She moved along to it with haste. Whistles sounded out as soldiers and train conductors called for everyone to board.

She made it to the door. "What's your name?"

"Arthur and yours."

"Naomi,"

"That's a nice name, I'm going to Boston." He said a little sheepishly.

She smiled, "If you don't get on your train, you're staying in Boulder."

He smiled; suddenly, the girl he thought he wanted to speak to wasn't the girl he wanted to talk to. His heart started to pump; it was this girl, Naomi.

"I hope we get a chance to speak again."

"We will, Arthur, but don't miss your train. It's leaving."
She looked a little more frantic.

Arthur looked ahead, and the train started to move. He smiled and waved at her, but in the process, slipped over. He got up, dusted himself off and gave a little salute, which he regretted as soon as he did it. Then he took in a big gulp of air and started to run; the train was starting to move quicker. Tom was hanging off the end guard carriage with his arm outstretched. Arthur just sprinted; all he could think of as he ran was how cute Naomi was, her soft lips, beautiful face and dreamy eyes. He was a little concerned he wasn't going to make the train, though and knowing the severe consequences this would have, he sprinted faster.

As he got close to the guard carriage, a hand came out. It wasn't Tom's. It was Corporal Heinz. He helped haul him up onto the steps. "Cutting it fine, Arthur." He smiled at him. "Who was the girl?" I think her name is Naomi; he paused as he caught his breath. "Thank you for helping me; please don't tell my mother and father."

"I won't, but please don't take any risks over this girl."

Chapter 15

Arthur sat on the carriage floor in a dream world. He had a big grin on his face and was proud of himself. Corporate Heinz said he would leave him in his thoughts and went off to join the other Engineers. After a few minutes, Arthur got up and looked out the back window; he watched the train behind them slowly start to pull away. He had butterflies in his stomach thinking about Naomi, and then he thought about having to tell Tom. He felt terrible as Tom had shown an interest in Naomi, and he had said he liked the blonde-haired girl, but that all changed with his short conversation with Naomi.

He left the carriage and went to find Tom. Arthur looked at the British soldiers in their khaki uniforms as he walked through the carriages. They were sitting and chatting, and the ones with families played with their children and generally relaxed. The great plains were on view as they trundled along, with their sweeping prairie grass gently moving in the spring breeze. A shout went up as a small child spotted a group of Buffalo wandering along, grazing as they went. This brought most of the children to the left-hand side of the carriage as they watched these powerful beasts feed.

He found Tom rushing back towards him. "I went up to the engine. I was going to ask them to stop if you didn't get on. Then, returning to the guard's carriage, he bumped into Corporal Heinz and said he helped you up. "

He could tell Tom was happy to see him and was eager for news on the girls. "Tom, I made contact."

"Yes, yes, what did you say?" Tom was almost hoping on the spot.

"Tom, before I go on, I think I should say that I fancy Naomi, the girl with the black hair." Arthur almost looked down after saying it.

Tom was a little puzzled for a second and then laughed. "Arthur, you broke the ice for us. I like the look of the blonde girl anyway; I just hope she likes me."

Arthur let out a gulp of air. "Thanks, Tom." "We need to see when we stop if we can approach them more."

Arthur felt relieved that everything was going so well. He sat in a spare carriage chair and leaned against the window. Tom joined him; they were both silent and stared out onto the plains.

The steam trains had gathered enough speed to move at a good pace. They were separated by enough distance to break and stop.

The journey settled down, with some soldiers falling asleep and others smoking outside on the open trucks carrying supplies. Charles walked through each carriage and truck, checking on everything as he went along. Sergeant Butcher caught up with Charles as he moved along.

"You seem a little on edge."

"I guess it's the map and what happened in Boulder." Charles looked out of the window as they moved along. "North Platte is where we stop for a few days, let the horses stretch and let everyone move around." He had agreed with Captain Steinberg that this was an excellent place to stop. Sergeant Butcher went to check on the guard carriage, and Charles went to sit with Rebecca and Emily. Emily had gone to play with her friend Nicola in the other carriage. Rebecca was reading a book and looking very relaxed.

"Sit next to me, Charles." He accepted her request and sat down.

Charles leaned over and kissed her on the cheek. "Start your book again; it's all going smoothly. I know you want everyone to be safe, but you must switch off sometimes."

He nodded and sat back on the carriage seat. He picked up his book, which he had left beside Rebecca, and started reading.

This was the pattern for the next several days. There had been a few stations they had stopped at along the way to stretch their legs and cook. Arthur and Tom were not allowed to leave the vicinity of their train. Only the officers were permitted to have a quick update on all of the trains.

Charles started to relax the longer the journey went on. When they pulled into North Platte, the town was full of people going about their business. The vastness of America always struck Charles; the train journey confirmed the sheer size of the country. He knew this could help in its defence or possibly hinder it.

The trains filled their tenders with coal and water. The passengers were relieved to get off and spend a few days moving about. It was decided they would decamp for two days. The horses would be allowed to graze and be ridden to exercise them. The families and soldiers could get some fresh air and move about.

Rebecca was happy to help set up a small camp for them. They would still post guards even though the townsfolk said they had not seen any flesh-eaters or walkers, as they called them, wandering around. They said it's pretty safe in "those parts."

Arthur and Tom had asked their parents about going to see a friend from the other train; they would be in the same camp, and it would be an excellent time to speak to them.

Arthur did not feel as brave as he had first felt; he was concerned about whether he could still talk to Naomi correctly.

Tom was just nervous and didn't want to say anything. Arthur said they had to find them and make contact.

Charles helped Hosah and his fellow braves get their tepees and other materials into the camp. Hosah remarked on the train's progress and how it was strange to sit and watch the world go by. He had seen the iron machine rolling across the great plains, its smoke leaving a trail as it went along. The braves were given British uniforms, which they modified to suit their preferences, but it at least helped them to be associated with his men.

Charles was impressed with their knowledge and skills in using natural resources, their ability to set up camp quickly, and their understanding of the land's flora and fauna. He wondered how this new world would suit indigenous people with adaptable skills.

Captain Steinberg walked over from the second steam train and spoke to Charles. They talked about how well the journey was going, but also about keeping their wits about them. The camp was set up not too far from the trains. Guards had been posted by them and around the encampment. The civilians were told to visit the town during the day but report back before dusk. There had been a roll call for everyone, and this would be carried out daily.

Arthur and Tom walked over to the second train, trying to see the passengers getting off. They both looked at each other when neither of the girls was seen.

"Do you think they were not travelling to Boston, Arthur?"

Arthur looked puzzled. "My father said everyone on the train was travelling to Boston."

"Then where are they?" Tom said, shrugging his shoulders.

"Let's go back to the camp and look."

They wandered back and sat on a wagon overlooking the soldiers setting up tents. A Gatling gun was placed facing out across the open prairies. Captain Somerset had taken a small detachment out to search the surrounding area for flesh-eaters and long limbs; even if there had not been sightings, extra vigilance was needed.

"I can't see them here, either said Tom."

Both boys laid back on the wagon.

"Arthur, are you helping out?" The soft voice made both boys jump up.

Arthur and Tom almost fell off the wagon when they heard the voice. Naomi and the other girl were in front of them. They were carrying bread and other supplies in two bags.

"My friend here is called Florence,"

Tom blushed on hearing her name and had to look down at the ground instead of making eye contact.

Arthur was still nervous, but hearing Naomi speak again put him at ease, which brought a smile to his face.

"Nice to meet you, Florence; this is my friend Tom." Tom was now bright red and almost shaking. He managed a soft "Hello", but it was barely audible.

Florence said hello back and seemed relatively quiet herself.

"Shall we take a walk on the prairies?" Naomi was straight to the point.

"Well, yes, that would be nice. I need to check with my father; he's the Major of the British Engineers." Arthur was concerned about walking onto the prairies and thought this would be refused. He planned to ask his mother.

Naomi was looking like she wasn't going to ask her parents. "I haven't seen any of those things on this journey." She paused. "I'm sure it will be fine if we don't go too far; the South Platte River is not far from here. If I speak to my uncle, who is transporting horses to Boston, we can borrow four."

Tom looked at Arthur. It was a look of wanting to do it, but I'm sure your father and mother would say no.

Arthur put his left hand over his eyes. "Ok, we all take a weapon with us, and make sure we're only gone for a couple of hours max."

Naomi smiled, "Great, give me thirty minutes, come back to this spot, and I'll have the horses. You bring what we need to protect ourselves."

Naomi came forward and brushed the side of Arthur's cheek. Her hands were soft, and it made him feel funny all over. He looked at her, not knowing what to say. The only thing going through his head was that he wanted to go on a horse ride with her.

The boys said a quick bye and went to get some things for the excursion.

"Arthur, your father will kill us if we go, and my mum will."

"Tom, I'm going to tell my mother we're heading into town for a couple of hours."

Tom nodded his head but stayed quiet for a while as they walked to find Rebecca.

When they did catch up with Rebecca, she was helping set up their tent with Emily. She was happy to see both boys and said Tom's mother was asking after him. Arthur said they would be heading into town for a couple of hours, and he would see them later. Rebecca told them not to go too far and asked Tom to speak to his mother first. Tom went and found her whilst Arthur loaded a revolver and rifle, plus a hunting knife, into his travelling bag. He had been allowed to take out these weapons when he went hunting. His mother and father had allowed him to learn how to shoot and train with Hosah, the Indians had life skills which would help them all.

Chapter 16

Arthur loaded the bag discreetly; he didn't want his mother to see him doing so. He felt terrible for not telling the truth, but also a little excited by the chance to go with Naomi to the river for a few hours. Arthur looked over his shoulder and saw his mother and sister continue to set up the tent. It made him question his judgment, and he was still thinking about that when Tom turned up. "I hope they do not find out what we're doing, Arthur."

Arthur reassured him that they would not be too long and that it would be a pleasant trip to the river. Tom brought some blankets, water canisters, and some fresh bread with butter.

They met at the rendezvous spot; Naomi had brought four horses with her. Florence was holding the reins of Naomi's horse, and Naomi walked the other two to Arthur and Tom. Tom admitted he wasn't the greatest rider in the Wild West, which raised a smile out of Florence. Tom noticed that, and it made him want to spend time talking to Florence.

Arthur handed a rifle to Tom and a revolver to Naomi. "Do you know how to use this?" She smiled and said she had shot tin cans a few times and would ensure he didn't get taken by wolves. Arthur smiled back at her; he liked her humour. Arthur had a dagger for Florence and showed it to her "Sorry, I do not have another gun". She shrugged her shoulders and then asked him to place it in the saddlebag. When this was done, they all mounted up. Naomi had a small map of how to get to the river, and she led the way; the heat was bouncing off the grass and coming upwards as they rode. Arthur had a Stetson hat, as did Tom, and the girls wore bonnets.

"I'm looking forward to having a dip," Arthur remarked.

"Naked?" Naomi said with a chuckle.

Arthur felt himself going red.

"No, the water will be too cold." He was happy with his comeback.

Naomi brought her horse next to his.

"You ride pretty well; where did you learn?" Naomi was impressed with his handling of the horse.

"I learnt back in England, but the Arapaho taught me to ride differently."

They spoke about his involvement in the war and how it had engulfed Europe and Great Britain. The story of his mother helping them escape Nazar's army of the dead under the catacombs of Paris made Naomi lean in even closer. She was amazed they made it out and said she felt for all the families that didn't. She was concerned that it was coming to America. The Europeans had arrived, and then the walkers came. She said they now knew that if you were bitten by one of the infected, you would turn unless you could chop that bite area off. Then there were the creatures with extra-long limbs, sharp teeth and sunken eyes. They moved in packs and were more dangerous than wolves.

The talk of Nazar drifted away as they closed in on the river. The spot that they chose was shallow, with clear flowing water. It wasn't too deep and was perfect to swim in. They dismounted and tied their horses to a collection of cottonwood trees near the riverbank. The girls had brought food as well, some fresh fruit and cake. This was all put under the trees whilst they went to the water's edge.

Tom was the first to dip his toe, letting out a yelp as it touched the water. The boys stripped down to their underwear; once they had done this, they suddenly remembered they were with girls they had only just met. The girls were giggling, but Naomi took the lead and took off her clothes down to her petticoat. Florence was a bit reluctant at first, but once Tom jumped in and shouted about how cold the water was, she followed suit.

Arthur dived in and was shocked at how cold the water was. He came up and let out a cry as well, "Damn, that is so cold." Naomi went under the water, as did Florence; their reaction was the same.

"We have to keep moving or freeze to death." Naomi led the way and kicked around in the water.

They spent a good while splashing each other and messing around. Arthur looked at Naomi, Tom and Florence; he enjoyed the carefree moment; they were teenagers having fun. He yearned for the world to return to normal, but first, Nazar would have to be defeated.

When they decided to come out, they ran to the blankets; the sun was warm enough to make the transition not too painful. They talked about how nice it was to get off the train and stretch their legs.

They laid out the blankets and took out the food to have something to eat. Arthur had checked his watch, and it'd only be an hour. Naomi and Arthur shared some bread and spoke about growing up in America and England. She was travelling with her uncle and Florence, who was her cousin. They were helping move the horses to Boston. Many were being reared to support the war effort; others were sold to farmers or cowboys.

Florence was starting to open up and chat more with Tom; he had lost some of his nerves and was reciprocating the conversation.

The food was quickly consumed as they sat there, drying in the warm sun. While talking, Naomi saw a farm building further down the river. Even where they were sitting, it looked run-down, and an old, dilapidated barn was next to it.

"Shall we check out the old farmhouse?" Naomi was looking at them all.

Arthur liked her spirit, but he was also acutely aware that they were already disobeying their parents; they were a few miles from the station, and the shadows from the trees were getting longer.

"I think we need to head back soon." Tom was thinking the same as Arthur.

Naomi nodded but then whispered in Florence's ear. They both smiled.

"If we go there quickly, each couple can get one minute to French kiss in the old house."

Arthur looked at Tom. Neither boy had had any experience of kissing. The idea of French kissing sounded exciting, but also worrying to them.

Tom stood up and beckoned Arthur to come over and talk to him.

"What do you think, Arthur? I wouldn't mind kissing Florence, but I know time is moving on."

He was moving on his toes, and Arthur had noticed Tom doing that when he was a bit nervous.

"I'm not sure; if we get back too late, there will be an uproar, but I really want to kiss Naomi."

They decided to go there for ten minutes max, then head back. The girls looked excited when the boys agreed; the only conditions were: if it's unsafe, they leave, and if time slips away, they head back. They loaded the blankets and leftover food in the saddlebags. The rifles were collected from the trunk of one of the cottonwood trees where they stood. Naomi had her revolver in the right-hand saddlebag. Florence had moved the dagger from the saddle bag and tucked it into a sheath strapped across her back. Arthur told Tom to keep the rifle across his back as well. He wanted them to be on guard.

Once mounted, they rode over to the barn. As they moved along the river, some areas started to flow a little faster. Gullies and crooks caused the water to flash up and bubble as the current intensified. They took the horses further away from the river's edge as they closed in on the farmhouse. When they arrived, the horses were tied to an old fence post. Arthur said he would go in first with Tom covering outside, and then the girls would guard the horses.

Broken windows and smashed wood adorned the outside. The front door was hanging on one hinge and looking tired. Around the yard, there were broken barrels and a wagon with three wheels. Bushes and weeds were reclaiming the land around it.

"Tom, cover the yard as I go in."

An Oak tree stood tall and proud near the barn; its branches and leaves helped shade part of the old farmhouse. The breeze was constant and refreshing; they stood downwind with the sun behind them. Arthur paused momentarily and then raised his rifle as he entered the house. He hit the butt of the rifle against the door before he went in. They had learnt that the dead reacted to sound. He waited a minute or two, and nothing came.

He then pressed forward through the door; it had dark-lit areas, even with the sun beaming outside. The corridors were narrow and had an aroma of dust and rotting wood. In the kitchen, there was an overturned table with broken chairs around it; the cupboards were empty, and whoever had lived there before had left long ago. Arthur did a quick sweep of the rooms and found nothing in them. Then, he left the same way he had come in.

"It looks safe; let's check the barn." Tom nodded his head.

Both boys opened the barn doors wide. The roof was partially missing, letting in light; a bird flew up in front of them, making Tom lift his rifle, ready to shoot. Arthur smiled and said, "It's okay."

"That was scary." He smiled

Arthur went in. Firewood had been stacked high to the roof on the right. At the opening of the barn door, on the left-hand side, lay a dead cow carcass. Further inside, at the back, was leftover farm machinery. Most of the things in there were broken or rotting. Tom searched around the wood, and it was declared safe.

"I'm a bit worried, Arthur; I haven't kissed a girl before."

"I feel the same. Hopefully, they will lead the way."

Arthur called Naomi and Florence to the barn. They came looking happy and eager. Naomi stepped forward.

"Follow me, Arthur." She walked behind the wood stack. Tom and Florence waited outside.

Once they were out of sight, Naomi and Arthur looked at each other. Naomi had large green eyes that sparkled in the light. Her skin was smooth, and her lips soft and raised. She caressed the side of his face and gently put her hand behind his head, bringing him closer. Arthur's heart skipped a beat, and he felt a weird sensation all over; he couldn't speak and let her direct him in. The sensation of their lips touching excited Arthur; it was something he had thought about, what it would be like to kiss a girl, and now it was happening. The kiss was slow and lasted just a few seconds, but it felt amazing.

When they stopped, he smiled. She then came forward, and they started to kiss again. It was faster than before; then, she began to put her tongue in his mouth. Arthur was taken aback at first because he hadn't kissed anyone before, and now they were French kissing, or his version of it. It was passionate, and he was excited by the whole experience. They broke off, and Naomi asked how he was. Arthur replied great, before they could kiss again, Tom called out.

"Ok, love birds. Times are up."

Arthur was wrapped up in the moment. He wasn't thinking about whether it was time to swap; he was thinking about what just happened. They both walked out of the barn, looking very pleased with themselves. Tom and Florence looked at them as they came out happy, and then they both walked into the barn to go behind the wood stack.

Naomi stood with Arthur; they were both silent for a few seconds. "I'm just going to check on the horses."

Arthur acknowledged this, but he was still in a dream world. The fact that he was in a dream world meant he didn't notice what was moving along the riverbank. It was slow and steady; now, it was closing in on the barn.

"Arthur, there's a giant wolf in the barn." A worried call crept out from the barn.

His heart rate sped up. The last time he thought about giant wolves was when they escaped from Europe and were attacked at the fort in the Carpathian Mountains.

Without a second thought, he moved into the barn. His eyes fell upon a giant wolf; its hair was up, and its growl was a deep, fierce rumble from the beast's belly. Arthur raised his rifle, Tom was already aiming, and Florence had unsheathed her dagger. "Where's Naomi Arthur?"

"She's with the horses, Florence."

The wolf rocked a bit from side to side. Its eyes were almost yellow, its teeth were shown as the growls grew more intense. "Start to back up, you two."

"Shall we shoot it, Arthur?"

"Wait a second, Tom, it's 2-3 times bigger than a normal wolf."

Florence looked around as they backed up and winced as her right leg scraped against a piece of wood sticking out of the wood stack. She kept in the pain, but blood poured out of her leg and down onto the barn soil below. She raised her dagger towards the wolf, as they kept moving backwards, the growls intensified. Arthur looked up to notice another normal-sized wolf on the woodpile. Two more appeared in the dilapidated barn and slowly made their way up the side of the barn.

"This is not good." Tom raised his rifle to shoot the large wolf in the head.

"There are at least four wolves in here, Tom; we must pick our moment."

Arthur then stopped moving. They had backed themselves into a corner; he aimed at the creature's head. Tom did the same.

"Now"

They both shot their rifles into the giant wolf's head. Tom's bullet hit the wolf's jaw and smashed it open; Arthur's bullet smacked in the right eye socket of the wolf. These bullets killed the creature, causing it to slump straight away. This instantly brought on an attack from the other wolves. The wolf on top of the wood stack started clambering to get at them.

The two wolves coming up the side of the barn went straight for them. Arthur did not have time to load another bullet. A wolf with a grey stripe down its face lunged at him; the power of the strike sent him flying backwards. Tom tried to load another bullet as Arthur used his rifle to block the bites, as he was on his back.

Florence tried to react to the other wolf coming from her side, but it knocked her down, causing her to let out a scream as it bit into her arm and body. This wolf was black, its fur matted together, and its breath smelt of rotting flesh. Tom kicked out at the wolf, which then turned on him. The third wolf had descended from the wood stack, sending old logs crashing to the ground. It went straight for Tom. He cried out for help. Arthur tried to move, but the other wolf was biting and snapping at him. Florence moved forward and stabbed her dagger into the leg of the wolf biting Tom. This wolf recalled back; it snarled at her and tried to get the dagger out. It then lurched towards her.

Tom felt the sharp pain as the teeth started to break through the skin. The wolf with the matted black fur was now biting into his side. Arthur could not think straight, but he wished he'd told his mother and father where they had gone. They started to lose hope as the soil around them began to be stained with wolf and human blood.

Bang!

The wolf on Florence yelped and slumped over to its side. Then, another two shots rang out, and the black-furred wolf broke off the attack and limped off. The grey stripe wolf on Arthur was still biting him. The following bullet hit its back legs, then the second hit its body. Arthur was able to push it away from him. Still growling, the final bullet from Naomi's revolver shot it between the eyes.

All of them were breathing hard. Florence came forward and hugged her cousin. They both had tears of joy and relief. Arthur and the girls quickly aided Tom. He had sustained several deep cuts, but all of them had got lucky with this attack. Naomi checked Arthur; she was concerned and looked at his wounds.

"I didn't think I would be literally saving you from the wolves." She half smiled.

Once Tom was back on his feet, they collected the rifles and pulled the dagger out of the dead wolf.

"Have you seen a wolf this size before, Arthur?" Tom stood looking at the dead giant wolf.

"Yes, over the past few years." He paused. "Nazar's army has many unnatural things in it."

Leaving the barn, Arthur looked back; he would never forget the barn for his first proper kiss with a girl, but also the fact it nearly cost him his life. There was a moment of reflection as they moved towards the horses. A howl broke this; no words were needed as they picked up their pace.

Once mounted, they left the farm as quickly as possible. There was no sign of more wolves, but they didn't want to risk another attack. They had got lucky, but maybe it would swing the other way next time.

The closer they got to the train station, the more people they saw going about their business. Arthur and Tom would need to be seen by a doctor. Arthur knew he would have to tell his parents about what had happened. Tom was anxious about this, but just wanted to see a doctor. Naomi and Florence helped them find an American army doctor when they arrived at the station. He looked over their wounds and cleaned them thoroughly with antiseptic. He asked what had happened, and they explained that it was a wolf attack.

He was concerned about the attack but, unfortunately, not surprised. The number of giant wolves seemingly leading other wolves had risen in the last year. They all thanked the doctor and returned the horses to Naomi's uncle. She gave Arthur a quick kiss, as did Florence to Tom. They hugged each other and said they would meet soon at the next stop. This time, no significant risks will be taken.

"Thanks for saving us, Naomi." Arthur looked her in the eyes.

"Good luck speaking to your father; blame me if it's easier." She hugged him again before leaving to find their tent in the camp.

Tom and Arthur caught up with Rebecca and Emily first; Tom's mother was nearby. Rebecca was busy cooking. When her eyes saw the boys, she stopped what she was doing. "Arthur and Tom, what happened?"

Tom's mother came over as well.

The boys sat down on a bench taken from a nearby wagon. They then told the story about how they wanted to have some adventure. They talked about the horse ride with two American girls and swimming in the river; they left out the kissing in the farmhouse and focused on exploring, and then the attack. Rebecca and Catherine both had concerned faces.

Rebecca was angry inside, but she masked her thoughts. She was grateful that Arthur had told her what had happened, but wanted to say to him that what he had done was wrong. She spoke to both boys about their actions. She could see that Arthur and Tom were carrying injuries. Tom was already sitting down and showed his bandages wrapped around his legs, waist, and arms. Arthur had arms and legs wrapped up, but was more fortunate than Tom.

"You were lucky, boys." Rebecca then let Christina speak on the matter. She was a bit more worried than angry. She talked about how the world had changed and how risks like this now resulted in injuries or worse.

The boys nodded; they felt sorry for themselves, and Rebeca and Christina recognised this. Arthur said he would speak to Tom later as he was helped to rest and recuperate.

Emily came over to Arthur and hugged him. "Do you have a girlfriend?"

Arthur looked at her in amazement; how did she know that? She said she had seen him ride off with Tom and two girls. "Does mother know?"

"I don't think so; you should have told her."

Rebecca brought him some warm broth and a hunk of bread. She sat next to him and gave him a gentle hug. "I'm not telling your father. He has enough on his plate; promise to tell me next time." Rebecca knew Arthur had survived the drone camp and could look after himself, but as a mother, she could never let go of the worries or fears ahead.

Later in the afternoon, Charles joined them after his patrol with the other officers. Rebecca had reported to the American soldiers that wolves were being seen by the South Plate River. Nothing was mentioned about the attack, but she did say that the pack had giant wolves in it. The guards were posted around the camp and trains; the town had its own detachment of soldiers who would also be patrolling it.

"All quiet; that's how I like it." Charles sat next to Rebecca on the blanket. The warmth of the small campfire she had made felt good in the chill of the night air. He pulled her in close. He had taken a buffalo hide from Hosah and wrapped it around both of them as they sat next to each other.

"The children are asleep, I take it."

"Yes, lots of fresh air today has worn them out." Rebecca nestled into his side. "How long are we staying here for?"

"Another day, then we must move on." He looked around at the camp; small fires were burning away, and people were talking and laughing. The mood was good, which made Charles happy. He pulled out a half-drunk bottle of wine from his tunic.

"You're still surprising me after all these years." She then leaned forward and affectionately kissed Charles on the lips. He kissed her back.

"Do you remember all those years ago when I met you at the ball?"

"Yes, look where that's got us." She smiled and looked over at the tent. "I'm glad we met; I'm glad we've been able to have this time together after Paris." A tear ran down her cheek.

Charles brushed it away. "I can't say how grateful I am for you being in my life. This world may be falling apart, but you all give me hope. I love you so much, Rebecca."

"And I love you too, Charles."

She broke off from their embrace for a moment and went to their tent. To the side of it was a casket. She quickly opened it up and pulled out two small glasses. Then returned to sit next to Charles. "Let's drink to the future and the fall of Nazar."

The wine was more palatable than they thought it would be, which prompted both of them to take another sip. Charles threw a log on the fire as it started to die down; this caused sparks to fly up into the sky. Their eyes followed the ambers as they rose higher, leading them to the beautiful night sky above. The stars were coming to life over the plains, and the sheer scale of the universe and its wonderful backdrop to Earth was breathtaking. Rebecca wanted to hold Charles there all night and soak up the night sky.

Chapter 17

The next day was spent walking and relaxing. The soldiers had been advised to have everything ready to load the following morning, and this message was also passed on to the civilians.

Charles met with Corporal Heinz and Sergeant Butcher after lunch. They strolled by the station and spoke about the escape from Tokay by train. The riders of the North would hopefully not be a problem this time, but Charles could not let the whole map incident in Boulder entirely go from his mind. It irritated him like a sore that would not heal. He knew Nazar had spies in America and would be planning disruption before their invasion.

Corporal Heinz had spoken about having snipers at the back of the trains. Sergeant Butcher and Charles agreed this would increase the defensive capability of the guard wagons. Corporal Heinz had been speaking with the Arapaho and appreciated their scouting skills. They had taken him on a hunting trip the first day they arrived at North Platte, and the way they moved through the grass and forests was an eye-opener. He was enjoying learning from their way of life.

Charles spent the evening with his family. They huddled together to look at the stars and ate by the fire. Everyone on the train needed a two-day break, and it would happen again along the journey.

Just after lunch the following day, they began to move again. The next stop would be Lincoln.

The journey ebbed and flowed, with short stops to fill the tenders with water or coal, passed the time. Arthur and Tom healed well; they spoke about the adventure and being with the girls. They hadn't seen the girls since North Platte; Arthur hoped they would spend some time with them in Lincoln.

Charles sat in a carriage with Hosah. The braves were relaxed and taking in the rolling countryside. They had grown used to the train and discussed seeing their country like this. Hosah wanted to know about Great Britain; Charles spoke about the Empire and how it had once controlled most of the world. They talked about fighting in battles and their now common enemy. Hosah spoke about how he felt the demons who now walked the earth would change it forever, regardless of whether they beat Nazar and his army. The nomadic lifestyle will suit the people who are left after the war. Charles knew he was suggesting that the American Indians would be better equipped to deal with the fall of civilisation. He hoped that if they won, they could build society back over time; he prayed Hosah's version would not come to fruition.

Lincoln was a growing city. It was first established because of the abundance of salt along Salt Creek, but it grew into a focal point. The state of Nebraska was vast, and the train lines were an essential part of its economy and the movement of goods and people. They would only stop here for one day as they tried to keep up a good time.

Arthur and Tom were allowed to speak to the girls. Charles had been told that Arthur had a girlfriend, and he thought it was fun for him. Of course, he did not know what happened in North Platte.

Arthur and Tom enjoyed some time sitting with the girls around a campfire. Naomi snuggled into his side and Florence into Tom's. They were happy everything was well, and no one had got into extreme trouble because of what had happened. Naomi had apologised to them for pushing for the kisses in the barn. Arthur and Tom said they wanted it as much as they did, which made the conversation break into laughter and giggles.

The stars were out again that evening, and they sat there with blankets. Naomi lifted the blanket over their heads and quickly kissed Arthur on the lips. "It's a lot safer this time." Arthur nodded his head. They kissed again; Arthur hoped Naomi would try the French kiss again, and she did. They stopped for a moment and checked on Tom and Florence, who had also gone under their blanket.

The evening passed as they discussed what they hoped would happen in the future. Naomi didn't want Arthur or Tom to travel to Canada. She wanted them to stay in Boston. Arthur started to feel the same way, but knew he must go with his mother and sister wherever they deemed safe.

The next morning, as the camps were being packed up, he hugged Naomi. Tom had walked to see Florence help her uncle load his horses onto the train.

"Naomi, I like spending time with you."

She blushed a bit, which was the first time he had seen her show that side. Nothing seemed to faze her; she was strong, determined, and fearless.

"I like spending time with you, too, Arthur." She walked with him to their train. The whistles went up for everyone to board.

"See you soon."

They kissed quickly before she got on the train. He then rushed towards his.

Charles was there with Hosah, smiling at him before helping him board.

Chapter 18

The next couple of weeks of travelling were going according to plan. They stopped for the odd night to stretch and restock the coal and water for the steam engines.

They had to stop to get water in a town called Erie.

Charles stood near the back carriage as they slowly pulled into the station. The station master had signalled to the train drivers to pull in slowly. As there were three engines, they pulled past the central station and allowed the middle train to approach and pull past. This meant the last train would have the platform to pull up to.

Bushes were concealing the side of the track to the right, and trees stood proudly around the outskirts of the town.

The station master called Captain Steinberg over and spoke to him for several minutes. While this was happening, soldiers and civilians were disembarking from the train. They were allowed an hour to stretch and go into the town. There were strict instructions about keeping free time to the hour.

Captain Steinberg finished speaking to the station master and then went to find Major Hayward. When the captain arrived, Charles was sitting in one of the middle carriages, speaking to Rebecca and his children. He looked concerned and gestured if they could talk privately. Charles ushered him to a carriage door, and they went to speak on the other side of the track.

The message was simple: fighting had broken out further along the track with sympathisers of Nazar. This meant they would have to be diverted via the Kinzua Bridge. It meant going through more mountainous terrain. Charles took a moment to ponder; he didn't like that they had to be diverted, but knew this was the advice coming from the American forces. Captain Steinberg said they should cut the time to twenty minutes and then leave. The town was being reinforced, and civilians loyal to the government were armed to help fight. The American Civil War was very raw in many eyes, and the general feeling was not to have this uprising split the country further if Nazar was planning to invade.

Fortunately, the rebel attacks had been more sporadic; they did not seem to have a leader on American soil. It was more Nazar's priests or spies stirring up trouble, but with a systematic growth in fear, the politicians did not want to lose their grip on the country. It would become easier for them to muster up forces if they did not show unity.

American and British Engineers near the station were ordered to gather everyone back. The trains were stocked, and the new route was explained to the drivers.

As the civilians and soldiers filed back to the trains, the officers were debriefed that all soldiers would need to be vigilant and ready for action. The mood changed when gunfire could be heard in the distance. The journey had been long but pleasant; this now took them back to the threats and dangers lurking in the wilderness.

A full sweep was done before they set off to pick up stragglers in the town. The American and British / European soldiers carried out roll calls. Then they started to move.

Arthur spoke to Tom; they wished the girls were in their carriage. He then went to his father and asked if he could have his rifle, which was turned down. Charles said enough soldiers were on the train to protect the civilians and that their two girlfriends would be okay.

Inside, he was mulling over possible scenarios; Charles was left again thinking about the map incident in Boulder. He had spoken to Captain Somersett, as many of his soldiers would be stationed in the third train. He suggested that the end train should try to stay within a manageable distance of them. The braking distance, yes, but not so that they become too far separated.

The route would take them around Allegany Forest. The train lines had been worked on in that area, and the station master had given an update as best he could.

As they started to leave the station, they felt a collective sinking feeling upon hearing the fighting on the outskirts of the town. The uncertainty was infectious, and while they felt safe in the trains for now, the impact on a larger scale stayed in their minds.

Corporal Heinz stood in the guard carriage. He watched the station shrink as they pulled along the track. The glorious weather that had accompanied them most of the journey had changed. A gentle breeze rocked the tree canopies along the rail lines. Moisture began to build outside the carriage windows as misty rain engulfed the train. This impaired the long-distance visibility, causing the last two trains to slow down.

The general feeling on board all trains was more relaxed as time passed. The officers kept the soldiers on alert, but now assigned guard duty times to keep them fresh.

Charles joined Corporal Heinz. He looked into the mist and saw that the sun was starting to beam through in places, but it hadn't beaten it back comprehensively.

"Do you think this will ever end?" For once, the ever-positive Corporal looked a little downbeat.

"I think he can be beaten, but will the world return to how it was?" Charles carried on looking out into the mist. "Probably not"
"We can learn to adjust how we live. The Arapaho have shown how you should only take what you need." Charles was in a philosophical mood.

"I agree with you, my old friend, but mankind is drawn to power, money, and all the problems that come with it."

Charles handed the corporal some bread and a tin cup full of coffee.

"We can have a game of cards soon; I'm tired of Rebecca beating me."

This brought a smile from the Corporal.

"I guess it's more fun to be beaten by different people."

Charles smiled and walked back to the adjourning carriage. Arthur and Emily were asleep, not noticing the forests, which rose and fell with the undulating landscape.
The Maple and Elm trees, as were the Birch trees, were coming into leaf. The trees, such as the Red Pine and Scots Pine, stood tall and helped shape the landscape.

They stopped briefly at several stations before working their way to the Kinzua Bridge.

The backdrops en route to the bridge were eye-catching. Charles tried not to overthink how hard it would be to cross this terrain on foot. It was a quick thought he buried deep within his consciousness again.

The plan was to cross the bridge slowly. It was built in 1882 and had weight restrictions. They approached at a steady speed. The mist was lifting, but it was still thick in some areas.

Hosah approached Charles and said he would like to sit on top of their carriage as they crossed the bridge. He suggested that some of the other Arapahos do the same and keep watch as they approached it.

The engines started to get closer to each other, and their speed dropped, allowing a gradual closing of the gap. The smoke from the steam engines covered the carriages behind them. Only as they started to pull away did the smoke ease around them.

Captain Somersett of the American 10th Cavalry gathered his officers by his side; Sergeant Boyd and Corporal Williams were his trusted hands. They had fought with him against the plains Indians, rustlers, and outlaws. This was a new challenge, fighting the flesh-eaters along the frontier.

"We need to keep all the soldiers on point." The captain was on edge since hearing of the rebel attack near Erie. He preferred to be in the saddle rather than cooped up in a train.

"I find it strange the Indians want to fight with us." Sergeant Boyd remarked.

The captain looked out the window, "Many opposing forces will come together against this world threat." "What happens after if we win will judge us."

The corporal raised his eyebrows a little. "Trust doesn't go a long way in my eyes. Some regiments are getting repeater rifles, and we've got the Springfield Model 1888 Breech-loading rifle."

"It's still a good rifle, John."

"Yes, Captain, but when the dead are bearing down on me, and I'm loading a bullet at a time, I would like to have the same rifle as some of the other regiments."

"Well, we will be getting some Winchesters, and I've requested some Krag-Jorgensen rifles."

The sergeant nodded his head. "We still have our sabres; the dead should fear that."

Corporal Williams laughed, "The dead fear nothing.

The 10th Cavalry detachment went to the windows and was ordered to stay vigilant as they approached the bridge. Having the guard carriage on the last train meant they had to check along the track. The Kinzua bridge drew closer; the civilian passengers looked in awe at the bridge over the valley. The views were stunning and made the carriages burst into life. The journey had been full of incredible views, but this was extra special because of the bridge.

The front engine came to a screeching halt. The noise of the brakes locking onto the iron wheels rung out around the carriages. Charles instantly went to Sergeant Butcher.

"Tell the soldiers to be ready and get the signaller on top of the train to warn the others." Charles took his Lee-Metford rifle and left the train with two other soldiers. They rushed to the front steam engine. The drivers were pointing ahead and saying there was a track missing. Charles ordered one soldier to remain at the front of the train and keep cover whilst he took another soldier to investigate the missing track.

The soldiers from the other trains were coming down from the carriages, but their officers ordered them back. They wanted to keep a small unit outside each train as a contingency plan.

When Charles reached the track, he soon realised they would need to replace several iron railings on both sides. They had planned for this eventuality by bringing extra track with them. The open storage trucks were attached to the middle and third trains.

It was now a matter of urgency to get the track repaired. They had British engineers who were ready to go and fix the missing track, as well as American railwaymen. The last train had a mounted Gatling gun on the middle trucks and was being pointed towards the forest on the left-hand side of the train. The problem was that they had a dense forest on the right, which was also a concern. The civilians in the middle train sat patiently; there was the odd cough and nervous laugh, but they were all thinking of the rebel attack near Erie.

Sugar maples, white ash, beech, and black cherry trees formed a thick backdrop on either side of the railway track. The mist was not helping; it lingered in some places, even if it was starting to clear. Captain Somersett climbed down the guard carriage on the third train with Corporal Williams. They had three 10th Cavalry soldiers with them.

"Go to the middle steam engine and see if they know what's going on." He continued away from the train and down the track they had come along. They stayed close together as mist swallowed them up for a minute or so. They could no longer see the end train as they came out the other side.

Texas had been riding with the middle train, and he climbed down with a shotgun, Winchester, and his two Smith and Western revolvers. Following behind him were Captain Steinberg and two more cavalrymen. He said he would walk to the front and see what was happening. The captain told the two soldiers to stay by the middle train and that he would check on the rear train.

Hosah and some of the other braves watched from the first train. They had rifles and bows with them. Hosah was the first to let out a war cry as he saw the trees forcefully sway from side to side under the pressure of something big moving past them. He had already fired an arrow into the oncoming beast. He was joined by three more Arapaho, who also began to fire arrows.

The creature emerged towards the middle train. The British engineers recognised some of the features of a razor tooth, which they first encountered in Europe, but that's where the similarities ended. It was a more enormous creature than the razor tooth, and its skin was leatherier. Its head was shaped like a wolf, with two tusks jutting from its jaw. Soon, they saw its hideous mouth, teeth like pointed knives, and a tongue that was longer than usual. It reacted to arrows hitting its body, roaring with each strike, but had one goal: to ram the middle train. The speed at which the creature came into the carriage side shook the civilians. They could barely escape the carriage as this beast smashed into it. Bodies were flung into the air, and women, children and men fell on top of each other, crashing into benches and tables within the carriage. Some were thrown out of the glass windows close to the train line's edge.

The creature used its weight to move the carriage off the railway lines. It was being hit by arrows and gunfire from the soldiers on either side of it. Still, it kept on attacking the carriage as if it had been trained that way. The bullets started to have an effect in the end; it pawed at its bloodied skin, letting out a roar before lifting itself onto its hind legs, and then began to rock the carriage. This didn't last long as an arrow hit one of its eyes; this sent it reeling back before it charged at the Arapaho on Major Hayward's train.

Texas was calm as he took a stick of dynamite from his saddle bag and looked at this giant creature, its powerful legs and muscles exuding through its tough skin. It was trying to get at the Arapaho, who were unleashing arrow after arrow into it. The Enfield rifle bullets were also taking their toll on its body. Blood oozed from the wounds, dripping onto the stone shingle below and the bare Iron track. The more injured the beast became, the more frantic it lashed out.

Its groans and roars were causing panic in all three trains, but Texas kept his cool as he lit the dynamite fuse and waited for a short while; he threw the stick just behind its legs and then shouted to the Arapaho to move. The guard carriage's soldiers also took heed and fell back through the adjoining carriage. This thing was oblivious to the burning fuse behind it, and when the explosion came, it tore into its flesh and bone. This time, it did fall backwards, clawing at the soil and stone around it.

The Arapaho appeared at the top of the carriage. Hosah had a spear in his hand and aimed it while standing on top of the guard carriage roof. Texas watched as the young Indian was like a hawk waiting to strike.

Whoosh

The beast was slain.

There was silence as the soldiers rushed to help the injured people from the carriage the creature had attacked first. There was a sense of urgency; now, one of the carriages was derailed.

Charles ordered soldiers back to get the railway lines and tools to fix the missing track. He had rushed back to the first train when all the commotion and gunfire had started. Rebecca had taken two rifles and armed Arthur with one of them, then moved Emily and Arthur to the front of the train with the other families.

Captain Steinberg and Captain Somersett had been updated regarding the attack, and Hosah had moved down from the top of the carriage to check the dead animal and retrieve the arrows. Several braves stayed on top of the train, keeping watch. A native Indian who went by the name of Mad Dog noticed the tree canopies moving on both sides. They weren't reacting as if blown by the wind; they swayed violently from side to side. This time, it was over a wider distance on either side of the track, and they shook as if scared. Mad Dog let out a call. Hosah told Texas something else was coming through the forests.

The forests were dense enough to hide the oncoming force, but everyone outside of the trains could hear the ever-familiar sound of hissing, glugging, snapping, and wheezy breathing. They knew flesh-eaters were on their way.

Captain Somersett ordered the cavalrymen on the middle train to concentrate their fire on the left-hand side of the track. He then ordered Corporal Jackson to get as many soldiers as possible to look at either getting the carriage back on the track or pulling it off. The carriage was slightly raised where the creature had smashed into it.

His mind raced with ideas: Could they use a leverage poll to lift it? Would they have to build something to do that? How long would they have before their attackers arrived?

Captain Steinberg said they may have to reverse the back train and leave the middle train where it was; sadly, this idea was short-lived, as in the distance coming up the track as far as the eye could see was a massive herd of flesh-eaters. Charles arrived by the middle train; he looked at the damage and spoke to the captains. He advised that he had already sent some of his British Engineers to start fixing the track, and he would also send some soldiers to help cover the right flank. He could hear the oncoming dead and looked at the officers around him.

"Time is of the essence", wiping the sweat away from his forehead. "We can assist with getting this carriage back on the track or off it."

"Captain Somersett nodded his head. Let's crack on and get things moving."

Charles got back to his train. Texas was helping collect sleepers for the track to lay on. He was a brute of a man, and his strength was exposed in this situation. Maybe adrenaline had added extra power, and the fear of getting eaten alive was a good motivator. Corporal Heinz and ten British engineers joined him. They were working furiously to get the material over to the missing section.

Sergeant Butcher had forty Royal Engineers ready with bayonets and Lee Enfield rifles. They started to move past Charles as he was coming back. "He shouted to them to stay sharp and stay alive."

Hosah was travelling along the top of the second train with six more Arapaho braves. They were well-armed with rifles, bows, and arrows. Charles didn't get a chance to speak to him; his natural fighting instincts were taking over. Their accuracy from a high position had already proved invaluable against the giant creature. Now, with the flesh-eaters coming through the forest, they could help protect the soldiers below.

The civilians amongst them were moved to the front train. Arthur stood on the guard carriage looking for Naomi and Florence, and when he saw them coming, he let out a sigh of relief. She kissed him as soon as they entered the train. Her uncle smiled and carried on further into the train. Tom joined Naomi and Florence in the guard carriage, and British engineers stood watch around the train. Arthur and Tom had been told not to leave the train unless asked to by an officer or Rebecca.

Captain Stenberg placed some of his soldiers at the end of the third train. They lined up in a three-line formation, hoping that volley fire would help slow down the army of the dead. Captain Somersett was doing the same on the left-hand side of the middle and third trains.

The noise increased as they came closer, branches snapping, groans wafting towards them from all sides. A 10th cavalryman named Mathew Johnson, a former child slave, stood firm. He had escaped the plantations at the end of the Civil War and later joined the 10th Cavalry. He had fought in the Indian wars and worked his way to Sergeant for his bravery and leadership skills, but old memories die hard. The bottle found its way into his life and started to take hold. He had started a family with a woman from South Carolina, and for a while, he was on top of the world, but his army postings meant he would have to be away for long periods. The alcohol would be less controlled, and the more he drank, the more volatile he became. This accumulated in many fights with his fellow soldiers and anyone else in the bars at the wrong time. One fight led him to nearly kill a wealthy southern man who made references to his past. It had been the wrong day and wrong time for this to happen, and the anger that boiled underneath exploded.

He was lucky not to serve longer than he did. The only reason he was accepted back into the army was Captain Somersett. He had lost everything during his time in prison. His wife left him and remarried, which made him contemplate ending his life journey at the Mississippi River.

By sheer chance, a 10th cavalryman was riding past the bridge he was standing on. It was enough to trigger memories of belonging to something. From that day, he found his former unit and Captain Somersett, who had to pull a lot of favours to get him reintroduced as a private.

Private Johnson loaded his rifle. He also checked his two Smith and Western revolvers and Bowie knife strapped to his back. The smell of the oncoming dead was hitting them before they arrived. His once jet-black hair now had grey strands running through it. Although he wasn't too old, he had enough experience in his life to age him twice. He was facing a new enemy that would force mankind into a fight for their lives.

The soldiers around him were of different ages; this was their first action for some, while others were more seasoned. A couple of young faces were showing signs of tension; it was one thing fighting men or women with guns and knives, but this was different. The flesh-eaters coming through the trees knew no fear. They had one thing driving them, and that was to feed on flesh.

"Steady yourself, boys." Private Johnson stepped to the front of the line. His presence helped those around him feel stronger.

"Pick your shots, aim for the head, and don't get bitten."

On the other side, Captain Stenberg readied his soldiers; they, too, felt their hearts racing, and the noise levels grew.

Hosah had made his way to Sergeant Butcher and spotted men dressed in black moving around the flesh eaters. Hosah did not know they were priests, but Sergeant Butcher did and told him they would help direct the dead towards them.

The machine gun crew covering the left-hand side bought extra ammunition for the truck. The soldiers on that side stood well clear of their firing range, allowing them to cause maximum damage until they ran out of ammunition.

Before the main attack arrived, one of the engineers on the bridge with Major Hayward saw something in the valley below. Several figures were scurrying around below; it was hard to count how many as the sheer height of the bridge dwarfed them. Their intentions quickly became apparent as a bullet smacked into one of the wooden beams near where they were standing.

Charles ordered two soldiers to lay down covering fire and then sent another back for more reinforcements on the bridge. They were now being stretched number-wise, and some soldiers needed to support the civilians on the first train. The civilians had been armed but would need direction not to hit the other British and American soldiers further down the track.

Corporal Heinz had climbed on the roof with the Arapaho and taken his Lisping sniper rifle with him. He wished he were a marksman in the same league as Alexander Chamberlin, or he would be with them now and not meeting them in Boston.

The first proper glimpse of what was emerging through the forest was soul-destroying. The flesh-eaters included a mixture of women, men, and children. The soldiers who had faced this many before knew the power the dead had in numbers. The battle for Europe was lost to the giant horde and Nazar's army. Great Britain had fallen to the same abomination. Now, slowly coming out of the dark forests, snapping at the air in front of them, was the driving force behind his bid for supreme rule.

The noise along the length and breadth of the trains was deafening. With flesh-eaters arriving from along the railway track behind them and both sides starting to reveal the dead as they broke out of the forests, the situation was intensifying. The machine gun facing the left-hand side of the middle train was the first to fire. The opening cackle made everyone flinch and indicated that the battle had begun.

Captain Stenberg was not interested in defeating the army of death because they did not know how many they were facing or whether they had enough firepower to beat them. It was all about getting that train back on the track and everyone to safety.

The Gatling gun began to tear through its victims as soon as they broke through the foliage. Arms, faces, and torsos exploded as the rounds cut through their ranks. Hundreds were dropping all along the left-hand side of the railway track.

The American soldiers fell into place once the Gatling gun had finished firing. The first rank raised its Krag-Jorgensen carbine rifles and took aim. Captain Steinberg told them to hold until they could see the heads of the oncoming dead. Their volley fire was mirrored on the other side of the train. The bullets were effective, piercing into the flesh-eaters. The body shots hindered their advance, but they would rise again. The soldiers knew to aim for the heads, but different-sized attackers meant this was not always possible.

The children's flesh eaters were starting to get closer. Sunken eyes and peeling skin made the firing soldiers think less about what they were doing, but it was still new for some of them. The herds they had encountered before had been small, but this one was larger than they had experienced before.

The challenge was to keep them from breaking through their ranks and not to be swamped from all sides. The problem area was the third train. The guard carriage had soldiers in it and on top of it, but the herd coming up the track was not obstructed by the trees as the other flesh-eaters were. They were coming in mass, and the American soldiers covering the rear started firing. The bodies of the flesh-eaters that were hit in the head helped slow down the steady advance, but if they hit anywhere else, they would eventually get up and carry on coming.

Texas was firing with the British Engineers. He had a Winchester rifle, which meant he didn't have to reload as often as the British used Lee-Metford 10-round holding cartridge rifles. He was shocked at the sheer ferociousness of this army pushing past the foliage to feed what was in front of it.

10th Cavalryman Mathew Johnson was laying down continuous fire with the rest of his detachment, the British were further along and also holding the line. The Engineers had one advantage over their allies: the experience of facing this type of force.

Captain Somersett steadied the poles that were being used to tilt the carriage back onto the railway track. The heavy clunk of the carriage wheels landing back on the iron rails was drowned out by the noise of gunfire and the dead.

Captain Steinberg's soldiers were running low on ammunition, and a cry went out to call for more; it was then that a dynamite stick was thrown from the oncoming horde. Amongst the flesh-eaters was a half-infected rebel. He could move amongst the dead undetected, and this particular individual got close enough to light and throw the stick.

The impact was enough to wound and kill three soldiers, but this meant the volley fire was partially broken on that side. Hosah had spotted the rebel attacker, but only after he had thrown the dynamite. He was quick to despatch him with an arrow. Hosah then frantically searched that side for more rebels, but no one else stood out.

Steinberg rallied the men around him as the dead closed in on them.

With each step, suffering from the impact of the explosion, a poor soldier stumbled closer to the ravenous dead who were still pouring forward through the forest. His demise came quickly as the flesh-eaters set upon him like ants on a potential meal. It shocked the onlooking U.S cavalrymen; they had seen these things feeding on animals and occasionally unfortunate souls, but it was the way they attacked the wounded soldier and tore into his torso, biting at his hands and arms as he tried to fight off the feeding frenzy, that distressed them the most.

This same fate fell on the ones that had been affected by the blast; shouts of desperation rang out amongst the chaos of the attack. Captain Steinberg tried to get some form of control over his unit, but they were quickly overrun. Hosah and Corporal Heinz quickly gave supporting fire as the American unit broke and pulled back. The other Arapahos also began to fire at the flesh-eaters coming around the back. The 10th Cavalrymen did not have time to reform their lines as the dead flowed around the middle train and onto them.

This meant hand-to-hand fighting was breaking out on both sides. Private Johnson was the first to react, spinning around from his position and bayoneting a flesh-eater in the head.

At that moment, he looked at the young girl he had just struck. Her outward appearance looked like she had only recently turned. The girl's hair looked as though it had been newly plaited, and she was probably no more than fifteen. Flesh-eaters who had just turned seemed more dangerous.

Private Johnson pulled out his bayonet from her head and brought the rifle butt into another oncoming flesh-eater; as he did so, he saw her fall to the ground from the corner of his eye. He couldn't help but think of his own daughter. Would she fall into the same fate as all those attacking them now? This image was quickly lost as the hissing and snapping sound grew louder around them. The dead had got a foothold in the battle and were causing havoc.

Captain Somersett took ten men and met Texas and three British Engineers between the gap of the two trains. Texas quickly jumped up on the storage carriage truck and called for the soldiers on the middle train to get the Gatling gun firing again as soon as possible. They did just that; the rhythmic rattle helped give the men some time to regroup as the dead fell to the heavy barrage of bullets.

Texas pushed into the oncoming sea of flesh-eaters; he had used all his rounds in the Winchester rifle and now pulled out his two Smith & Westerns revolvers. Using them wisely, he worked his way to different pockets of American soldiers fighting the dead, helping elevate some of the pressure by shooting a path for them to fall back through. When they were spent, he did not have time to reload and pulled out of his belt an axe.

The dead started to over-spill from the rear train as their numbers were forcing back the soldiers; some were clambering onto the third train, while others laid down covering fire.

Texas helped pull a soldier from the clutches of death and dispatched the two flesh-eaters who were about to administer that fate. The axe was useful for splitting their heads and then pulling it out to strike again. Texas used his size and strength to batter the decaying bodies that were coming his way. It was the first real action he'd had against this many; he got to see how they would overrun most men and women by their sheer numbers, and when the Gatling gun stopped again, the wave that was coming his way would take some stopping.

Charles signalled to his men on the bridge to fall back. They had completed fixing the railway lines, "fall-back to the trains."

He could see the smoke rising from the battle. They were still under fire from below, but there was enough cover for them to scurry back. Rebecca was with Arthur and Emily. She kept the families calm and got updates from the soldiers with them.

Sergeant Butcher had managed to keep the dead at the forest edge on their side of the middle train. Ammunition was getting low, bayonets had been fixed, and where they could, bullets were saved. A reverse line would step forward and bayonet the dead as they fell back.

Charles climbed onto the guard carriage on the first train and asked the bugler to signal the retreat of the trains. The steam engines had been prepped to leave, and the train drivers were shooting from the engine cab and helping where they could.

On hearing the call to retreat, Captain Steinberg and Captain Somersett shouted at their men to board the trains. Sergeant Butcher ordered the British to fall back to the first train. They had just enough bullets to carry out a steady retreat.

The screams of the soldiers who had fallen amongst the flesh-eaters died down as they were quickly ripped apart. Every effort had been made to pull them to safety, but the dead numbers were too much in some cases. Sergeant Butcher pushed his men back to the first train; a flesh-eater grabbed one of the soldiers as they climbed onto the train; it tried to bite into his back. Fortunately, his webbing straps stopped the bite from breaking into his flesh. Sergeant Butcher was helping another up and was quickest to react; he brought his bayonet into the dead man's side, spinning him around. He then withdrew it and plunged it into his head.

The dead were not swarming around all trains; they could not climb up the steps, but their numbers would prove a problem if they started to block the track, and the rebels could attack whilst they were stationary.

The relief of the first train moving and its whistle sent a wave of hope across all three trains. The Americans looked at their fallen soldiers as they started to move; the rebels and the dead had won this battle. The dead continued to flow out of the forests; a civilian on the first train asked how they had gathered in such a number. One of the British soldiers remarked, "It could have been one of the European camps that had been set up for the infected". Many who had arrived and had signs of being bitten were shipped out to various locations in the hope of containing it there. Some said a lack of funding and the will to monitor the camps correctly led to them probably being overrun by the priests and their rebels. It was an alarming prospect.

As the trains passed their ever-increasing numbers, the sheer realisation of what lay ahead struck all who looked upon the dead's gaze. They clawed at the trains as they slowly rolled forward, buffeting and crushing those wandering in front of the steam engine. Hosah and Corporal Heinz continued to fire down upon them as they closed in on the bridge. The other Arapaho focused on hitting the flesh-eaters before they got in front of the trains, where they could.

Arthur took Naomi's hand as they both looked out of the windows at the dead, their soulless faces and decaying flesh. She sniffed as a teardrop fell on the carriage floor below. Arthur squeezed her hand tighter. "It's going to be ok."

They stared at the dead's broken souls as they passed them and entered onto the bridge. It triggered Arthur's memories of the drone child training camp, where he survived with James and Sofie. He thought about their struggle there and how they had nearly died, and if it weren't for his mother and Hagen, they would have been either a flesh-eater or dead.

With the last of the soldiers climbing aboard the trains, Texas and Captain Somersett pulled themselves up. Sergeant Butcher had done the same with the British soldiers on the first train. The estimated loss was fifteen, but this would not be fully confirmed until they had checked with all three trains.

Charles hugged Rebecca and ruffled Emily's hair. Arthur stood with Naomi but acknowledged his dad as he walked past to speak to Sergeant Butcher.

The carriages were still on high alert, soldiers were crouching in the open carriage trucks, and each end guard carriage had snipers poised.

The morale was low amongst the American Cavalrymen; the loss of their comrades was a hard blow. In war, soldiers would die, but they weren't normally ripped apart and eaten in front of their fellow soldiers. The British and European forces were, of course, more normalised to this. It would have stirred memories of the fall of Europe and Great Britain.

The rebels below were firing at the trains as they went over this impressive structure. Charles was concerned about them detonating the bridge as the three trains crossed, but he believed Nazar would want the railways in some places to work to help ferry his forces quickly once they landed. This was a hunch; he still felt nervous as they rolled across it, but if they were to destroy this route, the journey through the forest and valley for Nazar armies would take twice as long.

There was a massive sigh of relief when the lead engine rolled onto the other side. They carried on moving forward at a steady pace until all the trains were safely off the bridge. Then Corporal Heinz and the other Arapaho hurriedly climbed off the carriage roofs and went to the guard carriage of the last train. Charles was there with Sergeant Butcher; the instruction was simple: to get some scouts further up the line and check for missing tracks or anything that could be a trap. This operation was quickly supported by them unloading four horses. It would be visualised that they could cover more ground, and trains could keep moving behind them. They wanted to get more distance between themselves and the valley.

A messenger was sent to each train to update them on the situation and take notes of the attack and casualties. It was a quick turnaround, and they got the trains rolling. Most had missed the wonderful backdrop across the bridge. Even if they could see it, their minds were filled with images of the flesh-eaters and their incessant need to feed.

The scouts rode ahead for many miles as the train went along at a steady, slow pace. Corporal Heinz and one British Engineer checked the railway tracks whilst Hosah and another Arapaho looked for signs of rebels along the route. No signs of tampering with the track were found, and there were no signs of rebels in that area. This meant that, at a safe vantage point, they loaded the scouts' horses back onto the trains. The railway line had taken them onto higher ground with good panoramic views of the surrounding forests.

The trains continued day and night to Binghamton, where they stopped and checked on the wounded soldiers. The gods had been shining on them regarding the injured amongst them, having no bite wounds. If they had been bitten, amputation would have had to of occurred where possible. This was, of course, only a small victory as the cavalrymen had lost fifteen. Sadly, the dynamite which was thrown had been the leading cause of the deaths; it had allowed the dead to swarm around the back, exposing the right flank.

It was a good few days until they reached the city of Albany, which lay roughly north of the Hudson River. They planned to stop and drop off some of the civilians with them. Arthur and Tom were happy that Naomi and Florence would not end their journey in Albany; both were heading with their uncle to Boston. It was a rest bite to what had been a long trip; information was passed to the local garrison regarding the rebel attack with the dead and the Kinzua bridge. The fact that there was a large number involved would worry the commanding officer in the region. He would have enough men and cannons to defend Albany, but the smaller towns and homesteads would suffer with those large hordes.

Congress had spoken about increasing the cavalry units to hunt them, but getting through the motions regarding increased spending was always difficult. The fact was that cavalry units alone would not work; you would need more firepower, artillery, Gatling guns, and a large army with cavalry. It also raised the question: Should they be supporting the European effort to take back Great Britain and assist in the future land invasions of Europe?

A large part of the political fraternity wanted to cut a deal with Nazar, and these attacks only reinforced this. They saw him as the supreme leader in Europe and knew that each year, his armies were getting more substantial; the mission to destroy the meteor in Russia had partially worked, but he had recruited from the countries he occupied. He used fear, join or be executed, or targeted the poor and disillusioned in society to help boost his numbers.

Chapter 19

The rest in Albany was welcome, which meant the families were allowed a few days to get away from the trains and soldiers to unwind in the city. They were all told they had three days.

Charles was keeping the British Engineers together and had told his officers where they were due to stay. They would be allowed to visit some bars in the city, but he did not want to leave anyone behind regarding the last leg of their journey to Boston. Arthur had spoken to Naomi and found they were not staying too far away. He had asked his mother whether they could meet with the girls at some point over the three days. It was arranged that they would go to a park near to where they were staying. Rebecca would bring a book, and Emily would play with her dolls.

Charles had time to arrange a meeting with the officers. The last part of the journey should be smooth, but he was slightly anxious now in the cities. Who was watching them? All of them spoke of being vigilant and wary.

Hosah and Little Bear walked back with Charles and his British officers. They were taken aback by the size of the city. With the noise and industrial size of everything, the people moved around like ants going about their business. Charles was aware of the shock for the Arapaho, going from rolling plains and the steppes to sprawling buildings and factories. Charles had seen some signs in front of the bars saying, No Europeans welcome, in a way he understood. It was human nature to react to change; what was coming in with the Europeans was the infections that turned them into flesh-eaters. Nazar and his armies were pursuing them; why would the public want that shadow hanging over them?

He had heard in some quarters that they wished that Europe had fallen without the mass evacuation of people and that the same fate had happened to Great Britain. The British were calling in her colonial forces to help take back their Island, but there were stories of outbreaks in India and Africa. How widespread Nazar was implanting of his explosion was not entirely known, but he was wise enough to have spies in the British countries and be aware of their preparation for continuing the war.

"Hosah, what do you think of Albany?"

The Arapaho Indian looked at him. "Too many people, not enough buffalo."

Charles and Sergeant Butcher smiled.

"Well, if things don't go our way, they're trying to eat you."

Hosah looked at him, then smiled.

When they returned to the building where they were staying, Charles asked for guards to be placed outside the main entrance. He said they could shift the guard duty from within during the evening.

The afternoon soon turned into the evening, and a small supper was prepared and eaten before they all went to bed early.

Charles held Rebecca tight in his arms as he curled up behind her; he nuzzled his head into hers; the modest bed they were lying in was adequate for their room. The walls had been painted recently in a mustard colour, and its smell lingered. This made both of them smile; it felt good to think about something other than war. The building would eventually be used as a hotel, but the local governors allocated it to the British for now; they were grateful to be off the train and not camping in a field. Families were allocated to small apartments, as the soldiers were sharing rooms. The children had gone to their bedroom and were busy being creative. Arthur had been making something out of wood for Naomi. He wanted to give her something, should they eventually be separated and was using the newfound skills he had picked up while they were living in America. Emily was drawing pictures of the dead, which Charles and Rebecca did not know how best to approach. She was trying to understand that they were no longer the people they were before, and all they wanted to do now, was eat you. Rebecca had told her to draw pictures of something nice, but even if she did, create a picture of a family house, there would be the dead walking nearby.

Charles felt Rebecca's hand rub his thigh.

"Time is going by too fast, Charles."

"I know. I think about the invasion more after the attack on the Kinzua bridge." He kissed her on the back of her neck.

"Seeing the dead in those numbers shows he is growing closer. The thought of what lies ahead when you land in Wales scares me, Charles." She turned to face him in bed. "What if there is more than what you faced in France? We know how his army's works." She paused and stroked his cheek.

"I don't want to go through this new world without you." Her eyes started to well up, "I'm scared of that."

Charles kissed up on the lips. "I will try and survive for you and the children, and maybe we can beat Nazar."

They spoke softly about the foothold that Great Britain would give them before attempting to capture Europe. The subject turned to the fact that Nazar would target America, and even if England was recaptured, how long could it be held? The problem was simple: The Americans were facing unrest about what was happening to their country. The Europeans had come over with all their problems, and now the very thing that beat them would follow.

The Senate argued that the war should be fought on British or European soil or that a pact should be made to surrender the main European leaders to this new Emperor.

The clock was ticking, and the unfortunate truth was simple: they had to be seen to be doing something. Staying in America and not trying to return to their homelands could possibly play into Nazar's hands. He had already sent many spies and Priests to raise more rebels to help stir rebellion.

The whole thing felt inevitable. Charles was at a rank where he had to go. Deep inside, he wanted to take his family to an island and leave all of the madness behind, but it would catch up with them one day. Arthur and Emily would want to grow up in a world different from this.

Later that evening, whilst the building fell quiet, a window facing out to the street below acted as a soundboard as rain could be heard hitting against it. Rebecca woke from her sleep and looked around the room. Charles was still asleep. She looked at his chest gently, rising and falling, and listened to the rain tumbling outside. A flash of light illuminated the curtains for a few seconds and then went back into darkness. Rebecca got up from the bed slowly, making sure not to wake Charles; she then went to the dressing table and poured a small glass of water. The refreshing feeling of the water touching her lips and entering her mouth was soothing. She then went to check on Arthur and Emily, who were both in a deep sleep. She spent a minute watching them sleeping before returning to her room. The lightning lit up the room again, creating shadows from the furniture.

Rebecca enjoyed listening to and watching storms and was drawn to the one outside; carefully moving across the wooden floor, she went to the window and looked through the curtains. A newspaper flew down the street below and briefly stuck against a lamp post. The sky lit up again, sending a forked bolt down from the clouds, then disappearing in the distance. The rain began to fall heavier; it was then Rebecca noticed a man in a hooded cloak walking along the street; he looked lost, as he stumbled a little. Her eyes followed him for a while. Just as he began to turn into a side alley, he looked up at the window. His face was hidden in the darkness, but then a flash of light saw it lit up; his eyes glowed yellow, and his teeth were sharp as he smiled. Rebecca only saw him for a moment; then, the street was returned to darkness. When the lightning struck again, he had gone. She closed the curtain with his face fresh in her mind.

Rebecca went to check; the door was double-bolted and locked. She didn't know whether it was one of Nazar's spies or priests, but it was enough to take away her calm feeling while staying there. Climbing back into bed, she pressed herself against Charles and tried to tell herself it was a bad dream.

Chapter 20

"The fleet is shaping up very well, my lord." Said General Georgiy.

"Is it Georgiy?" Nazar walked around the harbour, looking at the workers being whipped as they were pushed to achieve impossible targets. They then began walking down a jetty to inspect a landing vessel which was being completed.

One of the prisoners took offence at being repeatedly hit and grabbed the whip from the guard who was hitting him. He spoke in French before striking the guard. Nazar stood and watched as the prisoner began to beat the guard in front of him. Georgie looked at Nazar and then at the attack unfolding in front of them; guards standing at a nearby dock saw what was happening and ran over to help. The guard who was being beaten cried out in agony.

"Sire, should we not intervene?"

Nazar looked at him. "Nature is about survival of the fittest.

When the guards arrived, Nazar raised his right arm to indicate they should wait. The prisoner finished off by hitting the guard until he stopped breathing. Blood ran from his face through the wooden jetty planks and into the water below.

The prisoner braced himself for a fight, but Nazar spoke to him in French and said he had two choices: join his army or die. The prisoner replied that he would join Nazar's army.

General Georgiy looked at the prisoner as the guards led him off.

"Why, sire, he could fight for the enemy. How can we trust him?"

"Georgiy, we will need millions in our quest. When we land in America, it will take men and women like him to force our way into their lands and conquer the West."

Nazar pushed the guard's body into the water with his foot. He watched his body slowly sink into the murky water below, then continued to walk with the general. We leave in just over a month. This will be one of the largest armadas ever assembled. There was even a wry smile—this was one of the few times the general had seen his lord smile.

Chapter 21

Rebecca spoke to Charles about what she saw the previous evening as they had breakfast. Arthur and Emily were in good spirits. Arthur was looking forward to meeting Naomi in the park. Emily had been told she might be able to have a new doll as she had been so good on the journey. Rebecca was more conscious about what was lurking in the major towns and cities. Charles suggested they should still go, but be careful; he was due to meet the Engineers in the morning until early afternoon, then he would join his family for dinner later in the day.

The storm had cleared the air, and the sun was beaming through the clouds.

"Take care today, and we will meet back at the hotel at three O'clock," Charles said softly.

"Yes, we will do that, you don't think they are targeting this building?"

Charles looked at her as he cracked his boiled egg. "I think anything is possible, but we have guards at the entrance."

They carried on eating breakfast, thinking about this threat.

"Do I get to carry a revolver, Father?" Arthur was writing a note to Naomi as he said this. "I mean, I'm nearly fifteen years old. I can shoot really well."

This drew a look from both his parents; even Emily stopped eating her waffles and asked if she should also carry a gun.

"No one is going to carry a gun, Arthur. You will be allowed to carry a weapon if we get attacked like we did on the Kinzua Bridge. Emily, wait another seven years until you're the same age as your brother when he started learning."

Arthur looked a little disappointed. Emily carried on eating her waffles.

"Would you have to shoot me or Arthur if we turned into one of those things?"

"Emily, do not think like that." Charles was firm, but his voice had anguish in it.

"But I've seen children who were flesh-eaters attack us on the bridge."

Charles looked at Rebecca.

"I won't let it happen to you, Emily." Arthur was stern and positive about his statement. He reached over and took her hand. She smiled back at Arthur. "Thank you, Arthur."

"We are all going to make it through this. We must believe that. Your father will return from England, and we will all be together after that." Rebecca was emotional as she said this, prompting Emily to get up from the kitchen table and hug her mother; seconds later, Arthur joined her. Charles stood up and went over to the three of them, hugging and joining in; it felt good. The hug may have only lasted 30 seconds, but it was enough to give them all the strength for what was lying ahead.

The meeting with the British officers went well. They discussed the training that would happen in Boston and the small detachment of reinforcements who would be joining them. Charles had said they would be going in with the Royal Marines. The Marines would secure Newgale Beach in Pembrokeshire, and they would push on with supplies and tools from there.

The other forces would be landing along the west coast. St Ives would see the British main force push up through the southwest of England. Wales would be a middle staging post, with the British Engineers pushing on with the Marines and a smaller British force, coupled with European forces. Aberystwyth and Porth Colmon would see the American US-led army land there, mixed in with British advisers and European forces. The Plan was to force the defenders into splitting their units. The British and European forces had faced Nazar's armies en masse, and this was proving hard to beat. The tactics had to be adapted somehow, and this was hopefully the way to gain some control back in Great Britain.

The meeting looked at maps over a large oak table. There were very few reports on the numbers they would face. Spies had travelled to England, but very few returned. The civilians there were kept in towns or villages, and the dead walked around freely. The numbers were unknown. Corporal Heinz asked if he thought the occupied British people would fight with them once they knew they were trying to be liberated.

"I would like to think so, but as those of us here who have come face to face with Nazar know, he is not a man to suffer insurgents. If he found out at any time those who would rise up against him, he would punish them, their family, their village, and maybe the whole region."

They agreed he ruled by fear and was not afraid to kill whatever stood in his way. There was hope that if they could conquer enough of the country, the people would rally and help.

Rebecca walked with Arthur and Emily to the park. Tom and his mother joined them. The sunny weather made everything seem normal. The air was fresh, and the city was teeming with life. The birds were flying about, searching for grubs, and the mood around the city was one of great spirits.

That was the hardest thing to take on board; Rebecca had seen what happened to Europe and Great Britain, and the harsh realities of accepting this almost idyllic other side to America, whilst knowing that lurking in the shadows and dark forests were the dead.

Naomi was waiting with Florence to meet the boys at the park's edge. Their uncle had given them three hours to explore the park area and then return to their accommodations. When they saw Arthur and Tom, their eyes lit up. The girls looked at each other and smiled. Rebecca automatically smiled as well, saying, "Christina, young love ah." They both laughed.

Arthur and Tom went straight to the girls; there was a hug and a brief kiss on the cheek from each girl before they walked into the park. Rebecca and Christina went and found a bench; a large maple tree shaded the area perfectly. Emily placed herself on the blanket her mother had just put down and looked around the park. She looked for her brother and Tom; upon finding them, she relaxed and rolled onto her back. She thought about the journey so far, travelling on the train, living on the farm and their life in Europe and England. She wanted a friend to play with, and whilst the dolls were good, she wanted to have more fun. She thought about some of her old friends and whether they had been eaten or turned into flesh-eaters.

Her mind tried to shut out those thoughts like her mother and father had said, but they still lingered. The faces of the dead on the bridge gave her nightmares. She worried about her father going to England, but knew he had to. Her mind was diverted as Christina said she would go to the baker's and get an iced bun.

Arthur sat close to Naomi in the shade of a giant oak tree. Tom was perched against its trunk with Florence. Both couples were enjoying each other's company and thinking about how much they would see each other once they had arrived in Boston. Naomi had some good news: her uncle would be staying with family in Boston, which meant they would be there until early the following year. Florence told Tom simultaneously, and this was accompanied by a cry of yes from both boys. Naomi leaned forward and kissed Arthur passionately, and he liked the feeling of kissing her again. Tom took this as an opportunity to do the same with Florence. This was only broken by a young voice.

"Hi, I'm Emily."

Arthur looked up, a little shocked. He gave her the look of not now.

"I need someone to come to my doll's party."

"Awww, bless her, come on Florence, let's go. Boys, we should all go."

Naomi remarked how cute his sister was. Arthur initially nodded, but he wanted to say he enjoyed kissing more. They all got up and followed Emily to her blanket, where she had placed her dolls in a circle. Inside the circle were toy teacups and a small pot. Emily invited them to sit down and enjoy afternoon tea with the dolls.

Arthur thanked her and obliged. Naomi remarked on the lovely tea she made, which made Emily giggle.

Tom was able to use his acting skills and asked if he could have cake with his tea. He came across as a southern man, which made Florence and Naomi laugh at his accent.

The afternoon passed as they enjoyed time with Emily. When Rebecca said it was sadly time to head back, she thanked them for spending time with her. The girls said they would see them back at the train station tomorrow for the last Journey into Boston. There was a quick kiss on the cheek before both girls returned to walk back to their hotel.

Tom and Arthur were in a bubbly mood, walking back, Emily was skipping, and Rebecca was enjoying chatting with Christina. They stopped at a baker's that was making fresh bagels. Rebecca said she would treat everyone to finish off this fine day. The smell was alluring, bringing in a large crowd to buy fresh bread. The bakers were of Jewish descent and were busy turning the dough; they had come to America to start a new life and build a business. Their Bagels were the best in Albany, or so they said.

Rebecca told Emily and Arthur not to overfill, as their father would take them to a restaurant that evening.

Arthur said goodbye to Tom as they returned to their apartments. It was not for long, as Charles returned and said they would be going to an Italian restaurant near the Albany Pump Station. It served good ales and a hearty meal.

The family took time to get ready. They all wanted to wash and wear smart clothes for this treat. Charles had arranged for a Landau carriage to pick them up and take them to the restaurant.

The late afternoon air felt cooler after the warm sunny day they had experienced. It was still pleasant, though; Charles took a moment to look at Rebecca and admire his beautiful wife. Her resilience had kept the family alive, and it would be needed again whilst he was gone. He was proud of his children for helping him stay strong during this testing time. Rebecca came forward and kissed him on the lips; Arthur looked away a little; he didn't tell them to stop, but he was a teenager and didn't want to see his mother or father kiss in public.

"You look amazing, better than when I met you all those years ago."

Rebecca blushed a little.

"You too, I made the right choice, Charles." She pulled him in again.

This drew a cough from Emily. "I'm hungry, can we go?"

They both looked at her and smiled before boarding the carriage. The lanterns had been lit as they passed through the cobbled streets. There was still the city hustle and bustle around them, market sellers pushing the end-of-the-day fruit and vegetables. There was also the smell of street kitchens cooking various foods, which made Emily's stomach rumble.

When they arrived at the Italian restaurant, it was lit up with lanterns, and there was a healthy buzz around the restaurant. It was close to the brewery and was visited by its workers during the day. Families were flocking in, and Charles had been warned to arrive early to get a table.

Inside, there were candles everywhere, a man was playing music at a piano, and the waiters and waitresses were moving around at a frantic speed. The decor was Mediterranean and vibrant, with a large Italian flag next to an American flag. A large, round Italian man greeted them; he had a short moustache and well-groomed hair. He was loud and flamboyant; he kept saying his name, Stefano, as he sang an Italian song. Rebecca looked at Charles, and they laughed with the children.

He whirled over to Rebecca and kissed her hand. "A beautiful lady with a handsome man." Charles shook his hand as they were led to a window seat overlooking a courtyard. Stefano crouched down to be on the same level as Emily. "You have your mother's eyes. One day, you will break many hearts." Emily giggled a little, then squeezed into a seat next to Arthur.

Arthur was thinking about Naomi and their time in the park; he wasn't taking in anything.

"I see you are in love, young man." Stefano was now talking to Arthur.

He felt himself going red on his cheeks and didn't know what to say.

"Don't worry; you still need to eat even if you are in love." He clapped his hands, and a passing waiter passed him a menu. "Enjoy your evening here tonight", and with that, he was already welcoming in the next guest.

The menu offered different pasta dishes, some of which were seasonal. Once the family had ordered, they sat back and enjoyed the music and pleasant atmosphere.

"Charles, thank you for taking us here. I can live off this memory for a long time." She reached for his hand and held it tight.

"You've been through so much over the last few years, and I want to express my gratitude more than I do. This was the least I could do." They leaned in and kissed.

Arthur sighed loudly as if to ask them not to embarrass him. They kissed one more time and then ordered food. The evening passed too quickly. A carriage was waiting for them a few roads down from the restaurant. They thanked the staff and Stefano and wished them all the best before venturing outside. The stars and the moon reflected off the glass windows. They slowly walked to the carriage and pointed out different star signs as they walked.

Arthur and Emily thanked them for a lovely evening before climbing into the carriage. Rebecca hugged Charles before joining the children. Once he was in, they set off. Along the route home, Emily fell asleep, and Arthur studied the stars. Rebecca looked at her children and Charles and let her eyes gaze outside the carriage. They stopped briefly at a crossroads, letting two horse-drawn carriages pass them by; Rebecca sat up for a moment, wiped her eyes, and looked out towards an old shack. Standing beside it was the same man she had seen during the storm. He also had several people gathered around him.

His eyes lit up whenever the moon caught them. As he spoke to those around him, his sharpened teeth revealed themselves. His long and dark hair blended into his dark clothes. Standing to his immediate left was a tall, slender woman. Her eyes and teeth were the same as his. She followed his every word. The others were different. They looked scruffy, probably living on the street, but not carrying the same menace.

Rebecca felt a cold chill run through her body as the man's eyes looked over to the carriage. He squinted for a split second as the carriage began to move. Charles felt Rebecca tense up and asked what was wrong. She didn't want to endanger the children or him and said it was just the night air. As they rolled on, she allowed herself a quick look out of the carriage's back window. The men and women were no longer standing by the shack. She pulled Charles close and placed her head against his chest.

Chapter 22

The next morning, Charles spoke to Sergeant Butcher and Corporal Heinz; Texas had already gone with the Arapaho to the train station. They had all enjoyed the past three days, getting off the train and enjoying a break from the journey had been a relief. The attack at the bridge had made them realise what lay ahead, which was a sobering thought, but this time in Albany was just the tonic to help them believe in what could be.

Once they were all loaded on the three trains, they set off on the final part of the journey towards Boston. The weather was good, and the closer they got to Boston, the more the invasion force was revealed. Large military camps were stretching as far as the eye could see. European and British armies dominated this; they had been amassing for a year and going over invasion tactics. Rebecca looked at all the soldiers and put her hand on her husband's back.

They were due to stay in Malden, a town outside central Boston. From there, they could go over some drills before the planned departure. The date was being pushed back one week to make sure all the forces were ready to go. Finally, when the train rolled into Boston, there was a sigh of relief. It had been a difficult journey, and they thought about the soldiers lost at the bridge. Unfortunately, this would just be the start of it.

Boston was an inspiring city with its architecture and manufacturing growth. The usual chaos of everyday life was happening all around it, but this city was more impressive. The British knew of the Boston Tea Party and the start of the revolution from this great city. Now, it would launch another fight against the oppressive Nazar and his armies.

Once the trains had stopped, the soldiers disembarked and started helping unload the provisions for the coming months. Wagons had been transported with them from Colorado, but more were being supplied from Boston. The civilians left the middle train to go on their way. They thanked the soldiers as they passed them.

Naomi and Florence came over to Arthur to give them their address in Malden. They were staying in the same town, which meant both Tom and Arthur were super happy. They said their goodbyes and agreed to meet in a few days. Their uncle was helping with the horses for the British and American forces, which was why they stayed in Boston.

Once they had gone, Arthur spoke about how lucky they were to have the girls staying close. Tom smiled like a cat that had caught the cream. They were soon asked to help with getting their suitcases and the other suitcases that belonged to the families of the soldiers.

British General Greenway and American General McStevens greeted Charles. These two Generals would be part of the spearhead-led attack against Nazar's armies in Great Britain. General Greenway was leading the main British force landing at St Ives. General McStevens would lead the American forces when they landed at Aberystwyth and Porth Colmon.

Both men were buoyant about the planned invasion. The American General hadn't fought Nazar before but had witnessed the dead. General Greenway had seen some action during the retreat and fall of Great Britain. He was glad to have some veterans with him when they returned home.

The Generals were heading into town to meet some of the senior commanders at an evening function. Charles had been given an invitation but politely declined because they had just arrived in the city. Once everything was offloaded, they began to make their way to Malden. Large military camps had been set up with wooden huts, and they would be their home for the next few weeks until the soldiers left. Then, the families would move to civilian accommodation in a town called Lowell, and after that, they would eventually relocate to Canada.

The convoy of wagons began to move, and Captain Steinberg and Captain Somersett's infantry units would stay in Medford, close to Malden. They would provide cover and support for the British Engineers. The plan was to start training the following day. Much of that would involve going over where different units would be landing and what key points needed to be negotiated along the way. The British had not destroyed too much of the infrastructure as they retreated, as they hoped to one day return. Reports were a bit sketchy at best, but they did say that Nazar's forces had left most of the main bridges and roads intact. The railways were still carrying his soldiers around, whilst the dead could be moved anywhere or allowed to roam and cause fear.

Once the wagons had arrived at their locations, Hosah and his fellow Arapahos dismounted from their horses. They had brought Teepees with them and intended to camp outside instead of in wooden huts built for the British forces. Corporal Heinz went to speak to them and helped out where he could. Sergeant Butcher was getting the engineers to line up for roll call. The soldiers looked around at the barracks and the large gathering of British soldiers. There was a sense of pride in what was occurring.

Rebecca helped lead the other familie⸗
accommodation. Arthur went with Tom to speak
and asked if he could practice shooting a bo⸗
before leaving for England. Hosah said that would be ⸗⸗⸗
Charles joined in with unloading the wagons, whilst he was
carrying a box of ammunition with a fellow soldier, he got a
tap on the back. He looked around and was pleasantly
surprised to see some familiar faces.

Private Brown stood alongside Private Alexander
Chamberlin, and Lieutenant Kiesl was just behind him. He
would be leading a mixture of French, Prussian, and Austro-
Hungarians. To the side of them was a tall, muscular man.
Charles recognised him due to his size. It was Hagen the
Viking.

"I am very glad to see all of you. You have been with me
through this journey, and let's hope the next part will swing
in our favour." Charles took time to shake their hands and
acknowledge again his appreciation for them coming with
him. Texas, who was unloading a nearby wagon, came over.
Charles introduced him as a tracker and someone who would
help the engineers. Texas remarked on the size of Hagen and
how glad they were to have him on their side, although, in
truth, Hagen was only slightly bigger than Texas.

They all shared duties and helped offload all the supplies.
Then, it was back to the canteen, where a few barrels of ale
were waiting for them. Private Brown was able to fill in what
had happened since they arrived in America. Jon said that
Heidi would be coming over with the medical core. Charles
said that marriage would surely beckon after the war, which
brought a happy smile to John's face. It was only meant to be
a welcome drink, but a couple of hours passed, with the men
leaving in a joyous mood and not so steady on their feet.

Charles arrived back at the cabin and had to sit on the
porch for a few minutes to sober up. Rebecca came out to join
him and looked at Charles. "I bet it was good to see them
again." He looked up and nodded.

Then he went silent. "I worry for them coming with me, but I worry for you and the children more."

She sat next to him and brushed his hair. "We will be fine, and so will you." She then kissed him on the head. "You know your son has fallen in love."

Charles looked up at her. "I do; it's a good thing. He's growing up too fast, though." They hugged each other. That evening, Charles spent time with his family, as did the other soldiers who had family in the camp. Those who didn't lay in their beds and thought about what would be waiting for them in Wales and England.

The next few weeks were busy with training. Charles's detachment of British Engineers worked on making makeshift bridges. They also gave examples of how to build spiked wooden fences, which would offer protection against flesh-eaters around makeshift camps in Great Britain. Anything that would aid the rapid advance into England and Wales was discussed. They met concerning the beach landings and where they would go once they had a foothold in Great Britain.

Scotland had been discussed, but Wales and England must be secured first. Then, depending on the size of the army left, they would plan to push further north.

Heidi had come to meet John and the other engineers. She was in her nurse's uniform and looked very smart. A few nurses were travelling with the invasion force; they hoped for as few casualties as possible, but this was an invasion. The enemy was different and very dangerous.

The British Army had moved away from the red tunics for its soldiers, and they were now landing in khaki uniforms. The men liked it because it helped conceal them more in the undergrowth, and even moving through open fields aided their cover. They were trying out different tactics due to the nature of the enemy.

After a morning of going over manoeuvres, they finished at the shooting range. Alexander got to show why he was one of the sharpest shooters in the army. He was a killing machine; the more they practised with him, the happier Charles was to have him accompany them. Texas was joining with the preparations, as were the Arapaho. This would have usually been frowned upon before Great Britain fell, but now it was a case of getting an army together that could take on this formidable foe. Arthur and Tom had been allowed to go to the firing range under supervision. Rebecca had joined them, whilst Tom's mother, Christina, looked after Emily. Charles was happy to let them increase their weaponry skills.

Arthur spent extra time training with Hosah to use a bow and arrow. Hosah did not mind; he was impressed by how quickly he picked it up. He said to Arthur, "He would make a great Arapaho warrior." This put a big smile on Arthur's face for the whole day.

On weekends, the soldiers were given leave to visit Boston, and Charles used this time to visit the city with his family. Arthur and Tom had been meeting up with the girls when they could and were yearning for the next visit each time.

In the back of Charles's mind was the looming campaign departure. He was pleased with the soldiers going with him. He had seen the Americans training hard, as were the Europeans. The British forces would be crucial in helping guide their allies. Charles had recruited five Welsh fusiliers; a local private, Dai Evans, was raised near New Gale beach in a small village called Solva. He was there to help guide the Engineers and Marines to key strategic points they had earmarked to capture during the first day.

The Marines had been training hard on mock-up villages and clearing out small strongholds. Roch Castle was seen as a possible small enemy stronghold. This wasn't too far from Newgale Beach and would be targeted on the first day. Once they had landed and were pushing inland, they would have to keep lines of communication open. Charles was happy with everyone's efforts. Many factors would be out of their hands during the initial invasion, but they would try to control what they could.

While having coffee during a break from training, John went over to speak to Charles. He told him that he and Heidi had grown very close over the last two years and that he wanted to marry her after the war. John said he was honoured to fight with Charles and the Engineers and was hopeful they could turn the tide of this war.

Sergeant Butcher walked over to them and heard the last bit. "You've come a long way since the Carpathian Mountains, Private," John smiled at him.

"I still remember the retreat from Portsmouth and all those who lost their lives trying to save our great country." John was thinking about Charles's brother-in-law but did not want to mention his name. "Well, nothing like filling us with hope before the invasion." Sergeant Butcher said this using his dry sense of humour.

"I know! I know, sorry. I am hopeful we can beat Nazar. We all want revenge for what he's done." Charles nodded his head in agreement, as did Sergeant Butcher.

Charles changed the conversation when he spoke about Arthur and Emily growing up so fast; he had wanted to put all this behind him, work on the farm, and live out a simple life, but Nazar was coming; he was the common denominator shadowing over all of them. As they chatted away, Texas came over to join them. He took a mug placed on a fallen oak trunk and then grabbed a towel to handle a pot sitting on the fire. Inside was fresh coffee; he filled his mug and placed the pot back by the side of the fire.

"I feel we're going to kick some butt in Great Britain." He sipped at his warm coffee. "I haven't met this leader whom you're all talking about, but all men and women have weaknesses. We will prevail." The soldiers around him liked his belief and conviction, but they knew the Americans were yet to face the enemy in any significant number. They had experienced the attack on the bridge, which had resulted in them having to retreat. The problems would occur when you could not run anywhere and had to stand and fight to the death. That is when you would be facing your inner demons and fears.

The afternoon continued with further drills and explosive training. When Charles returned to the cabin, Rebeca spoke to Hagen and a tall, blonde-haired lady. She had strong features and piercing blue eyes. He was soon introduced to Hagen's partner, Elin. She greeted him and said, "What a lovely wife he had". Rebecca said Hagen and Elin were cooking Nordic-style food and wanted to know if they would join them to eat and drink. Charles looked at Rebecca, and they both nodded. It was only a week until they left, and every second with his wife and children mattered, but they had to carry on living, even with him leaving.

They agreed to meet in an hour at their cabin; Hagen had made a log fire to cook different meats. Elin had found new potatoes and various wild leaves and berries at a local market.

Arthur was reluctant to go with them as he wanted to make Naomi another wooden sculpture, an owl. He had chosen to make something more spectacular, but his skills were still limited. With his father due to leave soon, his mother convinced him he would have plenty of time to make things for Naomi, but only a week with his father around.

They set off from their log cabins to Hagen and Elin's feast. Charles was impressed with how the Americans had set up the camp, and the sheer scale of the operation had been handled well. The log cabins were freshly built out of Douglas Fir and had a distinct smell.

A lot of soldiers had to eat in the mess tents, which had been set up further in the camp. The feeling around them was one of hope.

Arriving at Hagen and Elin's cabin was an experience. They had put up bunting and a mid-summer pole, but it wasn't quite mid-summer. They said the Nordic communities would understand, as they would be away at sea at that time. Elin had her hair plaited back and was wearing traditional national dress. She stated it was a make-do dress because she left most of her belongings in Iceland when she came to America. Nazar's forces had attacked Iceland, but it was unclear if they had gained a strong foothold. It was thought they would use Iceland as a stepping-stone towards Greenland, then America. This had not been confirmed. The Icelandic nationals who had left their country said the enemy forces there were minimal. The dead had been frozen on the glaciers and were not moving around with the same effectiveness as they did in Europe and America.

Hagen took them to the fire pit he had made. He had also constructed a gridiron grill to go over the top of it. He had caught venison and paid for beef cuts from the army butcher; even a chicken had been plucked and prepared, ready to be cooked. Arthur's teenage eyes lit up. The food hadn't been too bad over the journey from Gold Hills, but this looked amazing and something he wanted to have immediately. Hagen said he could help cook the meat, which again got his stomach juices turning.

Elin asked if Emily would like to have her hair plaited, and the smile from cheek to cheek gave her an answer. She sat her down on a veranda outside their log cabin. Their cabin backed onto a wooded area; they had put up dried-up animal skins and various garments. Elin was very good at making clothes and fixing things; she had grown up on a farm and worked on the land. Many would have looked at her and thought she was part of high society, as her beauty masked her skills on the land. Hagen met her while helping the Danish community set up a camp near Boston. She had asked him to help her move some large boxes, and he remarked how strong she was. Then she joked that Icelandic girls were stronger than Danish girls. This was enough to get them to help each other.

Over time, they fell in love, and she agreed to come to the British camp. She did not want Hagen to join the invasion force, but knew he would be needed, as one day, he would like to return to Denmark and free it from Nazar's forces.

Arthur lifted two large strips of meat and placed them on the grill. Hagen then took some venison strips and put them on as well. They had been seasoned, and the smell hit them straight away. This carried over the whole camp, but fortunately, most were fed or drinking ale in the mess area. The only visitors to come over were the Arapaho. Hagen raised his hand to Hosah as he walked over. Hagen saw they were keeping themselves from the main army kitchens, so he invited them to his midsummer feast.

Charles and his family were happy to see them. Hosah instantly asked Arthur to come and shoot a target with his bow; Arthur looked at his father and mother for approval, which they gave. Emily enjoyed getting her hair plaited and watching Hagen and Charles turn the meat. The Indian braves also helped; they had brought a good supply of meat. The truth was now, they would probably not need to cook it all.

The Arapaho enjoyed the potatoes and other leaves and dishes on offer. Some of them were trying out their English, and Charles was impressed by how quickly they were learning. His Arapaho was very basic, and he felt embarrassed about how bad it was. Arthur was picking it up quicker. Rebecca had a bowl of food and joined Charles, looking into the fire. Some of the braves began to chant and sing songs from their ancestral past. The rhythmic sound was relaxing and powerful; Emily joined the braves, moving around another fire they had set up. Several sat playing the drums to aid the chanting. Rebecca got up and joined Elin as they danced around the fire.

Hosah told Arthur it was a war dance as they prepared to battle with their enemy. His aim was improving; with each shot, he began to hit the target where Hosah told him.

"Little Bear would be proud of you." Hosah then directed Arthur to a target he had set up on a rope. It was weighted so it could be swung from side to side. He then pushed it to get it swinging before telling Arthur to hit the target. Arthur looked at Hosah as if to say, "Come on, how can I do that?" But the look was ignored. "You can hit the target, young brave, but you must believe in yourself."

Arthur stood there; he listened to the rustling leaves around him. The breeze was soft, but he wanted to allow for that, so he took several breaths and waited. Then, drawing the cord on the bow, he looked at the target; Arthur waited and waited, and then he let go of the arrow. It flew fast and accurately in the swinging gut ball attached to the rope's end. Arthur let out a roar and jumped on the spot. He hugged Hosah and then ran over to the target. He couldn't believe he had hit it.

"Well done, Arthur, let's eat."

Arthur stood looking at the target for a moment with the arrow protruding out of it. Arthur pulled it out and went to join Hosah as they walked back to the campfire.

"Thank you, Hosah, for everything you have taught me." Arthur saw him as an older brother and didn't want Hosah or his father to go to fight in Great Britain. He knew they had no choice but didn't want it to happen.

Arthur arrived with Hosah at the campfire. He loved seeing Emily dance around the fire with the Arapaho. Rebecca and Elin were also lost in the chanting. Charles had a jug of ale and was enjoying the moment. He watched his family laughing and having fun; it was a memory he would hold on to in the coming months.

Chapter 23

Sergeant Butcher's family were leaving for Canada after he had set sail. He kissed his wife and daughter before picking up his kit bag. They would come to the dock to see him off later. He then went over to join the rest of the royal engineers.

Corporate Heinz came dressed in his khaki uniform and had his webbing and kit bag. His father, mother, and family had moved to Canada. He had seen them while they were in America, but it meant no one could see him off. Sergeant Butcher came over to him and said his wife and daughter wanted to hug him before they left. He instantly looked happier and went over to them. Sergeant Butcher's daughter told him to take care of and look after her dad.

The royal engineers were lined up to march to the docks. A military band was leading several units, and when they began to play, the soldiers came to. The bugler sounded the final call, and Sergeant Butcher barked out instructions for them to begin marching. There were crowds of people to see them off, a mixture of British, European and American families.

The British marched to the ships that were taking them. The engineers who were going in with the Marines lined up there. General Greenway addressed the British units one at a time. Many soldiers were taking part in the invasion. After his quick speech, they were allowed to say farewell to their loved ones.

Charles looked at his family. He was proud of what they had achieved and gone through. They had spent a lot of time together over the past two years. Charles was still reluctant to go, but he knew it was time.

The ship's horns sounded the official time to board. The Marines had a sergeant major waiting at the gangway with his roll call of names. He was a short, stocky man with a well-kept beard. It took a bit of time to board everyone, but they wanted to ensure those who were part of the invasion were documented. The high command did not fully know what they would face in terms of numbers in the enemy army. This was part of the reason they were taking several medical ships with them.

The new ironclad battleships could bombard the coastline defences and soften up the landing areas. The journey across the Atlantic was estimated to take around a week. Charles kissed Rebecca on the lips and hugged Arthur and Emily before turning to join the officers and seeing the soldiers onto the ship.

All the soldiers at the docks were saying goodbye to their loved ones, and those who didn't have anyone to say goodbye to were being cheered onto the boats.

It was a powerful sight when they set sail, seeing the cheering crowds, flags being waved, and the army bands playing rousing tunes. It put the soldiers in good spirits. Those who hadn't fought Nazar's forces felt encouraged by the pomp and pageantry. Those who had fought in Europe and Great Britain were more sombre, taking in the faces of the people seeing them off, looking for their family members, hoping they would be okay.

The message to the soldiers was simple: If the Allied forces could take back some of Nazar's recently captured land, this would help deter an invasion.

Charles sank into his bunk. He looked at a photo they had recently taken in Boston of his family. He wanted a moment to gather his thoughts before checking on the troops. The Arapaho were on the top deck looking at the sea below. The fleet around them was huge; Hosah and the other Arapaho were taking it all in. They have never been on a ship that big, let alone sail across an ocean. Hosah spoke to Little Bear about seeing a shoal of fish; they just wanted to stand in awe of what they were seeing.

Texas sat on a bench just behind them, reached into his jacket pocket, and pulled out a pipe and leather pouch. He cleared the old debris from the pipe's bowl by tapping it on the side of his boot. Then, out of the leather pouch, he took up some tobacco and rubbed a little between his fingers before pushing it into the bowl on the pipe. Shielding a freshly struck match, he lit the tobacco and drew on the mouthpiece to help get the tobacco going. He shook the match out and sat there in bliss, watching the American coastline slowly begin to disappear the further they pulled away from it.

Private Johnson from the 10th Cavalry Regiment sat down next to him.

"Can you spare some of your tobacco?"

"Sure." Texas gave him his tobacco pouch and told him to fill his boots.

They both laughed.

"My name is Mathew." He lent out his hand, to which Texas shook it and told him his name. "Texas"

"What, like the state?"

"Yep"

Mathew started to do a roll-up using the tobacco he had just received. He lit the cigarette and took a full drag before letting it out again.

"That was the first time I've seen the dead up close like that on the bridge." He rubbed his forehead. "I've heard stories, but most thought they were just that, more like infected people, but not actually walking dead."

Texas drew on his pipe. "I was the same until I encountered a disused house in Louisiana. I thought it would be a good place to stay the night; while I slept, some of those things wandered close by the house." He looked at Mathew, "I must have made some kind of noise, but they came through the windows, broken walls." Texas took another long draw on his pipe. "I was with my daughter."

Mathew just nodded.

"We got lucky. I managed to fight them off, but it changed the world as I knew it."

They both sat in silence for a few minutes, deep in thought.
"It wasn't long ago that I was fighting against these brave warriors. Now they fight with us." "It probably wasn't long ago that you told yourself you would never fight with men of a southern background."

Mathew looked at him and nodded. "I guess you're right; to survive, we must adapt."

"I cannot claim to know too much about the enemy we are going to fight, but if the dead are fighting with them, we are in for one hell of a war." Texas finished smoking his pipe.

"I'm sure we'll speak again before landing." Texas shook Mathews' hand again.

"I'm sure we will, Texas."

It wasn't long before America had disappeared out of sight.

Charles left his room and went for a walk on the top deck. He didn't mind being at sea but wouldn't describe himself as a sea lover. It had felt wrong to leave his family; he believed this was a plan that would not stop the impending American invasion, but the fresh sea air was helping to lift his spirits. He had pondered on the American government having to do something; the refugees were seen as a cost burden, and if they did not try and take something back, the feeling would be they would never return. With in-house fighting on whether to negotiate with Nazar still ongoing, this was an opportunity to clear the decks.

The American army was recruiting heavily and still preparing. Young British and European soldiers were in training. Some said they should have sent the largest force possible, but the top generals kept the elite soldiers behind. They wanted to be ready with a force to defend the country.

He was joined by two of his privates, John and Alexander. They asked if he was okay, and he replied he was adjusting to life on the waves. Alexander updated them on how he had been helping shoot flesh-eaters from afar. There was a group of snipers working with the American 7th Cavalry who would ride out and find small groups of flesh-eaters and eliminate them. With the more enormous hordes, the snipers could help cover the cavalrymen who would try and find places they could lead the dead to walk to. That could be cliff tops, ravines, or disused quarries. The problem was the Great Plains; it was harder to manage them effectively. The hordes were getting more significant, more dangerous and unpredictable. When Nazar's priests led them, they were a formidable conquering weapon. Their bite would infect more people; it was a troublesome problem and one they knew they would be facing in Great Britain.

The evening passed well. Charles wrote a letter to his family describing the journey so far; he planned to add more details when they reached Wales. Once they had a foothold in Wales and England, many of the escort fleet would travel back. There would be ships taking mail back to America.

He went up on deck with a mug of coffee. The fleet was inspiring, ships as far as the eye could see. Many carried troops and supplies, but had battleships at the front and sides. The main attack force would see the battleships clear a path of enemy vessels before the troop-carrying ships arrived.

After lunch, they made targets to place in the sea for some fun. It was a calm ocean, which allowed them to use it as target practice. Charles joined in using his Enfield rifle. He impressed himself by hitting a few of the targets floating in the sea. Corporal Heinz and Sergeant Butcher were having fun as well, it was good light relief. The engineers then challenged some of the marines with them. It was a close-run thing; Alexander was the top marksman amongst them, but points were gathered from all of those taking part, and the Marines took the top spot.

Charles had used his power as a major to allow some nurses to be stationed on their ship. John was very grateful for this, as Heidi was one of them. She was not allowed to go into his quarters, which was the same for John in hers, but it meant they could eat together and enjoy some time on the top deck.

On day four, the weather had started to change. The waves sent the ships up and down, and the spacing between the fleet grew for safety reasons. A lot of the soldiers were getting seasick and struggling with the harsh weather. Charles had a terrible night. He had travelled a lot before by sea, but this time, it affected him more. The ship dropped and rose repeatedly; Charles retreated to his bunk and closed his eyes as he hoped it would pass; the next morning, the oceans had calmed down. He gingerly went to sit on the top deck and take in the fresh air.

Private John Brown looked like he felt. He had gone to Heidi to get comfort after suffering from seasickness. She was not affected and made him an old remedy of ginger root, which he greatly appreciated. As the weather cleared, the seas became less volatile.

That evening, the ship returned to normal. A hearty meal was prepared for the soldiers and officers. It was another four days before they were closing in on mainland Britain. The weather had been overcast, and the sea was choppy but not like it had been a few days before.

An evening meal was planned, but the soldiers were broken into squads before that. Captain Steinberg and Captain Somersett joined the officer debrief. Hosah was allowed to be with them, and he had not suffered too badly from the bad weather, which was the same for the other Arapaho as well.

The map of the Welsh coast was laid out over two tables. It showed where the forces would land and where they needed to be. Communication was going to be difficult until they had taken key positions. Then, riders would be sent out to update the different units on the progress of each attacking force.

Charles looked at New Gale Beach; it was a long, flat beach with a broad, rising slope down the middle and steep banks on either side. This would mean they would have to push up quickly through the centre. They looked at the local villages and roads leading to them. Roach Castle had been marked as a strategic stronghold and would have to be taken. They spent time looking over the maps and discussing scenarios. The fleet was splitting, with some of it moving down to Cornwall. The main force would be pushing up from the lower west coast.

Ireland would not be touched at his present moment. There had been reports that Nazar took it, but it was unknown how many soldiers he had there.

The officer's next task was to relay all the information to their units. Once the beach was secure, the supplies and horses would be brought in. The European forces would land in Aberystwyth, and the American US-led army would land in Porth Colmon.

Later in the evening, Charles sat down to eat with the engineers and the allied units he would be commanding. Some joked that it could be one of their last proper meals for a while. He gauged the men's mood, and it still appeared strong. He had spoken to the Royal Marine commander, Major Samuel Briggs. He was a chirpy man who had seen some action in Europe and Portsmouth during the fall of Great Britain. He spoke about losing a lot of good soldiers in the fighting and was keen to re-engage the enemy.

Charles took time to work his way around the soldiers, talking about their role and reminding them of the long-limbs' speed and flesh-eaters' power in numbers. Beer was being served in jugs, and this brought out the singing voice of Sergeant Butcher. He treated them to some old Cornish songs, which then, in turn, brought out more songs from the other soldiers. Charles joined in whilst drinking beer; he thought, why not enjoy the moment? They spent the evening relaxing and talking about different stories about their lives. Some of the soldiers had relatives who did not leave Great Britain. No one knew if they were still alive, but they all hoped this invasion would help unite them again. Hosah and the Arapaho did not drink but performed some of their own war chants. Texas got the American soldiers to sing songs, and Captain Somerset's soldiers also added their impressive singing skills. "Captain Steinberg joked that if they could have a singing competition against the enemy, they would surely win." One soldier remarked on what song the dead would sing. Which brought the food hall to silence, and laughter followed.

The drinking went on into late evening, but an agreed-upon time to stop was put in place so they could rest and prepare for battle. The next day was spent waiting. The battleships did not want to begin bombardment until the following early morning. They stayed far enough from the mainland as not to be seen. The plan was an early morning attack; the shelling would begin as soon as daylight broke, and then the landing crafts would push onto the beaches. This was meant to happen along the Welsh coast and in Cornwall with the main British army.

That evening, Charles wrote more of his letter. He wanted to add that they would be landing in the morning and said he loved them all.

Not too much was known about how fortified the beaches were. From where they were waiting, they had not seen any enemy ships, which could have been different for the invasion force landing in Cornwall.

Hosah spoke with Little Bear and the other Arapaho about what was coming. They would put on their war paint before going into battle, as it was a tradition they wanted to continue. The British had supplied them with khaki uniforms, which would help ensure they were associated with the British force. Of course, they would be allowed to personalise them.

"Little Bear, keep moving once we hit the beach. If they have Gatling guns, we must get to cover." We all know what they can do if you are in the open." Hosah was direct.

"I will fight well and make my tribe proud; we all will." Little Bear was sharpening his tomahawk. They had spears, bows, and arrows stockpiled. They also had been training on Lee Enfield rifles and had Smith and Western revolvers.

They could not bring all of the weapons at once, as it would weigh them down. They planned to bring more equipment once they secured a beachhead.

They went onto the top deck and did a war dance. The British and American soldiers around them watched and respected what they saw. Inside, they all carried their own thoughts and fears for what the following day would hold.

John had gone to speak to Heidi. She was preparing for the wounded soldiers who would be coming back from the beach tomorrow. She had stockpiled bandages and field dressing and worked with the other nurses to organise everything. The doctors had met with some of the senior nurses, leaving the others to finalise the ward.

"Heidi, can we have five minutes?" he said, sticking his head around the door. The other nurses smiled and joked that she should speak to her lover. She came over to John and gave him a cuddle and a kiss. He went a bit red in his face, but with the planned invasion around the corner, no one was taking notice.

They found an empty storage room on the ship. "We don't have much time, John."

It was fun and wild, mixed with nervous energy and excitement. Heidi wanted to make love to him before he landed in Wales, and they were fortunate to get this opportunity.

Afterwards, she straightened his hair and uniform.

"Remember, keep your head down and stay close to others." She brushed the side of his face.

"I will, and you keep safe on this ship."

John kissed her on the lips. "I love you."

"I love you, too."

They hugged and embraced for a couple of minutes before kissing one last time.

"I will see you in a few days." There was conviction in John's voice as he left to join his unit.

Chapter 24

Charles awoke with the sound of battleships firing their first battery. The loud thumping vibrated around his room, shaking a small family picture he had put up on a sideboard. This was the start of the invasion. He swung his legs out of the bunk and took a moment to clear his head. Then he grabbed a towel that he had placed over the chair in the corner of his room. He went to the small, cramped washroom and freshened up before changing into his uniform. Whilst this was happening, the shelling continued along the coastline.

The louder the noise, the more encouraged the soldiers were. They wanted the enemy positions to be broken and destroyed before they landed. As daylight slowly crept along, the soldiers were given their last debrief. They had been shown where to head on the beach and where to wait if they got separated from their unit.

All the soldiers landing at Newgale Beach would not carry too many supplies. They were going in light; ammunition and weapons were the main port of call. The idea was to be quick and mobile. They would be resupplied once the landing area was secure.

The troop carrier ships moved closer to the mainland, enabling the soldiers to see the plumes of smoke rising from the coastline. They could visibly see the explosions of the shells landing on the hills around Newgale. The air carried the smell of cordite, which had a strong, sharp odour from the shells. It was mixed in with burnt soil and wood. Flames licked up from various locations. The soldiers said if the enemy didn't know they were coming, they would now.

The landing crafts were being lowered into place from the supply ships. The sea was a little bit choppy, but it wasn't as rough as they had experienced a few nights previously. The soldiers would be climbing down rope nets into the landing crafts, and then from there, they would be taken to the beach.

Charles would have the Arapaho and the Royal Engineers with him. Texas was also aligned with this detachment. The Americans were in their own landing crafts, as were the Royal Marines, who would be first out on the beach.

Letters were being handed to a staff sergeant with grey hair and a short moustache. He would be helping the wounded soldiers when they got taken back to the ship. Charles gave the man his letter and saw him put it into a large brown sack. The Staff Sergeant wished each man well before they left him to climb down to the boat. Charles then turned to collect his Lee-Metford rifle and strap it across his back. Sergeant Butcher and Corporal Heinz joined him; then Alexander and Private John Brown arrived. "Did you tell Heidi you'd see her soon?" Charles was calm and reassuring in his statement.

"I did, and she wishes us all well."

Their attention then turned to the coastline as artillery shells began to be fired from ground gun emplacements.

Texas broke the silence. "They found a uniform big enough?" he asked, causing them all to look around. The big man was just about fitting into his khaki uniform. It was a short moment to smile before filing down the rope ladder.

Charles was wishing them all well as they climbed down. A young doctor was joining them; his name was Christian Turner; he didn't look much over 25 and apparently hadn't seen too much action. He had worked in the hospitals in London, though, and came recommended for his medical skills. Charles hoped to keep him alive so they could benefit from his knowledge. He had been assigned to the Marines to start with, but they had some of their own medical officers going in with them. He had been debriefed on the objectives and carried a rifle and revolver.

They continued to fill the landing craft. Hosah stood next to Charles, looking at the beach and the Royal Marines leaving for it. "We asked the gods for us to fight well today."

"I'm sure we will." Charles patted him on the shoulder. Hosah, along with the other braves, then began to lower themselves down on the rope. The Arapaho were fast, agile, and in the landing craft in the blink of an eye. The battleship cannons stopped firing. This was now the start of the landings. The Royal Marines had already set off. Charles followed their progress briefly before turning to Sergeant Butcher and Corporal Heinz. "You both have been with me for all of this; please stay with me to the end of it." Charles shook their hands and began to climb down the rope ladder.

Once they were all in the landing craft, it was untied from the rope nets, and they began to push forward. Some of the Engineers had been with Charles from the Carpathian Mountains all those years ago. There were also a lot of new faces, some younger soldiers and older ones. Their thoughts and prayers were with the Marines going in first. Inside the landing craft, there was a mixture of nerves and anticipation. Those who had not seen action could see what was coming but tried to think of other things.

Charles watched the beach as the first landing crafts closed in. There was ground artillery shooting at the Marines as they closed in. Water burst up violently with each shell that landed in the sea.

Unfortunately, as the first craft landed, a shell landed directly at the front of the vessel. It sent wood and debris hurtling in the air and instantly killed all of the soldiers waiting to push out of the front of the landing craft. Those that were still alive jumped over into the sea and waves. They came under rifle fire from the hills above, making it hard to swim to shore. This destroyed vessel soon had company on the beach as more landed. The other landing crafts following behind could hear the vocal charge. Even with the heavy bombardment, the Allied forces still had artillery firing down upon them. The tide was coming in, so there was not too much beach to manoeuvre across before hitting the sand bank and pushing onto the slope and up the hill. It was more apparent for the Marines to see basic fortifications along the bank as they landed on the beach.

The Marines did well pushing on as mortar shells landed on the beach, bits of shrapnel flung up and into the air, mixed in with sand and water. It inflicted casualties as they pressed forward; rifle fire was also coming from the fortified defences and hills. The Marines had taken in each landing craft a homemade iron shield, the Idea being the strongest men within the squad would carry it up the beach and lay it down as a shield. Further in front of them were wooden spikes protruding from the defensive bank all along the Newgale beach, and other items used to stop them from advancing were strewn across the landing area. Nazar's clone soldiers had dug into this bank and fired from that position.

Several crossing points had been hurriedly filled in with sandbags and wood. Some defensive turrets were made out of soil and shingles. Maxim machine guns were stationed in those turrets. As soon as the marines were in range, they began to fire.

This started to take its toll on the advance. Major Samuel Briggs had got a large proportion of his men to the bank. Now, they were being hit hard by the Maxim machine guns. Wounded and dead soldiers were scattered across the beach. The Marines pressed into the bank and took cover behind anything that could shield them. The attack was being halted all along the front line.

Charles looked up as the sun started to appear through the clouds; the spray from the waves hitting the bow of the landing crafts splashed up on all the soldiers crouched in the boat. The shells were falling in the water around them, and the young soldier's anxiety was evident. Bullets thumped into the wooden sides and the front ramp the closer they got to the beach. Charles looked over the side briefly to check on the other landing crafts with the Americans and Royal Engineers. So far, so good, as they all closed in. It was hoped the marines would have broken through the defensive line, but the machine guns held them up.

Another wave of marines landed in front of the Americans and the Engineers. Again, they were coming under fire and struggling to get forward, which meant a build-up of soldiers almost caught in the breaking waves. Charles instructed his Royal Navy operator to steer them to the right-hand side of the beach, which was less crowded. As they were leading the third wave, the others behind them could follow their route.

"Alexander, I need you to start taking out the machine gunners in those turrets."

Alexander nodded his head. His rifle had been wrapped in leather and was well protected against the water.

Charles then said we needed to help break the deadlock. The drone artillery was directing its fire on the marines along the bank. It would not be long before the beach attack failed.

As they approached the swallower water, bullets began to hit the boat from all angles. A royal engineer was shot in the shoulder, but on inspection, it was a large splinter, which broke off when a bullet hit the top of the landing craft. The soldier wanted to continue with the attack and did not want to be sent back to the troop carrier ship.

Charles placed himself at the front of the vessel. He wanted to lead them as soon as the ramp went down. The second wave of Marines had pushed on but were halfway up the beach, trying not to get too close to the machine guns. The Engineers, led by Charles, gripped their rifles, and as soon as the ramp lowered, they rapidly moved forward; bullets were landing around them, but as they were in the third wave, rifle fire was directed more at the marines. Charles led the men to where there was some cover from the iron shields. He signalled to Alexander to take cover behind one of the shields. The other Engineers began to fire at the puffs of smoke on the hillside to their right and at the defences.

Alexander ran forward and took up a position just behind an iron shield. The sand was soft and wet under his body, and it seeped through his uniform. His heart raced as he removed the leather he had wrapped around his Lee-Metford rifle.

He then pulled back the bolt and loaded a bullet into the chamber. Taking deep breaths to control his breathing, he looked down at the scope of his rifle. In the turret nearest to them on the left-hand side of the beach was a group of drones manning the machine gun. The main gunner focused his fire on the marines pinned down on that side.

Alexander waited and dug the rifle deeper into his shoulder. Then, squeezing the trigger, he shot the main gunner. There was a squirt of blood from his head before he instantaneously fell backwards. Alexander then began to work his way through the turrets. With the machine gunfire being hindered, the marines started to throw grenades into the turrets. They also laid dynamite in sections along the defensive barriers. The explosions sent sand and rock flying through the skies. This was the signal for the Marines to press forward. Bayonets were fixed, and a huge roar went up as they burst through the gaps that were now created.

Alexander carried on targeting the turrets, killing any drone soldier that dared stick his head up. Some of the marines further back on the beach had set up motors and were firing at the artillery emplacements in the hills to each side of the beach. Charles had kept his men down, and the rest of the engineers joined the Americans who were by their side. The fighting on top of the embankment was ferocious; the drones were putting up a good fight, but as the second wave came up from the beach, the drones were starting to be overwhelmed.

The marines were gaining a foothold at Newgale, and the priests commanding the bank called for their units to retreat. This allowed the British soldiers to pick them off as they fled to higher ground. Mortars were set up from their new position at the beginning of the slopes. They began to fire on the hills on either side of the main slope leading away from the beach.

Alexander targeted the artillery on the slopes. They were better protected, but occasionally, he would capture a poor soul who moved into a non-shielded position.

Charles decided to push his units up to the main embankment. A marine sergeant was getting his wounded to be helped back to the boats. Charles looked around at the dead and dying as they took cover along the bank. A lot of soldiers had already paid a price for taking this beach. Texas looked on at the carnage; he was a hardened frontiersman, but this much death was new to him. They had to keep their heads down as shells continued to fall on their positions.

The Marine sergeant said scouts had gone out to see if there were more machine guns further up. The next push was to see them move in three directions. Some would take out the artillery positions on the hills on either side of the beach, whilst the rest would push up the middle. Captain Fairfax was leading the second marine wave; he said they were a few short of taking out the guns to the right flank. Charles said he would take a handful of his men and marines and see to the guns.

The captain thanked him for his help. Charles told Sergeant Butcher to keep the soldiers together. Captain Steinberg and Captain Somersett offered their assistance. Charles told them it would be better for them to hold the beach and stay in cover. With that, Charles selected two Royal Engineers and asked if Hosah and two of his tribesmen would assist them. They were also going up with fifteen marines. Alexander had pushed onto a grassed area with Corporal Heinz.

They nodded to the Major, saying he would get sniper cover from them.
"Let's move."

Using the side of the beach embankment for cover and then making their way along a long, dipping coastal path, they stayed low and scurried forward. Smoke from the explosions and burning ground favoured them as they slowly moved up the side of the hill, using it for cover. They could make out defensive sandbags around artillery pieces. There were also pockets of trenches where Nazar's soldiers were firing down onto the beach.

Charles could see drone soldiers further up a meandering dirt track and drones positioned in a sandbag square. His attack group lay down in the grass. Hosah crawled up to Charles, and they quickly discussed what needed to be done. Hosah spoke to the two Arapaho with him; one of them was to take out the guards nearest the cannons. The other one would go with Charles and help him take out the guards by the track.

Charles started to crawl forward, rifle in front of him as he walked through the grass. Hosah left his rifle with the soldiers. He preferred to take his bow. The other brave went at a steady pace towards the guns.

The marines and engineers would follow behind once the guards were removed. Hosah was first to strike; he sent an arrow into the neck of one of the guards next to the track; as his comrade started to move, Hosah sent an arrow into the drone's back. They then pushed further up the hill; as they crossed to look at the square sandbag fortification, a bullet hit the soil nearby, sending mud and stone in the air. This was quickly followed by more bullets flying past them and into the ground around them. Charles told Hosah to keep low, which brought a look of 'what else would I do?'.

Charles could see movement from within the sandbag square. A drone leaned out of the defensive wall to take aim at the marines and engineers moving up the other side. Charles's breathing was fast from the intensity of the battle; he took a moment to gather his breath, then looked down at the sights of his rifle. It had been a while since he had shot in anger against the living. When he squeezed the trigger, the drone soldier fell forward and slumped over the sandbags; blood began to stain the woven cotton material of the bags he was lying on. It had been a clean shot, something Charles prayed for.

The attack on the other side progressed quickly; the two drone soldiers outside the gun battery had been dispatched. Five marines broke from the group to help Charles and Hosah attack the defensive square. The rest pushed onto the artillery cannons. There was a thin, weaselly-looking priest who screamed out when it caught sight of the on-rushing British force. Drones came to the side of the defensive wall and began shooting; two marines fell as bullets cut through them. A marine who was shot in the leg fell forward but managed to light a grenade. He threw the bomb into the artillery battery; the explosion shook the ground around them and also disabled one of the cannons. The Arapaho brave was over the wall in a flash and used his tomahawk to dispatch a drone that came at him.

This was the signal for the attack on the cannons. The marines on that side of the hill rushed forward under fire. A marine who was shot in the leg fell but managed to muster the strength to light his improvised bomb, then threw it into the artillery battery, and the explosion shook the ground around them; it also disabled one of the cannons and killed many of the gunners. The Arapaho brave was over the wall in a flash and used his tomahawk to dispatch a drone that came at him. The British marines and engineers followed with Bayonets. They charged through the smoke and into the dazed gunners; some tried to fight back but were soon outnumbered and outfought. Those who surrendered were spared; the British high command had agreed with the European League of Nations and Americans that surrendering soldiers would be shown mercy.

Alexander and Corporal Heinz had pushed up the track and started taking shots at the drone soldiers in the sandbag square. Hosah sent an arrow through one of the drone's arms as he went to throw a bomb. This went off inside, killing the soldiers nearest him.

The gunfire from the Lee-Metford rifles was now focused on this defensive square. The marines and engineers had taken the artillery emplacement and laid down gunfire from that side. The Arapaho brave was using his rifle and shooting with the others. This was forcing the drones to take cover and not return fire, which enabled Charles to lead his forces up to the side of the sandbag wall and then two more bombs were lit and thrown over. Crouching down and waiting until after the explosions, they fixed bayonets and leapt over; the drones inside that were left alive raised their hands. Charles quickly scanned around and ordered the marines to lead the prisoners down to the beach.

The long-term plan for prisoners would need to be worked out, but for now, they wanted them out of the way and not close to the combat, where they could begin to fight again. Charles studied the faces of the dead and prisoners. Some had the grey-infected faces he had seen all those years ago when they were escaping Europe; others looked fresher-faced. Charles knew he would be fighting his fellow countrymen, as Nazar was known to give you a choice of 'join', or he would wipe out your entire family.

Inside the sandbag defence, there was ammunition and empty food boxes. The ground was sodden, and the mud covered everything. Corporal Heinz went over to check on the others; the wounded were being helped down the hill. The battle had progressed from the beach as the marines pushed further up the slope. The Americans and other engineers had settled in the defensive bank and were awaiting instructions. The hill on the left-hand side of the beach had been taken, meaning they were no longer being hit with artillery shells from the sides. There were still cannons further up on the slope, but it meant the bombardment had slowed down.

"Long limbs." An Engineer was the first to see a group of around twenty-five or more coming at them.

Charles shouted at the Marines to move the wounded quickly. He then called over to Corporal Heinz to get the soldiers to come over into the sandbag redoubt. They moved quickly, not having time to reload or think about what was coming. The soldiers threw themselves over the sandbags and joined the others, looking further down the track.

With their gangly motion, the long limbs were on all fours, moving at speed down the track and across the grass meadows. Their jaws open, showing their sharp teeth, saliva dripping from their mouths. The soldiers could hear the snorts and huffing sounds as they came closer. A roar went up from behind them, which caused a few of the marines to look over their shoulders to see where it was coming from. Charging down the hill was a detachment of riders of the North. Male and female giants, some seven foot and eight foot tall, strong and powerful. They came down on shire-size horses, brandishing swords, spears and rifles. The ground shook as they came forward; grass and soil were flung up from the horse's hooves, tearing into the soft, wet soil.

The Marines had pushed to a second line of defence but had no machine guns or artillery to slow down this cavalry attack. The mortars, which had been set further back on the beach, could not find the range quickly enough and were of no use to help stop this advance.

Charles's attentions were refocused on the long limbs as the first one was hit by a hail of bullets ripping through its skin and bones, causing it to fall and roll onto the grass below it. The Lee-Metford rifles had ten rounds in their magazines, which helped with this attack. Hosah and the Arapaho brave with him drew back their bows as four more long limbs came bursting towards the sandbags. One fell with an arrow through its left eye socket. Another stumbled as an arrow hit its hind leg, but still limped forward. The marines and engineers opened fire; they managed to kill the remaining three, but following behind were fifteen more. The marines with fixed bayonets helped force them back and stopped them from jumping straight into the redoubt.

This only made them circle the sandbag square, probing for an entrance. Some began to lift themselves onto the sandbag walls and start to climb in; Charles lashed out at one of the long limbs, which had two legs over the top sandbags on one side. He used his rifle butt to smash it in the head, it tried to swipe its claw at him, but before Charles could shoot his rifle, Hosah stuck a tomahawk in its head and withdrew it.

This only stopped one, others had already got themselves into the square. One marine was bitten in the back and arm; another had his chest opened up as he was set upon by two at once.

Charles knew they were in trouble; the long limbs were starting to get a foothold in this fight. Two engineers backed up to Charles, as did Corporal Heinz and Alexander. He dispatched a long limb as it came for them from the side, but their numbers were too great.

The battle through the middle had also swung in the Riders of the North's favour. The giant riders had pushed back the marines, killing several as they swept down through them. Texas watched what was happening further up the hill and over at the slopes. Private Brown had been offloading ammunition with Hagen. Once they had got the last box off, they looked at each other.

"We need to help at the front." Hagen was to the point.

"The orderlies can take the ammunition to the defensive bank."

They both grabbed their rifles; Hagen had an axe strapped across his back and a large dagger on his belt. They moved at speed to where the British and Americans were waiting. Texas had spoken to Captain Steinberg and Captain Somersett. He had asked if he could assist Major Hayward and his men. They had agreed he could and said he should take some of Captain Somersett's soldiers and British engineers with them. Little Bear said several Arapaho would join him.

Hagen and Private Brown arrived just as they were setting up the hill. Sergeant Butcher approved as they kept moving over the defensive bank and up the track. Captain Somersett led the 10th Cavalry regiment to support the Marines. Private Johnson fixed his bayonet and joined the others as they rushed forward to help the Marines. They wished they had horses to engage them in the saddle, but the beach was not secure enough to bring them in.

They advanced up the slope just as the sun began to break out from the clouds. The fighting in front of them was ferocious; two marines took down a giant rider of the North and bayoneted her several times. One marine was then struck in his back with a spear and fell forward as another female rider knocked into his comrade.

There was no time to wait as the 10th cavalry charged the riders of the North. Some northern riders had been dismounted and were fighting on foot. The Marines' energy was being sapped as they were thrown around and pushed back by these impressive fighters. The 10th cavalry came at them hard and fast. They added a much-needed push, hunting in packs like wolves taking down a larger prey. They formed a couple of defensive lines and began firing at riders of the North as they re-grouped to charge.

The Americans let off a volley of fire, which killed horses and riders alike. That meant those left charged back into the Marines and 10th Cavalrymen. Cavalrymen Johnson plunged his bayonet into an attacker and then kicked him off it; he had a marine on his right-hand side, who had a giant male rider punching and kicking him; he swung around, pulled the bolt on his KragJørgensen rifle and loaded a bullet into the chamber, then careful he took aim and shot the giant in the side, this allowed the marine to tussle the rider back and then finish him with his knife to his throat.

With the extra numbers, the riders of the North began to retreat. Some were picked off as they fled up the hill, leaving the remaining to return to the last defensive line at the top of the hill.

The redoubt was getting swamped with long limbs. Hosah had a knife and a tomahawk, scrapping with everything that came his way. Texas let off multiple rounds as he used his Winchester to good effect; the others followed onto the side of his position. They picked off the long limbs outside the sandbag walls, then fixed bayonets and climbed inside to help. Three marines and two engineers had been killed, and the long limbs had injured the remaining men in there. Charles was cut on his arm, as was Corporal Heinz and Pvt Chamberlin, but they were fighting hard. Hagen was in there with his axe, and his first action was to decapitate a long limb, which set the mood. Texas had a cavalry sword and struck it into the side of a long limb; it spun around to bite him, and as it tried to, Hagen brought it to a swift end.

Pvt Brown shot three times into a long limb that was pinning down a marine as it was lowering its jaws towards his stomach. The final shot was the killer, which caused the creature to land on top of the soldier, but John was there to help push it off. The fighting continued, but the long limbs began to disperse, and their bodies lay strewn around the artillery and defensive sandbags.

Charles asked Corporal Heinz to check over the wounded. Pvt Chamberlain was told to cover the track, and Hosah asked if they could scout ahead with two Arapaho. The wounded were led down to the boats again, and Charles took a quick moment to survey the battlefield with his binoculars. The Marines and the 10th Cavalrymen had started to gain control, and the Riders of the North that were left had retreated to the top of the hill. The Marines and the American soldiers had gone into a dip in the field, taking cover where possible. Sergeant Boyd from the 10th Calvary had arrived with reinforcements and the Welsh fusiliers. Pvt Evans was eager to join up with Major Hayward. The other Welsh fusiliers would be split amongst the detachments along the beach; all of them had some local knowledge, which would help with the advance inland.

Mortars had been brought up to Charles's position, and they managed to get one of the intact cannons prepped to start firing on the enemy position at the top of the hill. They had also done the same for the artillery on the other side. The cannons were captured British guns from when they had lost Great Britain. They had landed soldiers from the Royal Artillery Regiment for this purpose. The main attacking force in Cornwall had its own cannons, but they did not have enough to spare for each landing point.

Soon, the royal artillery detachment arrived at the hill. They got to work getting what shells they could ready and prepared the cannon. This was happening on the hillside on the other side of the beach. Once the artillery was ready, it began to fire on the last line of enemy defence.

"We need to move quickly to gain an advantage here." Charles loaded his rifle.

Sergeant Butcher was given the binoculars to look at the enemy position.

Dr Turner, the army medical officer assigned to Major Hayward, and several other medical officers had landed with the soldiers. A new Royal Medical Corps had recently been set up and was being used to help with this invasion. He had come up the hillside to check over the soldiers who would be fighting on with their injuries; he asked to let a couple of his MOs look over the soldiers there. Charles agreed it would be fine, but they had to be quick, as time was of the essence.

The army doctor examined his wounds and put a bandage around his left arm. "Keep the wound clean, Major."

Charles smiled and nodded. "Hopefully, I'll stay alive long enough for that to happen."

Charles thanked Texas and Hagen for supporting them at the right time. He also took time to speak to Hosah and his Arapaho warriors.

Captain Steinberg and his men joined Charles along with the Engineers.

"We must push on to Roach Castle. A message had been sent to General Greenway that they would push around from the right flank and take the castle. Fortunately, it was more of a defensive lookout tower rather than a full-blown castle. Captain Somersett and the 10th would push down the middle with the Marines. A young officer would take a detachment of marines with Charles. Captain Brewer had only recently got his commission, but the men liked him as he was unafraid to muck in and get involved.

The soldiers reloaded and took extra ammunition. Captain Steinberg would take the right flank, Charles would take the left and centre with the engineers and marines. Hosah would scout ahead with Corporal Heinz and two other braves. The Welsh fusilier, Pvt Evans, advised Charles of the track that led to the castle and how they could cut through fields and a small woodland to come up to the castle. As they finished preparing to move on, Dr Turner wished him well. He would be helping the wounded at the beach for now. Two MO soldiers would be coming with them.

Hagen spoke to Texas as he looked at the body of a long limb. He pushed his left foot into its side and looked at the skin and makeup of the beast. "It could almost be human in a way."

Texas nodded. "I hope we do not encounter too many of them." As he finished loading his Winchester rifle. Charles briefed the officers; he told them to keep the men spread out; they had seen what concentrated machine gunfire could do. They then started to move off in their squads. Sergeant Butcher was close to Charles, so they could share thoughts as they moved forward. Pvt Evans was close to the centre. The smoke drifted onto the slopes from the beach and the middle battleground. The explosions could be heard in the background as they moved forward. The marines under Major Briggs's command and the 10th cavalrymen had been reinforced and were now moving over the flat middle ground and onto the slopes around them. The left-hand hills, where the artillery was firing from, saw a detachment of marines pushing on from there. They follow Brandy Brook, a small stream that led them further inland.

The sun was now out entirely as they moved through the long meadow grass; it swayed in the gentle sea breeze, which helped keep the temperature down. Charles was glad for the khaki uniforms and the camouflage they gave them, but he couldn't help but think about the engineers and marines who had been killed in the fighting so far. He wanted to keep them all alive, but war was not like that; he would have to make the best decisions he could and hope they were the right ones.

Pvt Brown thought about Heidi and his family and how he had once been to Wales when he was younger. He let himself listen to the crickets as he walked through the grass.

A deep voice spoke softly, "Stay with us, Private."

"Yes, Sergeant." John looked at him and half smiled.

He remembered being pulled from the snow in the Carpathian Mountains all those years ago and was glad Sergeant Butcher was with them. He tightened his grip on his Lee Metford rifle and carried on moving.

Several dishevelled people were walking towards them. Charles raised his right hand, and the long line came to a halt. It soon became apparent they were the dead, four in total. Charles looked at Hosah and spoke to the Arapaho next to him. The silent flight of arrows stopped them in their tracks. Charles then waved his hand to move them forward. The Arapaho took their arrows from the corpses of the flesh-eaters, ready to use again.

The line of soldiers slowly approached the woodlands. The sight of the lush green leaves filled them all with inner joy. This pocket of trees consisted of Ash and Sessile Oak mixed in with hazel and wild cherry, but this is where the joy ended. It also made an excellent cover for the enemy. Charles was concerned that if there was a machine gun post in there, they might fall foul of it, so he sent Corporal Heinz to scout ahead with Hosah. Pvt Chamberlain would cover them from the open field.

The farm fields' hedgerows had become overgrown since Nazar had taken Great Britain. There didn't seem to be livestock in the fields adjacent to the beach, but the stone walls were still intact. The grass was long but not overgrown. Charles thought they must still be farming for the food supplies for his armies and suppressed subjects.

Corporal Heinz eased into the woods with Hosah. The young brave poised his bow, looking for movement or something that could be a threat. The deeper they went in, the more pungent the smell of rotting flesh hit their nostrils. Gorse and holly bushes were scattered around, hindering their line of sight. Hosah followed the smell to a dead deer carcass. Three more torn to shreds were strewn around the trunk of a large oak.

"Probably long limbs." The corporal was bent down as he examined the creatures.

Hosah broke his concentration by pointing over to something he had seen. Corporal Heinz followed him towards what he had seen, which became clearer the closer they got. A defensive sandbag machine gun post was further down the woodland edge. Four or five clones were preparing to fire. Hosah looked at the corporal and showed a five with his hand. He then took out four arrows and placed them on the ground. Corporal Heinz leaned against an Ash tree and raised his rifle; he had already loaded a bullet in the chamber and looked down the sights. He would let Hosah shoot first.

A whoosh was followed by shouts from the other drones as their comrade fell backwards. The British in the open hit the ground instantly. The drone behind the machine gun began to fire, but the targets were now on the ground and still out of range. Two of the drones began to fire blindly into the woods; they hadn't quite located where the arrow was fired from.

Boom!

A clean headshot dropped another drone soldier. This allowed them to locate where Corporal Heinz had shot from, and they opened fire on his position. Hosah was also spotted but sent an arrow into another drone. One of the remaining drones stayed low, and the machine gunner stopped firing and waited. A single shot through his neck caused him to slump over the gun. The remaining drone looked around at his dead and dying fellow soldiers and then decided to make a run for it. He managed to get past a thicket of bushes and into an open clearing made from a fallen tree before an arrow hit him in the back, forcing him to stagger and collapse to the ground.

Corporal Heinz called out that it was clear, and the soldiers cautiously got to their feet and continued into the woods. Charles was grateful for the scouting they had done; Hosah and the Arapaho were already proving invaluable. The background fighting noise had died down, which they hoped was a sign of the Marines and the Americans taking control of the last line of beach defences. If that was the case, Roach Castle was the destination now for the other units.

Charles gathered the soldiers in the woodlands and updated them on their route. As they approached the castle, they could use the woods for cover. He mentioned the importance of being vigilant and not firing at will. They want to scout as close to the castle as possible before engaging.

Pvt Evans from the Welsh Fusiliers spoke to Charles as they pushed forward. The young Marine Captain Brewer joined him. He seemed quite eager to get involved in more action. Charles spoke to him and advised them not to do anything rash. They did not know how many enemy soldiers would be stationed around the Castle and wanted to gauge the best form of attack.

They took a moment in the woodlands to drink from their canisters, then pushed on through the trees. As they moved along, they appreciated the cooler feel under the trees. The sun was beaming above them and onto the field below. Hosah and Corporal Heinz led from the front. Texas and Hagen were at the back of the group, checking that no one was coming to attack them from the rear.

Pvt Dai Evans said it had been to Roach Castle before, and he remembered it having good visibility over the fields around the surrounding area. He went with Sergeant Butcher and Charles to the edge of the woodland; lying in the long grass, they surveyed the castle from a distance with Charles's binoculars. He could see movement at the top of the castle tower and the defences around it. There was a small village that would likely have enemy soldiers in there. Charles spoke to Captain Brewer to send two marines to contact the main force and understand their plan of attack. He warned them to be careful and mindful of friendly fire.

Sergeant Butcher suggested that he could take five men and get closer to the village. The farm walls around the adjunct fields were intact and would offer decent cover. Then, if safe, he would signal for the rest to push up. Texas crawled up to where they were. He said he had dynamite with him and could help take out some of the houses if the enemy occupied them.

Sergeant Butcher gathered five men. Pvt Brown volunteered but was told to keep an eye on the rear flank of the woods with Hagen. The sergeant led the way with his rifle in front of him as he crawled through the long grass. Texas was one of the five selected; Pvt Chamberlin and Corporal Heinz covered them from the darkness of the woods. Charles watched them crawl off and told the other soldiers to be ready to advance.

Pvt Brown looked at a rabbit warren and the droppings outside it. He saw an entrance hole where the leaves had been pushed in and an exit point where the soil had been moved out. It took his mind away from the battle and into a childhood memory of playing in the woods with his friends.

"Hagen, who was your first love?"

The big Viking gave him a look of is this the time?

John smiled, "OK. Maybe it isn't the right time to talk about that."

"It's fine, John, but I try to bury thoughts about love deep in my subconscious while we're in a battle."

"I know, but it's been going on so long; maybe it will never end." He raised his shoulders as he said this.

"Mine was a girl named Emma. I was fourteen, and she was fifteen. I think we kissed in her house one sunny day, and I was in love."

Hagen looked at him. "What happened to that love?"

"She ended up kissing another boy called Antony."

Hagen laughed. "I'm sorry, but young love is hard."

They both stopped talking when a figure began coming through the woods. Its head was slightly down, and its clothes were dirty and torn. The figure moved erratically. The closer it got, the more they could see the flesh missing from his hands and face. He had brown hair, or what was left of it.

"Leave this one to me, John."

The flesh-eater slowly caught up to them, hissing and snapping his teeth. John stood still as it fixed its eyes on him. Hagen waited for the right moment and then brought his axe down on its head. He killed it with one strike and pulled it out in one motion before cleaning the axe on the dead flesh-eater's shirt.

"I have a feeling there will be more."

Sergeant Butcher kept pressing forward through the grass, looking to either side of him, checking on the men. They came to a hedgerow and waited until all five were ready to push on to the next field. This meant crossing a track and onto another field. One of the soldiers had made an opening through the hawthorn and gorse hedge. He signalled to the other soldiers he was going through and would take cover across from the track. Once he pushed through, Sergeant Butcher went forward. He watched the soldier dash across the track and use his bayonet to slash through the next hedge into the field. Whilst he did this, Sergeant Butcher looked at the tight, narrow track and thought it could be a death trap if they set up a machine gun post to focus fire down it. A lot of this advance would be crossing roads and tracks like this.

The countryside had been managed in some areas; in others, it had been left to go wild. The Sergeant and the other soldiers followed once the soldier had burrowed his way through. From this field, they could see the Castle tower clearly. The village and church were also in sight.

"We're going to push up to the edge of the village, check numbers, and then Private Pvt Baker will report back." The Sergeant had shaved his beard before the beach landings, but he went to stroke it as if it were still there.

"Do not fire if you see the enemy."

With that, they moved on through the field. He had told them to keep low and zigzag through the grass at a decent speed. Once they had arrived at a wall at the boundary of the field they were in, there was one more to cross before they were at the edge of the village. Sergeant Butcher led the way across the field and waited, crouched by the stone wall.

Charles was using his binoculars to monitor the situation. The woodland they were in was slightly elevated, but it was not enough for him to see the Sergeant and his men.

Sergeant Butcher waited until they all gathered around him. Unfortunately, the fields closer to the village did not have the same hedgerows around them; they were just stone walls. The grass was a little shorter in this field, indicating it had recently been grazed by livestock. Two engineers went over the wall and into the outskirts of the village; the two nearest cottages to them looked derelict. They observed further down the track, sandbags blocking off a street. Drones were moving around behind it. Worrying, they could see a cannon situated near the castle; it was hard to gauge the numbers they had defending it.

Sergeant Butcher nodded for Pvt Baker to leave them and report what they had seen to the main group. He went off at speed, bent over, trying not to be seen, following the same path he had taken before. He got to the track and didn't look before throwing himself through the hedge; as he landed on the other side, two drone soldiers patrolled further down the track. The noise of him falling on the ground was enough to get them to turn around. They then started to shout at him before opening fire; Pvt Baker tried to get through the hedge but was struck in the leg, sending shooting pains down his side. When he did find the entrance they had made, another sharp pain arose in his left arm. Using what strength he had left, he propelled himself through.

The gunfire alerted Charles, who sent Hosah and Corporal Heinz to investigate. Lying on his back, Pvt Baker waited for the drone to try to push through the gap in the hedge. Nothing happened; he was unaware they had turned and started running to the village. Sergeant Butcher had sent two of the Engineers to see what was happening. They opened fire on the two drones running towards the Castle, hitting one of them and causing the other to take cover and return fire.

Charles gave them the order to advance and engage if fired upon. He was firm that they should not move straight into the town. Captain Brewer took the Marines with him and said he would find and support Sergeant Butcher. The rest of the detachment followed Charles as he led them through the fields; the medical officer helped support the wounded. Pvt Brown said he would put Pvt Baker on a man-made stretcher using hazel branches and blankets and return to the beach. They carefully moved over the track to help support the soldiers by the village.

Captain Steinberg was bringing up the right flank and had come up further to where they were now pushing on. A royal engineer was sent to make contact and ask them to sweep around that side.

Captain Brewer and his small collection of marines had stormed down the track and were already bursting into the village. This seemed to have caused panic in the drone defences at first. Captain Brewer was a brave young man, a keen writer and was full of bravado; they charged into the village as several drones moved into the building around them. The marines began opening fire on them; some drones were killed before they entered the dilapidated cottages around them. This spurred the attack on, as the captain and his men approached the sandbag defensive line, they did not see a machine gun which had been placed in the cottage across from the barn.

The sunlight reflected off the machine gun's tip as it opened fire. Captain Brewer and his men were too close to take evasive action. It cut through them like a warm knife through butter; Sergeant Butcher was around the old cottages but could not get there to help them. The machine gun pinned back any soldiers who tried to move from their positions, leaving the Marines dead or dying in the street.

Charles could hear the dreaded cackle of the machine gun. He took cover, as did the soldiers around him. They then surveyed the village, the best they could. Bullets zipped past them, hitting the bushes in the hedgerows and walls they used for cover. Soil clumps flew everywhere, slightly sodden and mixed with grass and stones. Drones were firing from the second floor of the houses in the village; others were using the height of the church and the castle.

Charles wished they had some artillery to tackle the castle, but the horse artillery hadn't landed, so getting them up to the Roach village would take time.

The Engineers and the soldiers with Charles laid down, covering fire at the village houses and surrounding buildings. Captain Steinberg had been informed of the attack and began to attack the castle further around on the right flank. The main marine force was now secured on the beach; General Briggs had sent two detachments to assist in taking the left flank of the castle. As they approached from that side, they came under fire from machine guns and cannons. The plan was to take it as soon as possible to ensure Nazar's forces did not have time to wait for reinforcements.

Charles wanted to move forward to help check on Sergeant Butcher and the other scouts. He was unaware that Captain Brewer and his men had been killed in the village. The gunfire around the castle was intensifying; the drones were well bedded in, and the machine guns gave them confidence.

Charles spoke to Texas while crouching behind a stone wall. He asked if he could go with Hagen and several others and bring a field gun from the artillery post they had taken. It might take a while, but they had gunners with them, and it would give them a chance to take the castle with more firepower.

Charles perched himself against the wall and looked down at his rifle sights; he followed the movement from the windows in the houses. Then aimed and shot into a second-floor window of a house in the village. He then loaded another bullet into the chamber, picking another window; he squeezed the trigger and fired into that. They maintained their positions for a good twenty minutes. The enemy gunfire was now more focused on movement to save bullets. Corporal Heinz and Pvt Chamberlin targeted the castle tower; the rest of the engineers were behind stone walls or in good cover.

Hosah and the other Arapaho were close to the Major. He did not want to order them to attack the village until they softened the target. Hagen gave good news: They had brought with them a 6-pounder cannon. The gunners with them had found a clear spot to fire from and prepared to shoot at the castle. Little Bear suggested lighting fire arrows and targeting the houses with drone soldiers in the village. Charles liked the idea and said they should wait until the cannon had done some damage.

A moment or two passed before the first thunderous shot shook the ground. The shell cracked into the castle's lower buttresses. It took that first shot well. All the engineers and soldiers watch on. The next shell hit the top of the castle. This caused damage to the upper battlements; they then fired upon a house in the village close to the first defensive sandbag line. This house exploded into pieces of stone and slate; it killed five drones who were based there. The marines on the left flank started to close the gap around the castle.

The cannon was reloaded and fired again, hitting more buildings. Charles gave the nod to Little Bear. They had gathered wood and silver birch bark to light fires. He took three braves with him and got closer to the village. Mad Dog wanted to go, but Hosah told him to stay and join the attack when it was time.

The engineers gave covering fire as the Arapaho dashed across the fields. Sergeant Butcher guided them to a corner of a house where he stood with another engineer. It was shielded from enemy snipers, allowing them to start a fire. Sergeant Butcher was amazed at the speed at which they got the fire going. They then wrapped oil cloths around the arrowheads and lit them. With expert stealth movement, they popped around the cottage walls and started to shoot arrows at open windows and doors. Little Bear fired an arrow into a barn that sat further back in the village. The artillery was told to concentrate on shelling around the castle, not the village, as the British and Allied forces were closing in. It did not take long for the fires to start; several drones tried to put out the fire arrows in the barn, but they were being shot at from around the village.

Sergeant Butcher wanted to take the cottage close to them, but waited for the flames to take hold upstairs. Thick plumes of smoke wafted around the village, which provided the perfect cover. Two American soldiers had joined the sergeant, who waited for his order to go. Both were armed with Winchester Model 1887 shotguns. The sergeant looked at them and instantly wanted one. One of the Americans caught him looking at them and said they were repeat-loading shotguns. "You can have mine if I don't make it."

"Let's hope I never hold it then." Which brought a reassuring smile from the American.

Little Bear and the other Arapaho stopped firing the fire arrows. He put the bow over his shoulder and withdrew his tomahawk from his arrow pouch.

Then, Sergeant Butcher told them to follow him into the nearby cottage. With that, he sprinted across the road and through the front door, which was hanging on by one hinge. Inside was a wounded drone who raised his rifle; Sergeant Butcher was too quick and fired into the wounded man, killing him. The other soldiers followed in behind; a drone that was in the pantry burst out, but the American soldier with the shotgun showed how deadly it was at close range; it blew the drone back through the door he came through and left him on a heap in the floor, blood seeping from his wounds. Sergeant Butcher could hear movement upstairs, but the fire was taking hold. He pointed to the floorboards and peered up the stairs. He did not see the drone he had just killed start to rise behind him, but Little Bear did and was quick to use his tomahawk on the flesh-eater's head.

Two drones began to fire from the garden at the rear of the cottage; one of the Americans was shot in the chest, his fellow soldier pulled him to cover in the cottage kitchen. An Arapaho was also hit in the leg; Little Bear had drawn his bow and released an arrow into one of the drones, which fell backwards. Sergeant Butcher dispatched the other. As this unfolded, a drone began to come down the stairs; he did not see a young Brave with a rifle in the living room. He was quickest to react and shot the drone in the head, then watched the soldier fall down the stairs and land in an awkward position at the bottom.

Sergeant Butcher checked on the Americans; the one he spoke to earlier was holding his dying friend.

"Stay with him as long as you can." Little Bear helped lift the wounded brave as the fire spread and told the other Arapaho to take him back.

They were still some distance from the sandbag defensive wall, but three cottages from where the machine gun was stationed.

"We have to knock out the machine gun." Sergeant Butcher knew there were now only four of them. The American came in from the kitchen. My friend would want you to have it. He handed over his shotgun, with a pouch full of rounds.

"I'm sorry." Sergeant Butcher knew what it was like to lose friends in war.
The American nodded his head and got ready to move. Little Bear had covered his fellow Arapahos as they returned for treatment for the wounded brave's leg.
"We go out through the back garden and attack the cottage with the machine gun three houses up."

Sergeant Butcher looked at all of them; the gunfire outside was intensifying, and the shouts and battle cries grew louder.

"Good luck, lads."

They waited for the smoke from the barn to drift their way before bursting out of the kitchen. Sergeant Butcher had the shotgun primed and his rifle over his back. Low stone walls and various bushes along them separated the gardens. An old rocking horse had been left rotting outside the house. Its paint had fallen off its nose, and black, beady eyes stared at them as they passed it.

As they moved along, a drone soldier was firing from between two cottages; he was perched against the wall, looking down the street; within a flash, the Winchester shotgun was used to shoot the drone in the back. He did not take any chances and hit the dead soldier in the head to make sure he did not come back.

They started to come under heavy gunfire the nearer they got to the cottage; this was coming from its back windows and the area around the barn. It inevitably stopped the soldiers from moving forward. Little Bear shot at the nearest window, but the soldiers inside were holding firm. Sergeant Butcher and his men took cover while planning the attack's next phase. The British engineer with them had one stick of dynamite on him, which he took out and straightened the fuse. All four of them were crouched behind the cottage wall from which the machine gun was being fired. Sergeant Butcher said he would go around to the opening where the Maxim machine gun was firing and throw it in. The engineer interrupted and said it should be him, as he was quicker and more nimble than the sergeant, who received a scowl look back but reluctantly agreed.

With that, he lit the fuse and scrambled around the corner. The machine gun was aiming down the street, where there was movement from Charles and his detachment. A drone officer saw him, just as he came to the windows, which had been smashed out to act as the firing point. The engineer threw the dynamite in and hit the ground as he did so. The explosion covered him in stone, wood and glass. Sergeant Butcher leapt forward and came along the side of the cottage. Smoke was coming out of the broken glass windows. Little Bear and the American cavalrymen followed him. The machine gun crew had been killed, but there were several dazed drone soldiers from the blast; Sergeant Butcher and the soldiers with them finished them off before they could gain composure.

This was enough for Charles to start moving through the village. They began to pick off the drones behind the sandbag wall, utilising Alexander and Corporal Heinz's sniper skills. There would be a squirt of blood when a headshot claimed its victim. Some of the drones surrendered once they reached the defensive wall. Charles was relieved to see Sergeant Butcher and gave him a nod as he loaded a bullet into his rifle.

They still had one more machine gun left in the castle; the other one further down at the entrance had been hit by a shell. The cries and calls from the wounded filled the battleground, adding to the frenetic atmosphere. The barn, which had been utilised earlier, was fully alight and burning well; the smoke bellowing out across the castle, which was not helpful for the defenders. This meant the attacking forces could close in, and the drones left in the village had either surrendered or died.

The Allied cannon was brought up to the centre of the village. They had two shells left. The idea was simple: Hit the machine gun, and this would hopefully force the hand of the remaining Nazar forces. The first shell was close but landed in the soil between the castle wall and main tower. The cannon was then manoeuvred into another position, and all eyes watched in anticipation.

The gunners took some time to make a few adjustments and then fired the shell into the castle. The impact was thunderous and successful. It knocked out the machine gun and its crew. This signalled those in the village and around the castle to attack. The remaining defenders tried to muster up a final stand, but they were overwhelmed by sheer numbers.

Once the castle was secure, scouts were sent to watch the surrounding areas for reinforcements. The village was thoroughly checked, and the wounded were tended to. The captured drones and their officers were escorted to makeshift holding pens. They had not captured any priests. The mood was good amongst the soldiers. They had not lost as many men as anticipated once the beach had fallen.

Charles spoke to the officers and men in his detachment. He was grateful for not losing too many soldiers under his command. Texas and Hagen were involved in moving supplies up from the beach. The sight of horses being landed embodied the spirit of the attacking force. Wagons were also being landed, but the bulk of them would come from Fishguard, as that had a port. These would be needed to start the advance into Wales and mainland England.

Corporal Heinz came over to Charles.

"Well, that went really well,"

Charles paused.

"Almost too well."

The corporal looked at him. "Do you think we're missing something?"

"No, I think it's just part of his plan. We had to try and get a foothold back here, and maybe one day Europe." He took over his helmet, wiped the sweat and mud from his forehead. "There's still a long way to go before we can control Wales and England, but so far, this has gone well."

Charles then joined in with helping secure the village. Lookouts were posted all around, and patrols were along the lanes nearby. The Marines would be based near the beach and set up a defensive perimeter there. Hosah and two Arapaho would ride with Corporal Heinz to Hayscastle and scout the fields and woodlands around that area.

Chapter 25

"The ships are ready, my lord."

"Good, then let the invasion begin." Nazar looked over his armada, which spanned as far as the eye could see. He felt a huge wave of satisfaction, knowing that soon America would be added to his collection. His eyes had already been turned to Asia, and a new meteor had been found. He would pursue Africa once he'd first gained control of the other countries. He wanted his empire to be bigger than the Roman Empire and last longer.

Oksana would come across in the winter with the main cavalry force. This did not mean Nazar would be without cavalry and an assortment of his other fast-moving attacking creatures, but it meant he could spread his forces more. Oksana could sweep through Alaska and help attack North America that way. Nazar would tackle Canada at some point, but it was conceived that America was the main opposition to his quest for world domination.

He was taking two female priests with him on his ship. One was French priestess Eveline Arnoult, and the other was a Welsh priestess, Jane Llewellyn. He wanted to have company whilst he travelled across the Atlantic, and Oksana warned that if he fell in love with either of them, they would not survive long. Jane had short-cropped black her and was of slight build; she was quick and deadly with a spear and served Nazar well in burning villages in Wales, bringing them into line. Eveline was different; she was tall and had strong features, her eyes were light green, and she openly flirted with Nazar and Oksana. Both priestesses oversaw army regiments; Eveline had a sizeable French contingent under her wing and would be part of the force landing in California. Jane was commanding a regiment of Riders of the North and would help be the force that moves in quickly and hard.

Nazar stood at the ship's bow, looking at the water; he liked how it rose and fell and how whirls would appear and disappear. The crew worked tirelessly around him; they had been hand-selected to guard and steer him to America. Battleships were sent to distract and draw out the American and European navies. Nazar had been told most of the British navy was supporting the invasion of Great Britain, which meant they would have a chance to land their forces. He had built such an armada that even if the first wave of battleships were destroyed, they would still have enough to support the landing. He had increased his drone army by compulsory enlisting Europeans. They were not put in big enough numbers of the same nationally to guard against defections to the other side, and if they showed any signs of switching, they would be shot.

Several hours into the journey, Eveline and Jane waited for Nazar in his bedroom quarters on the ship. Both were naked and lying in his bed. Nazar looked around and laughed.

"We have not long left port, and you are already trying to gain promotion."

They looked at each other and laughed.

"Join us, sire, and enjoy some relaxing time with us both."

Nazar grabbed a goblet of wine and poured three glasses.

"Remember, I cannot enjoy it too much. Otherwise, Oksana will take your lives."
Both generals stopped laughing.
"Now, drink to your future king of America."

They grabbed their goblets and tipped back the wine. Then Nazar began to change; the two-priestess moved back into the bed. His face stretched, and his body mass grew. He was aroused by the two naked women in his bed; he let out a roar, which brought terror and excitement to Jane and Eveline. The noises coming from the room could be heard all around the ship. The destroyer drones knew better than to disturb him when he was entertaining. The raucous behaviour continued for hours; the guards and crew eventually relaxed when it settled down.

The ships were moving through the sea at a good pace. General Georgiy ensured pigeons were being sent to keep contact with the main flagships. They had been trained to return to the different flagships and were proving useful in maintaining a line of communication. Time passed as they pushed along; Nazar trained with his sword and spear daily; some of his opponents were prisoners he had brought to practise fighting with. He wanted to give them a chance to attack and kill him, as he felt it had to be authentic. Nazar did not shape change; he fought as himself. He was injured several times during the journey, but he almost enjoyed the better opponent; Nazar wanted the challenge.

The female generals would also train with male and female opponents. Both priestesses were skilled with swords and spears, but on days when the sea was dead calm, they would do shooting practice; Nazar had rifles made in his factories across Russia and France, and they had also captured many weapons during his campaign to conquer Europe and Great Britain. His Drone armies were a mixture of forced recruits and veterans; the veterans needed an antidote to stop them from turning into flesh-eaters. Some of his generals wanted to infect all of the soldiers, but Nazar felt this would not be necessary. He reasoned that vast numbers of soldiers would turn if they did not have enough remedies. They could still be used as a weapon, but not as well as a non-turned force.

The weeks passed with the same process: Nazar would drink and spend time with the generals. When he got bored, he would change and find something to destroy. The final part of the journey drew them closer to Boston. The first wave had already begun, with the navy engaging with the Americans, and battles had broken out all along the American coast. This limited their chance of encountering a fleet of battleships as they were already tied up.

The invasion fleets had their landing destinations set and made their way towards them. Nazar was in a boisterous mood. He wanted to be on land, feel the earth beneath his feet, and take what he believed was his.

He knew his generals felt empowered. They had an overwhelming force and an array of creatures that could move at speed or hunt in packs. The power of a herd of flesh-eaters was lethal. They also had drone soldiers ready to fight to capture America.

As they neared the American coast, deep rumbles made the ships vibrate. The fleet that had arrived before them was causing havoc. As they were being engaged, it left space for the second fleet to start the land invasion. Nazar wanted to use the same tactics as he used against Great Britain: lead as many of the dead as possible onto the beaches, let them absorb the bullets, and then send in the long limbs and razor tooths.

Whilst they were engaging the defences, the drone soldiers would land. He would use the destroyer drones for the key targets and smash the main artillery encampments.

Nazar wanted to lead from the front, but General Georgiy had advised against it, stating it would be better for him to work his way into battle after the beaches had been taken. This provoked a disgruntled response, almost to the point where the general feared for his life, but he abated his anger and agreed to let the drones capture the beach first. The American defences were strong around Boston. They had a large port there and built the defences accordingly.

Nazar sent envoys weeks earlier to ensure rebels and governors would side with him once they had landed and established themselves.

Nazar looked on from his flagship as the battleships bombarded the coastline. The Americans had raised the alarm as soon as the naval attack had started a week earlier; the fear and panic were infectious as they began to move civilians from the city. The Americans had some heavy batteries firing back, but Nazar would tackle them with his destroyer drones.

The first landing crafts set off towards the dock area. Fort Andrews and Long Island would need to be taken, as gun batteries were entrenched there. All of the Islands had been fortified to some degree; even if there were small field cannons, they would still have to be knocked out. Nazar was not too concerned about losing flesh eaters; they were expendable. He had forces landing in the whole area and would be landing further up from the dock. Reports had come back about an area of land which was starting to fall.

With the smoke rising from the beach, Plum Island offered Nazar his first taste of land in a very long while. Several waves of flesh-eaters had gone in first. Their bodies floated in the water, the closer inland they got, and the beaches were strewn with them. Nazar had sent in the long limbs and a detachment of destroyer drones to take out three-gun batteries along the Island.

The rumble of fighting and explosions made the hair on his skin rise; it excited him; he stood at the back of the landing craft, the breeze lifting his long black hair as they moved quickly through the water. He watched them draw closer to the beach and landing crafts in front of them disembark; they did come under fire, but it was not in the same way as the flesh eaters had endured. The destroyer drones were busy fighting the soldiers guarding the cannons, so they no longer fired on the incoming crafts. The drones began to ascend the beach and charged inland.

A machine gun hidden in a gully opened fire. The oncoming drones did not see the bunker and were cut to pieces as they pressed over the dunes. This did not deter Nazar. He jumped in the water, tasting its salty flavour in his mouth as the landing craft closed in on the shore. His sword was strapped across his back, and daggers were sheathed to his belt. He had not changed his size; he wanted to save that until later.

Wading through the water with waves breaking over him, Nazar emerged from the sea. The landing crafts touched down as he moved up the beach. Officers and priests soon joined him. General Conway was leading the European forces and was bringing up his troops to the right of Nazar units. He was joined by General Eltsina, who was commanding the artillery for the Boston attack.

The destroyer drones around Nazar kept a close guard as he walked up the beach; he would snarl if they got too close. The machine gun in the gully had been overrun as Nazar's forces swept in front of his units. The distant cackle of gunfire and artillery firing was all around them.

The priestesses Eveline and Jane had joined their forces further up the coast and had been ordered to meet Nazar in Boston once it had fallen.

A small fort was holding out at the main connection point to Plum Island. The American soldiers dug in and used their ammunition wisely. Nazar grew excited by the holdup and knew it would be his chance to engage the enemy.

"I will lead this attack." He began to change in size. Those who had not witnessed it before stood back; it was a shock to hear the bones crunching and growing, and the priests around him smiled. Others had this power to change body size, but their numbers were still few. He was happy to keep it that way, as they could become a future threat. Once complete, he stood towering over everyone; his clothes were ripped and torn by his sheer size, his face had extended, and his teeth were sharp and long. His voice was gravelly and thicker.

"Follow my lead."

General Richard Conway wanted to change, but knew he could not match Nazar's impressive size. It was not the time to attempt it; he would wait till later in the battle. Nazar had begun his advance across the dunes and into the creek; they had chosen a low point to cross, and the water was refreshing as they marched forward. Following closely to Nazar's side were his destroyer drones. General Conway took the right flank, and on his left flank was a division of drone soldiers, which officers and priests were leading.

Nazar's force was near the fort as they made a beeline for it. The sandy soil beneath each step sunk with the weight of each soldier.

The closer they got to the fort, the heavier the fighting became. Strewn around the brooks and gullies were dead or wounded drone soldiers. Nazar carried on past the fallen towards the battle. They began to come under fire as they closed in on the defensive earth mounds around the fort. Drones began to fall as bullets struck them as they advanced.

Nazar crossed into one of the offshoots from Plumbush Creek. Waiting along the bank were hundreds of drone soldiers crouching down, looking for cover along the bank. He withdrew his sword and brought it down next to an officer who was cowering in the sand.

"I'd start the attack if I were you."

Without another word, he withdrew his sword, pulled out his revolver, and charged at the fort. Running alongside him was Nazar. He let out a roar, inspiring all the forces around them to charge. The Americans in front of the defensive earth mounds opened fire with a machine gun they had. It cut into waves of onrushing soldiers, dropping them in their tracks, but they kept on coming.

The officer, who was encouraged by Nazar, tried to catch his eye again to reconfirm his commitment to attacking the enemy when a bullet hit him in the head, knocking off his helmet and causing him to fall unceremoniously to the ground.

Cannon and rifle fire from the defensive fortifications took its toll on the advancing soldiers; soil and sand rocketed into the sky as the shells landed amongst them. Nazar didn't care; his adrenaline was pumping through his veins. He loved the fighting, the mayhem, and the carnage.

Soon, he approached the first earth mound with wooden spikes sticking out of the soil; the Americans had fixed bayonets and were waiting for the drones to come over the top. Nazar did just that, scrambling up the earth mound like a rabid dog, snarling, growling, exuding anger. He had a sword in one hand and a club in the other; as soon as he entered the American ranks, they were shocked by his size. A young corporal lunged at him with his bayonet and pierced his left leg above his kneecap. Nazar let out a roar and then brought the club around on the soldier's head. Bits of scalp and hair flew past his fellow defenders. Two American soldiers opened fire into Nazar's body, but he turned and came at them with this sword. He brought the sword down across their midriffs, slicing their stomachs open; as he did this, a soldier came across with an axe and took a swipe at Nazar, but he missed. Before he could reset himself, Nazar bit into his shoulder, tearing off a massive chunk.

While this unfolded, the destroyer drones poured over the earth mounds like ants invading a foreign nest. They were bigger than humans, but nothing compared to Nazar. The drone army revered their fighting skills, and their loyalty to Nazar was why they were his personal guards. Soon, the Americans were falling back into the fort to make a last stand; dynamite was thrown at the attacking force, but it could not quell their numbers.

Inside the fort, a young Captain named Thomas Williams rallied the troops; they turned over two wagons by the front gates and had sandbags around the middle of the fort. The last of the ammunition was dished out. A single cannon was wheeled into place to face the entrance. Nazar soldiers brought up a razor-tooth to smash through the fort. It charged at full speed; the first hit loosened the wood hinges, the second dislodged them, and the third caused the thick wooden panels to collapse under the beast's power. It did not get a chance to move inside as a cannon shell was fired into its head.

There was a small gasp from the gunners as the creature's head exploded into thousands of bits. This was short-lived as the drones began to pile in.

Axes and swords were hacked into the fort's sides. Three sticks of dynamite were thrown into a tower situated on one of its corners, and flames burst out from the tower following the explosions. The soldiers around the fort's walls fought valiantly but could not stop the attackers from streaming over the sides.

Captain Williams gathered the last of his men into a circle in the middle of the fort. Their blood-stained clothes and broken uniforms expressed the battle they had just fought.

The fighting died down as the soldiers looked at their attackers, gathering around the defensive battlements. Nazar climbed on top of a broken tower.

"I am the future ruler of this country." He sheathed his sword.

"You all fought well, but the end is inevitable."

Captain Williams stepped forward. "You, sir, will never be our ruler."

With that, Nazar climbed down like a creature they had not witnessed before. His soldiers parted for him as he approached the young captain. The handful of American soldiers left gazed at this half-human, half-beast before them. They had heard the stories from the Europeans, and some had witnessed the dead walking, but this was the final confirmation that he was real.

Nazar had his club loosely gripped in his hand and dragged it through the sandy soil over to the Americans. Captain Williams tried to stay calm, but inside he was feeling extreme anxiety.

"I will let your men survive, but you must surrender your life."

The captain looked around at his men, who shook their heads.

"Do I have your word?"

"I will make it quick."

He lowered his rifle and put it on the ground. He walked closer to Nazar and looked up at the sky before looking back into his dark, pupil-less eyes. Nazar raised the club over his head and rested it on his shoulder.

"I've changed my mind." The destroyer drones had gathered closer inside the fort and mixed in with General Conway's drone soldiers.

"Kill the soldiers" and string up their Captain outside the fort."

Captain Williams reached for his revolver and pulled it out. As he did so, the drones rushed at the remaining soldiers in a circle.

"You will not win." He then began to fire at Nazar. The bullets hit his body whilst wounding him, but they did not kill him. He could only be killed by losing his head and being stabbed in the heart. The young officer felt his actions had little effect, but what could he do? Nazar swung his club into Thomas's chest, knocking him down. Nazar did not unleash another blow; instead, he made the young officer watch his men being ripped apart. They fought to the bitter end, and even in agony, Thomas tried to raise himself to help them, but with the last of his soldiers dying, he slumped into the soil below. As he was being dragged to be strung up outside the fort, he slipped in and out of consciousness. The last thing he saw of Nazar was his face breaking into a smile at his demise.

Chapter 26

Arthur looked out of the window in his room. "We have to move, Mother; the gunfire is moving closer. The docks have fallen."

Rebecca left the log cabin and walked on the veranda, seeing the smoke pouring from the docks, before going back in to speed up their packing. The heavy artillery from earlier had subsided. A British staff sergeant from the Royal Household Guard came over to their log cabin on horseback. He looked like he had been involved in the fighting. His uniform was dirty, and his face was covered in mud. He quickly dismounted and knocked on the cabin door. Rebecca hurriedly went to open it.

"Madam, the docks have fallen." He paused to get his breath. "Nazar's armies will soon be sweeping through the city."

Rebecca composed herself. "Thank you. We will leave now. Godspeed to you."

He nodded his head and quickly made his way back to the horse. Then he remounted and left in the direction of the docks.

Rebecca had finished packing everything they needed. Two wagons were situated nearby and hurriedly loaded with supplies. Naomi's uncle, who went by the name of Vincent, was sitting on the first wagon, ready to lead them out of Boston. Elin was helping Christina and Tom with their belongings. She had a Winchester repeater rifle strapped across her back and a Smith and Western on her gun holster. Rebecca also had a Winchester rifle and an Enfield revolver in her gun holster. They had experience of what was coming and knew that the invading force would contain creatures that craved flesh. Vincent looked at the docks in the distance; he had a shotgun tucked into the side of the footwell in the wagon. Arthur checked his Bow, then his Krag-Jørgensen rifle. He had been given this from the Captain of the Fort in Golds Hill. Emily had asked to be given a weapon, which was refused. Instead, she was given a sharpened stick, which did not please her one bit, but sometimes, these things come into their own.

Naomi and Tom sat in the back of one of the wagons. Florence would be joining them shortly, but she was gathering the last of her belongings. The wagoner was an elderly gentleman called Reginald Devlin, who had worked for Florence's father's horse business for many years. He had no family and said he was happy to take them away from the danger; no one knew his age; he said he was born in the old country a long time ago but hadn't been schooled, so he was unsure of the date. His hair was grey and thinning, but he was as strong as an Ox.

A French family and a Swedish family were joining them. The French mother had two young girls, and the Swedish mother had a nine-year-old boy whom Emily liked. They would be travelling with Rebecca and Emily. Rebecca would sit next to Vincent and Elin at the front of the wagon.

Gunfire grew louder, making Vincent call out to Florence, "It's now or never." Tom had hopped off the back with Arthur and Naomi to help carry her stuff to the wagon, and as soon as it was onboard, they left. Vincent had four horses walking behind each wagon; he had given the rest to the army for the war effort but wanted to have some in case they lost horses along the way. Their destination to start with was Brattleborough; the fighting was gathering pace as they entered the road away from the barracks. Most of the civilian population had fled over the past few weeks, but there were stragglers. Some of these were store owners desperate to save as much of their stock as possible, but moving at a snail's pace in doing so. In the distance, they could see a checkpoint. Rebecca looked back at the children sitting there silently; they looked calm, but all the faces bore a worried look.

The explosions had become more muffled the further they travelled from the city. Rebecca was busy looking in the woods on either side of the road leading up to the checkpoint. Vincent brought the horses to a slower pace as they approached the wooden barrier. Rebecca looked at Elin and then softly said to Vincent that she didn't like the fact that they could see no soldiers guarding the checkpoint. She looked back to make eye contact with Arthur, as soon as she did, he picked up her concern in her eyes and face. He then whispered to the others in the back of the wagon about being alert.

Vincent pulled on the reins, bringing the horses to a standstill. Reginald did the same behind. The checkpoint had a cabin next to the side of the road and a sandbag dugout on the other side. No one came out to greet them.

"They could have fled their post or been recalled to their regiments." He said this whilst climbing down from the wagon. He was about to leave the wagon without taking his rifle, but Rebecca leaned forward and handed it to him. He smiled and loaded a bullet in the chamber.

Vincent looked back several times at the wagons before walking towards the cabin entrance. The wooden door was half-ajar, with a gaping hole where the handle used to be. He put his hand on his heart, concerned that something would hear it thumping; using the rifle to manipulate the door, he pushed it further open. It wasn't the largest wooden hut, but it had three rooms. The dingy light inside meant Vincent had to let his eyes adjust to what he was seeing. He moved into the hut one step at a time. Each step felt peculiar; there was a slippery substance underneath his feet.

The first room had a half-open shutter; the desk was overturned, and paper was strewn across the floor. Vincent turned and kept moving. He paused and wanted to call out, but the crunching and tearing sound held that thought. He felt his shoulders tense and his hands grip the rifle tighter. He tried to turn around and walk away from the sound, but his nagging voice had to find out what was happening. Moving along the short corridor, he advanced to the room from which the sound seemed to be radiating. The tearing, crunching sound suddenly stopped. Vincent held his breath; his throat was dry, and his hands were sweaty; he froze for a second. A groan and a shuffling noise followed; his eyes adjusted slightly to the dark, but he could still not see what was coming towards him.

Out of the darkness came a figure with half its head missing; its teeth were grinding together, rasping and wheezing with each step. The shock caused him to squeeze the trigger on his rifle. The bullet struck the flesh-eater in the chest, and the impact propelled the decaying man back into the room, but to Vincent's side, another flesh-eater emerged. It was a young girl, maybe only ten, who had a bite on her neck, which was probably the cause of her turning. Her eyes had sunken into her face, and her skin was peeling off it. Lumps of flesh still hung from her mouth as she lurched towards Vincent. Upon seeing her, he fell back into the corridor wall. Using his rifle, he kept her at bay as she tried to bite him.

The situation was compounded as the male flesh-eater Vincent had just shot began to come out of the end room. He nervously looked to his side and tried to keep both at bay. Using his weight and leverage from the cabin wall, he turned to get his back towards the entrance and began to move backwards. He did not see the broken debris behind him; as he shuffled back, his foot got caught, and he fell; the rifle slipped from his hands, landing next to him. The dead were onto him in a flash. He kicked at the male flesh-eater and held the young girl with his arms. She slowly came closer to his face; her breath smelled rotten, and bits of skin fell onto his face.

"Father" Boom, the first shot hit the girl flesh-eater in the head. The second hit the male in the jaw, but Florence reloaded and took a deep breath. She made sure it counted, hitting him in the head before he could get his teeth into her father's leg. Standing by her side was Rebecca; she rubbed the side of Florence's cheek. "You just saved your dad's life." She smiled and then helped him up.

"We have to move." Rebecca turned to rush back to the wagons.

Vincent stood up with help from his daughter. She collected his rifle and handed it to him. He leaned forward and hugged her. "Thank you." He looked at the far end of the room. We have to leave now, Dad."

With that, Vincent followed Florence out of the cabin. Arthur and Naomi lifted the barrier together and held it there whilst the wagons were driven through. As soon as they were through, a war cry rang out.

Rebecca was helping Arthur and Naomi onto the back of the wagon when she saw riders coming their way. Amongst them were long limbs and wolves. Elin helped and grabbed her rifle as they began to move forward with speed. Vincent was still recovering in his head after the attack by the flesh eaters in the cabin, but now had to navigate the road at speed.

Screams and shouts echoed around the forest on either side of the road as the riders behind them began to gain ground. Reginald could see the families looking anxious behind him as he glanced over his shoulder. "Keep low, everyone." Which was a good shout, as the riders behind them fired at them from the saddle as they rode along.

The Swedish mother climbed into the front of the wagon. "Give me a rifle, and I can help." Reginald looked to his side as his hands were focused on keeping hold of the reins. He had his shotgun wedged into the corner, but next to that was a rifle. It was a breech-loading gun, and the bullets were in a pouch next to it. She quickly climbed next to him, making sure not to fall as the wagon bumped and sped along the road.

Picking up the rifle, she leaned over the side and fired at the pursuing riders. The shot missed, but it caused them to break off the road and head into the trees for cover.

Wolves emerged alongside the wagons, snapping at the horses' legs as they galloped along. Elin steadied herself as they hurtled along, looking down at the rifle, she picked out a wolf that was running closest to them on her side. Bang, a good shot into its back sent it tumbling onto the road beneath it.

Rebecca was on the other side, using her Winchester to good effect. The strike rate was high, causing the attack to lessen. Arthur and the others were also taking shots at the wolves as they came in close. It was controlled firing, and possibly, they were conscious of not causing the wolves to fall under the horse and wagon behind.

The riders reappeared from the woods, firing from the saddle again. The Swedish boy was hit in the shoulder and let out a scream. His mother stopped firing and climbed back to aid him. He was in the arms of the French woman travelling with them. He looked at his mother, still in shock from the wound. She had tears running down her cheeks, but wasted no time cradling him.

The French woman took the rifle beside her and began firing at the approaching riders. She carefully aimed at a large, bearded man coming at them with a fixed grin on his face. The bullet struck him in the waist, sending him spiralling out of his saddle; he crunched into the ground below, still with the same fixed expression on his face. She reloaded and fixed her eyes on a large wolf gaining on the wagon. Its tongue was flopping out to the side of its mouth, with saliva drooling from its gums. Her first shot missed, and the wolf increased its speed as it prepared to leap at the back of the wagon. Her children's eyes focused on their mother, then again on the wolf. She gritted her teeth and let it gain on them. Its eyes met hers before she squeezed the trigger, sending it tumbling into the dirt road they were hurtling along.

It brought a grimaced smile from them as they looked at two female riders charging at them with spears. The nearest rider to them managed to come alongside the wagon, climb onto the side canvas, and work her way along to Reginald. The Swedish mother was full of rage; she shook with anger, her son's blood covering her midriff and hands. She gently lent her son against a grain bag and watched this silhouette of a figure close in on the front of the wagon. Clenching her fists, she moved towards the person on the outside of the wagon; as the female attacker began to manoeuvre herself to climb into the front, she was hit by force from the inside, which sent the attacker flying off the wagon and into a tree by the side of the road, the thud was enough to confirm her demise.

The other female rider launched a spear into the back of the wagon. It flew past the children and embedded in the side of the Swedish woman. She slumped down, holding the spear. The French mother, who had been firing at the front, looked behind her. Seeing the boy lying there, worried and concerned for his mother, was unsettling. She wanted to go and support them both, but she knew she had to keep firing at the riders closing in on the wagon.

"Reginald, they're closing in." The French mother told her children to help the wounded boy and his Swedish mother as best they could.

Bullets rattled the wagon frame; some popped through one side of the canvas and out the other. Reginald looked around and could see the injured boy and woman. He knew they were in a dire predicament.

Arthur and Naomi looked on with concern and frustration. They could not help more from the front wagon. They shot at the riders from the back of their wagon, but it was hard to aim at them when they stayed behind the other one.

Rebecca looked to her side, and her eyes fell upon a rider closing in on them. She recognised the face from the stormy night in Albany. His eyes glowed a cavernous yellow, piercing across the open ground that lay between himself and Rebecca. He steered his horse towards her and whistled as he did so. Emerging from the forest around him were ten or more riders. Rebecca's heart sank. She looked at Elin and Vincent.

They started firing as they came closer; Vincent felt a sharp pain in his side; he looked down to see blood seeping through his shirt; he grabbed the reins harder. Elin saw him wince and asked if he was ok. She looked down to see the blood on the seat and soaking into his trousers. She touched his arm and squeezed it tightly, then returned fire as they closed in on them. Rebecca tried to shoot the leading rider, but he weaved in and out of the adjacent red maple trees on both sides of the road.

Several more riders appeared on Rebecca's side of the wagon, drawing her fire.

"We're getting low on ammunition back here." Arthur looked at his bow and arrow, but decided it wasn't the right time; he then counted how many rounds he had left.

A whizzing sound flew past them and into the woods to the right side of the front wagon. The following explosion took out four riders, and another shell then landed on the opposite side. The man Rebecca had seen in Albany looked over one last time at her and broke off the attack. A wolf jumped and landed on the back of Vincent's wagon; half its body was hanging over the rear tailgate and half off the wagon. It snarled at Naomi and the others; Tom reacted quickly by grabbing and bringing a hatchet down on its head. He had to wiggle hard to release it from the animal's skull. It slumped on the back of the wagon, and the sight of it hanging there made the teenagers stare at it.

The last of the riders and wolves broke off and began to disperse in the forests on either side of the road. The further they travelled along the road, the quieter it became. They eventually came to a crossroads guarded by an artillery position. A US Army detachment was holding that location. A middle-aged army officer came over and introduced himself as Captain Greaves; he was well-spoken and asked how they were. He had ordered the small detachment to prepare for the rebels and the Nazar forces.

He took a moment to check on the group's injuries in the attack. He had a concerned face after checking on the Swedish mother and her son.

"I have a unit moving on to a field hospital near here."

Rebecca looked at Vincent.
"It's ok; the bullet nipped me and hasn't done too much damage.

The officer looked at the wound and said it should be cleaned quickly and dressed so they could move on. They pulled past the onlooking soldiers. The atmosphere was tense; littered around the guard point were dead bodies; some were rebels, and some were US soldiers. Mixed in with them were wolves and the odd long limb.

"The rebels are striking along the coast to cause disruption and help Nazar's landing forces."

Rebecca shook her head. "Why aid a monster like him?"

The officer looked around and then back at her. "Probably the promise of land and money." He sighed, "Power corrupts even the best of intentions."

Gunfire broke out behind them.

"We can take the wounded mother and son, and then you should keep moving."

Rebecca thanked him and wished them well in their fight against Nazar forces. Vincent had his wound quickly cleaned, and alcohol poured over it. They applied a bandage, and he climbed back up onto the wagon. Reginald came over to speak with them, but first, he helped the soldiers lift the Swedish mother and her son onto stretchers and then into another wagon. Rebecca and Elin held her son's hand as they transferred him. They spoke to his mother as they gently carried her into the back. The son looked pale but was awake and happy to lie beside his mother. The soldiers helping move them said the military hospital wasn't too far away, and they would receive the medical help they needed.

Rebecca climbed back up on the front wagon, as did Elin. Reginald said he would check the horses and reload his shotgun. They had two soldiers who would travel with them to Brattleborough. Both young men were new to the army and had only joined six months earlier. Private Samuel Hawkins and Private Dean Baker would travel in Reginald's wagon.

Arthur leaned forward and asked his mother to see if they could get more ammunition. Private Samuel overheard them talking about this and quickly spoke to Captain Greaves. Within a couple of minutes, more bullets were brought to both wagons. With that, they set off.

The explosions began to get louder the further they travelled along the road away from the checkpoint. Private Baker and Hawkins sat looking out the back of the rear wagon. They had their rifles poised, scanning the forests and fields for movement.

Arthur hugged Naomi and kissed her on the cheek. She responded by brushing the side of his face.

"I'll be glad when we get further away from here. I hope the Swedish mother and son make it."

Arthur nodded his head. He had experienced the retreat from Europe and the fall of the British Empire, and now he was witnessing the invasion of America. Florence was sitting next to her father. She kept checking to see if he was okay, to which he replied he was and told her not to worry. Tom sat just behind them on an empty tea box, Elin and Rebecca on either side of Vincent and Florence. Rebecca looked back to check on Emily, who was talking to her dolls; she felt an overwhelming nervousness about what lay ahead. Her husband was now fighting aboard with no way of contacting them; she wouldn't even know if Charles was ok. She prayed for him every night and longed to see him again.

Her focus was drawn back to the road ahead. The soil from the horses' hooves was being kicked up as they pulled them forward, leaving a dry sensation in their throats. The long meadow grass swayed from side to side in the gentle breeze, and clouds overhead started to disperse, allowing the sun to poke its head through them.

The late summer warmth was still felt on their skin. Looking at the pockets of blue sky above them also offered a moment of hope.

"Look ahead, ladies." Vincent pointed to two figures moving through the long grass. Their movement was erratic but familiar to Rebecca and Elin. The closer the wagons got, the horses began to veer away from them. They were moving at a slow, steady pace and would not reach the wagons as they moved past.

"Do not shoot them, kids. We don't want to attract more to the area." Rebecca kept her eyes on the two figures stumbling awkwardly forward. Both of them had been turned a while; their flesh was hanging off, and their clothes were shredded. She did not think they were part of the land invasion, as they would not have been able to cover that distance that quickly; they were more than likely brought in by the rebels to help with the invasion from behind the American lines.

The horses that were tied behind the front wagon stirred as they slowed down. Rebecca had asked Arthur to jump off the back of the wagon and tell Reginald and the soldiers not to shoot the flesh-eaters. She was concerned the two young soldiers would shoot them once they had passed them by. Reginald received his message and quickly told the American soldiers to hold fire as they passed the dead. Arthur turned and sprinted back to his wagon. Naomi, with a smile on her face, was the first to help him up.

"I don't want you being their lunch." She let out a little laugh when she said that.

"Thank you for caring, at least," Arthur said as the wagon passed the two walking dead. They were still far enough out of reach not to trouble them. Arthur and Naomi looked at these poor souls, hissing and snapping as they passed. The soldiers did the same as the two flesh-eaters came onto the road behind their wagon. They watched them for what seemed an eternity as they slowly became small dots on the horizon.

As they travelled from Boston, the pockets of fighting started to quieten. They pushed on for hours before stopping to have a break outside a small town called Greenville. The soldiers both went to check the deserted town as far as they could tell from the outside. Pvt Baker joked with Pvt Hawkins that they could see if there was anything in the bakery they could eat. Samuel kicked at Dean's feet as they walked, which caused him to fall on the grass verge next to the road. They laughed too hard to notice a long limb move across a street within the town.

"Come on, Samuel, let's get to the town; the civilians are waiting."

They both put their rifles over their shoulders.

"I like the English woman; wow, she's attractive." Dean looked into the clouds above as he said this.

"She's too old for you." Samuel then stopped them. "I do like the one with a funny accent."

"Do you mean the lady from Denmark?"

Samuel nodded.

"Imagine if they get lonely and want some fun time." Dean laughed as he said this.

"Were both only nineteen years old? That would be amazing!" Samuel looked at a town sign to see if he could determine where the bakery was.

They both decided to walk down the main street that led through the town. The buildings looked like they had only recently been deserted; doors were open, and stoves were still burning. Dean pointed to a hardware store further along the street. They got to the door, which was shut. "Have a look through the window." Dean did, "It's clear". He twisted the handle, but the door was locked. He turned to leave, but Samuel used the back of his rifle to break the glass shop window.

"Geez, we can get in trouble for that."

Samuel cleared the glass with his rifle. "Dean, the dead are walking here in America, were already in a shit load of trouble." He then proceeded to climb into the shop. Dean looked around, tutted to himself and climbed inside. The store was full of various tools and goods. There was a jar full of lollipops to which Samuel stuck his hand in and grabbed two straight away.

"Should we check upstairs, Samuel?"

"No, let's go to the kitchen area."

They both wandered into the kitchen. The aga stove still had a log smouldering away, and on the bench next to it was a black pot.

"Dean, check inside; it smells like coffee."

Dean wandered over to it. "Samuel, we are in luck." He then put the pot on the stove to heat it.

"Look, we can't spend too long here, but we can get a cup of coffee for everyone." Samuel was pleased with himself and put his rifle against a corner table. He removed his cap and placed it on the same table, then pulled out an oak chair beside it. He lowered himself into the chair and swung his legs onto the table.

Dean leaned against the wall next to the aga. "Do you think we can beat this invading army?"

Samuel swept his hair to the side after it had been tightly packed under his army cap.

"It's a hard one to answer. They've already landed in Boston, and by all accounts, they've taken it." He swept his hair again whilst thinking about the question. "Do you think we can win?"

Dean looked for two cups, which he found in one of the cupboards, and then placed them down by the stove. He opened the front of the aga and put in a couple of logs.

"I would like to think so, but I've seen the dead walk... I mean, walk again." He took off his cap. "The creatures now walking in the fields and woods are from the devil himself." He paused. "How can you beat that?"

They both sat in silence.

After five minutes, Dean poured them a cup of coffee each. They sat there holding the cups, looking around the room. A picture of a family on the wall made them think of their families. Both lads had come from Portland, Oregon, and the silence was only broken when Dean asked if Samuel thought Nazar's armies would land that far up.

Sipping his coffee, he shook his head. Inside, he prayed they wouldn't.

"We'd better get back to the others." Samuel put his coffee cup down.

"Maybe we should do a quick sweep further in the town, then head back."

Samuel nodded and grabbed his rifle to put over his shoulder. As he did so, a loud crashing sound made them jump. It came from the shop floor, and both of them stood still. Dean could feel his heart pounding hard; he thought it would burst. Samuel brought a finger up to his lips.

A deep growl was heard from behind the closed shop floor door. Both soldiers raised their rifles. Something scratched at the ceiling above them, which soon turned into aggressive clawing. Whatever was up there wanted to get through to them.

"Dean, go tell the others," Samuel said quietly. He pointed to the door which led out of the kitchen.

"Don't be stupid, I'm not leaving you."

"Dean, you have to go."

He shook his head but saw the fear in Samuel's eyes; he was just about holding it together.

"I'm coming back." He backed up to the door slowly and opened it with his left hand. As he left, the noise from the ceiling was intensifying. Once outside, Dean began to run to the main street. A flock of starlings sitting in a Red Maple tree suddenly flew up, causing him to flinch and stop moving. He was about to start again when his eyes fell upon what lay ahead. Sniffing and licking at a fresh kill, stood a large, long limb. It had a dog under its right front paw. It began tearing at its hind legs, ripping and eating the flesh as quickly as possible. Dean raised his rifle and was about to squeeze the trigger when a strange barking call rang out. Soon, another long limb joined in the feeding frenzy. Dean lowered his rifle and rushed to the nearest cover he could find: a side of a fabric shop.

He paused and thought about what to do.

Samuel could see the ceiling starting to give way a bit. The growls outside the shop floor had stopped, which began to unnerve him. He started to back towards the kitchen door. He did not know what was happening outside. A piece of wood dropped from the kitchen ceiling onto the floor. Then a head started to appear, poking down from the freshly made hole. Samuel raised his rifle and took in a deep breath. He then gritted his teeth and pulled the trigger. He missed the long-limbs' head by inches, with the bullet travelling into the wooden board next to its head. This then made it focus on him; it began to scratch and claw at the ceiling in a frenzied way; it desperately wanted to get its body through so it could attack Samuel.

He loaded another bullet into the chamber and focused again on the ceiling. This moment of concentration was lost as the shop floor door was hit hard, causing splinters to fly into the room. The other long limb rammed that door as it tried to get to the young soldier.

Dean pressed his back against the wall, his chest rising and falling quickly. The question was where to go next. He thought about going around the back of the shops and houses, but he wondered how many more long limbs were out there. He thought about fixing his bayonet, but changed his mind. Dean just stood still; he didn't know what to do. The noise of the long limbs tearing the dead dog apart started to quieten down, which began to worry Dean.

Samuel held fire until the long limb smashed through the door and crashed into the table in the corner of the room. He then pulled the trigger whilst it tried to regain its composure.

This time, he hit the beast in the stomach; its eyes rolled with pain and then refocused on him. It let out a deep belly snarl and came at him. Samuel had loaded another bullet into the chamber and brought his rifle up; the other long limb was still halfway through coming down from the ceiling. The wounded creature came at him gingerly, moving side to side, but before it could sink its teeth into Sam, a shot pierced the kitchen window nearest the door. The bullet struck the long limb in the neck, but its body movement kept it coming forward. He held out his rifle as it smashed into him. The impact flung him against the wall, knocking off his cap and causing him to drop his rifle.

The other long limb had nearly pushed its way through the hole he had made in the ceiling, but its foot had got caught, its arms now touched the kitchen floor, and its legs were still in the room above. Dean opened the door and saw his friend underneath the dead long limb; he also saw the other beast desperately trying to break free to get at them. He wasted no time in fixing his bayonet; Samuel was pushing the dead long-limb body off his whilst Dean lunged forward at the other dangling one. He scored a direct hit in its neck, pushing the bayonet through one side and out the other. He then withdrew it and attacked its body multiple times; blood spurted out with each strike. Dean lost control out of fear and anger, and only stopped once the creature stopped moving.

"You should have kept running, Dean."

Dean smiled. "I tried to get to the others, but more of those things are out there." They heard strange calls from outside the building as he finished his sentence.

"They're here."

Dean went to the broken door and quickly looked at the shop floor. It was empty; they both jumped when two claws appeared at the kitchen window. One of the long limbs that had been eating the dog was now sniffing through the broken window. The young soldiers ducked down and waited a moment. Dean gave hand signals to Samuel that they should try to get upstairs.

They were unsure how many were out there, but both were getting stressed about their group coming to find them and getting attacked by a pack of long limbs.

Once the creature had dropped down from the window, the soldiers scurried out of the kitchen and across the shop floor. They saw stairs in the corner leading up and made a beeline for them. As they moved at speed across the shop, they knocked over tins and brushes which had been stacked up. They did not care about the noise it created; as they rushed up the stairs, glass could be heard breaking in the other room. They both paused at the top; Dean surveyed the open store areas from the top of the stairs. To his horror, four to five long limbs came into the room from the right; they stood on their hind legs, sniffing the air. Both soldiers stood still; the long limbs from the kitchen joined these.

"Shit, we're up the creek," Dean said under his breath.

Samuel nodded

The long limbs sniffed the ground and picked up the scent of the two soldiers. They all seemed to look up at once. A larger one of the group let out a cackle and led the rest towards the stairs. Sam looked at Dean. "Let's kill as many as we can." They raised their rifles at the largest long limb coming their way. It had enormous eyes, which were sunken a little into its giant head.

While concentrating on the long limbs gathering to come up the stairs, they did not see Arthur leaning in the window with his bow prepared. An arrow flew past the fallen tins and into a long-limb hind leg. It squealed in pain and tried to bite at the arrow protruding out of its leg. Another arrow flew past the wounded creature and into the long limb next to it. The shot was accurate, striking it in the head.

The other creatures started to stir. The Alpha was still working its way up to the two American soldiers when a thunderous shot hit it in the back. Rebecca was outside the broken shop window with Elin and Vincent by her side. Naomi and Arthur were further down by another window, poised to fire again.

Dean and Samuel, both encouraged by their support, refocused their attention on the giant, long limb coming up the stairs. "Aim for the head."

Dean nodded and looked down the barrel of his rifle before squeezing the trigger, bang. It was a good hit, right between the eyes. Samuel fired as the creature recoiled back, and the bullet struck the side of its head. Remarkably, it still managed to turn itself gingerly around and advance up the stairs with blood gushing from its head. The gunshots from the others downstairs started to disperse the other long limbs. Some ran towards them; others smashed through a window from the shop floor.

When the giant alpha reached the top of the stairs, both soldiers moved backwards along a narrow landing. They reloaded their rifles but were nervous that their initial shots had not killed it. Its bloodshot eyes fell upon them with menace, and it began to creep towards them.

"Dean, let's aim for the legs."

It reared up with claws out, they both braced themselves to fire again, but in a flash, its legs went, causing it to roll to the side and then over the top floor bannister, sending it crashing onto a counter below. They took aim at another long limb making its way up the stairs. Both of them fired at once, hitting the beast's right-hand side; it tried to raise itself but was mortally wounded. The floorboards shook with the constant gunfire, but slowly, they began to take control of the building. Once the last of the long limbs ran off, Vincent shouted to the soldiers it was clear to come down.

Tom, Reginald and Florence were waiting with the wagons, everyone was on edge. Dean thought about mentioning the coffee, but didn't want to stop them from escaping the town.

"Thanks for helping." Samuel and Dean both said simultaneously, which caused them to look at each other.

Rebecca loaded her rifle and looked around. "This commotion would have brought more of them to the area."

They all set off together at the same time.

"Arthur, you're getting pretty good with that Bow." Naomi leaned in and kissed his cheek. Arthur smiled back.

"Thanks. I hope I do not need to use it for a while now."

She nodded her head.

The group arrived at the wagons. Tom was up a tree surveying the surrounding area. Florence stood at the bottom with a Smith and Western strapped to her side.

Elin suggested they pull through the town and take more supplies from the store. There were pelts and furs in there and some leftover ammunition; the gun rack had been cleared, though, which wasn't a problem for now as they had weapons. Some tin foods could be taken, but they didn't have long. Rebecca was concerned that Nazar's mobile units would be pushing on around the outer towns around Boston.

Once they arrived in the town, they quickly loaded what they needed from the store and moved on. As they left, four flesh-eaters began to stumble their way down a dirt track next to the hardware store. Elin shook her head. "Is this the future?"

Vincent sighed, "It is if we do not beat him."

Tom sat next to Florence, looking out of the wagon.

"I wish we had a dog with us." Tom was looking at the horses when he said this.

Florence let out a little chuckle. "I'm sure we will find a stray on our journey."

"They would also help bark if the dead were approaching." Tom smiled at the thought of having a pet.

"Or bring in more by barking."

"Come on, Florence, they would be more useful than not."

Naomi leaned forward with two lollipops.

"Enjoy these, and we'll find you a dog, Tom."

She then leaned back to sit with Arthur. He was a little quiet and in his own world. "Are you ok?"

"Yes, just thinking of my dad. I hope he's ok."

She rubbed his arm and sat close to him. "Have a lollipop."

"Thanks, Naomi, it's hard with everything. This felt like we could make a life of it here." He looked at the lollipop. "But every time that happens, Nazar and his army of death arrive."

They both leaned back onto grain bags placed in front of the wagon. Naomi then rested her head on Arthur's shoulder. The gentle motion caused Arthur to begin to close his eyes.

Chapter 27

The night sky lit up over Boston.

Standing next to General Richard Conway was Nazar. Blood was dripping from his soaked clothes.

"I love War, and I love winning."

"You are good at it, my Lord." As soon as Richard said this, he felt nervous.

Nazar looked at him. "We have a foothold in America, but I am not stupid enough to believe this is the end of the fight. This will take time. Oksana will land in the north and help us take control of this country." He spat blood out of his mouth.

The General carefully thought about what he should say next. "I would like to lead the assault north of the city of Boston."

"Would you." Nazar's tone was flat, neither giving encouragement nor denying it.

Richard stood there again in silence.

"Not long ago, you fought for the enemy, but you have shown loyalty to me and treachery to your people. I have a need for those who want to be part of the new world. The rewards will be endless. You have been gifted with your ability to shape change, but this is just the start of your journey, General." Nazar's eyes widened as he watched the enemy soldiers being marched past them while they stood on a hill overlooking Boston.

"Will you execute them all?"

"Not all; some will be used as cannon fodder, others turned into the walking dead. We will see if any will join the cause. It's a good place to be." Nazar half-smiled, which allowed General Conway to see his sharpened teeth.

"I do have something you may be able to help me with."

Richard waited on what would be requested of him.

"There is an English soldier, a leader I met in France several years ago." Arching his back and rolling his shoulders, Nazar looked like he was twitching as if shaping up for a fight. "I like a challenge. This soldier went to my lands and destroyed something dear to me."

"What would you like me to do, sire?" Richard said enthusiastically.

"He has to pay. I have a feeling he may not be here in this country, but something dear to him probably will be."

"Do you want me to search for his family?" Richard said.

"I want you to get a group of your best soldiers and bring them to me. I have a feeling we will meet Major Hayward again at some point during this War. I want to be the one to take his final breath."

"I know of an officer who would serve this request well. She is ruthless and dogged and would love to bring you your prize."

"Good General, Good. The British army left from Boston. I would imagine they are fleeing north."

With that, Nazar turned and left to speak to his other generals. Richard stood there, contemplating what this could mean to him. He thought about gaining more power. He might be given a state when they beat the Americans and Europeans. Maybe, just maybe, he would be given a country to manage, and he could become a king. With these thoughts in mind, he left to find General Eltsina to hunt the Hayward family.

Chapter 28

Major Hayward awoke with the morning birdsong in full chorus. He was staying in Roach Castle on the lower floors. The main force had started to move inland and was pushing towards the Brecon Beacons; Swansea was now under siege from the Welsh fusiliers and European forces. Charles was going to help push forward with his unit towards Hereford. Early reports had been coming in that the Cornwall force was doing well; they had made huge gains and had not encountered a sizable force yet.

Hosah was standing on the castle roof. Parts of it had been destroyed in the battle for Roch, but there was enough for him to perch and look out over the sweeping fields. The Engineers and marines with Charles had taken over the cottages and buildings that had not been affected by the fighting. Supplies had been brought ashore and stored in the accessible barns and farms.

Texas was outside, splitting wood and singing to himself. Corporal Heinz had gone out with Little Bear to patrol the surrounding area. Standing close by was Dai Evans, holding a lamb. "I've missed Wales, and I've missed my family's sheep farm."

"Well, we're here now, and if things keep going the way we hope, you'll have that farm back."

The sun was creeping over the hills, lighting up even the darkest forest. Texas finished cutting the wood and loaded the remaining bits into a cart. They were joined by Pvt Brown and Pvt Chamberlain, who were both laughing about something. Texas asked what was so funny, and Alexander said that John reckoned his next girlfriend would probably be a flesh-eater, as she would be the only one to put up with his snoring. Texas half-smiled and then shook his head. "I think you'd find that relationship would get messy." Then he laughed to himself.

Sergeant Butcher arrived, eating an apple. He was not wearing his greyback shirt, which exposed his broad chest and large arms in the morning sun.

"I like these Welsh apples, Dai. They are not a patch on the Cornish, but still."

Dai looked at him and said, "Well, I suppose you do not want to have some Welsh pig tonight."

Sergeant Butcher threw his apple core at him and turned to walk off to make sure the morning patrol had nothing to report.

Charles went down to speak to his men. The following day, they would be moving towards Hereford with the Marines, and he wanted to check that they would be ready. They had set up flesh-eater defences around the Roch village, which would be the same for all British and Allied camps.

Sergeant Butcher saw Charles speaking to some of the Engineers and the Arapaho. He made his way over to discuss the departure the following day. Both men were given a mug of coffee and began to walk and talk. A red oak tree creaked as a soft breeze pushed at its leaves, swaying it slightly. There was a freshness to the air; it carried the warmth from the end of the summer but was sharper and clearer.

"Sergeant Butcher, we need a machine gun on the rear wagon." Charles surveyed the wagons, which were lined up outside a barn.

Thomas nodded his head. "I still think we haven't met their main force yet."

Charles agreed. "I don't think we will meet their main force here. Hopefully, it will not be going to America until next year." Charles looked at the clouds.

"Do you think they have landed already?"

Charles looked at Thomas. "I do." He patted his friend on the shoulder and said he would continue walking around the troops.

Hosah had come down from the castle and reported that there was nothing on the horizon. Charles asked if he wanted to ride out with him. He said he would like that.

They mounted up and headed out towards a village called Wolfs Castle. There had been a battle there a week before, as this was a strategic crossing point. From there, you could travel to Fishguard or carry on to the Preseli Hills. Hosah had a rifle, bow, and arrows strapped across his back. Charles took with him his Enfield revolver and sword. He was about to leave without a rifle, but Sergeant Butcher stopped them on the edge of the village.

"Best to have this Major." He said this with a smile on his face. He then passed him a Lee-Metford.

"You're not often wrong, my old friend."

They then rode out across the open fields. A couple of hours passed without any sighting of the enemy, and they stopped along the way at various checkpoints; both men had agreed to stay clear of thick woodlands and use the roads where possible. They arrived around lunchtime at Wolfs Castle, crossing the Western Cleddau River. The area had been a strategic point for the Normans when they invaded Great Britain in 1066. They had built a castle motte, which had become an earth mound over time, but the location was still significant. The village had the hallmarks of a recent battle; the defences around the perimeter had been destroyed or charred by shelling. Some of the buildings which had been used as a stronghold were obliterated.

The allied bodies had been buried, but the bodies of the enemy had been burnt. It was known that some of the drone soldiers were infected and would come back if they had not been shot or stabbed in the head.

The brightness from the sun was coming and going as the clouds rolled past it in the sky. Charles looked at the picturesque stone cottages that had not been destroyed and thought about the people who had been living there. He thought about what life under Nazar's rule would have been like for them once the British forces had been defeated. He felt as though they had let people down by leaving them behind, but knew at the time there had been little choice. They had not come across too many Welsh civilians but had heard rumours they were being kept in larger towns for their protection from flesh-eaters.

As they were riding along, Hosah brought his horse to a stop and then dismounted. He had spotted something that looked like tracks in the soil.

"Charles." Hosah was feeling the soil between his fingers. "Something big has been here today; its tracks lead through the village."

Charles brought his horse around.

"How big?"

"Looking at how deep the track is, it's very heavy."

Charles lifted his helmet. "It could be a razor tooth." He considered what to do.

"Shall we track it?"

"Not today, my friend. We can search the village quickly, and then we can head back." Charles waited while Hosah remounted before they set off.

To their right was the Afon Anghof River, which was well-covered by various deciduous trees. The black alder dominated along the riverbank, with sessile oak trees tucked further through the fields. Charles did not want to spend too much time away from his men. He was slightly concerned he hadn't seen a checkpoint guarding the village. He was aware they wouldn't be able to station soldiers at every location throughout South Wales, but this had been a key route to Fishguard.

Dark clouds had covered the sun, and it looked like it would start to rain shortly. Charles called out that they should think about heading back. At that moment, his horse began to stir and step backwards. Hosah raised his finger to his lips. He then pointed over to a corner by a side road where there seemed to be a sandbag defence layout. Leaning against the front of it were two rifles.

Hosah dismounted and slid out a spear he had wrapped in an animal pelt on the horse's side. He then walked slowly and carefully to the sandbags. Charles took his horse and rode it over to a fence. He then dismounted and tied both of them up. He took the Lee-Metford rifle from his shoulder and quietly loaded a bullet into the chamber. Hosah had already gone over the bags and was heading down a street to the side of it.

Charles surveyed the houses around them; he looked for tracks in the road; moving past the rifles, he saw an open ammunition box. The bullets from it were scattered on the sandbags and the ground. He leaned against the bags and looked for Hosah further down the street.

There was a strange stillness around the village; no birds were darting from house to house, or wildlife moving through the empty roads. Charles scanned the road behind him; the clouds overhead started to yield a light rain shower. As he turned, a large creature crossed from one field to the next with a body in its mouth. His first thought was a razor tooth, but this was different; it was more muscular. The head had similarities to the long limbs, but it was slightly less human in appearance. The nose was elongated, and the face was narrow at the forehead; it had sharp-looking eyes with ears that were pointed upright. It was something of a mix of a long limb and razor-tooth. Charles stayed still and did not move; he did not want to get its attention.

The creature dropped the body from its mouth and sniffed the air. One of the tied-up horses let out a neigh; this instantly caused the giant beast to turn its head in Charles's direction. Its eyes just stared at him; it lowered its nose to the corpse and licked it, then nuzzled it. Charles still had his rifle in his hands, but was statuesque. The creature sniffed the air; Charles thought it looked like a dinosaur he had seen in the London Natural History Museum. Similar to a Stegosaurus, but different as this was a meat-eater; it didn't have the armoured plates across its back or spikes on its tail, but it did have teeth that looked like they would rip through flesh and bone. It clawed at the ground with its front right leg.

Charles let his eyes fall to his right slowly. He couldn't see Hosah to warn him, but his heart rate was up. Both horses let out a concerned snort and began to pull at the rope they were tied with. As he let his eyes roll back, the giant creature came at him; it smashed through a hedge, losing its footing briefly. Charles jerked forward and swung his legs over the sandbags. He did not take another look at where the beast was; he kept running towards a cottage nearest to him. The door was shut, but he had no time to wait and threw himself at one of the ground windows. He dropped his rifle as he went through; the impact was masked by the creature smashing into the wall and window behind him.

Charles did not have time to think; he picked himself up and scrambled past the sofa behind him, and the wall shook under heavy pressure from the creature. It awkwardly stuck its head through the broken window, snapping at the air and letting out bellowing grunts. He moved past a corner table and flung the living room door open. He then began to make his way up the stairs. The sound of stones falling gave away where it was; Charles moved up the stairs, tripping on them as he went. The door behind him burst into bits, and the giant beast clawed at him like a cat grabbing a mouse. Charles kept moving; he didn't have time to think as the creature edged into the small hallway.

He could smell its rotten breath as it snapped and tried to reach him. Charles entered the first room on his right, a bedroom with an unused bed sitting proudly in the corner, the sheet still crisply folded. Charles looked at the window and then made a beeline for it. The sound below went quiet, which forced Charles to stop in his tracks. At first, he thought maybe it had gone after Hosah; then, he wondered if it was waiting for him to move. The floorboards sprung up as the creature shattered the wood underneath his feet. Charles fell to the side as more of the floor fell away; he kicked out at the head of the beast. Its tongue licked out at Charles's legs as he tried to get his footing; it then fell heavily backwards. He managed to push himself off the wall nearest to him and went through a bedroom window by kicking it open and lowering himself down. The creature continued to break its way towards him through the house.

He hit the ground and fell forward, but was up in a flash. Moving at speed, he sprinted down the road, looking for another house to enter. The sound of glass breaking meant it was now on his tail. Charles reached for his revolver but couldn't get it out as he ran. Breathing hard, he arrived at a house on the corner of a side road. The door was ajar, so he ran straight inside. The charging creature behind him did not smash into the door this time. Charles withdrew his revolver and raised it; he saw its large frame move past the living room window. It was now stalking him; it raised itself onto its hind legs and pushed at the wall.

He wondered what to do; shooting at its underbelly was an idea, but the skin looked armoured to a degree. The one thing that stuck in his thought process was to try and shoot it in its head from the roof. He decided to climb upstairs and break through one of the bedroom

ceilings. Looking around the room, he saw a chair; instinctively, he smashed it against the bedroom wall and then used a chair leg to dig a hole into the ceiling above. Once it was big enough, he climbed up, moving around the beams, and he used the chair leg to make another hole in the slate roof.

Charles waited a moment or two for the creature to circle the house. He pulled out his Enfield revolver and aimed.

Bang

He hit it in the jaw, just below its cheek. Blood trickled down from its mouth onto the grass around its legs. It kept on moving its mouth as the wound irritated it. It then raised itself on its hind legs, its front legs now resting on the top of the roof. Charles stared into its eyes; they narrowed when it focused on him. It then began to try and climb up the side of the house.

Charles lifted the gun and aimed. Sweat began to fall from his hairline and cheek onto his tunic. Slowly, the beast got its claws into the side of the cottage and started to haul itself up. Charles knew he might not be able to kill it with one shot, but he also contemplated how long it would take him to climb back down through the roof.

Its head started to get closer to where he was situated, leaning out of the roof. He now had it in his sights; aiming, he squeezed the trigger repeatedly. The bullets thumped into its forehead; one hit its nose, and this took its aggression to another level. Blood was pouring from the bullet wounds, but it was still coming. Charles did not have time to re-holster his revolver; he just dropped it and went through the ceiling hole.

The creature's body was completely on top of the roof, and its weight soon caused the wooden beams supporting it to collapse. Charles was picking himself off the bedroom floor when the beast's lower body crashed in around him. Instantly, he reached for his sword, but to no avail; it was still strapped to his horse.

The creature started to wriggle; it sensed it was close to its prize.

Footsteps could be heard running up the stairs, and in a flash, Hosah ran in with a spear; he almost glided across the floorboards as he rammed the spear into its chest area. The force he needed took him right into the swinging legs of the beast. Charles was quick to pull him back as they both turned and moved to go down the stairs. Hosah led the way to the horses; Charles allowed himself one glance over his shoulder, and the side of the room at the top looked like the wall was starting to buckle.

"Quick, let's mount up and leave. Hopefully, it's wounded enough not to follow."

Hosah was in his saddle with an effortless lift; Charles had to steady his horse before he pulled himself up.

"Shall we not try and kill it?" Hosah looked determined.

"I've shot it in the head six times; you've stuck a spear in its chest; something says maybe we leave this for another day."

As they spoke, it started slowly appearing from upstairs of the house. Stones fell from the outer wall as its head and body emerged. Before jumping down, it pulled at the spear sticking out of its chest. Once out, it let out a deep bellow and whooping sounds.

"I hope it's not calling in more of its kind." With a concerned tone, Charles said.

Hosah nodded his head and agreed to move back to the camp. They turned their horses swiftly and drove down the road from which they came. The giant creature jumped through the hole it had created and began to give chase; fortunately, it gave up after a short distance.

"You need to find a new rifle." Hosah smiled

Charles smiled back. "Thanks for helping me back there; I'm not sure I would have made it without you."

"I fear for my people on the Great Plains. Everything has changed; the more this darkness comes onto our lands, the more my hope fades." Hosah had a forlorn look.

Charles realised that witnessing what they were up against was soul-destroying. This new creature was another demon in Nazar's ever-increasing arsenal of weapons. He doubted whether they could stop him. His army had been defeated in battles, but he was slowly winning the war.

They took a slightly different route back. In doing so, Hosah was the first to see a structure in the distance. It looked like a wooden fort, running for three to four fields in length. Charles wondered why they had not been notified of this before.

"I'll check what's going on over there." He pulled out his binoculars from his saddle bag and studied the fence line. Nothing was happening; no guard towers or drone soldiers patrolled the outer perimeter.

"It looks safe."

"Let me ride around it and double-check." Hosah got the nod from Charles and left at speed.

Charles carried on surveying with his binoculars. He saw a muntjac deer roam around the side of the fence line and begin to eat the grass growing there. Hosah had used the nearest field to get close to the structure. He moved his horse in a controlled, stealthy way, leading it through the soft ground. Charles marvelled at his horsemanship and counted his stars—he had the Arapaho with him.

Hosah came in close to the fence, pulling his horse in tight; he then stood on his horse and looked over the fence before raising himself over it. On the other side, he saw empty paddocks, a few outhouses and a barn. Near the centre of the fort was a wooden-looking house. Hosah withdrew his knife and moved silently along the outer paddock stock fence. No animals were inside the large area; wool strands hung from the splintered bits of wood in fence posts. In the paddock, there were cowpats but no livestock.

Hosah concluded it was how they kept the animals from being attacked by the flesh-eaters.

He cautiously approached the wooden cabin, feeling an outside fire pit to check for warmth, which helped him gauge that there hadn't been activity for a while. He moved along the outer veranda and then to the window; a glance was enough for him to move to the front door. He banged on it twice and stepped to the side. Hosah then moved around the back and found a back window. He looked in again; it looked empty; he was satisfied enough that he could enter from the front. He moved inside with a watchful eye.

It looked like it had been used as a farmer's shack, with tables and chairs pushed into the room's corners. Farming equipment lay scattered around the room, on the floor and shelves. Moving through the cabin, he passed the living quarters; the beds still had sheets and blankets. There were other supplies in a back-end room within the cabin. Hosah quickly checked them and then moved outside; the outbuildings just had hay and empty pens. Without wasting any more time inside the fortification, he moved to one of the gates nearest to him. It was straightforward, too open, and he closed it behind him. Letting out a whistling sound, he called his horse.

Charles could see Hosah's horse moving around to the other side. This was enough for him to kick on and ride over.

Hosah soon appeared.

"Nothing in there. It's where they kept their animals."

Charles took another look and realised they would need structures like this to help keep the flesh-eaters from killing everything. As they rode back, his mind drifted to life under Nazar rule, which inevitability made him think about his family back in America.

"I'm sure they'll be ok. Your wife is a fighter, and Arthur is half Arapaho now."

Charles nodded. "You have good perception."

Hosah looked at him, not fully understanding what Charles was implying. "You must be thinking of your family as well, Hosah."

Hosah said they were always with him in his thoughts and heart, the birds and animals, the wind and sun. Charles was so impressed with the whole philosophy of the Native American Indians, especially the Arapaho. They only took what they needed from the land and tried to live in balance with it. They had one more stop; Hosah had noticed a small farm with smoke wafting out of the cottage chimney. They both rode cautiously to it. A wooden sign stood outside the entrance, and the farm's name was carved in the wood—little Rhyndaston. Hosah and Charles dismounted and looked around; it was a homely place with lots of character; everything was still fresh, with a log still smouldering in the aga. The men did not spend too long, but they took a moment to look at the rolling fields behind the farm and the calmness this gave before they continued to ride back to the others.

Captain Somersett of the American 10th Cavalry rode alongside Sergeant Boyd and Corporal Williams as they patrolled around the castle. Charles was grateful to see them as they approached the British and Allied positions.

"Major" Captain Somersett smiled as he said this. "We have something to show you."

They rode together, following the American soldiers to the side of the village. Raindrops started to fall, and the dark clouds above dropped the light levels. Sergeant Boyd dismounted and walked over a corpse of trees. Charles did the same. The Sergeant led him into a thicket of trees, and lying about twenty yards in was a large body.

"We've nicknamed it rough back razor tooth." He walked around it slowly. "The Engineers talked about razor tooth, but this was different, so we named it."

"How did you kill it?"
"We got lucky; it killed a horse and dragged it to the nearest hedge to feed. Whilst this happened, we got a small artillery piece and hit it." He had a smile on his face as he pointed to the wound. "It's a big old beast; I hope they don't have too many of them."

Charles lifted his helmet and eased it off. "We had a run-in with one at Hays Castle. We couldn't kill ours, though." He took a branch and stuck it into the mouth of the roughback, pulling back at the gums and exposing the large teeth.

The American soldier scratched his head. "Just how?"

"It's a long story, but somehow they have, over time, harnessed the ability to use the fungus of a meteorite not from our world." Charles felt the soft drops of rain now hitting his uncovered hair. "You know we have a fight on our hands, Sergeant. Nazar has the devil riding with him."

"Major, my beliefs in God have helped me in my darkest moments when I was a slave and afterwards with my family. I have to pray God will prevail."

Charles put back on his helmet. "I want to believe as well. Let's head back; we need to double the patrols.

Chapter 29

The next morning, the sun was out early. The evening had passed without major incidents. Several flesh-eaters were spotted but never came close to the perimeter defences. The soldiers had a good feast the night before and were ready to push on to Hereford.

Charles rode to the front of the column and was greeted by a young Marine Captain. Behind Captain Hedges was Captain Somersett and the other officers.

It was a strange sight that Charles had to look at along the line. There were British Engineers, Marines, Arapaho, American Cavalrymen from the 10th and 17th regiments and then Texas and Hagen as scouts. He didn't mind, as they were not fighting a war in the conventional way. They had to adapt and change to the enemy they were facing.

The convoy moved out with multiple wagons; the other soldiers were mounted for rapid movement. The first destination was Llangadog, just on the outskirts of the Brecon Beacons. Charles had reports that the British and Allied forces had pushed on through and were now laying siege to Hereford. They had secured the defences around Pembrokeshire and along the beaches. Fishguard and Tenby had small detachments there now. Scouts had been sent to Ireland, but they did not want to engage in another front, even if the forces there did not seem to be of significant numbers.

Corporal Heinz set off with Hosah and Pvt Alexander. They would check the paths ahead and report on the villages and towns.

Major Hayward travelled along the line; he wanted the soldiers to see him and know he was actively there with them. He was reminded of some of the officers who put him in the glasshouse prison. It was vital for him to have their respect and for them to know he was looking out for them. The number of soldiers under his command was an increase for him, and he wanted to keep them all alive if possible, but in the dark corners of his mind, war was not letting anyone have their wishes regarding lives.

Alexander mopped his brow with his handkerchief, and the skies were still clear. He continued that way throughout the day. They had decided not to stop and wanted to get as many miles done as possible. As the day drew to a close, it was decided to set up camp near Llys-y-Fran. This was a village on the southern slopes of the Preseli hills. The Engineers were quick to build a defensive fortification around the village. Alexander, Hosah and Corporal Heinz were instructed to scout the surrounding area. There were a few bullet holes around the village, but no indications of artillery shells, which suggested that not much of a force was based here.

"Where do you think all the Welsh are?" Corporal Heinz was riding slowly in front of the others, "Maybe they've all been eaten or turned", Alexander said with a half-serious smile and shrug of the shoulders. He added that he thought they had been moved further inland, possibly to camps.

"We've seen how they protect their animals; they've built forts for them." Hosah was straight to the point.

Corporal Heinz nodded his head as if to say that makes sense.

They continued to ride up into the hills. The forests started to thicken, meaning visibility became restricted. The oak trees were mixed in with other broadleaf trees, and it was a beautiful sight. The lower slopes had more woodlands, unlike the higher Preseli Hills, which were windswept and used for grazing. Hosah suddenly stopped them. "Look at the broken branches. A few larger animals have moved through here."

They all stayed still. The general chat the night before was on the roughneck razor tooth. These things would take some stopping. The fear was, if you came across a large number of them, what would you do?

Hosah slid off his horse and went over to the broken branches. He felt the branches and looked at the paw prints; they matched the ones he had seen in the village. "It's the roughnecks, maybe four to five. It looks like they have a small one with them."

"We should warn the others!" Corporal Heinz began to turn his horse.

"The branches have been broken for a while; they are no longer fresh," Hosah added. He thought they could have passed through there days ago. "We should go and check a high point."

Heinz loved the Hosah's worldliness and considered himself a good scout, but the Native American Indians were at another level.

They passed along several narrow sheep tracks, which undulated back and forth. The tracks slowly rose higher as they climbed to a peak. At the top, they looked out over a low-lying valley. There was no sign of a roughneck razor-tooth.

They spent a good thirty minutes scanning the horizon for anything threatening. Alexander enjoyed seeing a deer come into an open glade and graze for a while. To Hosah, that was a clear sign that nothing dangerous was lurking in the woods nearby.

The three of them returned to the village and reported their findings. Charles was wary of these new creatures but knew they had to press on. They were moving into September, and while the weather had been good, it could quickly change.

The following week, they travelled steadily and stopped where they felt safe and secure. Scouts and patrols were sent out regularly.

The journey was progressing well. There had been some rain, but it had been good going overall. They would stop in a village called Trapp, and from there, they would push on to Llangadog.

Pvt Dai Evans pointed out that they were in the "Robbers Valley" and that it used to be an ambush point, which made everyone slightly more concerned.

As usual, the defences were set up around the village. Patrols were doubled as they bedded in for the night. Charles spoke to Hosah and several other Arapahos; he wanted to thank them for all their help so far. Mad Dog would ride out in the evening to check the foothills around the Brecon Beacons.

A roaring fire inside a Welsh cottage greeted Charles as he went to his quarters. Texas and Captain Somersett were sitting at a table playing cards and laughing about stories of the Wild West. A pint of ale and some freshly cooked venison were waiting for him on the table.

He pulled a chair close to the fire. "Thank you. This is like a dream."

Captain Somersett turned to him. "It's a cold night."

Sergeant Butcher came into the room with a plate for Charles to use. Charles thanked him and took some meat and bread to have next to the fire. The warmth was soothing on his face and body; the evening air had a chill in it, which was a welcome relief. The fresh bread and the taste of well-seasoned meat were heaven-sent. He wondered, whoever cooked it, how they had made it so tasty. Texas could see he was enjoying it and was quick to point out he had prepared the meat and cooked it.

"Compliments to you, my friend."

Texas laughed, "I was surprised to find so many herbs." He paused, "I guess the dead don't mind eating us unflavoured." The room fell silent for a second before bursting into laughter. It felt good to hear laughter. Charles was able to relax for a moment and not think about his family and the war. The mood in the cottage was buoyant and hopeful. He sat back and took a large swig of ale. The evening passed with stories of the past and present. Corporal Heinz and Captain Hedges joined them. The drinking and discussions passed on into the early hours.

Charles awoke with a sore head. He went to the privy and relieved himself before heating some water over the stove to wash with warm water. It helped refresh him immensely. He then found some coffee on the stove in the kitchen. Captain Somersett was up; his sheer size and height made him hard to miss.

"Morning, Major."

"Morning, Captain, great coffee."

"You're welcome." He excused himself, and he went to check on his men.

Charles took his coffee and walked outside. There was a slight dampness in the air, but it wasn't raining, which made Charles smile. Pvt Brown was cutting wood outside and raised his hand to Charles.

"Morning, Major."

"Morning, John," he stopped and asked whether Heidi and the nurses had settled into Tenby. John looked happy to hear her name.

"I think they have, sir; I'm hoping the more we conquer Great Britain, the more I'll see of her."

Charles took another sip of his coffee. "No one can argue with that logic, John."

Charles walked around the village, checking on the Marines and Engineers. He stopped by the American cavalrymen and the Arapaho. He hadn't seen Hosah or Little Bear, but the others said they had gone out looking for food.

Just as he finished walking around, he saw Hagen standing close to a tree.

"Are you ok, Hagen?"

He just stood there.

"Listen to the wind."

Charles first thought Hagen was deep in thought and just speaking out loud. Then he began to listen. It was a strange sound, almost like a steam train going at speed. Then again, it changed on the wind, like chattering teeth. He couldn't work out if it was getting closer or moving away from them.

"It's like we've heard it before, but it's different."

Charles took a gulp of his coffee.

"I don't like it."

Hagen looked at him. "We haven't encountered a sizable drone force here in Wales." He sighed.
"I think it's coming our way."

The next sound to pierce the airways was an Arapaho war cry."

Coming their way at speed were Hosah, Little Bear and Mad Dog. They brought their horses to an abrupt halt by Hagen and Charles.

"The dead are coming."

"How many?"

Hosah paused. "They are coming like ants; the ground shakes with them."

Charles turned straight away and shouted at an engineer who was carrying a pail of water. "Sound the alarm. Get the bugler to call to arms."

The soldier dropped the pail, sending water streaming onto the ground below. He sprinted over to the nearest unit that could raise the alarm. There was a young cavalryman out tending to his horse. Within seconds, he quickly found his bugle and let out a lung-bursting call to arms.

The whole camp came to life and began rushing around to prepare. The wagons had not been fully unloaded and were in a state of readiness. Charles didn't have time to grab his kaki tunic or helmet and asked for it to be loaded into a wagon. He went to get his horse, which was quickly prepared for him, as he ordered Corporal Heinz and Alexander to check the area to the west. He asked Sergeant Butcher to speak to the officers about getting the convoy ready to roll out.

Texas had come out to the sound of the bugler and was scratching his thick blonde hair. Hagen was already riding his horse over to Charles. "We will go with Hosah and two Engineers to see what is happening."

Mad Dog had gone to speak to the other Arapaho and spread the word. As Charles mounted up, Pvt Brown and Pvt Simpkins joined him and the others.

"Hosah, take us to them."

As they began to ride out of the village, a herd of deer hurtled towards them, jumping over hedges and racing through the surrounding field. Some had severe wounds, with intestines hanging out; all looked petrified. Still loading their kit onto wagons or preparing their horses, the soldiers stopped to watch this herd of a hundred or more deer run through the village.

The sound of hissing and chatting teeth was growing louder, like a wave of noise across the horizon flooding towards them. Charles turned his horse and joined the rest of the riders. They rode to the North until they reached a suitable high point; it wasn't long before the wall of noise hit them. Hosah was right; all along the valley, there were flesh-eaters. Charles had never seen so many in one place. The land seemed to be moving directly towards them. The stench of death filled their nostrils; Pvt Simpkins gagged a little and covered his mouth.

Charles looked along the oncoming horde. There did not seem to be any gaps they could exploit. He spoke out loud, saying as much, and shook his head.

"This is what Nazar had controlling Great Britain, an army of the dead." He was angry with himself for not suspecting as much.

"We should be quick. They are starting to come around to our left." Hagen pointed to where they were emerging through the trees. The original plan was to head northeast to Llangadog, but now it wouldn't be possible; they would have to head east. Charles steered his horse around and told them to return to the village rapidly.

They arrived back to a line of American soldiers laying down fire to the west of the village. The flesh-eaters were appearing from the woods, across the fields, all along the line of sight. Charles stopped his horse alongside a US Cavalryman who was holding the horses for the soldiers. They were doing a good job of being accurate with their fire, but the numbers were too many for them to stop the flow. "Get the men to mount up. We have to leave."

He then rode towards the centre of the town.

Captain Hedge was speaking to Captain Somersett; both were in a rush as the noise of the oncoming horde swept over the village.

The wagons were lined up and ready to move. The noise was so incessant that Charles found it hard to think. Shouts rang out, and the horde was flooding into the south of the village. Captain Hedges said he would take some marines to buy time. Charles nodded his head.

He then called Sergeant Butcher and Corporal Heinz over to him. He dismounted and went to the nearest cottage, and went inside. His trusted friends followed him in.

"I'll make it quick. The dead have the upper hand. This horde is the biggest I've ever seen. We have a decision to make." Charles paused for a moment to think.

Shouts and gunfire broke out nearby; time was of the essence.

"I think if we stay and fight, we will all die here for sure; the trouble is, if we run, I'm not sure where the end of the line is for the dead." Charles looked directly into the eyes of the men in front of him.

Sergeant Butcher felt his beard. "Pvt Dai Evans knows these parts; he could help us."

Charles did not need to say anything; Corporal Heinz said he would find Pvt Evans and turned and left immediately. Sergeant Butcher lifted his rifle and did a quick inspection.

"Shall I take a small detachment and assist the marines as they fall back?"

Charles looked at him.

"Please." "Don't get surrounded."

With that, they both left the cottage. The fighting was taking place as the dead pressed against a stone wall; it was only a matter of time before it gave way. The fear on the soldiers' faces could not be hidden; the numbers were beyond belief. A marine corporal asked if they should uncouple the cannons and bring them into action.

"Major, we can head to Carreg Cennen Castle." The voice was shouting due to the noise.

Pvt Evans ran over with Corporal Heinz.

"Pvt, how far?" Charles shouted back

"Just over a mile and a bit."

"Sound the retreat. Let's get to that castle."

The bugler did a good job sounding out the retreat. He was hoisted onto a cottage roof and let out a piercing call. The wagons started to move. Pvt Evans led the way from the front. He had given instructions for Corporal Heinz and Hosah to search their expected route to check how safe it was.

Charles brought his horse, but he still did not have his tunic or sword; there was no time to find which wagon it was in, so he continued as he was. He rode over to the retreating Marines.

"Quickly mount up." The oncoming flesh-eaters were stumbling towards them in mass. The only direction left out was the north-west, which was the direction of the castle. If the dead ended up coming from that direction, it would mean a final stand.

He saw the Marines mount up and follow onto the last wagons. The engineers who were mounted rode alongside the column. Mad Dog appeared next to the Major.

"Crazy man to take them all on." He said this with a straight face.

In this desperate situation, it made Charles smile.
"Are all the braves mounted and leaving?"

"Yes."

As they turned to ride, a flesh-eater stumbled in front of them; it had come from a gap between two cottages; before it could get any closer, Mad Dog had drawn his bow and unleashed an arrow into its head. The blood squirted onto the track below. Charles acknowledged Mad Dogs' accuracy and speed as they kicked on and rode along the village's main road.

Captain Somersett galloped over to them. "Major, all my men accounted for."

"Good, I do not want to leave anyone behind." The three of them watched as the village was slowly overrun by the dead. The horses were disturbed by the noise but were kept under tight control.

"Let's join the others; this isn't over yet."

The convoy moved forward at a good pace, and scouts were keeping a watchful eye on all flanks. Corporal Heinz and Hosah took turns reporting back on the route ahead. Little Bear and Texas patrolled the rear flank. The flesh-eaters were still moving their way across what seemed like miles.

Charles discussed this with his officers as he rode up and down the column. The main concern was whether they were being encircled without their knowledge. Pvt Evans was leading from the front and was soon joined by Charles. They spoke about Carreg Cennen Castle. Pvt Evans said he remembered it being on a steep hill and would offer them somewhere to lie low whilst the horde moved past. The mood amongst the soldiers was calm; those who were not mounted sat quietly in the wagons as they trundled along.

It was decided they would not stop until they reached the castle. The sun was out, but the sheer number of dead moving had created a dust cloud that was following them. Charles was still riding in his shirt. Sergeant Butcher offered to get his tunic and helmet, but he said it wasn't the time.

The track they were following started to rise gradually as they began to climb the hills. They could see the castle in the distance and the surrounding fields moving as if a flood was engulfing them. The dead stretched across the valley as far as their eyes could see.

Hosah and Cpl Heinz arrived to update them on the castle itself. It was clear and ready to be occupied. The corporal said they would have to cover some of the gaps in the front, but it offered a place to stay out of the way of the horde. The column sped up once they approached the track leading to the castle. The noise of the horde carried through the hills like a siren calling for boats to come to the rocks.

The soldiers were led by their officers quickly to the front of the castle. Horses were led inside the castle walls, and wagons lined up outside the front of the castle. Supplies were brought rapidly in, and cannons were uncoupled and moved inside. Three-quarters of the sides were too steep for the dead to climb, but the other sloping side would hopefully deter the others.

Charles had given his orders to the officers to carry out. While they did so, he followed Pvt Evans up the castle walls to the viewpoint. The castle itself was a ruin, but it was still the best bet for now. He looked out at the flesh-eaters sweeping through the valley; their numbers were shocking.

"Pvt Evans, well done for leading us here." He smiled as if pleased with himself.

Sergeant Butcher joined the Major and looked on with horror at the moving army of death. "We need to make sure no soldiers are moving around the battlements or outside the castle walls; we must do nothing that would draw them here."

The soldiers were quick to settle inside the castle. The ground felt like it was trembling under their feet. Outside the castle walls, every snarl or snapping hissing sound felt closer; it sent shivers down their spines as they waited quietly inside.

Texas spoke softly to Hagen about the castle itself. He was impressed at its structure, as there was nothing like it in America. Private Johnson from the 10th Cavalry Regiment joined them.

"The walls look strong enough to hold out in places, but the front of the castle would pose the problem."

Pvt Johnson sat on a ration box and cleaned his rifle. Hagen took out his axe and checked its sharpness.

"If they find out, we cannot escape through this horde. The Major has taken the only option we have." Texas sat next to Pvt Johnson.

The hours passed, and shadows moved around the castle. Nothing was spotted on the front side of the castle. The Arapaho were stationed along that side; they were tasked with any flesh-eaters who came close to the British force; they would take them out with arrows.

Charles spoke to the captains and told them they would wait it out until the morning. They would send out patrols once the last of the dead had gone. The issue now concerning Charles was where that horde was heading and whether they would run into it again. The whole conflict for the British Isles was based on beating the drone armies that Nazar had established there. They knew he would have flesh-eaters and other creatures, but not in this sizable force.

The evening passed without too much going on; some flesh-eaters had wandered near the castle entrance, but the Arapaho had dealt with them swiftly.

Charles made small talk with the soldiers before they set off in the morning. The plan was to move forward at a steady pace, but they could not guarantee they would not meet the horde again. If they did, they would have to think on their toes and react swiftly.

Alexander was standing on one of the walls overlooking the valleys below. The fields looked like a herd of elephants had gone through them. There were broken stone walls and collapsed trees. The soil was churned up as if it had been ploughed. A few flesh-eaters were wandering around. Some had been squashed under walls or by fallen trees. The main thing Alexander reported back was that it was safe to begin moving again.

The convoy slowly lined up and prepared to leave; the route was to take them around the Brecon and on to Hereford. Gradually, the horses began to pull the wagons forward and onto the tracks, leaving the castle behind them. Captain Somersett looked back at this old ruin. The falling light rain helped set the sombre mood surrounding the troops. The realisation that the army of the dead was more powerful than anyone imagined. The unspoken census was what would happen if there were two or three more of these hordes, and how would they be stopped?

Scouts were already gathering intelligence of what was out there, but only fifteen minutes into the journey, Hosah and Mad Dog accompanied a group of riders towards the column. Charles broke off from the front and rode to the approaching group, joined by Cpl Heinz and Pvt Chamberlin. The riders were dressed in kaki and were from the Queen's Royal Regiment. They had a Cpl who rode forward, a friendly-faced man who asked to speak to the commanding officer. Charles said it was him.

"Sir, America has been invaded and is under a huge threat from Nazar forces. We believe Boston has fallen."

Charles momentarily lost his train of thought; all he could think about was his family and whether they were safe. He was brought back to the situation on hearing Sergeant Butcher's voice. He was prompted if the wagons should come to a stop. Charles gave the order for the column to stop and asked what their orders were.

"It has been requested that all the American forces return, and half the allied forces return to help with the conflict in America."

Charles kept a calm face, but inside, his stomach turned. He wanted to hear what his Engineers and current force would be required to do next. He almost felt sick thinking about what he had to ask, but he knew the question would determine their next move.

"What has been requested of my Engineers?"

The Cpl took out a piece of paper and unrolled it.

"Your orders for you and all of your men are to return to America and help with the conflict there."

Charles let out a cough, an automatic reflex to the news, as he had to mask his relief. They spoke briefly, and he thanked the Cpl and wished them well in their continued fight for Great Britain.

The officers were quickly summoned together, and the news was spread quickly that they would return to America. Some soldiers without families were disappointed not to have taken the whole country back, but they would follow orders and return to America.

Pvt Brown was happy to return to Pembrokeshire and see Heidi. The nurses would be split down the middle, and John said a prayer, which seemed to be answered. She was coming with him and the engineers. The journey back had been smooth, but they had passed a flock of crows cawing around a carcass of the roughneck razor-tooth. Charles and Hosah looked at each other; they didn't have time to inspect whether it was the one they had injured. The soldiers were just happy to see its giant frame humbled.

Within a week, they were packed and heading back to America.

Chapter 30

Rebecca was almost falling asleep as the wagon plodded along. They were closing in on Richfield Springs and would stop there en route. As they moved along, they had seen pockets of people fleeing the invasion but hadn't encountered any more rebels or flesh-eaters.

Vincent's wound was healing well, and the group had settled down into the journey. Naomi and Arthur giggled like teenagers should, and Tom and Florence were busy discussing her plans for a horse ranch after the war.

Elin took over driving the front wagon so Vincent could rest in the back. Reginald had also swapped with Pvt Hawkins to share the wagon's steering.

"Arthur, I was thinking about the girl you were imprisoned in Europe. Do you think if she were with us, you would be tempted to have her as your girlfriend?"

Arthur rubbed his eyes. "No, Sophia is a lovely girl, and we survived the camp together, but you and I have been through so much together, plus I'm older now" " he said with a smile, "I really like you, Naomi, I can't think of anyone else I would like to be with as we fight for America."

She gushed with happiness, hugged him, and kissed him on the lips.

Tom remarked at that. "Steady, there are children here."

Florence stopped thinking about the horse farm and hoped they would have a regular bed to sleep in once they arrived in Richfield Springs.

Tom leaned forward to kiss Florence.

"Aww, that's sweet, Tom, but you don't have to copy just because that couple can't keep their hands off each other. I don't mind, but let's get back to planning."

Tom felt slightly rejected, but Florence sensed that and quickly leaned forward, put her hand behind his head, and kissed him long and hard. When she broke from the kiss, he felt very good about it. He looked over at Naomi and Arthur, who looked happy for him.

"Tom, focus if you want another kiss." Florence went on to talk about her favourite breed of horse and how they would need to build a defensive barrier for the animals due to the flesh-eaters.

The conversations continued throughout the day as they closed in on the town. The closer they got, the more people appeared. Their anxious faces carried concern over to the group; Rebecca told Vincent to take a side road and maybe keep on the outskirts of the small town. There were no soldiers to ask what was happening.

The track they chose along one side of the town was fairly quiet; the odd stray dog ran out in front of them and sniffed the air, almost seeing if they could scavenge food from the passing wagons. The dust kicked up from the horses and made it stick in their throats. To the side of them was the Ocquionis Creek; it carried a gentle sound of water rushing over rocks and pebbles. Eventually, they came to a clearing made by a small detachment of soldiers.

Private Samuel Hawkins and Private Dean Baker had meant to travel with them to Brattleborough, but they diverted their route via Greenville due to the fighting. After the attack by long limbs, they had now travelled onto Richfield Springs. The group had stayed clear of Albany because of the large population there, and the US army was preparing to fight for the city. Both soldiers were now going to speak to the officer in the town and see what their orders would be.

A young Captain introduced himself as an officer from the 5th Infantry Regiment. He said they only had a handful of men and were trying to set up a defence perimeter.

Rebecca was the first to ask what the enemy reports were. The young Captain looked like he wasn't going to answer this direct question, but Rebecca added that her husband was a Major in the British army, and the families with her had loved ones fighting for America. Emily stuck her head around the canvas sheet covering the wagon.

"Hello"

The young officer was instantly thrown from his train of thought.

"Hello, I hear your father is fighting Nazar's armies?"

"Yes, I hope he comes back to America. I miss him, and I think we'll need him here."

The soldier smiled. "I'm sure they will be back soon to help us."

Emily liked that response and nodded her head

"Ma'am, there are reports of rebel and destroyer drones coming our way."

"We ran into them before, just outside of Albany. Why are they moving so far away from the main army?" Rebecca asked the question, but inside her head, she was thinking about what to do.

"I guess it's normal to advance as far as you can with some units to take strategic locations."

They continued talking about where they could pitch up. The officer said they could use some of the tents put aside for the civilians who were arriving. Rebecca thanked him.

The two privates asked him if they should join the 5th, as they could not get to their regiment in Brattleborough.

The young officer thought momentarily, then said they should still stay with the major's family and guard all of them until they could rejoin their regiment or join a more extensive US force. They thanked him and drove to the tents. People were moving along towards the cleared area. The fence around them was not large; its primary purpose was to stop the dead from wandering in and attacking them in their sleep.

Rebecca was concerned, so she aired this to Elin and Vincent.

"I think they are coming for us!"

Vincent looked at Rebecca. "I think they're coming for all of us."

"No, it's not that, Vincent; I think they're coming for us, as in me and my children."

Vincent pulled the wagon alongside several empty tents.

"Why would they target you out of everyone in America?"

"I think it's because Nazar has not forgiven my husband for helping destroy the meteorite in Russia. He would want to make an example of us."

Elin rubbed Rebecca's shoulder; she could sense she was concerned.

"Look, it's not safe for you to be around us. If they are looking for us, you will be taken or killed." Rebecca pushed her hair away from her face and turned around to look at Arthur and Emily.

Vincent put his hand on her shoulder. "We stick together now; if they come, we will fight them together."

Rebecca turned and had a tear running down her cheek. "Thank you both; I just wish none of this was real. I worry for our children. I'm not sure Arthur would survive another spell in their children's prison. Emily, well, she's so young."

Elin hugged her. "We will do our best to protect all of them."

They began to climb down and out of the wagon. The tents were a good size and were divided amongst them. Fire pits were dug, and wood was close by. A note pinned to a post read Please cut down more wood to refill the supply.

Reginald and the two US privates joined them, standing outside the tents. They all spoke about staying in Richfield Springs for a night, packing, and moving on the next day. Suggestions were made to go to Binghamton; reports indicated New York was still in American hands and would be defended, hopefully slowing the advancing Nazar army.

Emily took Naomi's hand whilst the adults spoke and led her towards one of the tents. Florence came to join them. "Can we girls share a tent tonight, please?"

"Maybe ask your mother first, and if she agrees, that's fine," Naomi said.

"I will, I will." Emily then went to stand behind the adults. She played with her bear's ears as she stood patiently.

Once they had finished talking, Emily pulled on her mum's top.

"Yes, my love."

"Can all the girls sleep in one of the tents tonight, please, please, please."

Rebecca looked at her soft eyes and saw how much it meant to her.

Private Samuel Hawkins and Private Dean Baker were walking towards their tent.

"Dean and Samuel, would you please share with Vincent and Reginald? The girls want to share."

They both said that was fine and called out to Vincent, who also said it was fine. Reginald was already leaning over against the fence, checking for its strength. He looked over and gave a thumbs-up. He walked along the fence line and found a somewhat wobbly section. He dug his heel into the ground to mark where the loose part was. Then he turned and walked to the wagon to find some wood to strengthen it.

Elin spoke to the French mother. She had decided to stay in the camp with a group of French families. She thanked them for helping them get this far and wished them well in their journey away from the invading armies.

The fire pits were soon filled and lit. The remaining group members gathered around them, talking about days gone by. The two young soldiers talked about how they used to race horses and fool around in the forests. Dean said a brown bear had chased him, but it gave up because he was too quick. This brought a look of disbelief from the adults, but he shrugged his shoulders as if to say it was all true.

After they had all eaten, they continued to sit by the fire. Rebecca took Emily to bed and left her in the tent. It was nice for Rebecca to look around at the smiling and laughing faces. She liked seeing Arthur holding Naomi close and how he was turning into a young man. She knew Charles would be proud of them, and for now, she could put the thought of Nazar and his army of death to the back of her mind.

That night, she felt relaxed as she let her head sink into a rolled-up blanket on the makeshift beds. Tom asked Arthur if he would help him practise shooting arrows over the next week when they could. He agreed, which made Tom smile and fall asleep with the thoughts of shooting arrows into flesh-eaters.

The first screams did not wake them from their sleep; it was the gunshots which woke them. Rebecca's heart started to pound straight away. She put on her converted trousers and slipped on her top; she grabbed her gun holster and rifle. The others were busy getting ready. She did not wait, bursting out of the tent; the scene was chaotic; people were running around, grabbing what they could. The noise was familiar to her; flesh-eaters' constant asthmatic breathing and hissing could be heard all along the fence line behind them.

Vincent came out of the tent with a rifle.

"We need to get the children and go."

Two soldiers from the 5th Infantry were ushering people away from that area. Rebecca went into the girls' tent; Naomi was busy dressing Emily. When she saw her mum, her eyes lit up. "Are they here?"

"I think so; we must be quick."

"The fence has broken behind us." A man carrying a young child ran past them, shouting those words as he went.

Arthur joined his mum's side. "Shall we go to the wagons?"

"There may not be time." She raised her rifle as a flesh-eater stumbled towards them; it was a rotting soldier, a US cavalryman who looked to have been attacked a while ago. She looked down at the rifle and pulled the trigger; a clean headshot saw the dead soldier drop to the ground. More were following behind him. Vincent made sure Florence and Naomi were out of the tent. Pvt Hawkins and Pvt Baker stood by the side of their tent and began to fire. Screams from people being caught by the dead and eaten alive travelled around the night air.

Reginald had his shotgun and a large piece of wood. The first flesh-eater to come at him got that lump of wood wrapped around his head; the second felt the force of the shotgun.

A soldier from the 5th rode to where some families were trying to flee from the oncoming dead. He drew his sabre and quickly dispatched several heads. Suddenly, a bullet struck him in the chest, causing him to fall from his horse. The flesh-eaters wasted no time falling on him like flies on an open sore; his calls for help were drowned out as they began to claw him apart and devour his skin and organs. The families from the camp were trying to get towards the town, but the horde was causing chaos.

Bullets started to fly through the tents. A war drum sounded, booming over the screams and cries; a roar went up in the distance.

Vincent said they had to fall back to the village. Rebecca told Emily to stick with her; Arthur was with Tom and the two girls. Arthur had a Krag-Jorgenson rifle; it was a bolt-action rifle. They moved back together. Pvt Hawkins and Pvt Baker covered the right flank. They could see rebels and drone soldiers starting to climb over the fence behind the tents. Some of the tents had been pushed or carried into the fire pits by dead-walking through the camp. They instantly caught alight, creating a disturbing scene. Burning flesh-eaters began to walk randomly into other tents, setting them ablaze.

The smell of burning, rotting flesh filled the air. The 5th Infantry steered a cannon into space at an entrance to a road. They hurriedly prepared the cannon and fired it at the oncoming flesh-eaters. Once the shell landed, it obliterated a giant wave of the dead. The problem was that they kept on flooding towards them.

They angled the cannon towards a corner of the camp, where drones and rebels had begun to open fire on the civilians and soldiers. The gun crew hurried around the cannon to reload it; one of the young men carrying a shell was struck in the leg and fell forward. His fellow soldiers helped him to the side, picked up the shell he was carrying, and loaded it into the cannon. They started to come under increasing fire; another soldier in the artillery unit was struck in the head and was killed instantly. The remaining soldiers knew this would be their last chance to inflict some damage on the attacking force. Once the shell was in, they aimed and fired. The shell landed between several rebels and drones. It had the desired effect, inflicting a lot of casualties on them. The soldiers grabbed the wounded soldier and fell back into the town.

Rebecca and the others had to move past the wagons and continue down Elm Street. There was gunfire in the street next to them, causing mayhem among the fleeing civilians. Flesh-eaters were pouring through the camping area and were starting to come down the street behind them. The group kept moving forward, but the concern was that they could not escape quickly without horses. It joined the main street when they reached the top of the road. People were running everywhere; it was chaos, and the main force of soldiers from the 5th infantry was trying to help where they could. The young Captain was further down the main street. He had two lines of infantry firing on the flesh eaters as they came along. The soldiers would take it in turn to fire and then retreat.

Rebecca looked to her left along that side of the street; again, flesh eaters were coming towards them. There were also mounted drones coming out of the darkness, attacking anyone who was American or European. Arthur took aim as a drone cavalryman homed in on an elderly gentleman.

He rested the Krag rifle butt into his shoulder and looked down at the sights. He then pulled the trigger; it took less than a second before it struck the rider as he was in the motion of swinging his sword. He fell off the horse whilst trying to strike the old man below. Arthur reloaded another bullet into the chamber and moved with the others towards the middle of the town.

Emily looked at her mum; even in the early morning darkness, she could see the worry on her face. She wanted to hold her mother's hand, but settled for Naomi's.

Vincent and Rebecca looked up and down the street. It was carnage and a desperate sight. Rebecca felt her throat had gone dry and was almost beset by panic. They had always had options, but this attack had thrown that out of the window. Vincent looked at her and the children. Pvt Hawkins and Pvt Baker were standing ready with bayonets fixed. Elin raised her rifle, but it became apparent they could not stay in the open where they were.

Reginald was the one who saw an opportunity for them to get off the street. A building which had shops below it and apartments on the upper floors was directly behind them. He could see soldiers going into it and ushering people inside. Reginald told everyone to follow him; as they made their way to the building, Rebecca saw a female rebel running at them with an axe; as she got closer, she could see the hate in her eyes, almost foaming at the mouth; she pulled out her revolver and fired twice into her torso as she came forward. The woman fell to the ground; her odour was foul, as if unwashed. Rebecca did not spend any more time looking at her lying there and followed the others rapidly into the building.

Once inside, they passed many frightened faces. Those who could use a weapon were handed something to use. The soldiers in the building were firing on the enemy from the higher floors. Rebecca checked on Arthur and Emily. She then looked around the building. They were now stuck inside.

"Vincent, I'm unsure where we can go from here."

"I'm hoping this is just a rebel and drone attack, more of a distraction to the larger force that is coming; they couldn't have their main force here yet," Vincent started to lead them up the stairs.

Elin helped the children move up in front of her and onto the stairs. They could hear the fighting outside as they followed Elin to the top of the stairs. Elin had a glance out of a middle-floor window. She could see houses burning as the rebels and drones swept through the town. The soldiers held fire and told the civilians with them to do the same. Vincent also looked out of one of the middle floors' windows. The rebels had captured some of the 5th Infantry and led them away. The dawn sunrise was making the aftermath of the attack easier to see.

Rebecca and Elin asked if he thought they would disperse and leave the town now. He thought that could be the case: a quick night attack and then onto another town or settlement. The dead started to clear from the town, and the mood in the building lifted. Arthur held Naomi tight; she still held Emily's hand. Pvt Hawkins and Baker had gone to the top floor to check the surrounding area.

Smoke swept around the town, carried on a breeze. It masked the fallen for a short while. They couldn't determine how many had escaped the camp or who had been captured. A sergeant with the 5th said they should wait another ten minutes before sending out a couple of scouts.

Vincent came and sat with the rest of them. He looked at their faces; they looked tired and concerned about what lay ahead. Emily was asleep in Elin's arms.

A thunderous explosion shook the building. Dust and debris fell from the ceiling above them. They were all shocked by this attack; the second explosion was downstairs. It blew open the front windows, shattering glass and brick, which caused multiple casualties on the ground floor. The gunfire drowned out the calls for help from the poor, wounded souls. Vincent had gone down the stairs to check on the situation on the lower floor when a roar went up; soon, there were drones and rebels mixed in with flesh-eaters coming at the building.

Vincent tried to help a few dazed people who were scattered around after the explosion. Those who were okay to fight took what they could and rushed to the windows and the main door.

The drones and rebels steaming into the building had been half-infected, meaning the flesh-eaters would not attack them. Nazar had used this in the beginning of his campaign of terror in Russia. Then, he reserved it for special attack parties. He didn't want to infect his whole army, as they did not have enough antidotes to stop them all from changing.

Vincent leaned against a wall and used his 45-calibre trapdoor rifle to open fire on the attacking force. His first shot hit a rebel in the leg, causing them to tumble down. His second shot struck a drone in the neck; as he reloaded for a third shot, rebels had already started fighting with the 5th infantry and civilians downstairs. Most of the children had been moved upstairs to the second and third floors. Vincent moved away from the broken window; as he turned, a drone lunged at him with a bayonet.

Vincent used his rifle to block the bayonet partially; the drone looked ill; his skin was greyish, and his hair matted and dirty. He snarled at Vincent and spat in his direction. Vincent did not have a bayonet and used the rifle to help protect himself from each lunge. A large rebel woman standing over 6ft 4 joined in the attack. She was ferocious with an axe and caught Vincent in the shoulder; he was fortunate, as it did not embed into his bone, but the pain still shook him as blood poured from the sliced skin on his shoulder. Vincent's problems were further compounded as he was struck in the leg by the drone with the bayonet. He fell back onto the wall behind him; the rebel lady laughed as she raised her axe to finish him off. She never brought it down; a bullet shattered her left eye socket, sending bits of bone and skin in the air. Elin reloaded as the drone turned to target her. She was swift to fire before he could raise his file; a chest shot was enough to kill him in his tracks.

Reginald had moved down the stairs and was quick to help his old friend. Elin covered them as they drove past her and up the stairs; she screamed out for the others on the lower floor to retreat upstairs. The flow of attackers continued to stream into the ground floor. The numbers were overpowering those that were left; some managed to flow past Elin, and soldiers stood by her side as they continued firing on the advancing drones, rebels and flesh-eaters. A soldier next to her told her to get the others to secure the top of the stairs; she touched the side of his face before swiftly moving up to the second floor. There was frantic movement; everyone took what they could to block the stairs. The soldiers at the bottom of the stairs fought tooth and nail to give them time on the upper floors.

Rebecca helped Reginald to the top floor. Florence had tears in her eyes as she saw her father being helped past. He touched her hand and muttered under his breath that he was okay and that she should help fight with the others.

Soon, drones and rebels were coming up the lower staircase. Reginald had come down to help the others, and Pvt Hawkins and Pvt Baker began firing from the staircase landing. The enemy was coming under heavy fire from the landing and behind the barrier, but they kept on coming. When their bodies started to block the route, they were dragged out of the way, and more rebels pressed forward.

Rebecca stroked Vincent's cheek. He looked at her and winced when he tried to shift his position. He had his revolver out and sat back against some storage boxes. "Please see if you can get Florence and Naomi out." He paused. I know it might not be possible, but please, if you can?"

Rebecca felt her eyes well up, "I will stay strong, Vincent." She turned and loaded her rifle. She had her revolver strapped to her left-hand side and a large knife on the other side. Before she went downstairs, she went to Emily, who was huddled with other children; elderly men and women were looking after them. All of the children looked frightened and concerned with the fighting below. Rebecca hugged Emily tight, "Whatever happens, I love you so much." Rebecca did not want to let go, but she had to help.

"Please be careful, mummy"

Rebecca nodded and moved towards the stairs; something made her stop and look out one of the large windows to her right. She could see drones and rebels rushing forward to attack the building, but further back, she could see Nazar priests sitting on horseback. There was also a man gesticulating, giving what seemed to be orders. He had a woman on his right-hand side who was also giving out orders. Rebecca was about to turn back when she saw something that made her lose her breath. It was the long, thin man she had seen in Albany many months ago when they fled Boston. She stood back; inside, she was convinced they were after her and her family. Rebecca put her mouth to her arm and let out a silent scream. What could she do? She felt lost and feared for them all now.

Gripping her rifle, she moved downstairs. Arthur and Tom were on one side, firing from the windows, and Naomi and Florence were close by but further along.

"Destroyer drones coming." Was the shout from Arthur. He tracked one with his rifle and got a clean shot in its head. The rush of the destroyer drones pushed the attack further up the stairs. They were armed with swords and axes; some even had spears. The stairs barrier could not withstand their force, so Rebecca called Elin to get the children and move to the last floor. A destroyer drone smashed its way through the remaining chairs and cupboards placed at the top of the stairs. A 5th infantry soldier stepped forward to push him back, but he was too strong and quick, blocking him and bringing his axe down on his neck. The other destroyer drones pushed on through behind him, snorting and snarling as they moved.

One soldier shot the nearest drone to him, but he kept on coming. The force of this half-beast, half-human creature impacting him was enough to take the soldier into the wall behind. The destroyer drone bit at his face and neck; his nearest comrade tried to pull the drone off but was speared in the back as more drones followed up the stairs.

Arthur told the others to move to the last floor; he put his rifle over his shoulder, and as the first drone soldier came into their room, he was hit with an arrow in the chest. Arthur drew another arrow; some of the soldiers left with them used their bayonets to make a hole in the wall. Once it was big enough to climb through, they rushed through it. Arthur called to his mum and Elin to join them. Reginald brought up the rear behind them, and simultaneously, three destroyer drones burst into the room. "Keep going through. I'll hold them back." Arthur looked at him as he lowered himself through the hole.

The first one came at Reginald, thinking he would smash him like the other soldiers who had got in its way. Reginald quickly brought his axe around as the destroyer drone came charging forward. He side-stepped and caught the beast across his chest. It sent blood spraying up from his wound and off the end of the axe head. In the same motion, Reginald pushed the drone into the wall to his left.

The other two let out growls and came at him with anger. He held his axe tight with his left hand and did not swing until they were on him. The drone to his left plunged his spear into Reginald's stomach, and the one on his right swung his axe towards Reginald's neck but missed. The drone did not see the dagger in Reginald's right hand, as the momentum of his attack carried him into the knife, which was rammed into his chest.

The destroyer drone with the spear lifted him up and held him aloft. The drone with the dagger in his stomach was crouching on the floor alongside the one with an open chest wound, who was gingerly trying to get to his feet.

"You have done well, old man." The destroyer drone laughed at him, hanging there. "But you are all weak."

Reginald let his arms flop to the side. The pain of being held on the spear almost caused him to pass out. He gritted his teeth, tasting his own blood in his mouth.

"If you destroy everything, nothing will be left worth living for." Reginald looked into the beast's eyes, searching for humanity.

He answered with his deep, gravelly voice, "Ha, I'm not part of this world anymore; I'm different. I do not care for humans. There will be one true leader, and he is named Nazar."

The pool of blood on the floor below was the life draining out of Reginald. He knew his time was passing but wanted to act one final time. Strapped to his belt were two small hunting knives he had been given on a hunting trip with his father. As the destroyer drone began to lower him, he summoned his final strength, pulled out both knives and quickly plunged them into the neck of the drone. The beast looked at him in the eye for a second, then collapsed onto his knees. They both maintained eye contact until the end.

Arthur made sure Naomi and Florence had moved up the last staircase. Tom was helping soldiers and civilians get to the top. "Arthur, we have to fall back." He loaded a bullet into the chamber, checked his ammo pouch, and found roughly ten bullets left.

Arthur could see soldiers still fighting; he was waiting for Reginald. "He's not coming, Arthur." Tom's voice was calm but assured. Arthur gripped his rifle tight and turned to move up the final staircase. They helped him move over the chairs, tables, and boxes that were being piled up. Rebecca came over and hugged him. Looking around the room, he could see the wounded and frightened children in the corner. Elin was looking out the window and could see a selection of drones and destroyer drones coming in with a white flag.

Leading them were Richard Conway and General Eltsina. They had not tried to storm the last staircase and lingered out of firing range. Richard changed his size as he approached the last floor. He sent three drones in with the white flag to the bottom of the stairs to see if they were shot at. Once he believed it was safe, he appeared at the bottom of the stairs.

"Lower your weapons, please. I come in peace." His voice was gravelly due to his shape change.

Rebecca leant over the banister. "Why would we trust you and your army of death?"

He let himself reduce to his human form. "Think of your children; surrender now, and we will let you all leave here as prisoners of Nazar."

Rebecca turned around with an apprehensive face; Elin looked at her. Arthur and Tom also looked at her. The soldiers around them spoke amongst themselves.

Richard Conway called to say they would have five minutes to decide. He advised them to look out of the windows; he would not wait any longer than five minutes. With that, he turned and left the building with General Eltsina. Rebecca rushed to the nearest window on her side. She scoured along the road but could not see anything at first. Eventually, though, she did see a cannon being wheeled into position.

Then, drones appeared in a line carrying burning torches. Richard Conway stood by the cannon with General Eltsina.

The remaining soldiers and civilians gathered at the top of the stairs; some thought they should fight on, others looked at the children and shook their heads. Rebecca looked at Emily and Arthur, and her heart sank. Their faces looked tired and unsure of what was going to happen. The worried eyes followed each other around the group. One soldier said he could create a distraction whilst the families try and run for it. Elin said she didn't think they had a choice but to surrender. They would fire the cannon at the building and then burn it.

Rebecca sighed; she knew they had no choice. If the children were not with them, maybe a distraction and escape, but there were too many drones and rebels. A show of hands was quickly carried out to see the general consensus. Surrender won. They took away the barriers they had made at the top of the stairs and slowly began to file down to the ground floor. Vincent wanted to check on his dear old friend. He was helped by Private Baker and Private Hawkins to his body. He nodded his head in respect for having killed two destroyer drones. He knelt beside his body for a second and said a prayer. Then, he was helped up and assisted down the stairs.

Two priests stood on the ground floor. Both looked smug and happy to see the defeated group pass them. The children who had parents with them held onto their hands, and those who didn't held onto the soldier's hands.

They were told to lay down any weapons on the ground outside the building.

General Conway stood further away, talking with several officers. General Eltsina stood much closer to the building. She looked at the children as they passed her. She smiled, which sent shivers down the children's spines. Emily was walking with Rebecca when her eyes fell upon General Eltsina. The general knelt down to Emily, brushing away her matted hair from her face. Rebecca tensed up but knew she had to play it calm.

"You have a pretty face, young lady." Her Austrian accent was strong, but her English was clear enough.

Emily looked at her. "Why are you attacking us?"

The General was taken aback by her question, "It's because we will all soon serve the emperor of the world."

"What happens if he fails?"

She made sure she was on the same level as Emily; her eyes were a sharp blue and complemented her doll-like face, but Emily noticed her lips were red and a little dry. She had gloves on, so she removed the glove from her right hand. Then, forcefully grabbed Emily by the jaw, "Watch what you say, stupid little girl" Her grip on Emily's face was hard; she stayed brave and tried not to show anything. Rebecca began to clench her fists. General Eltsina saw this and quickly remarked that she should hit her and see what happens. She let go of Emily's face, almost pushing her backwards.

She looked for Rebecca's reaction. "That's right, nothing. I could feed her to the dead and make you watch."

Rebecca looked down at Emily and smiled in a cool, calming way. "Apologise, Emily, to the officer."

"I'm sorry. I'm sure your emperor will rule the world."

General Eltsina smiled and then spoke in Russian. Four destroyer drones came over and stood by her. Two of them grabbed Emily. She might have been small, but she kicked and fought hard. Rebecca struck the nearest drone to her. She then pushed the other back and managed to wrestle one of them off Emily. Holding onto her arm, she looked at the General. "She apologised!! Please let her go. Please, please, please."

She drew her revolver and pointed it at Rebecca. "I can end both of you now; your actions will kill you."

Rebecca could hear hissing, snapping, and heavy breathing. Two infected rebels led a group of seven to eight flesh-eaters towards them. Rebecca looked around. Arthur was readying himself. He looked at Naomi, and she looked back. Rebecca shook her head.

The rebels brought the dead close; five more destroyer drones joined them. General Eltsina slowly put back on her glove and looked at the prisoners.

"You're about to see a lesson I'm sure you will all remember." The destroyer drones let Rebecca grab Emily and then stood in a circle around them. Emily held her mum tight. She had her teddy bear in one hand. The rebels brought the flesh-eaters into the circle.

"You will learn that our great leader can show mercy when he wants to! But he will not tolerate any form of disobedience; this mother and daughter have shown that they care for the old ways; these old ways will help you meet your maker." She laughed out loud; her laugh was a cackle, like a hyena calling out over the savanna. Drone soldiers gathered around the prisoners, their rifles pointed at them. Rebecca looked at Emily and then let her eyes focus on the dead in front of her. She took several breaths and dug her feet into the soil beneath her.

The General raised her left hand.

"Stop, General." Richard Conway walked towards them.

"I recognise you; I believe your father was an officer in the Grenadier Guards."

Rebecca's heart was racing.

"He was how do you know that."

"Well, I was looking forward to my officer disciplining you and your daughter" He looked at Eltsina and smiled, "She was doing the right thing, but we might have something here more valuable than we realised."

He walked over to Rebecca and Emily.

Rebecca studied his face, and something twigged inside her.

"I have seen your face before. Weren't you a British officer?" Rebecca's face looked disgusted, although she tried to hide it.

Richard looked pleased that he had been recognised from a previous engagement. "That was a long time ago, Rebecca; it is Rebecca. He flicked his hair back; that would mean you are worth more than all these people here." He pointed around at all of the poor souls standing there. Richard did not know Arthur was her son; he was happy to have Major Hayward's wife and daughter. All he could think about was how Nazar would reward him. He would like to be the king of England or even America.

While he daydreamed, a tall, gangly man arrived. His shape and features were distinct, centered on his pointed nose. A foul odour surrounded him. When Rebecca saw him, he smiled, exposing his crooked teeth. She knew it was the same man she had seen in Albany and who had led the rebel attack on them.

Richard saw him staring at Rebecca and introduced him as a French regional Priest, William Boucher. He pointed out his effectiveness in getting information and ensuring people got in line. The man lurched towards Rebecca.

"It would have been a different story if I had found you before they did." His tongue was split like a snake, giving his voice a lisp. His eyes were completely dark, with no white surface at all. He smiled again and reached out to touch Rebecca's hair. She grabbed his forearm.

"Now, we need her in one piece, her child. Well, that depends on how she behaves." General Conway turned to face the others.

"I have no real need for the prisoners at the moment. I cannot put them straight to work as we are behind enemy lines." Boucher leaned in, as did General Eltsina, toward General Conway. They spoke and laughed a little.

Richard couldn't hide his excitement.

"Look, normally I would let the dead feed on your wretched souls, or the drones have their way with the fine women folk in this group, spoils of war and all of that, but I am actually in a fulfilled mood. The wounded will be left here to fend for themselves. The able-bodied and, of course, our prized asset, will be coming to meet her new lord."

He clapped his hands, and the rebels and drones separated the survivors. Vincent hugged Florence and Naomi, calling on Rebecca to look after them the best she could. Arthur and Tom could only give him a nod, as their cover still had not been exposed. Once separated, Richard Conway stepped forward.

"Consider yourselves fortunate; in the name of Nazar, your wounded have been spared." He walked over to them, sitting on the floor or leaning against each other. "Remember to tell others of this day, for woe betide those who forget his generosity."

He then turned and beckoned over a corporal from his drone unit. "Bring my horse. We must move quickly; the fighting could have alerted local units."

"Sir, what about our wounded?"

He shrugged his shoulders as if to say Why was he being asked this question.

"Put them in the nearest building, and they can ambush the next enemy soldiers that come along, whether they are alive or dead." With that, the corporal was prompted to get his horse quicker now.

The corporal did not question it further; he knew most of the wounded could not move and would turn once passed. He had been forced to join Nazar's army from Poland, and then he was infected. He was given a serum every year to stop him from turning. Rumours were rife that this was running low since the destruction of the meteorite. Either way, he kept his thoughts to himself; he did not want to join Nazar's forces, but the young men and women were told to join or watch their families being slaughtered.

General Eltsina had taken what wagons she could find from the allies; she would have made them all walk, but she wanted to move quicker as they were behind enemy lines. The prisoners were sat in these wagons, hands tied and told not to speak. Tom and Arthur were split from Rebecca and Emily. Naomi and Florence were seated in another wagon; Elin was, fortunately, sitting close to Rebecca; they could not speak but tried to communicate with their eyes and bodies.

A column of mounted drones was riding at the very back of the convoy. General Conway and General Eltsina were at the front of that group. Behind them were around twenty or more destroyer drones. The rebels were riding on either side of the wagons. Some had put on US soldier uniforms. They would ride out to meet any scouts or Allied forces and help not draw too much attention to the wagons until they reached their own lines.

They travelled through the night and did not stop to rest or eat. The next day, they passed a vast battlefield, and many bodies lay strewn across it; most were Nazar's forces. Those sitting at the back could see the aftermath of the battle; their faces lit up on seeing so many enemy casualties. They travelled for a further couple of miles until the column was brought to a halt.

Richard Conway told them they could all get out to stretch their legs. Guards were placed all around the wagons. He said anyone who felt compelled to run would be caught and fed to the flesh-eaters. Most of the flesh-eaters had been wiped out in the attack on the town, but some had been put in a wagon. They were tied together and snapped at the air when they got the scent of the prisoners.

"You probably got your hope up seeing so many of our brave soldiers lying dead in the fields. Do not be mistaken. A lot of them will be walking again." He had a huge smile on his face, "Your new emperor has foreseen your desire to fight the unknown and not embrace this new world. This is a forlorn hope and will only end in failure." He continued to ride his horse backwards and forwards as the prisoners stretched their legs.

General Eltsina looked at Rebecca and Emily and smiled at them. It was not a pleasant smile. It had insinuations behind it. She knew what lay ahead and was happy to see them going in that direction. Rebecca averted her eyes; she did not want to give her an excuse to do something to Emily. She continued to ride around the group, almost looking for a reaction.

Pvt Baker and Hawkins whispered, but this did not escape her eye. She brought her horse between them. "Who said you could talk?" Both the young soldiers looked at her.

She whistled over to four destroyer drones.

"Tie their hands and make them walk behind the wagons."

Both soldiers wanted to tell her something to her face, but knew it would only get worse for them to talk back. They had to quickly take water from a ladle before the water carrier was told to move on. The group was ushered back into the wagons. Tom and Arthur filtered behind Rebecca and Emily, Naomi and Florence. Arthur managed to touch Emily's hand; she looked around, concerned, but raised her eyes in an affectionate way. Rebecca had warned Emily not to give away Arthur, her brother; she took this seriously.

As they climbed back into the wagons, an elderly gentleman was being helped up. Arthur lent out to help him make the last bit, but a female rebel stepped forward and kicked him in the back of the leg. He tried in vain to steady himself, but another well-placed kick in his lower back forced him to fall down. Another rebel, a middle-aged man with missing front teeth, joined her. He cackled at the situation.

"You gonna get up, old man?"

The old man looked around. He had anger and fear in his eyes.

"If you stopped kicking him, he would be able to get up, prick." Arthur lost himself for a split second. As soon as he said it, he knew he shouldn't have.

The female rebel looked at her counterpart. "You ain't letting him get away with that, are you?" He looked confused; he kicked the old man again. The female rebel started to slide her hand to her Smith and Western; Rebecca saw this from where she was sitting. As she drew the revolver, Rebecca leapt from the wagon, knocking the male rebel to the side; she landed on top of the woman. Unleashing pent-up anger, she struck her in the face; blood spurted out of her nose. Arthur jumped down to stop his mother from hitting her again.

Two drone soldiers rode over to the commotion. They quickly withdrew their rifles and told them to stay still. The female rebel got to her feet and pulled out a knife.

"I'm gonna cut that pretty face up really good. "

Rebecca pushed Arthur behind her as the rebel moved forward with blood dripping from her nose.

"Stop; this is not the time to kill her." General Conway was sitting on his horse, the September sun making his silhouette glow. "Rebecca, I cannot keep saving you like this." His face turned aggressive. "You're starting to be a problem like your husband, and believe me, my lord would love to see him again." With that, he kicked on his horse.

He told the rebels to move to the last wagon and not go near her again. The female rebel, with blood running from her nose, spat on the soil beneath her feet but was led away by her comrade.

Rebecca and Arthur helped the old man into the back of the wagon. He looked at them with gratitude in his eyes. Rebecca looked at Arthur with a scornful expression. Arthur tried to look sorry as he helped the old man onto the wagon bench. Rebecca was proud of him inside, but knew this was not the time to take risks. None of these rebels or drones would think twice about killing him.

Naomi rubbed Arthur's arm and squeezed his wrist. She let go once the drone soldiers got into the wagon. Pvt Baker and Pvt Hawkins were tied to the back of the wagon and began to walk behind it as they moved forward. Everyone felt sorry for them, particularly when it started to rain. The drones laughed as they slipped on the mud and were pulled along in some sections of the journey before they could upright themselves. The further they moved back towards Boston, the more evident the heavy fighting had happened.

Some villages were still smouldering, with houses riddled with bullets. There were piles of bodies in fields; some had fresh eaters around them, eating what they could. These would have been fresh kills, as the dead fed on the living. Nazar wanted to show the general population what happened to those who fought back. Some soldiers would be executed; others would be put to work for his war machine.

Many poor souls were being marched towards Boston; they looked up at those taken in the wagons. Every face told a story of despair; Emily nuzzled into her mother's side upon seeing this and closed her eyes as she moved along the muddy track. Arthur put his hand near Naomi's; she looked frightened, as did Tom and Florence. The problem was that Arthur knew what was coming, and for the younger ones, you should be scared. He, of course, kept that to himself.

They travelled for another hour before shouts and calls went up in Russian. The number of drone soldiers increased. The defensive barriers started to appear. Packs of wolves with long limbs could be seen in pens; there were also sizeable wooden holding pens for the dead. They could not see the full scale of it due to the restrictions of sitting in the wagon. A lagorian stood chained to a tree; some Europeans had seen them before, but the American soldiers and citizens who hadn't looked on in horror. Its size was enough to cause doubt about the chances of success in defeating Nazar's army of death.

The longer they travelled, the more and more hope started to fade. Soldiers had been tied along the roadside and left to starve to death. Eventually, they passed two wooden gates; work was being undertaken everywhere; wood was being cut, and animals were cooked on open fires. There was drinking and fighting breaking out everywhere. Richard rode to the front and brought the convoy to a halt. He ordered the soldiers to escort the prisoners out of the wagons. They were screaming at them to move quickly; Pvt Baker and Pvt Hawkins were exhausted and had open sores on their wrists from walking behind the wagons. Both were told to join the others.

General Conway stood next to General Eltsina and told the two priests who had arrived to greet them that they must go and grab the women and child waiting in the wagon. Elin and the others looked on as Rebecca and Emily were escorted from the group. Arthur wanted to reach out to them both, but so many eyes were watching them. Rebecca just looked at him and smiled. Emily had tears in her eyes but stayed strong to her mother's word and did not call out her brother's name as they were led away. Naomi squeezed Arthur's hand tight; she could see the anguish on his face. Florence was comforted by Tom; she was worried about her father and the loss of Reginald. Tom said Vincent was better away from this place, and they would escape.

They were then told to line up and report to the workhouse. A mixture of priests and rebel guards escorted them towards a forest nearby. The people they passed looked broken. They did not even raise their eyes to look in their direction; they just kept working. Different smells wafted around the camp, some strong and pungent, others of freshly cooked meat. The group had not eaten for a day; they had had water, but they all wanted to taste food.

On the edge of the forest, they were greeted by a round woman. She introduced herself and welcomed them to the new world, sounding like she had an American accent.

"My job is to get you working for the greater good." She had a whip in her left hand.

"If you fail to work hard enough, you will be dealt with. Does everybody understand?"

There was a quiet yes.

"I cannot hear you speak up, or someone will be shot." She said this with a smile, showing her black teeth.

A strong "Yes" followed.

"Good. Now go to the wooden sheds and eat something quickly. We need some rocks loaded onto wagons before you can rest tonight."

They followed a short, mousey-haired woman to where they would eat and sleep. She said she had been a prisoner there for four weeks and helped build the wooden huts. They looked fresh outside but were grubby inside due to the heavy rain and mud that had spread everywhere. There were a few stoves in each hut, but they were all overcrowded, and with the winter to come, the future arrivals would have to fight to be near the stoves.

The short-haired woman said her name was Norma and told them to line up to get their broth. The queues were quiet, and rebel guards watched over each line.

"I'm worried for my mum and sister." Arthur felt sick in his stomach, but Naomi, Tom and Florence supported him.

"Your mother is tough and will be clever to ensure they both are ok."

It helped calm him down. Their presence was encouraging and reassuring, and it meant he would not do anything on the spur of the moment until they had understood the situation first.

Rebecca and Emily were led along a well-guarded path. All eyes looked at them as they walked down it. General Conway and General Eltsina had a spring in their step as they led from the front. Standing outside a large, impressive tent were several Destroyer drones and four Riders of the North. The Generals stopped and waited for one of the destroyer drones to enter the tent. He quickly came out and then ushered them in.

Rebecca squeezed Emily's hand and kissed her on the head as they walked behind General Conway. The entrance to the tent was through a long canvas tunnel with lanterns hanging from metal poles every meter or so; the light from these lanterns caused shadows to reflect and dance around them as they walked towards the main entrance. Emily's eyes followed each one, intrigued and nervous inside. The smell of burning oil made her breathe in through her mouth. There was a curtain pulled aside as they entered the large tent. It had many sections, and her eyes looked around for movement. Rebecca held her hand tightly.

"Welcome," The voice was dark and rough.

Something was talking from deep in the shadows; the voice was intimidating.

"Take a seat."

Rebecca and Emily were shown a sofa which was loaded with cushions. Richard Conway just stood there and said nothing.

"So pretty, so, so pretty." This time, a female voice could be heard from the darkness, with a slight hiss.

"Step out of the darkness so I can see who I'm talking to." Rebecca was strong, but she was scared inside.

Emerging from a corner of the tent was a large man. His physique was enough to make most take a step backwards.

"You will know my name, and I believe I have met your husband." He paused and pulled on his long beard.

"He took a lot away from me." He almost smiled to acknowledge what Charles had done, but could not hide his anger for long. He moved towards Rebecca and Emily, almost not seeing a chair in his way. His leg brushed it aside as if it did not exist. Standing before Emily and Rebecca, he looked down at them both.

"What to do with his family." Nazar almost laughed as he spoke.

Emerging from the shadows behind him was Oksana.

"I could imagine a hundred things, but not all are nice." As she said this, she brought her hand to her lips and looked at Emily.

"Oksana, there is plenty of time for that after he's dead." Nazar also looked at Emily.

"What is your name, little girl?"

Emily looked at his hands and long, sharp nails; his eyes were as dark as night as she lowered herself back into the cushions behind her. He then lent forward.

"What is your name, little girl? Answer, or I'll cut off your mother's hand."

Tears ran down her cheeks. "My name is Emily; please do not cut off her hand."

"See how a little push works wonders in this world."

Rebecca edged herself closer to her daughter.

"Why would you care about us? My husband is fighting in England, and we do not know when he will return."

Nazar nodded his head. "Yes, yes, yes, I know the allied forces have attacked my country. They will pay for that in time, but you know your husband came to my lands and destroyed something precious to me and my family."

He covered his eyes with his left hand. Then uncovered them and looked at Emily.

"What would you do if you were me? Forget it happened. Show mercy? Show compassion?" Nazar walked around them as they sat in his tent. Oksana stood by a small round table. Sitting on the table was a jug of water and a cloth. She started to wash her face and hands.

"Emperors who rule must always make hard decisions." He clapped his hands

Four destroyer drones came in. Reichard Conway stood back.

Rebecca began to stand as they came in. Nazar looked at them and then at Emily. They moved for her in a flash. Rebecca let out a scream, withdrew a hidden knife, and lunged for Nazar; she managed to thrust it into his chest, causing him to move backwards. Oksana did not move.

He grabbed her hand, helping her push the knife in deeper. Her eyes looked at him; he did not smile or say anything. He slowly began to increase his grip on her hand; the pressure was so powerful she let out a cry; he then redrew the knife and spun her around. Holding her tight so she could not move, he ensured she could see the destroyer drones holding Emily. Emily kicked and fought hard, but they were too strong, and she was carried over to a table beside the tent.

Rebecca continued to struggle and fight.

"I like your drive." Nazar was too strong for her; she felt his warm blood seeping into her hair and down her back. She couldn't control her emotions as she watched Emily being held on the table. Her screams and calls for her mother were too much for Rebecca. She begged and pleaded for them not to do anything.

Oksana looked at her and smiled.

"A bit late for that, don't you think? " Her Russian accent came across thicker than before. She was carrying a small box over to where they were holding Emily.

She looked at Rebecca as she slowly opened it. "You will never look at your husband in the same way now." She lowered her hand into the box and pulled out a scalpel.

"Please, please, she's just a little girl. If you have to have your pound of flesh, take me."

Oksana spoke in Russian to the soldiers. One tied a cloth around Emily's mouth, and then all four held her down.

"You should never interfere with what you do not understand." She then raised Emily's top, lifting it to expose her ribs. "Please be silent, or this could go a lot worse for her."

Rebecca felt faint, but Nazar held her in place. She tried to make eye contact with Emily and told her how much she loved her.

Oksana began to cut her ribs. The blood began to flow onto the table, and Emily was crying in pain. Oksana stopped cutting and cleaned the scalpel with a cloth. She then pulled out a glass bottle and a syringe, placed the syringe in the bottle, and drew out the liquid. Oksana smiled at Emily and brushed her cheek before injecting the liquid into her ribs.

"There, you see, it wasn't that bad."

Oksana closed the box and told one of the soldiers to call the army doctor. He arrived and was instructed to stitch the wound. Once this was complete, she let Emily return to her mother. Emily ran to her mother, holding her side, and they both fell into each other's arms.

"What have you done to her?" Rebecca was crying, but her anger travelled through her trembling voice.

Nazar stood looking at Rebecca.

"She will now need us; she has become one of us." Oksana placed the box back into a large chest near the bed. Rebecca looked at her, trying to understand what that meant.

"She is infected, just like many of our drone soldiers." Nazar started to move towards a south-facing exit from the tent. "Your husband will pay for what he did, and so will you." He then left the tent.

Oksana came over to where they were standing, causing Emily to cower. Rebecca had to control her rage. She wanted to attack her, but she knew it would result in retribution that she would regret. It wasn't the time or place for such an action. Oksana stood close to Rebecca and brushed her hair back, revealing her neck. She then lowered her mouth to the back of her neck and kissed her.

"What are you doing? Get off me?"

Oksana laughed and moved back.

"You're a beautiful woman; why should you suffer for what your husband did? I could take you to a place where you've probably never been before."

Rebecca looked at her in utter disbelief.

"You have just infected my daughter with poison. Do you even know what you're saying or suggesting?"

Oksana shrugged her shoulders. "This is the new world; get used to it or die, and in your case, death will not be the end of it. The first six months are free. She handed over the serum in a small bottle.

"You must earn the next one; don't play hard to get." With that, Oksana left the tent.

Rebecca and Emily stood in the large tent, holding each other. Richard Conway was still in there, pouring himself a goblet of wine.

"That went very well, don't you think?"

Emily had calmed down and sat on the sofa.

"At what point did you surrender your soul to them, Richard? You were known for being a fine officer, and had the world before you?" What has become of you to fall this low?" Rebecca shook her head.

"What do you know of this new world? Nazar has blown away anything that stands in his way. The British army could not stop him, so what would my sacrifice mean in the greater picture?"

"Your sacrifice would mean the same as the rest of us fighting against evil."

"Rebecca, the world has changed forever; sacrifice would not have got me here; it would have given me nothing but death. A name mentioned only for a short while, lost in the new world." He drank from the goblet.

She shook her head in a despairing way.

"You have a chance to survive with your daughter. If you stay on his good side, maybe he can cure you; I've seen them reward some of the best soldiers with it." He finished his drink and called for the guards with wine still on his lips.

"Don't be a fool and try and fight against something you cannot beat."

He turned and walked out. Emily looked up at her mother, already looking weaker as the poison entered her petite body.

"Mummy, I'm feeling tired."

"It's ok, little one; you can rest soon."

Guards came in behind Richard Conway as he left. They went to Rebecca and Emily and aggressively told them to move. Rebecca carried Emily in her arms as they moved through the long tunnel leading out of the tent. Standing next to a flaming torch was a lady dressed in a black uniform.

"My name is Claudia; I am the commanding officer of the prison guards. You will not be staying in the main prison block. You have been chosen to work light duties; consider yourself lucky."

Rebecca gave a vacant look, then hugged Emily.

"Take them to their quarters."

Claudia turned and started to walk away from them. Rebecca wondered where she was from. Her skin was olive-coloured, but she didn't seem to have a Mediterranean or Russian accent. She had long black hair and was a beautiful woman. She wondered what had enticed her to join the Nazar forces. Was she motivated the same as Richard, or was something else making her join?

Chapter 31

"Major, we've landed a search party, and the ports and shores are in allied hands."

Charles looked along the shore. There was no smoke or gunfire, which felt comforting.

Captain Somersett stepped forward, "It's good to see Charleston. I have mixed memories of the place, but this is a future we can build together if we win."

Charles put his hand on Captain Somersett's shoulder. "We have to"

Texas moved over to them. "It's good to be home," he paused, "I think." All of the soldiers and officers had troubled thoughts.

Captain Steinberg led the first group of soldiers into rowing boats and headed to shore. Charles watched them land just outside the port. Even when the search party gave the all-clear, they did not want to sail directly into the ports if the search group had been duped. Captain Steinberg would lead forty men into the docks and do a large sweep before they would sail in.

Charles thought about his family and hoped they were safe from the front line. He had to cast aside those thoughts and concentrate on being back in America. He was grateful they had crossed the Atlantic in one piece, and the soldiers' spirits were high. The battle for Great Britain was still raging, but it felt like a small victory to many men. Charles knew Nazar expected and planned for that invasion; the hordes they encountered would take years to deal with, but these were his own thoughts, and he knew the army would have felt some encouragement from fighting back.

A flare went up, and the ships began to sail towards the docks. The soldiers still manned the guns and were on top deck, ready to be called to action if needed. Charles's eyes looked along the docks as some people had gathered to watch the fleet coming in. His heart jumped a few times as he thought he had seen Rebecca and the children, but unfortunately, each time was soon met with disappointment.

Once they had landed, the senior officers of the invasion army met with several American and allied commanding generals. The Allied forces were being sent to a camp outside Charleston, but there was a meeting taking place at Drayton Hall. Major Hayward was asked to join the other officers there to discuss the war effort in America. You could feel the tension in the air as they passed through the town. People were still going about their business, but you could sense that the war was growing closer; reports that Boston had fallen and the American forces being pushed back had sent shock waves around the country.

The forces around Drayton Hall were sizable; this was to protect the senior generals from rebel attacks. Two buildings flanked this impressive Hall. Soldiers stood guard outside the buildings, and cannons pointed outwards in all directions.

Charles went inside and joined the others. Once everyone was present, Brigadier Thomas Baker stepped forward, and Major General Bartholomew Green joined him.

"Gentlemen, this is a grave time for us all." Brigadier Baker was clean-shaven, with his hair swept from right to left. He was clear, well-spoken, and had a calm tone to his voice.

He was not an oversized man—five feet ten at most—but had seen action in the Civil War and was known for organising an army.

"We have reports that Boston has fallen, and Nazar's forces are taking New York and pushing into Pennsylvania. Most of our forces are gathering on the West Coast and planning to meet him with extreme force. Make no mistake about it: this is a war for the very soul of the world." He paused and looked around the room.

"We have officers here from Europe and around the globe. Some have faced this enemy head-on in large battles; so far, they've worn us down with attrition, using the dead as a wall to soak up bullets and shells. They have huge numbers of infantry, un-god-ley creatures and a way of conquering everything that stands in their path."

He leaned forward, picked up his coffee mug, and took a sip.

"I would like to introduce Major General Green."

He was short in stature, with receding hair, but he had a presence. On the left-hand side of his face, there were scars; they ran from his ear to his jaw. Charles wondered if they were from fighting or something else.

"Our armies have fought well, but they are still advancing. Washington will be fighting for her very survival." He looked around the room.

"Nazar has a force which could be double ours. He has got into the souls of many of our own people. If America falls, the world will fall."

He then turned and walked over to a map pinned to the wall behind him.
He took out a marker stick and pointed to the map.

"We have to slow them down as we try and work out where we can best face them full on, " he pointed out on the map using the stick. We will slow them down here." The non-Americans did not know America's geography as well, so he said it would be Harrisburg.

"We will hope to kill as many as we can when they cross the Susquehanna River. I would love to say this will be a decisive battle, but they outnumber us ten to one, at a guess. He is still growing his forces; we believe his mobile Cavalry units have not fully landed yet."

There was a collective sigh, a realisation that the task ahead would be difficult and possibly unachievable. No one spoke in those terms, but the mood was sombre. The general let the room digest the decision for a moment, then discussed their next move. He said they would be moving to Harrisburg as soon as the army was mobilised. He discussed how they would set up the defences at Harrisburg and which regiment would be stationed along different parts of the river.

Afterwards, tea and cake were served, with the officers mingling around the room. Captain Somersett and Captain Steinberg stayed close to the Major.

He was joined by his old friend and fellow veteran, Lt. Kiesl. They spoke about the war and how things have unfolded in America so far. He asked if he had heard anything about the army families in Boston and whether they had been evacuated to Canada, like many Europeans. Still, Charles shook his head, saying he was unsure. Lt Kiesl could see he was concerned with not knowing and tried to reassure him that they would see their loved ones soon. Charles understood the question was for himself as much as it was for Charles. The speed at which Nazar forces move would catch many out and lead to a lot of them being captured and either killed or put in work camps. Charles did not want to think about that; he had to focus on the job at hand.

After they had finished having tea and cake, Brigadier Thomas Baker gave a short speech. Charles felt he had the interest of the nation in his words. He would take his makeshift regiment to Harrisburg in the morning, and at some point, they would face his old enemy on the battlefield.

Charles looked around the room at the different officers; the Americans were in good spirits, the Allies a bit more subdued. They had fought and lost to this all-consuming force. Just as they were about to leave, an American officer entered the room. He was loud in apologising for his timekeeping. He had long blonde hair and a strong accent. Charles had heard of General Custer and what happened at the battle of Little Bighorn, and whilst General Custer was killed in action, he had inspired this officer.

He introduced himself as General Baxter Washington. He was tall but stocky. He liked the sound of his own voice and moved around the room, telling everyone he had the best Cavalry regiment in the United States Army. He had a full beard, which he liked to stroke as he spoke. Brigadier Baker and Major General Green were busy talking to themselves as General Washington strutted around, as he had already won the war single-handedly.

He stopped in front of the British officers.

"You will see how we deal with these invaders here in America." He smirked as he said this.

Charles looked him in the eyes.

"I pray that you are right."

"Why, you sound defeated already in your very words." His voice grew louder, exuding the smell of alcohol as he spoke. He paused, looking around the room and making sure his audience was attentive. "As an American, that is not something we think about; if we had thought like that, the British would still be our masters." He let out a deep belly laugh, but it did not get the full response he wanted. Some of the younger American officers smiled, but they were the ones who had not seen combat; the ones who had fought the enemy knew differently. This got his back up a bit.

"I suggest our allied friends do not carry that defeatist attitude into battle, or you will surely fall foul of the enemy blade." With that, he turned and left the room.

Charles looked at his officers. They did not say anything, but there was a concern that this general was in charge of the mobile cavalry units. He came across as brash and a risk-taker. In battle, you wanted to think the people making the decisions had some grasp of the enemy and their capabilities.

They left Drayton Hall and approached where the British invasion force had been waiting. "Do you think this is a good plan, Major?" Captain Steinberg looked at him as he said it, trying to gauge an open, honest response.

"Captain, with every hour that passes, Nazar moves closer to his goal."

He stopped short of a carriage summoned to take them to their units. "We know what he is capable of, but we have tried to stop him and failed. Maybe your nation is the nation to stop him finally."

Charles lifted himself into the carriage.

"I pray you are right, Major, but it will take her allies to help us see this through."

Charles nodded his head.

Chapter 32

Pvt Brown had snuck to see Heidi in the early hours. She was with the medical corps and resting with the other nurses. He awoke Heidi with coffee and asked if she wanted to take a short walk. It took her a few minutes to come around, and then she put on her nurses' uniform and followed John to a small thicket of Red Maples by a stream. They leaned against a tree and pressed against each other. Heidi took a sip of coffee and looked at the gentle, meandering stream.

"It's going to be a beautiful day, John, and I'm happy to have this moment." She leaned in and gave him a passionate kiss. "Be careful. I've heard from the injured Allied soldiers we're treating that Nazar's forces are two to three times bigger than what they were in Europe." John brushed her cheek and kissed her again.

"I've been lucky to have you through all this, and if we could run away and escape it, I probably would ask you to come with me." He looked her in the eyes. "There will be nowhere to run in the end; he is swallowing up the world."

Heidi had tears running down her cheeks. "I want to have a family with you." John started to well up as well.

I'm sure we will have it when we beat them. They pulled each other in tight. A bugle call broke the moment. Heidi held him tight, "A minute more won't hurt."

When they arrived back at the camp, there was much movement. Heidi kissed him again before letting him go to the Engineers. He looked back and placed his hand on his heart. She did the same.

The Engineers were mobilised to destroy bridges over the Susquehanna River; the Cumberland Valley Railroad Bridge was one, and the Walnut Street Bridge was another. They would target anything that would help slow the enemy's advance.

Charles sat in his tent alone. He looked at the canvas sheets over the tent poles and his bed with the neatly tucked-in sheets. It took him back to Paris when he was separated from his family. Those dark demons were hard to bury in the back of his mind. He did not entertain the thought of them for long because he knew it would cloud his judgement.

A corporal said he had a fresh pot of tea with bread and jam.

After finishing his tea and bread, Charles fastened his tunic and went to his men and officers. The scouts had been bringing news that the defences were holding strong from New York to Philadelphia. The idea was to keep those cities as long as possible. The generals predicted Nazar's forces would try and swoop around the back of the cities, a bit like how the Zulus came at the British troops in a buffalo formation; the horns would encircle whatever force was in front of them, and the main bulk would then wipe them out.

Harrisburg would not have been seen as the city to stop them, but it was in-visualized that they could inflict many casualties as they crossed the river. Charles was debriefed on what they wanted from his Engineers and soldiers with him. The Bridges were to be destroyed once the forces had retreated across them.

The officers falling back would update them on how close the enemy was. Charles knew this would be a tight call, as the soldiers and civilians left on the other side would face the wrath of the invading force.

When they arrived at Harrisburg, the weather was bright; the defence works were being prepared all along the banks of the Susquehanna River. On the other side of the city, machine guns were being hoisted into houses, and cannons were put in strategic locations. The main reports were a couple of regiments of drone soldiers, and cavalry was coming their way. This force had rebels, razor tooths, and possibly roughback razor tooths. It also had some Riders of the North and Priests. A sizeable force of flesh-eaters was herded towards Harrisburg, but all reports still indicated the main force was looking at taking New York.

There was still a flow of civilians leaving the city, heading West. The Senate had moved to San Francisco, and large refugee camps were springing up along the coast. Mexico had tried to help but was worried it would be drawn into the war. Nazar's forces had not attacked Mexico, and they did not want to send soldiers, as it would be seen as a sign of them choosing a side.

Charles arrived with his force and began to get to work. Hosah, along with Corporal Heinz and Texas, was instructed to ride to the city's edge and be the eyes on the enemy movements. He wanted his own men to guide him when the bridges should be destroyed, so they could maximise the time the retreating soldiers would get.

It was a sunny Autumn morning, the men working in their shirts as they dug ditches and prepared defences. Charles sent engineers onto the bridges to prepare dynamite for when they would be destroyed. Tension was evident in the air, which was ramped up when heavy cannon fire could be heard. It was distant, but a reminder they were closing in. A lot of the soldiers stopped to look across the river, and even though the enemy wasn't there, it made them double their efforts.

Chapter 33

"The reports are coming in, my sire. They have fortified New York and Philadelphia."

"Good work, Priestess Arnoult. We are closing in on Harrisburg."

She smiled on hearing the praise, moving closer, her body rubbing against his.

"Can I be rewarded for my efforts?"

Nazar looked around at the soldiers marching by.

"You are playing a dangerous game, but I like it."

He led her towards an embankment and then into a woodland edge. The canopy of trees overshadowed the sun's light, making it darker the further they went in.

The Priestess followed behind Nazar, moving through the woods where the dead were. They did not venture near Nazar or her, but she was still cautious of them. She muttered in French under her breath. He turned and pressed her against an oak tree, then began to kiss her neck, working his way to her lips. She embraced and kissed him back aggressively; she bit him on the lip, making him smile. They began tearing each other's clothes off and made love under the tree. When they had finished, Nazar got up and walked naked into the open glade. Priestess Arnoult followed him, and they both stood there on a mound, watching the dead being led past them by Priests on horseback.

The sounds and movement of this marching army excited Nazar. The Priestess could see his eyes light up, and she stood close to him.

"It's a powerful sight, my lord."

She got a look back, which instantly made her fear for her life, but his eyes relaxed.

"It is a powerful sight, Eveline; they are marching to defeat our enemy." Nazar carried on looking at the army of dead trudging along, soulless and un-waving in their search for fresh meat. The Priests did not even look in their direction, nor did the destroyer drones close by. Eveline wanted to come closer to him, but did not dare to move. A Priest riding in their direction was quickly brought into action, "fetch some gowns for us now."

He turned and raced towards a column of wagons being pulled to the side of the flesh-eaters.

After speaking to the driver, he dismounted and climbed into the back of the wagon. He found two long furs, probably taken from a manor house during their advance into America.

With haste, he returned to Nazar and Eveline, keeping his eyes focused on Nazar. He handed them over. Nazar flicked his wrist, and the priest re-joined the herding of the dead.

Eveline slipped the fur on and pulled it around her body as the wind picked up. Nazar gave her his coat and walked down the slope. He stood next to the dead, looking at them as they moved past in different states of decay. He then ventured into the masses. Eveline looked on in horror; she knew he was linked to the dead but could not hide her fear of them. He pushed past them as they brushed against his naked body.

A large, dead male bumped into him, almost knocking him to the floor; Nazar took exception to this and bit into his throat, tearing out the rotten flesh and then spitting it into the sky. The large dead man moved past him and kept on walking.

"You are only truly alive when you are close to death, Eveline." He shouted at her as if drunk on the moment.

She smiled back, but it was a worried smile. She was frightened he would ask her to join him amongst the dead. Nazar pushed himself through the sprawling masses of bodies as they followed the priests. He went to join Eveline at the top of the mound and took the black fur she held in her arms.

"Take a small detachment and ride ahead to gather information."

She nodded her head and left Nazar standing, observing his army.

Chapter 34

"Naomi, wake up; we need to get nearer the queue for food." She took a while to wake, which worried Arthur; the guards would be in soon, and already a large, stocky woman they nicknamed the beast was taking a dislike to them. They always tried to avoid eye contact as she didn't need an excuse to lash out with her stick. Tom was with Florence, and they helped Naomi up; once she was up, they stood waiting for breakfast. The morning air was nipping at their legs and kept them standing close together.

They did not normally get breakfast, but Tom had seen the guards making the cooks bring in large pots. Everyone had to make a wooden bowl for use when eating. It was one of the first requirements if you wanted to eat: make yourself a decent bowl. Some of the prisoners were very skilled with woodwork and had helped out in many cases. Once they arrived at the front of the queue, they heard a familiar voice.

"Get a fucking move on." It was the beast; she was eating bread, which muffled her voice as she spoke.

The porridge was tipped into each bowl; they then moved to sit closer to the stove. As Naomi moved past the Beast, she looked at Naomi and pushed into her; Naomi dropped the bowl onto the wooden floor below. This brought a belly laugh from her, which angered Naomi. Arthur could see that she started to clench her fists, but before anything could unfold, he took her hand. He helped pick up the gloppy, thick porridge off the floor and put it back in the wooden bowl. Naomi whispered 'thank you' to Arthur.

The Beast was not impressed. She raised her stick and brought it down hard on Arthur's back. He winced in pain but did not react and kept on ushering Naomi away from her. She went to hit him again, but a guard called for assistance in moving someone who was too ill to work.

Naomi asked if he was ok and thanked him for helping her. Arthur smiled. "A little sore, but nothing like a bit of porridge couldn't heal." She smiled back at him, and they moved nearer to one of the stoves. Tom and Florence asked if Arthur was ok. He remarked they would have to try and escape soon before they'd become too weak to attempt it. He looked around at his friends and girlfriend. He could see their undernourished faces staring back. Nazar did not care about the cost of his work camps; humans were in abundance, and this was the best use of them. Once they had fulfilled their purpose, they either joined his cause or perished.

Later that morning, they were ordered into a work group to cut wood for Nazar's forces. Naomi was nearby, carrying logs that Tom and Florence were cutting up to place in a wagon. Arthur was sipping water out of a barrel using a ladle.

"Boy, don't drink too much." The Beast waddled her way over to them. "That water is meant for the real workers, and you four are definitely not them."

Arthur put the ladle down and started stacking the logs again. He said nothing and carried on working. Naomi walked over with more logs to give to Arthur. The beast stood there and kicked her from behind as she passed. She fell forward onto the woodland foliage, which helped to soften her fall.

"Ha ha silly bitch." She kicked her whilst she lay on the floor.

Naomi let out cries with every kick she received. Arthur was standing on top of the wagon and quickly turned when he heard her cries of pain.

"Please stop, she's done nothing wrong."

The Beast could detect anguish in his voice.

"Aww, young love." And kicked her again.

Naomi let out a scream and started to beg for her to stop.

Arthur reached down and picked up a long log.

The beast stopped for a moment and looked at him.

"Do you genuinely think you could strike me?" She let out a deep cackle. "There are guards all around these woods. They would shoot you before you could raise that log."

She looked at Arthur and smiled before preparing to kick Naomi again; the shallow thud made her arch forward, and her eyes looked up at Arthur in puzzlement before blood began to spill from her mouth. Standing behind her was Florence, her hands still gripping the handle of the axe sticking out of her back. The Beast tried to pull it out, but as she panicked, she saw Arthur swinging the log at her head. The blunt force knocked her down onto her knees. She muttered something as she was on all fours. Naomi had stood up, holding her ribs; she wiped the blood away from her brow. She looked at Arthur, who then delivered the final blow, causing the wood to break in half.

"We need to hide her body quickly." Tom was aware that they did not have much time. He asked Arthur to help grab her legs whilst he took her arms. Naomi helped with her torso. Florence took both her hands and levered out the axe. She brushed the soil and leaves on the floor to cover the blood from the beast.

Naomi went to where they had stacked logs a day previously. Making a hole through the middle, they put a rope around her ankles and dragged her in.

"We shouldn't cover the whole thing; maybe the long limbs or wolves will come and eat her?" Tom was talking and looking around as he did so.

"You're right, Tom, but we have to escape tonight. They will come looking for her later. We can pray for rain, which generally keeps them in longer." Arthur looked at the cloudy skies above.

Naomi nodded her head. "Thank you all; you saved my life." Tears rolling down her cheeks, Arthur came forward, hugged her gently and kissed her lips. He wiped away her tears. "I must see if I can get to my mother and sister." She agreed.

As they spoke, rain started to fall from the heavens.

Florence smiled, "We have a window."

They quickly loaded the wagon and turned it around to return to the camp. The rain was running off their soaked hair and wet clothes. A guard started to walk up to where they had been working.

He stopped the wagon. "Where is Beast?"

Naomi stepped forward. "She checked on us earlier in the day, then said she was going to go to the other side of the camp to get fresh chicken for you all to eat."

The guard, with no front teeth and matted black hair, spoke with a slight Spanish accent. "Ummm, sounds about right, letting others do her job, useless bitch." They just stared back at him.

"Well, don't just stand there; get a fucking move on."

The rain created small streams flowing down the muddy track. Tom allowed himself a glance over his shoulder. The guard looked like he would walk further up the track, but instead changed his mind. The rain was too heavy, and he rolled up his collars and called out to more prisoners to get their asses back to the camp.

As they rolled into camp, the guards walked to the hut to dry off and eat. The group went to the barn to unload the logs and then back to the hut. Arthur stopped them as soon as they were inside. He kissed Naomi and hugged Florence and Tom. "If I do not return, leave without me. Head to Colorado and seek shelter there.

"How will you get them to let you out of the camp to find them?" Naomi held his hand.

"I will tell them I am her son."

Tom let out a nervous laugh, which brought a puzzled look from the weary souls around them. "Arthur, they're not going to believe you, and if they do? What, then, how will you help them escape?" Tom paused. "Maybe you should just come with us now; your mother and sister are tough to have survived this long. They will find a way to escape."

Arthur looked at their concerned faces. "Hosah taught me how to move in the shadows, soft on foot and quick on feet. I have to try, at least."

They looked down, knowing he would not change his mind.

Naomi came forward and brushed his hair away from his face. "Please come back to me." She leant forward and kissed him long and hard on the lips. He kissed her back and said he would do his best not to become a Nazar spy, which received a strange look from Tom and Florence but a smile from Naomi.

The rain outside was strong enough for the guards to move inside, but one was lingering by the gate leading out to the rest of the vast camp. He went inside a small hut beside the gate, which sheltered him from the rain. Arthur planned to distract this guard and get the others out. Stables were nearby that kept horses for the guards to be mounted and prisoners to pull carts. As they made their way towards the hut, the heavens opened up even more, unleashing a torrential flow of water onto them.
"Follow me." Arthur led the way.

He approached the hut earnestly and called out to the guard as soon as he got close. He stood inside the wooden frame, looking at the rain dripping off their soaked clothes.

"What are you doing here? Get back to the huts. I'm not getting wet for you, useless kids; now move."

Arthur carried on standing there. "I have something to say."

The guard looked at him with growing perplexity. "I do not care what you have to tell me. It's late, and I'm tired. For the last time, move, or I will have you thrown in the pit."

"Nazar has my mother and sister in his tent."

"I'm sure he has a lot of ladies in his tent. What does that have to do with anything?"
The guard picked up his mug of coffee.

"My father is a British officer who has fought many times against your leader."

The guard shrugged his shoulders. "Boy, I don't give a damn about your story. I'm not going to get permission for you to meet Nazar." He started laughing to himself, "Stop wasting my time."

Arthur wondered if they could overpower him, but this would not give them much time, as the other prison guards would check on him.

"There would be a reward, I'm sure, but that's okay; let someone else have that."

He paused for a second, "Wait here, boy."

Arthur got the others to hide at the side of the hut; when the gates were opened, he hoped he would not lock them behind him. The rain was coming down so hard that he did just that and pulled them together. He then walked over to the main cabin, barely visible because of the weather; this had more guards and had access to the main camp. Naomi stepped forward and kissed Arthur on his wet face. He then pointed at them to move; Tom and Florence touched his shoulder as they left his side. They ran into the darkness, and Arthur pulled the gate shut again.

The guard returned to him and told him to follow him to the other guard's house. Arthur arrived at the porch dripping wet from the heavy downpour. He was shown inside; pipe smoke and a roaring fire filled his nostrils.

"This is the boy who's made me get bloody wet."

A group of men and women were sitting around the fireplace. They looked up. Most were scraggy in appearance, with torn clothes and unwashed faces. Some drone soldiers were drinking out of tankards. They looked grey, which indicated to Arthur that they were infected.
One of the women got up and walked over to Arthur.
"How old are you, boy?"

Her face looked like it once carried beauty; now, her frown line was deep, and her eyes were sunken and uncaring.

"I'm fifteen years old."

"Have you ever been with a woman before?"

Arthur shook his head.

She approached him and put her hand around the back of his head, squeezing his hair and rubbing his shoulders.

"Kathleen, once you've done the boy, how about sending some of that my way?"

"You ain't getting anything, Thomas; you lied about the chicken the other day and ate it yourself."

Arthur looked to see if he could see a weapon. He felt uneasy and threatened.

She continued to circle him, touching his face and lips with her hands. Her breath reeked of alcohol. She pressed her body up against his back. Arthur felt sick inside, but knew if he reacted in a negative fashion, she could make it worse. The woman took his hand and pulled him behind her, only stopping to grab a half-full bottle of wine. The others jeered as he was led off into a corridor to the side of the main dwelling. Arthur tried to think of what he could do to escape the situation. His heart rate began to speed up, the woman mumbled to herself as they walked.

"You'll always remember your first." She then took a swig of wine, staining her teeth dark red. Some of the wine dripped out of the side of her mouth, causing her to laugh. "I'll go gentle the first time; after that, it's how I want it."

"We don't have to do this." Arthur's voice was mild and calm.

"It's not what you want; it's what I want. That's the spoils of war, boy."

She began to undo her top, exposing her breasts; Arthur looked away. "Ha, I don't care if you're embarrassed, you'll love it".

"I don't want my first time to be with you."

She grabbed him by the cheeks in an aggressive manner. "I don't care what you want."

She then began to pull his trousers down. Arthur held onto his belt, fighting against her actions. She was laughing as they struggled. He looked around the room to see if there was something he could hit her with. She was physically strong and countered his resistance.

Slowly, she started to pin him down. Her following reaction was to kiss him on the lips and around his neck. The smell of alcohol and tobacco made him feel sick.

Arthur tried to stay calm, but he was panicking inside.

"Kathleen, Kathleen, a Priest is here to get the boy."

"Oh, for the love of god, can't they give me five minutes to have some fun?"

She stopped kissing him and looked at Arthur.

"Once you've been to see whoever you're going to see, I will find you, and we will finish this."

She spat out the tobacco she had in her mouth and wiped her lips with the back of her hand. She then let him wriggle away from her; her eyes just looked at him as he adjusted his clothes. Standing half-dressed, she did not move; as he left the room, he allowed himself to look back once. She blew him a kiss and smiled as he left the room. This made Arthur clench his fists; sweat and water ran down his forehead, and he could taste it in his mouth. He thanked God for the intervention, thought of his family and Naomi, and prayed he could help his mother and sister escape.

Standing in the main cabin, drying off next to the fire were two more drone soldiers and a priest. The guard who had shown him in spoke to the priest, explaining "that he brought him here to be checked", hoping there would be a reward if the boy turned out to be of value. Arthur said nothing as they told him to follow them to the main camp. He was glad to leave the guardhouse and tried to compose himself mentally and physically. The coolness of the rain hitting his face was refreshing outside, and there was little movement as they went through more gates and passed mounted guards. Arthur knew they were riders of the north by their size and presence.

The priest just waved his hand, and soldiers would stand aside. Arthur looked around the camp, assessing if there was an escape route, but it was larger than he had anticipated. They walked for thirty minutes or more before coming to a house. It wasn't too big, but it was well-guarded.

"Wait here, boy."

The priest went to the front door and knocked on it. A guard half-opened the door and spoke with him for a minute. The rain had eased up a bit, but Arthur was soaked through. Fires burning as far as the eye could see highlighted the size of the camp. They had made temporary covers to stop the rain, and there was a muttering of voices and laughter. There were also arguments and shouting, carrying on in the night air.

A figure came to the door, but Arthur couldn't determine who it was. He was then ushered forward; he could not help himself and ran towards the person at the door when he saw his mother's face more clearly. He flung himself into her and hugged her tight. The priest was standing next to them, just observing.

"So, he is your son."

Rebecca was cold. "I have seen him before we were captured. He is just a boy who wants to get out of the work camps."

"I told him about my husband and the fight with your Emperor before we were captured. He must be clever to have remembered all of that."

Arthur looked shocked and anxious. Had Nazar won over his mother?

"He can help us, though; I have things that need cleaning and fixing."

The Priest looked unimpressed. "This has been a waste of my time. He can stay and work with you tonight, and then he will be punished for wasting my time."

He then pushed Arthur into the house and looked at the two drones, which indicated they would follow him. The house door was closed by the guard with them. He then went and sat in a room next to the dining room. He tucked into a roast chicken and was content to let Rebecca lead Arthur away. Once they had moved through the house and upstairs, she took him to a room in the far corner of the house, opened the door and ushered him in quickly; she looked around to see if anyone else was watching before closing the door behind him. She then grabbed him and held him tight. Her tears fell onto his head. "We must speak quietly."

"Where is Emily?"

A little voice called out behind him. Moving from the shadows was Emily. She looked slightly grey and tired but smiling. She rushed over to join their family hug. Arthur bent down, "Good to see you trouble." He kissed her on the forehead and ruffled her hair.

"You have to come with me. Naomi and the others are already outside the camp. We can escape and find Dad."

Rebecca still had tears in her eyes. Her hand caressed Emily's head.

"What's wrong with Emily, he felt his eyes filling up. Has she been bitten; has she been bitten?" He pulled her in close.

"No, Arthur. She has been infected by Oksana, the same as the Drones." We cannot leave; they have the medicine; she will need it every six months."

Arthur shook his head. " No, no, no, no, there has to be a way!" He knelt and looked at Emily. "I love you, little sister. We will find a way to make you better." He stood up and looked at Rebecca.

"I can stay with you."

Rebecca shook her head whilst keeping her emotions intact. "They will come and take you away, and more than likely kill you."

Emily pressed herself against him. "I love you, Arthur, but we will be okay. Mummy will look after me." She took his hand and squeezed it. "I don't want them to hurt you like they did me. Escape with the others."

Tears ran down his cheeks, and he found it hard to talk. "For you, I will find a way."

Rebecca said he must leave immediately, in case the priest spoke to a senior official and the word got back to Nazar. She then pulled him in close, and Emily joined them.

"Tell your father how much we love him. Please stay safe and do not take unnecessary risks." She kissed him on the cheek and forced herself to let go of him.

"I can get you to the kitchen door. From there, head along the road south. It will take you close to the camp where you were kept. There are drone uniforms near the pantry. We can see if we find one that might fit. It will help you escape."

She then took his hand. "Stay here, Emily." Emily tried not to cry, but a few tears fell. "I love you, Arthur."

"And I you." Rebecca then carefully led him out of the room and downstairs to the kitchen area. She helped him find a suitable uniform and hugged him.

"Listen, once you go, do not come back. They will go looking for you with wolves and long limbs. Keep moving and find the Allied forces. You may even find your father."

Arthur breathed him. "Please stay safe, both of you."

"I will make sure of it, Arthur." She then opened the door in the kitchen.

"Now run, my angel, run, do not look back"

Arthur hugged her one last time and kissed her on the cheek. He then left the house through the door and into the damp, cool night air. He did not look back and continued along the road she had told him. The rain had started to fall heavily again, but he was happy with this; it meant there would be fewer guards patrolling the road. He had been given an army cap, which he pulled down; Arthur put mud on his face to help disguise his youthful features.

Time passed quickly as he moved past the tents and burning fires. The odd mounted guard rode past but barely acknowledged him in the rain. Lighting cracked in the distance, and the soil flung upwards as the rain fell heavier to the ground. He looked at his boots splashing through the water and gravel beneath him. He thought about Emily being infected and his mother staying in this god-forsaken place.

His eyes fell upon the cabin. He could see lights flickering inside and figures moving behind the glass. Pulling his collar up, he continued to walk past. As he was entering the path behind it, a call went up. It came from behind him. Arthur did not look back. He then heard a bell being rung and raised voices.

The path he was rapidly moving along wove in and out of clumps of trees. He could not afford to look over his shoulder to see if he was being followed. He carried on the path for several more minutes and then began to enter a farm field adjacent to it. The ground was sodden, and his boots sank into the soil below it. He moved at speed, following the road until he saw a small cabin. It was being used as a checkpoint.

A rebel soldier was standing outside smoking a pipe; approaching him were several rebels with rifles pointed at three captives being ushered towards the cabin. Arthur could hear their voices.

"Come on, you useless kids, escaping the camp will cost you dear."

The captives said nothing as they were shown inside. He crept closer to the fence line to confirm what he was thinking. It was Naomi, Tom, and Florence. It would not take long before the commotion in the camp caught up with them. Arthur took a moment to compose himself. He looked up, and the raindrops ran off his face and onto the ground below him. Behind the clouds, a moon was trying to break through.

Pulling himself over the fence, he moved to the cabin. The rebel smoking outside had finished and joined the others inside. He glanced through the window as he came closer to the door. They had Naomi and the others lined up, shouting and laughing at them. A woman was holding up a shepherd's stick and had it pointing in their faces. Arthur turned the cabin door, pulling down his cap as he did so. He had rubbed more mud on his face just before he walked in. He had a plan, and it was risky.

The warmth of a fire burning in the corner was the first thing to hit him. The rowdy voices fell silent upon his arrival.

"What's going on at the main camp? Are they looking for these worthless souls?" The man asking the question was the same rebel who had been smoking outside. His features were disguised in his long, overgrown beard. As he spoke, he cleared out his pipe and let the used tobacco ash fall to the ground below his feet.

Arthur looked around the room quickly. To his left, he saw a gun holster placed over a desk chair with two revolvers sitting on either side. "I'm training to be a drone soldier." The room fell silent.

"Good for you, but what's happening in the main camp?" He was a bit more forceful in his tone.

"These shits have escaped and deserved to be punished." Arthur's tone was aggressive. Tom and Florence didn't look up, but Naomi did. She kept a stone-cold face, but her eyes looked at Arthur.

"Quite the big man then. Show us what you can do. Shoot one of them now." He paused to light his pipe. We will say they tried to escape. "

The other three rebels' eyes lit up. "Do it then. If you're going to be part of this new Empire, show us what they are training you." His eyes looked at one of the revolvers sitting in the holster. The female rebel went and sat on the lap of a guy who was warming his hands; she still had the shepherd's stick pointing at the three prisoners. The fourth rebel leaned against the fireplace in the centre of the room.

"Come on, boy, or I'll beat one of them to death with my stick." She then brought the stick around hard on Florence's head. Tom reacted and raised his hands to make sure she did not hit her again but was stopped by the rebel standing beside the fireplace. "Stand there, or I will gut you like a fish."

The long-bearded man puffed away. "Last chance."

Arthur looked up, "I'm ready."
He stepped forward and grabbed both guns. He directed both of them at Naomi. "Sometimes people get what they deserve" Looking down both barrels, he held the revolvers steady. He moved in a flash, turning both guns on the bearded rebel first, who looked on in horror as the first bullets hit his throat and chest. The noise was deafening inside the cabin, and the rebel, leaning against the fireplace, reached down to his holster. He was not fast enough as Arthur re-aimed both Smith and Western revolvers and squeezed each trigger. Both shots hit him, forcing him back into the wall behind him.
Arthur continued to move forward, turning the guns on the female rebel with the shepherd's hook and the rebel she was sitting on; she desperately tried to raise herself up, but was pushed back as a bullet hit her shoulder and into the man behind her. They both fell to the floor.

"You little bastard, what have you done?" She was on all fours; she had been shot in the stomach and shoulder.

The other rebels lay dead on the floor or dying.

Arthur took his cap off and raised the gun next to her head.

"Let's go, Arthur, save the bullet; she won't make it anyway. They'll feed her to the dead." Florence wiped the blood away from her face using a rag that was lying on the table.

Naomi moved forward and kissed him on the lips. "Thank god it's you."

Arthur hugged her tight. "We do not have much time. Gather what you can, and we should move."

He clipped the gun holster around his waist before slipping both guns back in. The others rushed around, finding what food and water they could. Some rifles and pistols were taken. They could not overweigh themselves, as they would be travelling on foot.

The alarm bells were ringing around the camp, and they could hear a lot of commotion. Tom said they should head to the river where they had been working recently. He had seen boats moored there and thought this was their best chance of survival. The rain began easing as they moved to the cabin through an adjacent farm field. There wasn't time to fully thank Arthur or ask the obvious question regarding his mother and sister.

They pushed through a cluster of saplings rising in an area vacated by a fallen oak. It did not take them too long to reach the Hudson River. Light bounced off the water, and the clouds moved at speed, revealing a large moon behind them.

Tom looked around for where they had been sent to cut wood for the prison camp. The light from the moon was helping him find areas they had worked in. Arthur stopped Tom with a careful hand on his shoulder. He whispered that something was coming. The familiar sound grew louder once it homed in on them: the chatting teeth and wheeziness of his breaths. "Flesh eaters."

The girls steadied themselves, "No guns if we can?" Arthur was clear as he pulled out a Bowie knife he had taken from the bearded rebel in the cabin.

A man and a woman were moving slowly towards them. They looked to have only passed recently, as their skin hadn't decayed. Both of these flesh-eaters focused on Tom; they weren't aware of the others moving around them. Tom carefully stepped backwards, enticing them forward. Swiftly, Naomi and Florence grabbed the woman. Arthur quickly stuck the blade in her head and withdrew it. They did the same to the man who was closing in on Tom.

"Thanks, Tom; what you remember about this area and the river could save our lives".

Tom took them to where he had seen some rowing boats. Several were pulled ashore, and soon, the four of them waded out and were gently rowing down the river.

Naomi brushed the hair of Arthur. "I'm sure you will see them again."

"Emily has been infected the same as the drone soldiers. My mother had to stay with Nazar to be near the antidote. Thank you for waiting for me, but maybe you should have left without me; they would have hung you all."

"I think we can only make it through this if we all stay together," Tom said, stopping rowing and grabbing his shoulder.

"Thanks, Tom, thank you all."

The water carried the face of the moon, and they pushed it. They could hear the bells softly disappearing the further they got away from the camp. The plan was to move down the Hudson River towards New York, but Florence suggested they leave the river at a town called Newburgh, head onto land, and try to meet the Allied forces.

Chapter 35

"Major Hayward, the explosives are in place.

"Thank you, soldier."

Charles looked at his pocket watch and slipped it back into his tunic. The wind was picking up, but the Autumn sun still hung in the sky. He looked at the skyline of the town. The defences were in place. It was now a waiting game before Nazar's first wave arrived.

Texas arrived with a cup of coffee. "It's hard waiting for it all to begin."

Charles thanked him for the coffee. "We must be ready at some point for a battle which will hopefully turn the tide of this war."

Charles sat on a rock close to where they had been working.

"You have fought them in a large-scale battle; do they have a weakness

"It's a fair question, Texas, but one we haven't really found an answer for." Charles looked at his watch again.

"It will take a collective effort from all of us to defeat evil; sometimes, you must face it head-on."

Texas nodded his head and looked out across the Susquehanna River. "It's hard to sleep at night. This new world does not agree with me. I dream of the dead walking towards me and slowly feasting on my body."

Charles looked at this large, powerful man admitting his own fears; it took courage to do that.

"It's hard to clear your mind of them; when I first saw them in Austria, it was a shock, and you never really lose that thought."

Their conversation was stopped by a rider bringing news that the enemy forces were closing in outside the city.

Charles tipped out the last bit of his coffee, "Harrisburg has a battle on its hands now."

The next few hours brought a flood of messages from the frontline. The fighting was heavy, and the American and Allied forces were putting up a great fight.

Hosah and Little Bear joined him in a makeshift battle tent overlooking the river. Corporal Heinz followed them in.

"Good morning, gentlemen. Before we destroy the bridges, I will travel across the main part of the town to check the withdrawal is finalised. This attack is not Nazar's main force, but it's a powerful one."

Captain Somersett and Captain Steinberg joined them; Charles showed on a map how the enemy forces had passed Fort Indiantown.

The forests were teeming with rebels and drone soldiers, but the main force of the attack was the dead. Nazar harnessed their drive and hunger to incredibly good effect.

Stories emerged about how a detachment of cavalrymen was overrun by wolves and made a desperate last stand, whilst one rider escaped to warn the convoy they were protecting. Charles knew what it was like to face the gigantic packs of wolves. He had witnessed men and women being torn to pieces. They had evacuated most of the civilians from the city, but they were running out of states to fall back to, and with winter coming, the struggles would be set to continue.

Major General Green and General Washington were already fighting at the front with their soldiers. The Engineers and the other soldiers with Charles would help gauge the retreat and sabotage where they could. All the soldiers were in full combat fatigue and ready to leave after the meeting. If they did not make it back, a number of them would stay back to carry out the bridge destruction.

Once the briefing was concluded, they began to cross the Walnut Street Bridge; from there, they would go onto Mulberry Street Bridge and further into the city. Charles split them into three groups: Captain Steinberg had a cluster of American soldiers, Captain Somersett had cavalrymen and a handful of British Engineers, and Major Hayward had British Engineers and a mixture of his new fighters. The thunderclaps of artillery fire and the smell of battle were carried on the airways.

The soldiers had a mixture of weapons; some had Krag-Jorgenson rifles, others carried Lee-Metfords with ten-round magazines, and a few carried a new rifle called the Lee Enfield. Charles had a Lee-Metford strapped over his back and his trusted Enfield revolver by his side. His Khaki uniform was now standard with the British soldiers. Some Americans had a mixture of Khaki trousers and blue tunics, but a significant number were dressing in full Khaki.

Once across the bridges, Hosah and Little Bear led them along Mulberry Street and closer to the front. Stretchers carrying the wounded were funnelling past them; their missing limbs and shattered torsos gave away what was happening at the front. The further they moved through the city, the more the destruction became apparent; fires fiercely rose out of the broken houses and shops. Dead rebels lay strewn across the streets. American soldiers from the 10th Infantry stood near a shell-hit townhouse, drinking coffee. "They haven't just died." Shouted one of them, "They died last night in a raid. That's what they're doing at night. I'm glad these traitors are lying in the street." The soldier then went back to drinking his coffee as the detachment with Charles moved by.

"How further forward should we push, sir?" The young soldier looked concerned about what he was seeing.

"We'll push up to Pembrook and assist where we can."

There were still civilians moving with processions through the streets.

The young soldier leant towards Private Brown. "Why haven't they left already?"

"It's not that simple; some are too old, and some think we will beat them back."

The young soldiers' eyes lit up momentarily, and then he saw Private Brown's reaction. His face gave the impression they were only here to help the retreat, blow up the bridges, and cause disruption to gain time.

Charles had the soldiers spread out and take cover. The fornications were still in place, and the gunfire in front of them was growing louder. He had sent soldiers to lay dynamite in a warehouse which was adjacent to the road they were next to. Anything that would now aid the retreating soldiers would help. The next half hour saw the fighting creeping closer; Pvt Brown looked at the young lad next to him; he was breathing out deeply. He kept on adjusting his hands on the rifle as they became sweatier, as the fear grew inside him. Hosah and Little Bear returned.

"Major, the enemy are close. Corporal Heinz is still monitoring the retreat and bringing soldiers back with him."

"Thank you, Hosah."

To the side of them was a burning house; smoke poured out of the windows from the top floor. As they looked further down the street, a giant rider of the north burst through a window, covered in armour and carrying an axe. He charged at the retreating American soldiers, knocking three to the ground. Charles's men were spread out around the area, but he looked over to Sergeant Butcher, who was close by; the soldiers with him tried to aim, but the giant was amongst the Americans as he fought, making it hard. He struck one soldier in the chest and lifted the other into the air. The young soldier with Pvt Brown charged the giant with his bayonet and stuck it in his chest; this man fell to his knees; his eyes looked up at the young soldier and then closed. Retreating American soldiers helped the wounded from the attack and carried on moving. Pvt Brown went to the young soldier, "Are you ok?"

"It's the first time, I don't like it."

"Unfortunately, it won't be your last. Follow me."
They moved back to the side of the road.

A shell landed close to their position, which prompted Charles to give the order to be ready to destroy the buildings. Corporal Heinz appeared, running down the road they were on. Texas stood up and waved him in, so he ran to their position. Out of breath, he said the dead were coming their way en masse. Most of the Allied forces had retreated or were fighting a rear-guard action.

"Light the fires and fuses."

A cry of "attack" moved through several streets near them. A collection of rebels was present. Charles said not to engage and ordered them to fall back quickly.

The men moved along the side of the road. Texas looked at the houses, their doors open and their insides now lifeless.

They came to a halt; Sergeant Butcher pointed to their right flank, a sea of dead moving past houses and on towards the city. "We must be careful not to get sounded major."

A shell landed close to where some of the group were crouching down. Pvt Miller was hit. He was losing a lot of blood from his stomach wound. Hosah and Little Bear tried to help by compressing the wound. Close by was the army doctor. Cpt Turner quickly got over to him; he looked at the wound and looked over to the major.

"Get a stretcher ready." Corporal Heinz then took three men to help lay down, covering fire as the dead started to come towards them.

Bullets ricocheted off a stone wall to the side of them as rebels and drones moved along the street.

A voice called over to them in a strong French accent, imploring them to move his way. Then, the sound of a machine gun cut through the battlefield; the dead fell on top of each other, it momentarily stopped the assault from the rebels. Charles ushered the soldiers with him into a townhouse; they followed the soldier who beckoned them into the back room; there, a small group of soldiers were scattered around the house and a long wall outside. My name is Captain Roy Dechant; you should keep moving, Engineers.

The gunfire grew louder, and shouts and screams from the advancing soldiers closed in. Sergeant Butcher ushered the rest of the soldiers into the ruined house. Wooden beams protruded into the air, and bricks lay scattered across the once well-kept garden. Private Brown brought the young soldier to his side, "They're coming around the back, Sarg."

"Keep them at bay, Pvt Brown; there's a good lad."

With that, Pvt Brown took the young soldier up what was left of the staircase, climbing onto broken floorboards. It gave them an advantageous point from which to shoot. "Pick your target." The rebels were pushing through fields and backyards. The dead were being funnelled along the main roads to soak up bullets and drive the attack. The young soldier brought his Lee-Metford up to his shoulder and tucked it in. He then focused on the on-rushing rebels; squeezing the trigger, he let a round off. "I got one, I got one,"

"Refocus and keep them back." Private Brown saw three drones moving towards the house close to theirs. He picked out one and fired a shot. It missed his intended target but hit another in the leg. The injured soldier was pulled to the side. The drones crouched down and began to fire back at their position. The rebels were also holding back as more engineers opened fire on that flank.

Captain Dechant said Major Hayward and his men should keep moving as the Bridges must be destroyed to slow down this army of death.

Charles put his hand on the man's shoulder.

"Fall back with us," Charles said firmly.

"It is impossible; someone must keep the machine gun firing as long as possible. We are handpicked, and my men have nothing left. Go now, my friend, and win this war!"

The broken house was coming under heavy fire from three sides; Pvt Brown kept on firing, one round after another, and he heard a cry next to him. The young soldier fell backwards, "I need help; he's been hit."

"Fall back, full back." Pvt Brown moved down the broken stairs; the young soldier lay dying at the bottom. The roar of the next attack grew louder. The Pvt asked to be laid down, "For the love of god, I don't want to die being moved through the streets; give me my rifle" John leaned into him, "You will see the valleys again." His reply was short.

"Run, run." He perched himself against a back wall, loading his Martini-Henry rifle. Hosah grabbed his hand tight. "heniihoho'neiht", meaning brave.

They turned to move and left the back of the house, leading down the road. Hosah came out first and sent an arrow into a rebel approaching from across the road. He let out a war cry as they moved back. Little Bear covered them as they moved. Texas had his Winchester rifle and kept firing as they fell back.

Charles led the men further down the street. Behind them, the machine gun kept firing, and the noise of the attack grew louder. He tried to block out the faces of the men he had just lost, but it was something he had to bury deep down inside of him. They moved to St Francis Catholic church, where he stopped his men to re-group. There were more allied soldiers spread out along a defensive line. General Baxter Washington was saddling up; he had a hundred or more riders with him.

Charles spoke briefly to Sergeant Butcher and Corporal Heinz. General Baxter Washington rode over to them, "How's it looking at the front? Are we giving them a good beating?"

Charles knew this type of officer: "We are inflicting heavy casualties on them, but we need to think about how much longer you want us to defend this side of the river."

This caused him to look puzzled: "Defend, dear man? I'm here to push them back. I hear this hasn't been done before."

"Sir, you might need a few more men. The dead are moving down the main streets. They are not scared of cavalry or anything. May I suggest you try and find an opening for a raid behind them?"

"So, the good things I've heard are true: an Engineer with a tactical brain. Why are you just a Major?"

"I've heard about your bravery. Your men know you will die for them, but I applaud you for not attacking them head-on."

"Charles Hayward, as you've been fighting at the frontline, I will heed your advice and bring my men around Walnut Street."

Charles nodded his head and patted the horse.

"Good luck, General."

"You too,"

Charles did not waste time and got his men to rest in the church. He sent Hosah out with Corporal Heinz to bring Captain Steinberg and Captain Somersett to them. Pvt Chamberlin arrived as they left; he was glad to rejoin the main group. Charles asked if he could go to the bell tower and help suppress the enemy advance the best her could. Thirty minutes passed before the other men and officers arrived. The fighting had increased as the rebels and the dead pushed on. Drone soldiers were only being used in pockets of the attack. A shout went out, "Wolves and bears", "Giant Bears with two heads."

Market Street was blocked off with sandbags and carts—anything that would delay the advancing enemy. The American 12th Infantry and a mixture of civilians held this line. On hearing what was coming, Charles went to the bell tower to get a better look, but the other buildings along the road restricted some of the line of vision.

"We need some sort of artillery piece by the road or a machine gun."

Captain Steinberg shook his head. "Nothing like that left on this side of the river."

A shout from the bell tower rang out, "They are closing down the street."

The thunderous shots echoed outside; Pvt Brown looked at the walls and roof as bits of dust fell into the pews, which had been stacked on either side of the church.

"Do we have any spare explosives? We need something quickly."

An engineer came forward with several sticks of dynamite, "These, sir."

"Get close to the action and take out as many as possible when they break through." Charles paused. "Remember to watch where our men are."

Sergeant Butcher said he would accompany the soldier, following him out a side door of the church. Charles told the officers to have their men ready to fall back if need be. He then went outside to join the others on the frontline. Hosah and Little Bear took positions by the windows overlooking the street. Pvt Brown stood next to Charles,

"Is Heidi on the other side of the river?" Charles asked the question.

"Yes, sir,"

"Good, let's try and keep them on this side as long as we can!"

Pvt Brown nodded his head. Sergeant Butcher came alongside him, with Captain Somersett and Pvt Johnson.

Captain Somersett looked at Pvt Johnson, "Have you ever faced a bear before?"

"No, sir"

"Well, at least you can say these had two heads."

This brought a smile from Pvt Johnson. It was short-lived as the remaining scouts came rushing along the road; one soldier was shot in the leg as he tried to make the barricade. The men around him tried to go back for him, but at that moment, a larger-than-normal wolf rushed rapidly along the edge of the street and sank its teeth into his back; his screams were drowned out by the mass of wolves and bears coming towards them.

"My god, have pity on our souls." Captain Somersett said it under his breath.

"Fire at will" was the call. The 12th Cavalrymen began firing on the spalling animal mass coming their way. The bullets struck their bodies, legs, and heads and caused many to collapse and be crushed by the sheer number behind them. The bears with two heads smashed into the barricade, causing anyone on it to be flung into the air; three of these beasts were biting and snapping at anything around them. Wolves quickly scampered over the broken sandbags and crushed furniture. The larger wolves hung back and let the others engage; soldiers fixed bayonets and fought ferociously to control their attack.

Charles withdrew his sword and stuck it into a wolf as it bit a soldier close to him. Texas came out of the church with a hatchet and a shotgun. The first wolf to come his way got the hatchet in its head. Hagen joined him; they fought side by side as the beasts poured over the collapsing barricade. Charles turned and tried to react to a bear coming towards him. The creature was too quick, and a single swipe from its paw sent him flying into the scattered sandbags near the barricade. His sword was lost during the impact, and his revolver was left in the dirt two feet away. One of the bear's heads was drawn to a soldier as he ran to bayonet him; again, in a quick motion, it snatched him in its jaws and bit him in half; blood gushed out of its mouth and onto the ground below. The bear carried on lashing out at anything that was close by.

Charles reached for his revolver as a wolf flew into his side. It sunk its teeth into his officer's strap, which was attached to the gun holster. The creature's fur was dirty and smelt of urine and rotting flesh. It was a strong animal and pulled him around as it tried to get him in another position to continue the attack. It eventually managed to work its way onto the top of him, slowly lowering its jagged teeth towards his face. Using both arms, he kept it off, but the animal had the advantage; Charles moved his body from side to side, pushing his legs into the soil below for leverage. The smell of his breath was putrid; Charles could not reach the blade he had attached to his belt.

Slowly, the jaws began to clamp onto his face; the acute pain was terrifying; his warm blood began running down from his forehead onto his nose and into his mouth, then down his chin onto his neck.

A violent jerk was felt through Charles's body, and the creature on top of him instantly let go of its death grip and fell to his side.

Charles wiped the blood from his eyes and picked up the revolver; all around, there was chaos, soldiers with wolves on top of them and bears smashing and crushing bodies. Charles looked up to the bell tower; it was a clean shot, and he knew Alexander had saved his life. He picked up his sword and sliced at a wolf which was feeding on a wounded soldier. He shouted out for the explosives to be lit.

Two bears in close proximity to each other were an ideal target. Sergeant Butcher and the young soldier took their chance; they ran at them after lighting their dynamite sticks. The young lad put his under the first bear but was set on by wolves as he passed it. Sergeant Butcher grabbed his knife and flew at the other bear; it attempted to grab him and reared up, roaring at the man in front of him. It then came down on Sergeant Butcher; at the same time the explosives went off, the effect was crippling on the animals. Charles tried to move closer to check on him, but the wolves' numbers prevented that from happening. He picked up a rifle with a bayonet attached and jabbed and fought with those around him. Hagen and Texas managed to come in behind the last bear. It was busy tearing into a fallen soldier. Hagen struck his axe into one of the beast's hind legs; Texas did the same with his hatchet to its other hind leg. Pvt Johnson came from the front with a spear as the beast swung around in pain. He lunged it deep into its chest, causing it to refocus on what was just stuck into it. The blow was fatal; a few steps were taken before it fell forward.

The killing of these giant animals was lost in the continued onslaught of wolves. The sound of a bugle and a mass of horses coming in behind the wolves was a welcome sight; they had attacked the rebels and drones, bringing up the rear and pushing them back. The next assault was to help the battle-worn frontline soldiers fighting the wolves. The larger wolves broke off from the attack first and followed a call from Priest's near to the attack. These creatures were of more importance to them and were deemed not worth sacrificing on this occasion. The remaining wolves slowly began to break off the attack; Hosah and Little Bear were amongst the soldiers fighting at the front; their skill in hand-to-hand combat was evident, drawing arrows at ease and taking out wolves as they ran around the broken defences. Corporal Heinz was the first to where Sergeant Butcher had fallen.

He was holding his side.

"Are you OK?"

Sergeant Butcher looked up. "Check on the young lad."

Charles crouched down by his side with some water. "Hold in there, my friend."

Orderlies started to arrive with stretchers and army doctors. Charles looked over Sergeant Butcher's wounds; he had lacerations and cuts from the blast and bear swipe. He was bleeding quite heavily, but they managed to get him onto the stretcher and move him from the street.

Charles said, "Stay with me, my old friend; I need you."

Sergeant Butcher looked up. "You know what to do if that time comes."

"It's not our time now, it's not now." He held his hand for a second as they moved him down Market Street.

Charles stood there for a minute, watching them load him into a wagon along with the other injured soldiers.

Hosah came up to him. "He has fought well; I am sure the gods will look on him favourably."

Charles looked blank. Losing his closest confidante was something he struggled to accept. He thought of his family, and his head went dizzy. Only Hosah's words brought him around.

"The general approaches"

Sitting on his horse, covered in blood, was General Washington.

"Are you ok?"

Charles nodded his head.

"Your advice worked; you've gained us more time, but there is a larger second wave coming, those things you call long limbs mixed in with the dead. I've never seen bears like that before?" He was less jovial and more pondering his own words. He turned his horse. "I've asked the artillery to start a bombardment of this area soon. Move your forces across the river."

"We will, General; you saved many lives with that attack." They both looked at each other out of respect and turned to get things moving.

Corporal Heinz came up to Charles, "He's as strong as an ox. I'm sure he'll be fine." Charles patted him on the back. "I'll pray so."

"We need to get moving before the artillery starts the bombardment."

The soldiers gathered the wounded and continued to fall back along Market Street. Charles spoke quickly with Captain Steinberg and Captain Somersett; it's time to get as many back as possible, as he said that an enemy shell landed close to the church.

"Fall back, fall back!! "

Pvt Chamberlin came out of the church and entered the main street. Charles caught his eye. They nodded to each other before moving on further down the street. The smoke thickened behind them, and the skies darkened with the destruction coming their way—it was equivalent to a wave of fire.

The noise of drums and chanting was unsettling and seemed as wide-ranging as the smoke slowly engulfing the city.

Charles had re-sheathed his sword and re-holstered his revolver. He had taken a Lee-Metford rifle off a fallen soldier from the broken barricade. The bayonet was still attached, and he wrapped the rifle strap around his wrist. His thoughts were with his men and the other soldiers they were helping. Moving along Market Street, Captain Steinberg said he would help cover for the retreating soldiers. Charles told him not to dwell too long in one area; he stressed that they could not stop what was coming. With that, a handful of Americans, under Steinberg's command, fanned out across the road and beyond what was deemed reasonable. The noise coming from the smoke grew louder.

Units from other American divisions ran past, shouting Allison Hill had fallen, and the dead were moving along State Street. Captain Somersett was asked if he could move his men to the bridge over Paxton Creek,

"Hagen, go with Texas and the others and get across Walnut Bridge. It will not be long now. Corporal Heinz retreated to the Walnut Bridge with a handful of men. Alexander, cover them from the bridge as planned; we must get as many as possible back across."

The men agreed and wished his small group well.

"I can stay, sir."

"No, Private Brown. I need your experience on the other side. Remember Portsmouth. That was a close shave."

"Yes, sir, God's speed."

He smiled and told those around him to keep the soldiers moving. The remaining American forces and allied soldiers filed to the bridges to leave this faltering side of the city.

Charles looked at the sight of so many souls moving towards the river; it was time for the enemy to strike. Drones and rebels came through the smoke. Riders of the North charged towards them. The ground trembled under the sheer volume of this marauding mass. Fear and desperation gripped all those as they fled. Charles cleared his throat and called for the bugler to sound the retreat. A field cannon to his right, tucked in a street corner, prepared to fire; its thunderous shot smashed into the charging army. Limbs were torn off bodies and flesh flung into the air; screams were lost in the noise of the many.

He withdrew his sword again, feeling tight from the previous fight. It did not affect him as his adrenaline took over. Captain Steinberg kept his small detachment firing by rank and falling back. Charles looked over at Captain Somersett. He had moved his men onto the Susquehanna River. Priests appeared next to their units, which indicated to Charles that this was the push to secure the city and bridges.

Some of the Americans from another regiment had climbed up into a nearby house and were shooting from any high point they could get to. Charles tried to tell them to fall back, but the calls were drowned out in the fighting. He pulled the bugler close and told him to sound the retreat again; the lad cleared his throat and began to belt out a call when he was hit in the chest. He fell backwards onto the ground behind him and looked at Major Hayward once with despair on his face before closing his eyes. Charles felt anger erupt, but controlled his emotions as the Riders of the North charged into them.

The giant men and women were having success smashing into the retreating soldiers. Their axes and swords cut the men down in a brutal fashion, lopping off arms or heads. Charles continued down the road, moving close to the debris when he could. A rider was catching up with him; he had a lance, which meant facing him front on would not be wise. He cut into an alley and waited, his rifle strapped across his back. The fighting meant it was hard to hear if a horse was approaching, but sure enough, it emerged around the corner, but it was not alone; there were two more riders with him. A man and a woman. The Riders of the North saw Charles and smiled before dismounting.

"Let's tear his legs off and feed him to the wolves."

They then spoke to each other in Russian and began to move forward. Charles did not think about confronting them; instead, he lifted himself through a gap in a broken wall and into the burning house.

"He runs like a coward; I like it when they do that."

He moved through the smouldering rooms. In the dining room, a table and chair were turned over, along with other pieces of furniture broken into pieces on the floor. Scattered around were family pictures depicting a time that had now passed. A painting miraculously still hung on the dining room wall. It showed a rolling landscape, which disappeared into the hills and mountains behind it. Charles's eyes only rolled over this briefly as he could hear the bellowing calls of the Riders of the North coming after him.

"All the English pigs die eventually." This attacker had good English and was closing in on him.

Charles re-sheathed his sword and revolver. He cautiously took the rifle from his back and pointed it towards the door where he hoped the first rider would come in. His heart was beating fast, but he stayed focused. The only sound that he could hear was the background thumping and gunshots. The fire burning upstairs drifted out of his mind as he concentrated on the entrance, his finger poised on the trigger.

A scream rang out, followed by an almighty thud on the wall beside him. He warily moved forward, and to the side of the door was a large body; one of the riders lay there holding an arrow in their throat, talking slowly and losing consciousness. Another cry broke the eerie silence. It was a higher pitch. Charles rushed into what was left of the kitchen; his eyes fell upon a female rider of the north; she had been hit with something, and her skull was split open. A war cry rang out in the house, and at the same time, a prominent figure pushed past him; it did not try and strike out but fled to the same place they had come in.

Charles raised his rifle as they moved to climb through the hole in the wall. He squeezed the trigger, hitting the rider in the back. The uncomfortable movement indicated the pain of the bullet shattering in his body. He continued to try and move forward, but his efforts were futile; Charles loaded another bullet into the chamber. He did not even see Mad Dog emerge from the shadows; within moments, he struck the rider in the head and let him fall back. He then took the blood from his victim and wiped it across his face. Bringing a finger to his lips, he looked to the side before moving in that direction. Charles followed behind, and as Mad Dog moved almost without effort through the burning house, he led him back onto the street.

"Come." That was all he said.

Fighting was erupting everywhere, bare hands grappling with the would-be killers, and shells were landing around them, as Nazar did not mind firing on his own soldiers. The roar of a second wave coming their way added to the feeling of desperation to get to the river.

Captain Somersett had his men holding Walnut Bridge, helping soldiers cross and suppressing the enemy foothold in that area. Pvt Johnson saw a wounded soldier who was staggering their way. He instinctively put down his rifle and ran towards him. Tuffs of grass and soil flew up, and bullets landed around his feet as he ran. He got to the man and lifted him over his shoulder; coming from the smoke was a drone soldier; his bayonet sparkled as he emerged from the smoke into the light. Sergeant Boyd had tracked his run and looked down the barrel of his rifle; his shot was good enough to cause the onrushing drone to fall to the ground; he wasn't dead, but he had dropped his rifle.

"Keep coming, Private, keep coming!!"

Another soldier from the 10th spoke up, "Shall I go to him?"

Captain Somersett shook his head. "We must hold this position.

A shell landed close to Pvt Johnson, breaking his steps towards the bridge; he had to kneel before getting up again. Blood could be seen coming down from his cap; it flowed onto his face and then his tunic; another shell momentarily seemed to evaporate them, but he resurfaced again. When he arrived at his unit, an army doctor and soldier helped take the man. Sergeant Boyd looked over his wounds, "You've been lucky. Get patched up, and we'll see you on the other side. "I can stay and fight."

"Don't waste time; we'll need you to hold that side before the engineers blow the bridge. Now go."

He turned and moved with the other wounded across Walnut Bridge.

Captain Steinberg's detachment was now engaged in hand-to-hand fighting. They had fought a gallant rear-guard action, but the enemy numbers were too many. Rebels were moving in from the left to reinforce the drone soldiers already amongst them. Shouts of pain and anguish filled the battlefield, but the arrival of destroyer drones with a large, powerful figure meant it was time to flee.

He could be heard bellowing out to those fighting to stand and fight.

"Call the retreat, it's time."

Captain Steinberg moved his soldiers and everyone else with them towards the bridge. Mad Dog had taken Charles to Hagen and Texas, where they were fighting by the bridge.

"I thought you'd be bloody across this by now." Charles had a wry smile.

"Good to see you alive. I see it took Mad Dog to save you."

"He certainly did that. How are the others doing?"

"We have seen many cross, but there is still a lot on this side. Captain Somersett is holding over to the west of us. The wounded on City Island are stacking up. They're working on getting them off, but it's a slow process." Texas looked concerned.

"Captain Steinberg?"

"No sign of him or his men?"

Charles pulled out his pocket watch.

"Give me fifteen minutes, then give Captain Oxford these written orders to blow the first part of the bridges along the river." He handed over a letter.

Pvt Chamberlin stepped forward, "I'll come with you, sir. You'll need a sharpshooter." Mad Dog also said he would help, but Charles said it would be better if he got the message to the other Arapaho and soldiers on the Island to move across fully. Corporal Heinz said he would like to join him with two other Engineers. With that, they pressed off. Charles had taken a Krag-Jorgenson Carbine rifle; he had enough rounds to get them through, he hoped.

They moved along the river, making sure all visible soldiers moved.

"We still have soldiers from our detachment fighting in the buildings. We can't leave them." This was from the 11th Brigade.

Charles knew this would be true, but said the bridges must be destroyed, or the enemy would sweep across and destroy the retreating army.

They moved along the river's edge until they got to where Captain Somersett was fighting with his men. Scattered around were bodies from his unit and the enemy. They focused their fire on the buildings further along the river's edge to the west. "They're closing in."

"It's time, Captain, it's time."

The brave men of the 10th started moving towards Walnut Bridge; as they closed in, they could see a small group of soldiers fighting their way backwards. "It's Captain Steinberg and his men."

"Pvt Chamberlin, give us some covering fire; we need to see if we can get to them."

He moved forward with Corporal Heinz and some of the 10th. They instantly found themselves coming under fire from the buildings that were along the riverfront, "Keep moving, fire at the smoke from the windows; it was then that riders of the North came sweeping down the streets next to them; they had with them drones and rebels, wolves and long limbs were unleashed.

"Dear god, no."

Charles shouted to Captain Steinberg to run. He turned to look his way, but Lev came forward from the onrushing horde; this beast and man towered amongst the others. He raised his axe and brought it down hard against the sword of Captain Steinberg. His men around him were forced back, fighting valiantly; they were stabbed or shot as they held their ground. Charles watched on helplessly as they fought out a vicious fight. Pvt Chamberlin tried to aim for Lev, but the grappling men around him made it not a clear shot.

"We need to move; they are sweeping along our side.

"Alexander, help Captain Somersett."

"Yes, sir, He breathed in, which was hard, as his heart rate was beating so fast; he began his destructive work. Shot after shot dropped the drones and rebels as they approached.

Charles ordered them to move towards Walnut Bridge as other bridges began to explode along the river. His instructions were for the last remaining soldiers to get across the bridge.

Bullets ricocheted around them; one soldier was shot in the arm, another in the chest. "Corporal, get the men moving". Pvt Johnson was carrying two men across Walnut Bridge. Charles and Alexander were left crouched by the side of a sandbag defensive wall at its entrance.

Eerily, the attackers stopped for a moment as a horn was blown. The mass of enemy soldiers parted as Lev strutted forward. He had a freshly cut head dripping with blood, dangling in his left hand. Charles sighed; it was Captain Steinberg.

"You see, this is WAR!" He laughed out loud with the soldiers around him banging their weapons.

Several priests rode behind him with spears in hand.

Charles looked over at the sorry sight; none of Captain Steinberg's men were alive. He ushered everyone behind him to move quickly.

Lev brought his axe into the air.

"Kill them, kill them all."

The noise was terrifying as they charged forward.

The engineers on the bridge lit the fuses as the soldiers fell back. Charles aimed into the onrushing wall of hate and let off round after round. Captain Somersett and his men stood side by side as they fell back as quickly as they could. Some were hit by enemy fire, and others grappled with the drones, who managed to catch them.

A colossal boom shook the bridge, causing many parts of the structure to fall into the river; this also took with it the advancing Nazar soldiers; some were blown into pieces from the explosion, and others into the river below. Lev did not charge onto the bridge. Instead, he walked to the riverfront edge, followed by the priests behind him. Charles's eyes were drawn to his position; he did not know this man was Nazar's brother, but he knew he held power over this force. Alexander kept his firing rate up and helped make the drones along the riverbank seek cover as they opened fire on the retreating Americans and Allied soldiers.

Sergeant Boyd was helping the wounded fall back whilst Pvt Johnson fought a large rebel man; his face was missing an eye and ear, and judging by the colour of his skin, he looked infected. He held the Pvt in one hand and brought his knife up to his neck.

"Buffalo soldier, you'll wish you never joined their side." Before he could finish what he intended to do, Charles ran his sword through his neck. The rebel's eyes looked at the Major for a split second before closing, and he lost control of his body. Charles helped steady Pvt Johnson and pushed the body into the water below.

"Thank you."

"Keep moving back; they'll have our range here soon."

Charles asked for an update once the remaining soldiers had reached City Island. He was told General Washington had last been seen fighting on the city's outskirts. He had decided not to take his horses across the bridges as they would take up the little space they had.

The evacuation of the Island was in full swing, and it was only a matter of time before they turned their attention to bombarding them with artillery. Charles gathered his men and thanked them for their heroics in destroying the bridges. He paid respect to Captain Steinberg and his men; he knew their sacrifice helped more men escape the grip of Nazar's forces.

Hagen and Texas used their size to carry as many men as possible to the carts lined up to take the wounded. Within twenty minutes, shells began to land on the island. They had some mortar artillery pieces, which they used to fire back, but it was hard to locate all the gun emplacements as they were not firing from the river's edge.

The island was evacuated, and the final part of Walnut Bridge was destroyed. The soldiers stood by the river's edge, looking at the burning city. Pvt Brown brought news that Nazar's army had crushed the main American forces as they tried to relieve Washington. The plan was to retreat to the Great Plains for one last stand.

Charles sat on a rock which jutted out towards the flowing river. He took off his helmet and pushed his hair back. He thought of Captain Steinberg and the men he had lost; he let his mind go to the dark place where his family was. He felt unsteady in himself, almost sick; using his arms, he leaned back. The autumn sun was trying to poke out from the smoke clouds engulfed the riverfront. The enemy cannons had ceased firing, as they would save ammunition for better targets.

He lay there looking up. Part of him felt how he did at the start of this war when his family was stuck with the oncoming flesh-eaters. He was ready then to end it with them, but fortune took their side, and they escaped the clutches of death. This time, everything was beginning to feel final. They were running out of places to retreat, too.

"Father, is that you?"

Charles sat up. He could have sworn he had heard his son's voice. Then, looking straight up, he saw Arthur's face.

"Dad, it's me." He moved forward and hugged him. They embraced each other for several minutes. He brushed the side of his cheek.

"Where are your mother and sister?" He felt sick asking the questions as he could only see Arthur and the other teenagers.

"She is in Nazar's camp. Emily," He paused, "Emily is infected like some of the drone soldiers."

Charles pulled him in close, "Has she turned?" His voice was wavering.

"Not yet, Father; that is the reason they stayed with Nazar; he has the antidote."

He put his hands on his head. "We are drawn together in an impossible web."

"Why does he want you so badly?"

"I destroyed the meteor, remember, son? He will not forget or forgive." Charles looked up as the soldiers prepared to move from Harrisburg.

"He holds all the cards to our family now."

Arthur looked at Naomi, Tom, and Florence and said, "There's still hope, Father; that's all we need."

With that, Charles ruffled his hair and went to speak to the others. He hugged all of them. "We can get you some food, but they will soon try to cross the river in a day or two."

Naomi came forward as they turned to go.

"I am sure Rebecca and Emily will be by your side soon."

"I pray so, Naomi, I pray so."

Chapter 36

"Harrisburg has fallen to my brother Lev." He quaffed a large jug of ale, letting it run from the sides of his mouth. Then threw it to the ground. "Bring me my horse." Behind him, as far as the eye could see, was an army fit for an Emperor. It marched to giant drums played by riders of the North.

General Conway and General Georgiy joined at the front of the column; they were soon joined by General Pavel Grengo, French Priestess Arnoult, and Welsh Priestess Llewellyn.

Nazar was in a good mood and looked happy with their progress in America. "Soon, New York will fall, and so will Washington. They will have nowhere to run!"

"I have heard rumours of the enemy gathering their forces in Colorado." General Conway was calm in his tone. He did not want to upset his ruler, as he knew the fate of others who had befallen that mistake.

"This is why Oksana has travelled to the north to bring around our main cavalry forces. They will travel this winter, and we will attack them in spring." He pulled up a black bear skin to cover his shoulders. "Sooner if we can, but they are hardy fighters."

"What of the husband of Rebecca and the infected child?" Again, Richard chose to ask wisely but in a subservient manner.

"Richard, Richard, so many questions." He paused.

"Major Hayward will pay for his crimes in good time." He still did not break from his buoyant mood.

"Make sure my destroyer drones guard them from now on. If they try to escape, bring them to me. If they do escape, well, you know what I will do to the captain of those guards and his men."

"Now, leave me to speak to Georgiy."

"Yes, sire," Richard pulled his horse backwards to ride with the others behind Nazar.

"Georgiy, we have fought a long campaign together, and soon, we will be closing in on controlling America." His smile unnerved the General.

"You seem to be happy, my lord."

This drew a stern look.

"Why would I not be happy with our progress, Georgiy? Are you holding back news from me?"

The general shook his head. "Of course not; it's just that the war is not over yet."

"This is why I like you. I should be thinking like that. Have a thousand prisoners executed at our next campsite."

Looking smug with himself, he rode ahead alone. "Remember to take their severed heads and distribute them around the four corners of this country.

"Yes, my lord."

Chapter 37

"Captain Rimmel, can you confirm Harrisburg is now under our control?"

"Yes, it is Lev, my lord."

"Good, our forces are sucking the life out of New York and Washington."

He stood looking over the burning city.

"Winter is coming; we must be ready to move to the Great Plains to finish them once and for all."

"Send scouts to look ahead, send messengers to share the good news, and get me my spoils of war. We will feast tonight."

Lev rode his horse to the highest point and made a bellowing call, almost the same as a wolf, but with more menace and graveness. His tent was set up that evening and was joined by a host of female priests; all around as far as the eye could see, fires burnt, sending sparks into the night air, singing and fighting broke out, there were screams from those in peril and cries for help as prisoners were slaughtered in drunken rage.

He passed the evening gorging on food and wine, then began to have fun with those who were there to entertain him. The guards outside his tent stayed focused and did not move, even with the hollers and screams.

Lev left the tent, followed by Priestess Catherine Bonnaire. She was his General in command and also his preferred night-time guest. She planned to marry Lev, but it wasn't the time to suggest such a thing. For now, it was to do his bidding and win his favour more.

"Catherine, my trusted Catherine, you looked like a princess in there tonight. You showed them how it was done."

"My lord, I'm sure your brother will be impressed with your progress."

There was an awkward silence.

"He's never really satisfied, only when he has won the battles himself." Lev seemed to ponder his remarks momentarily before turning to her.

"I'm doing the hard work here, winning the war, and I'll get fucking Britain as a reward." He laughed out loud.

Catherine stayed quiet. It wasn't the time to question his mood.

"I mean, General Conway is being promised more than me—his own flesh and blood? His own flesh and blood?" His anger saw his size grow, and he began to change, but a gentle brush on his back started to calm the process down. He looked at her with his changing face, and his elongated jaws with razor-sharp teeth began to recede.

"I am sure you will have your time, my lord."

"I hope you will stand with me when that time arises, General Bonnaire?"

She smiled. "Of course I will."

"Good, very good. Soon, their major cities will fall, and we can squeeze the last drop of resistance out of them."

He then took her hand and led her back into the tent. He sent the other priestesses out so he could enjoy her company for the night.

Chapter 38

The news broke that New York and Washington had fallen to the advancing Nazar armies. They also had updates that Lev was commanding the most forward of those armies, and Nazar was bringing the other forces up behind him.

Charles sat with Arthur, talking to him about what had happened since they last were together; he told them about the campaign in Great Britain; it had been successful, but the sheer number of dead would take a long time to conquer. Arthur spoke about their retreat from Boston and how they had seen the tall, thin rebel again. He had tears in his eyes as he explained he had tried to get his mother and sister out of the camp, but it wasn't to be because of what they had done to Emily. Charles pulled him in close, and they held each other for a moment.

"You did the right thing; I'm sure your mother will keep her safe."

"I just want things back to how they were before all of this?"

Charles looked at him and said, "One day, I'm sure it will." He called for the soldier steering the wagon to stop. He climbed down from the wagon and untied his horse, which was walking behind it. Hosah arrived next to him. He smiled at Arthur and the others.

"You are becoming a warrior, Arthur. We will ride again soon." Little Bear and Mad Dog came alongside them.

Naomi snuggled into Arthur to comfort him. He put his hand behind her head and kissed her on the cheek. "Thank you," he said.

Charles rode with the Arapaho to join Cpl Heinz, Texas and Hagen.

"Do we have news on Thomas and our men?" Cpl Heinz stepped forward. "There's nothing more to report; he's been moved on towards Colorado."

Charles looked down, rubbed his beard, and pushed back his hair. "I'm grateful I have you around me. We will enter into this final chapter together."

They all nodded and looked at each other.

Captain Somersett walked up to join them. He was warmly greeted. "Where to now, Major?"

"We must enter the forest of Monongahela," Charles said, taking a deep breath.

"I wish we could move around it, but the rebels are amassing near Pittsburgh, and they'll push on from Washington. The forests we know are where they will push the long limbs, the razor-tooths, and possibly the rough back razor-tooths. They will be pushing the dead into the darkness of the forest. We must pray that God is with us."

He put his helmet on.

"We set off tomorrow"

The others began to disperse, but Hagen came forward.

"Did Arthur mention anything about Elin? Did he see her?"

Charles put his hand on his shoulder.

"She is alive and moving with Nazar's army; as Arthur said, she wanted to help Rebecca and Emily; she will be some sort of handmaid, which means she will be close to them."

Hagen breathed in and out.

"I'm sorry to hear what they have done to Emily. We will make them pay."

Charles breathed out.

"Get some rest, my friend."

Chapter 39

It was a glorious October morning as the wagons and men entered the forest. The track they had chosen looked well-trodden; it wasn't cut up or causing them too many problems due to the lack of rain. They were not the last regiment to go into the forest, but were separated from the primary columns. Red Spruce trees were the dominant species in the forest, mixed in with White oaks and Hemlocks. Their sheer size was a challenge, but they were fortunate to have guides to help them navigate their way through.

Moving at a steady pace was encouraging, but Charles could not help but look at every hill or clearing they had to cross. He wanted to be ready for any sign of the enemy. Days passed without any reports of untoward sightings. Charles had let Arthur and the other teenagers ride out in front of the column with Hosah and Cpl Heinz. They were told not to engage in anything they saw and to report any findings. The further they went along the track into the forest, the more they began to see broken carts and wagons left scattered alongside it. There was the odd makeshift grave with branches used as crosses, but the Arapaho said the footprints and animal tracks were still human and not the beasts of Nazar.

Hosah rode back with the teenagers; he stopped by the major.

"We are not alone; a hunting party is following us."

Charles turned his horse and rode to the back of the column.

"Should we prepare for an attack?"

"They are not Nazar forces."

"Rebels?" Said Charles as he reached for his revolver.

"No, Shawnee and Ioway tribes."

"Is that a good thing?"

"I am not sure; they are not great friends of the white man, but they would also see what Nazar brings to their lands. The dead are walking, and the demons run through their ancestors' lands."

"Should we wait to meet them?"

"No, they will come to us."

"To fight or ..?"

Hosah turned his horse as if to return to the column.

"We will find out."

The next few days followed the same pattern; they doubled the scouts, but there were no sightings of Indians or Nazar's forces.

Arthur and Naomi were perched next to a fallen oak. They looked out to a clearing—for the first time in a while, it wasn't just compacted forests.

"It's my sixteenth birthday today."

Arthur looked at her.

"Oh no, did I forget? I'm so sorry. I've lost track of time and.."

She brushed his face.

"Don't be silly; it's okay. The new world makes time disappear. I mean, no school, no chores, or general stuff."

Arthur still felt terrible.

"I'm soon sixteen as well."

"You're growing into a man and a warrior."

He laughed, "Not sure about the warrior part, but thanks anyway."

A yelp went up.

"What is it?"

Little Bear came riding up.

"Go back to the others and tell them to be ready."

They mounted quickly and set off in haste, weaving in and out of the trees, which was difficult. They arrived back at the column, but it was already getting ready for an attack. Charles came over and told them to join Florence and Tom in the middle wagons. Arthur had a rifle across his back. His father put his hand on his shoulder and told him to stay safe.

Some of the Arapaho warriors arrived at a steady speed, the air of initial threat receded, and now it was more of a subdued one; following behind them were Shawnee and Ioway Indians riding proudly on their horses. They looked fierce and ready to fight, but Hosah was relaxed as he spoke to an elder Indian in front of them. Charles dismounted and walked over to them; he didn't have a gun or sword and wanted to come across as open. The elder Indian rode forward and acknowledged Charles as he walked towards them.

"You are taking a risk coming through these woods."

Charles tilted his head as if to say what choice did they have.

"We are fleeing the invaders from Europe."

The elder laughed.

"They are already here!"

Which brought a rousing response from the Braves behind him.

"Your English is very good."

"It pays to understand the white man's tongue and the lies that flow from it."

Charles started to feel this conversation was not going the way he hoped. He thought about whether this was a trap and that the Indians would attack from all fronts, but then his mind also thought Hosah would not allow that, and surely, he would sense if this would not turn out well.

"Can we continue through the forest safely?"

"Yes, you can, but I cannot speak for all the tribes ahead. The Arapaho are great warriors, and you are fortunate to have them on your side; Shawnee and Ioway Indians will fight against these demons, but we have lost faith in Europeans."

Charles looked at a scar that ran from his left eye down his face to his jaw. His age was hard to tell—fifty or sixty, Charles did not know. He wanted the best for his people, and Charles knew that the Europeans had not done that over time and asking them to fight for them would almost be an insult to those who died under the previous regime. The choice would come down to the lesser evil: Nazar or the Americans and Allied forces.

Hosah animatedly spoke to the Shawnee Chief, pointing and gesturing a lot. He then put his arm across his chest and broke off from them.

"We are allowed to continue, but they will need twenty rifles to help with the battle against the dead."

The chief rode forward after they agreed on the exchange.

"You have come across the water, and death has followed you; at some point, you will have to face it."

The major looked back at the Shawnee Chief and said, "We'll need the nation of Indians with us to help us survive this."

He turned his horse as the rifles were handed over.

"Beware, there are enemies amongst your friends." He said nothing more and spoke to Hosah and the other Arapaho before letting out a call. They disappeared into the forests as night turned into day.

Charles rode over to Hosah, "What does he mean about enemies amongst our friends? Is he talking about the rebels?

Hosah was quiet for a moment. "I think he means something else, but I'm not sure who yet." I will call the spirits tonight to receive answers. Charles thanked him.

"Captain Somersett, keep an eye on the men in our command."

The captain looked a bit confused but acknowledged the request.

A week passed slowly as the tracks were smaller in places, and debris littered the route. They had encountered the odd flesh-eater walking, but no packs of Long-limbs or other beasts.

That night, the wagons were pulled into a defensive position, and fires were lit. Pvt Brown sat next to Heidi. The air was as cold as the clear sky, and they both looked at the stars above.

"They are hypnotic, don't you think?"

John took off his helmet. "They are pure and distant. They remind me of childhood moments when I would sit in the garden and look up at the stars."

Heidi leaned in and kissed him on the lips. "That's what I love about you; you are different."

"I hope a good different?"

"Don't be mad; you know I mean a good different."

They continued to look at the stars above.

"I used to love being in woodlands and forests; now, every twig that cracks or branch that breaks makes me feel on edge."

Rubbing Heidi's arm, John told her he would make sure they escaped this.

"I think we're going to need a miracle to stop him, them."

"The major has fought with Nazar; he helped destroy his power source. His wife and daughter are with that monster, but he's still trying to get us to safety. We have to believe."

She smiled and kissed him again. "Follow me to my tent."

John looked around. He was not assigned guard duty, and there was no Sergeant Butcher to spy on him. "Look, I will have to return to my section later."

"Sure, let's go."

Chapter 40

Hagen awoke that morning, went to the water barrel to fill his canteen, and took some to splash his face. It was refreshing. He took a moment to look around. The camp was silent; the odd guard checked the track and forest. They were close to a small town called Buckhom; the hills meant they had to check all around them. He thought about Elin and Denmark as he drank water from a barrel they had at the side of a wagon; a deep voice sounded out whilst he did so. "Don't drink all the water, you oversized Viking"

Texas was coming his way. He seemed to be in high spirits, which helped lift Hagen, but he still had thoughts flying around.

"Texas, do you think they will stop if we eventually beat them here in America, or will they just wait and come again?"

Texas filled his canteen with water, which rushed in, creating bubbles around the top of the canister's opening. He then brought the canteen to his lips and took four hearty gulps.

"Yes, they will come eventually; even if we beat Nazar, someone will always want to control everything. We cannot do much about that, but I hope we find peace in our time."

Hagen leant back against the wagon and pulled out a pipe. He stuffed it full of tobacco and lit it. The smell wafted under Texas's nostrils, and he got out his pipe. Hagen offered his tobacco pouch, and Texas thanked him and filled his pipe.

"She's a fighter, Hagen; you will see her again."

Hagen took a deep breath before exhaling and watching the smoke rise to the sky.

"I would like to start a family with her, raise some children, and grow some crops, but it is a dangerous time to dream because she could already be in Valhalla." Hagen stopped for a second.

"What about you, Texas?"

.

"There have been women, but I have only loved one. I have struggled with my chosen path." He carried on smoking his pipe.

"Could you find the one again? Do you know where she went?

"She married a man in New Mexico; they have children and run a small business. It's my own fault. I drank too much and gambled too much. I should have tried harder."

Hagen could see him struggling to continue,

"It's okay, big man, to feel pain.

He half smiled. "I'm sorry to bore you with my past. I'll check on the Major."

Hagen stopped him as he left. He grabbed his hand, "You'll never be alone. We will live through this time together or die together fighting for what is right."

Texas squeezed his arm back. "Thank you."

Private Brown awoke next to Heidi, "John, you'd better get back to your post."

"Oh Lord, I fell asleep with you afterwards."

"I know, so did I."

Before anything else was said, voices could be heard outside the wagon's defensive circle.

Charles was further down from Heidi's and John's tent. He was half asleep, dreaming of tea and scones, when a soft voice called out.

"Major, come."

He got up, a bit stiff and groggy. He put on his khaki trousers and blue shirt.

Mad Dog appeared and put his finger to his lip. "The soldiers who have arrived with Pawnee scouts are not to be trusted!"

Charles was trying to process everything. He went to step outside without his revolver or rifle, but Mad Dog stopped him.

"Blood will be spilt; be ready."

Charles felt himself tense up. He grabbed his revolver with the gun holster belt and then his Lee-Metford rifle. He didn't have time to ask more questions as Mad Dog was moving at speed around the wagons. He had awoken several of the soldiers as he ran past them. Corporal Heinz was out, with most of the Arapaho warriors searching ahead.

Charles came to a small clearing where two American soldiers from the 10th were discussing something with cavalrymen who looked like they were from the 7th. They sat alongside them in their saddles, and there were four Pawnee scouts. Mad Dog had taken him to a collection of small saplings. He drew an arrow from his pouch, which was strapped across his back. Charles touched his shoulder to check what he was going to do; as he did so, a cavalryman pulled out his revolver and shot the two 10th Cavalrymen guards. Charles wanted to shout out, but his throat was dry from the night before. Mad Dog had already released his arrow in response to the attack. His accuracy was deadly; the arrow flung into the chest of the soldier who fired his revolver, and as he fell off his horse, all hell broke loose.

It was hard to count their numbers as they poured forward. The Pawnee scouts let out war cries and started firing arrows at the onrushing soldiers who had come out of their tents on hearing the gunshots. The Pawnee rushed forward, firing arrows and rifles from their saddles. Charles raised his rifle and fired at a 7th Cavalryman as he charged forward with his sword in the air. It was not a clean hit, but the bullet hit him in the torso, causing him to sprawl forward. They quickly got amongst the group; British engineers were slightly confused about why the American forces were attacking them.

A Pawnee Indian threw a spear into a British Engineer, knocking him back; he then threw a tomahawk at another soldier as he came out of his tent while pulling up his braces. The soldiers from the 7th Cavalry were quick to charge through the waking soldiers. Texas moved himself against a tree, and as a rider passed him, he swung a branch he had picked up, knocking the soldier to the ground; he then brought the branch down hard on his head. He felt a pain in his side, looking down; an arrow struck from his hip. A Pawnee Indian came at him from his horse; Texas blocked the spear with his branch but fell backwards in the process. A soldier joined in the attack on him. Texas tried to rise from the ground but had to dodge the soldier with his sword. He now had the Pawnee brave attacking from one side and the 7th Cavalryman from the other; using just his fists, he struck the soldier, knocking him down; the brave was quick and pushed him back, pushing the arrow further into his side.

Texas let out a yelp and spun the brave to the floor. He was slight in build but as strong as an ox. Texas did not see another rider come in behind him and shoot him in the back.

Hagen came flying out of the tent with his axe and stuck the soldier on the horse in his leg. He then pulled him off the horse and brought the axe around onto his head. Texas had managed to pin the brave down, pulled out the arrow, and brought it down on his chest. He then fell forward, blood pouring from his wounds.

"Stay with me, Texas." Hagen grabbed his slumped body and dragged him to a nearby wagon; he scrabbled around for something to stem the bleeding; there were some shirts tucked into the back; he took the cloth and ripped it to use as bandages. The fighting was erupting all around them.

Charles aimed again and shot another cavalryman as he rode past. Mad Dog pushed the injured soldier off his horse and remounted it; he then chased down a Pawnee brave and came alongside him at speed; they lashed out at each other with knives. Mad Dog grabbed his opponent's arm and pulled him closer before stabbing him in the chest and letting him fall away. The attack started to break off; this was more of a raid than a full-on battle. Charles looked as the attacking riders dispersed into the forests around them.

Tents were burning, and bodies lay strewn around the tents and the defensive ring.

Pvt Brown came running over. "It's Texas, sir."

Charles called for Cpt Turner, the medical doctor. "Pvt Brown, pls check on my son and his friends."

Pvt Brown asked where Texas was and left to look for Arthur and the others. As Charles approached, he saw Hagen on one knee, holding Texas's arm. He knelt next to the big man and shook his head. "Why now, our own soldiers turning on us?" Charles looked at the wounds, and they did not look good.

"You have to beat them, we have to win, or this will be the end."

Charles put his hand on his shoulder. "Save your energy. I need you to help fight them."

"I think this is my time, Charles." He looked at them both, reached out with his left arm, and took Charles's hand. He squeezed it hard, but slowly, his strength started to disappear. Captain Turner joined them, but Charles put up his hand.

"It's too late, he's gone."

Hagen stood up, picked up his axe, and buried it in the tree next to them. Charles felt drained from all of it; he put his hand on his brow and sat next to Texas.

Captain Turner said he would be back as there were more wounded to attend to. Charles thanked him for coming so quickly. Hagen was busy dragging two of the 7th Cavalrymen to a tree. His rage was unabated, and he was almost shaking with anger.

Charles closed Texas's eyes and covered him with a blanket. He lost his balance a little as he moved towards the two soldiers now tied to an oak tree. Hagen went to get his axe whilst Charles came closer to them; the morning sky had changed, and the clouds above let light rainfall across the simmering battlefield. Charles had blood on his blue shirt; he knew it was not his but that of his trusted friend. The soldiers did not look that old, early twenties at most; one had a black beard and long black hair, the other had short blonde hair and a square chin, and both had cuts and bruising from the earlier fight.

"You might as well join them as well." The soldier with the black hair was the first to speak.

Charles adjusted his belt.

"Why have you turned against your people? Has the whole regiment turned?"

The man looked up. "Nope, but if they don't, they'll die like you're gonna do."

"Where have you come from?"

"I ain't telling you more shit now."

Charles looked at him. "That's a shame." He then looked at Hagen, who walked slowly over to the black-haired soldier.

"You don't scare me, big man."

He did not say another word as an axe came down hard on his forehead. The crunching, splitting sound vibrated into the tree.

Hagen withdrew the axe from the other soldier's head and stood next to the Major.

"My name is Max; please do not kill me."

"Why have your detachment defected to Nazar's army?"

The young soldier looked at the blood dripping off Hagen's axe.

"We didn't have a choice; our Captain said they would kill us all if we did not change our allegiance. There was also a rebel, a tall, gangly man, who said he was from Albany."

Charles breathed in and out.

"How many of you swapped sides?"

He again looked at Hagen. "Please don't kill me if I tell you?"

He got a nod from Charles.

"About a 100, maybe more."

"What's the name of your Captain?" Charles leaned into him.

"Captain Alberton sir."

"The Pawnee scouts with you, how many turned?"

"Just the four; they have been with us for many years."

Charles looked at him, then at Hagen. "Take him to Captain Somersett; make sure he's watched all the time."

Pvt Brown returned to him and reported that Arthur and the others were fine. He was then given instructions to check on the wounded and dead. Heidi was helping the doctors and other nurses. It had been a flash raid and caused a lot of damage. They couldn't afford to lose tents or supplies as winter was approaching; as this all unfolded, Corporal Heinz and Hosah, with the other Arapaho, arrived back; they all looked concerned and ready to fight; they cited the smoke and returned as quickly as they could.

Mad Dog went to Hosah and spoke about the raid. He would track the attackers to make sure they had left the area.

Charles broke the news of Texas and the casualties they had suffered. The Cpl dismounted and leant against his horse. He didn't speak for a while.

"That's a hard one to take; I feel we're slowly losing the war."

Charles looked around and then back at the Corporal.

"I know how you feel, but we are gathering for one last fight. If we are going to lose, let this be the battle that decides it."

It made the Cpl look up and agree.

"We need to pack up and keep going."

Over the next month, the weather began to get colder; they moved to the edge of the cities and sent scouts in all directions, not to get ambushed or attacked as they did in the Monongahela forest.

Charles spent time each evening talking to his soldiers and officers, and also with Arthur. He wanted to utilise all the spare moments he had. After losing Texas and other soldiers in the raid, he felt the desperation of the situation and the despair as they headed towards winter and a possible final showdown.

That evening, he sat by a campfire and took out Texas's old pipe. Gently loading it, he pushed in the tobacco with his thumbs and lit it.

"I haven't seen you smoke in a while, Father."

"Well, I know, Arthur; it feels like an old memory of living in Sunninghill and taking walks in Windsor Great Park."

"I remember you telling me the story of King Arthur when we walked in the park. You liked the story so much that my name was derived from it."

Charles smiled, "Yes, it was a different time then; the old world was full of myths and legends, now monsters exist, and we could do with the power of Excalibur."

Arthur reached down to grab his water canteen. He took a long gulp and laughed. "We're going to need a miracle to stop them." They both pulled their animal skins closer around their shoulders.

Cpl Heinz joined them by the fire with a pot of coffee. "We've looked around the area and sent out more scouts, but it's looking clear, Major."

"Thanks, Cpl, are the Arapaho joining us?"

"Yes, Hosah has sent braves to the other tribes asking for support. He has also sent some back to Colorado to check on his tribe."

Naomi joined them; her hair was down past her shoulders now. She went and sat next to Arthur and snuggled in tight. Charles looked at them; he was happy they had found each other and longed to see Rebecca and Emily.

The Cpl started talking about a bread loaf his grandmother used to make and how he used to eat it with cheese. He laughed about growing up in his small village and playing tricks on the local policemen. They would steal his bike and hide it a few cottages down. He was a kind man and never told them off; he just waggled his finger and smiled.

Cpl Heinz's tone dropped a little after that. "I got the news he had been taken by Nazar forces when they invaded; some say he was fighting to the end, protecting orphaned children." He looked away and then back at the fire. "Too many good people have paid a price for this war. We have to stop him."

Charles knew the mood was a little sombre and asked if Naomi knew any songs to lift it. She asked if her cousin could join her. Florence came over with Tom, and they both agreed on a song they used to sing when they were younger. As they sang, more people gathered to enjoy the music. One of the soldiers had a banjo and played along; when they finished, a round of applause went up. There were shouts of more and encore. Naomi giggled with her cousin, but they agreed to sing a few more songs.

Arthur looked at the sparks lifting up to the sky above and then at Naomi and Florence singing. It made him feel warm inside his stomach; he felt so proud. She looked beautiful and had an amazing voice. The night passed with songs and laughter as the cold started to creep in.

Chapter 41

"The snow is falling hard, and the coves are starting to freeze on the lakes."

A rebel soldier moved closer to the tall, gangly man.

"When do we attack, Captain?"

The tall, gangly man shook his head. "We don't; we gather as many of the dead as possible and lead them their way."

"We would do more damage raiding them and destroying their food supplies?"

The tall, gangly man moved towards a clearing where several dead were tied to a tree.

"Look at them; they were once normal people like us, but now they follow us and do as we command. They thirst for flesh, and we will give it to them."

The rebel soldier scratched his head. He understood using the dead to attack and cause disruption, but thought attacking would be a more destructive option.

"What's ever going on in that head of yours? Keep it in there. I've told you what's happening, and that's it."

The rebel soldier gathered as many men as he could and told them to round up the dead.

Nazar rode around his camp on a horse given to him by a senior official from Washington. The horse saved his life. The stallion was a thoroughbred, and Nazar enjoyed showing it to the other priests. He was not ordinarily interested in any of the trappings of the spoils of war, but this horse caught his eye.

"Georgiy, Georgiy, look at this fine beast!"

Georgiy had been drinking but sprung up out of his tent when he heard Nazar was calling.

"It is a fine horse, one worthy of your greatness."

"Ha-ha, enough with the praise; bring me three prisoners to fight whilst riding this horse."

Georgiy came back with three poor-looking souls; an African American stood there with ripped clothes; next to him was a man from the south, and an Irishman.

Nazar rode close to them, saying, "It's simple. You knock me off this horse, and you'll live; if you fail, you will be fed to my dogs."

The men looked at each other and were then presented with wooden poles. Nazar pulled a sword he had strapped to his back and let out a raucous laugh in the morning air. He then ushered a destroyer drone to come and take it. He said a sand timer would dictate how long they would get to achieve their goal or face the consequences. Nazar said the timer would give them ten minutes.

He started riding around, easing into his saddle and swinging himself from side to side. The three men looked at each other and then at Nazar. He nodded his head to the destroyer drone to turn the timer.

"Begin."

The men rushed forward and swung at Nazar as he used his horse to slip in and out of the men. They tried spacing themselves, coming at him from different angles, but he was at one with his horse, moving it in and out of them. The African American managed to get close and strike Nazar across his body, leaving a scrape across his face. The blood dripped from the wound and onto his cloak. He smiled and licked at it, revealing his extra-long tongue.

"Five minutes" "Try harder, try harder."

The Irishman was short but had spent years working on the railways; his legs were the size of tree trunks, his shoulders were broad, and his neck merged with them. He took it upon himself to go for the horse as the other two men swung in vain at Nazar. On one of his runs, he easily manoeuvred past the other two men, knocking them over. As he came close to the Irishmen, instead of swinging his pole at Nazar, he sprang at the side of the horse, using his weight and power to knock the horse off balance; Nazar fell from his horse as the animal took a tumble and crashed into the soil below. Nazar stood up and began to change in size, doubling his already impressive frame. The men stood back at the sight of him changing; the horse tried to raise itself, but could not put pressure on its back leg. Nazar let out a roar and hissed in anger that he had been felled. He then went over to the horse, took it by the neck and looked at the men before swiftly snapping its neck.

The sheer power of what was in front of them caused each man to step back. Nazar picked up the Irishmen's pole and snapped it in half.

Georgiy looked over at the dead horse and expected the punishment for the three prisoners to be more severe than normal; after all, Nazar loved that horse.

There was an awkward silence. The three men backed towards each other as Nazar stood looking at the dead horse. His body size began to return to normal. He looked at the men and then at Georgiy. "Return them to the work camps."

Georgiy was surprised but said nothing. Two destroyer drones came down to escort the men away. The Irishman looked at the other two men and saw the fear in their eyes. They said nothing as they walked away.

Nazar took out his knife and cut the horse's heart out; he then proceeded to eat it.

"Georgiy, we're moving to the winter camp soon."

Georgiy came closer.

"I have news of Oksana landing in the north; she has come from the motherland and will move through Alaska and down the coast."

"Good, good."

He then turned and walked to his tent. French Priestess Eveline greeted Nazar. She looked confident in her stride towards him, but when she saw blood around his mouth, she lowered her expectations.

"My lord, I have excellent news,"

A finger in the air from Nazar stopped her from continuing her update. He walked past her and into his tent. The Priestess stood there, unsure of what to do next. She waited outside his tent for five minutes before moving inside. Nazar was sitting in a throne-like chair, drinking out of a goblet.

"Why do you disturb me when you know I'm busy?"

She lowered her head.

"I couldn't wait to tell you."

Nazar filled his goblet again.

"Tell me? Is this to do with the opposing forces massing in Colorado?"

She stood there with an almost horror-like look on her face. "How has the news arrived so fast? The dispatcher only just arrived, my lord."

He sighed and leaned back, "Do you think my ear is tuned to just your gabble? I am a king, an emperor! I will control the world, do you understand?"

She started to shuffle backwards.

"Eveline, I want the Hayward wife to dance for me; bring her to me."

"Yes, sire"

Eveline took great pleasure in instructing Rebecca to leave Emily and follow her to see Nazar. Emily did not want to leave her side, but Rebecca had requested someone to help during their travels and was allowed to pick a servant. She chose wisely and now had Elin by her side. Elin reassured Rebecca that she would take care of Emily, and Emily clung to her as Rebecca left their tent.

Rebecca followed the priestess through the camp. Nazar had two razorbacks guarding his tent entrance, and two priests stood on either side of the tent opening. Eveline pushed her through and stepped back.

Inside, the torches lit the tent. The drapes surrounded the tent's edges; his throne was positioned in the corner, but he was not sitting on it. A voice from somewhere in the darkness said, "Dance for me, Rebecca."

She stood there, not moving.

"Why should I dance for you? You're a monster!"

"I am a monster, everything you hate in this world. Did you know your husband nearly killed me? Imagine how the world would have been different, but he failed like those before him, and now here I am, closing in on taking another part of the world."

"I wish he had; I wish you never existed."

"The problem is, Rebecca, I do, and nothing will change that. How is Emily coping with the illness in her veins?"

Rebecca felt the rage inside her well up.

"You fucking know that it was you that put it there, a child, how could you infect a healthy child."

"Spoken like a true mother, caring and willing to do anything for her."

He paused and moved into the light.

"Do you want her to get the next six months of medication? Maybe even reverse the illness?"

Rebecca felt sick to the bottom of her stomach.

"You are just saying that you have no cure; you just have the disease."

Nazar just shook his head.

"I am what this world needs. I am the darkness that follows the light; I am what Mother Nature intended to happen to control mankind from destroying more of this planet."

She just looked at him. Music began to play from outside the tent.

Dreading and fearing this megalomaniac overlord and the control he had over Emily's life, she began to sway from side to side.

"Give me wine." It was the only thing she could think of that would help her through this process. He clapped his hands, and two female priests came in with wine and a thin, see-through gown.

"Change into that now and dance before I have no use for you."

Rebecca closed her eyes and drank the wine from the bottle, letting it spill over her. The female priests left, and she undressed and put on the gown.

"I don't know how to dance; we do not dance as you would wish in Victorian society."

"Queen Victoria is dead, as is the Victorian age; I ended it." He went and sat on his throne.

All she could think of was some of the Indian dancers she had seen perform at various parties before the war. She did not know the full dance but started to move as she thought would suffice.

Nazar carried on drinking. He did not say whether he liked it or not.

As she swirled around, Eveline came in behind her naked. Rebecca carried on dancing, trying to ignore her, but she came in behind her, moving like an Arabian dancer. Nazar sat up, looking more interested now. She moved from side to side and squeezed up close to Rebecca. She wanted to push her away, but knew he was now aroused, and it was not the time to anger him.

The music became faster and more furious; Eveline spun her around and moved her close to her naked body; she grabbed her from behind and pushed her breasts against hers. Rebecca was trying to move backwards, but Eveline pulled her in and kissed her hard on the lips.

"Bravo, Bravo, this is more like it."

Rebecca smelled the vodka on Eveline's breath. She didn't want to be kissed again and tried to push her back. She then came in behind her and danced from side to side in motion with Rebecca's body. Her hands moved up and down as Nazar stood from his throne.

An officer entered the tent as he began to take off his top.

Nazar's glare had the officer stop in his tracks.

"This better be good because I will tear you from limb to limb, if not?"

"I have a message from Lev, my lord; he has a request."

Nazar turned to throw over a table but stopped himself.

"Eveline, take Rebecca away." His voice was disappointed.

Rebecca pulled her gown around her shoulders tight. Inside, she felt a massive relief as she left the tent. She did not know what would have happened next, but this was a huge let-off. She did not look back as she left the tent; Eveline threw her clothes in the snow. She acted as if it were Rebecca's fault for ruining her chance to advance higher up the chain of command. It did not take her long to put her clothes on as the fresh snow pushed in between her toes. The coldness was sobering, sharpening her senses as she left into the darkness and falling snow.

Chapter 42

Corporal Heinz checked the ice around the edges of the cove. It was frozen. Within the next few weeks, it would be plausible to walk across the ice. The last of the Allied forces was camped around the Ozarks; most were now gathered around Colorado. The battle plans were being drawn up for the 'Last Stand'.

Hosah and Hagen had gone with the other braves to bring fresh meat, particularly whitetail deer or elk. Charles had the civilians and children near the engineers to keep them under close watch. Captain Somersett had his men and the late Captain Steinberg's soldiers under his wing.

The other units were scattered around the lakes so as not to concentrate an attack. General Baxter Washington was in charge of these forces and sent regular scouts out to keep the lines of communication open. The heavy snowfall that followed made it difficult to move around; the pockets of Allied forces were cut off from each other and kept themselves busy by cutting wood and helping store the food, which the hunting parties returned with. Charles watched Hosah take Arthur out hunting; the Native American Indians handled the extreme weather well; their skills in such conditions were needed.

As the evening fell, the first call from a nearby camp signalled the arrival of the dead. Gunfire could be heard around the Ozarks, and screams of those who had been caught and torn apart were carried across the frozen water. Charles asked the soldiers to check their weapons to see if they had frozen in the icy conditions. The snow was coming down heavily, which limited the amount you could see. The soldiers around the makeshift camp looked into the woods and open areas for movement; Charles told Arthur and the other children to be ready, and as he spoke, the call went up that they were amongst them. Hagen came to Charles' side with his bear skin on and axe in hand. Instantly, Charles felt more secure having the Viking alongside him. The sight of a frozen flesh-eater coming towards them was unnerving. A British soldier stuck his bayonet into the stomach of a flesh-eater who resembled a man; it was hard to determine his age, as the rotten flesh was partly frozen, and a lot of his features were distorted with bits missing. The soldier fought to hold the flesh-eater back, but coming through the snow was another one, this time maybe a woman or teenager. It came to his side and grabbed at his arm.

Hagen stepped forward and chopped both the dead woman's arms off. He then kicked her back and stuck his axe in the head; he was surprised it needed another hit for the flesh-eater to stop moving. The frozen weather had helped toughen their outer layer. Charles brought his revolver around and shot the other in the head. The attacks were random and not a sustained assault. They continued throughout the day and evening and were demoralising for the forces camped around the Ozarks. The heavy snow meant they could not leave their encampments and had to continue fighting these small attacks; the idea was to wear the forces down. Charles thought that if they had more flesh-eaters in place, they would mount a significant attack, but it was more than likely that they gathered what they could and set them in the direction of any allied camps.

It meant food-hunting parties had to be extra vigilant. Charles had the civilians working on getting wood for the fires, and the soldiers took it in turn to go out and gather food with the braves. Arthur came forward and told his father he was heading out with Hosah and two of the engineers to hunt elk. The weather was clear and still early morning; he reluctantly agreed to let him go. Naomi kissed him on the cheek and told him to be careful; he asked her to look after Tom with a cheeky smile on his face.

They moved through woodland and onto a small hill. They could see a cluster of elk grazing and waited for them to get near a frozen cove, and then they pounced; the two British engineers took watch whilst Hosah and Arthur prepared to use their bows and arrows to take down two elks. Hosah took down a steer with a shot to the body. Arthur waited for Hosah to give him the nod, and when he did, he let fly with an arrow which hit a large female elk in the head; she fell onto the ice hard, and the sound underneath the ice reverberated and twanged across the cove. Hosah led them down the hill and told Arthur to stay close as the other elk fled the attack. Hosah moved carefully across the ice and looked weaker in certain areas; he pointed this out to Arthur as he followed behind. When they arrived at the fallen animals, he noticed the ice was cracking under the weight of the animals.

"We do not have much time; the ice could give way", he also pointed to the dark, marauding clouds which were moving in; Hosah quickly got to work tying the legs and attaching the rope they would use to drag the elks off the ice. Their horses were tied near the cove edge, and before Arthur could go to them with the rope, a cry of pain echoed out from the hill. One of the British soldiers who was waiting at the top came running down; he was out of breath and pointed to the hill. "A small herd came up behind us, a rebel and a priest was leading them, whilst Henry was relieving himself they crept up behind him and stabbed him" he paused, then they let the dead eat him alive, "I tried to help him and fight off the dead, but there was just too many."

Hosah looked up at the hill as the flesh-eaters started to push through the undergrowth and venture towards them. There was no sign of the rebel or priest; they had probably snuck off back into the forest, was the soldiers' reckoning. Hosah told the soldier to guard the horses the best he could, and he would try and lead the dead onto the ice. He told Arthur to fall further back on the ice.

Arthur looked at the frozen dead's faces, twisted even more by the extreme cold. The situation was compounded by the first flurry of snow, which began to fall hard.

"Carl, be ready" The soldier looked at Hosah and brought up his rifle with a bayonet attached.

Hosah banged his knife against the small axe he held in his other hand. This helped focus the flesh-eaters on him and not on the British soldier. Arthur counted twenty or more of the dead and brought his bow up in anticipation; Hosah focused on luring the first one towards him and then dispatched his victim with a quick hit to the head with his axe. He then walked slowly backwards as they followed him across the ice. Carl began shooting at the four flesh-eaters in front of him. Hosah kept moving back and killing anything that came into range. The echoing under the ice was making Arthur wary,

Hosah continued leading them further onto the ice, which began to crack under their weight as their numbers increased. The first couple at the front fell through; seeing them thrashing around, trying to get at Hosah before going under the ice, was strange. A large male flesh-eater came at him, and his rotting stomach protruded out of a dishevelled shirt. He managed to grab Hosah's arm, and as he lowered himself to bite it, they both went through the ice.

The dead man thrashed about, trying to reach the flesh in front of him. Hosah could only push him back as he attempted to pull himself out of the ice, but it kept breaking away. Several more did not take long to fall through the broken ice. Arthur called Hosah to say that he was coming to help. He drew his arrow, but Hosah had already swum under the ice and was moving towards Arthur. Two flesh-eaters made their way towards Arthur; he looked at them and tried to gauge how much time he had. His heart rate increased, and he felt overwhelmed with Hosah trapped under the ice. Hosah had frantically started to use his knife to cut into the ice underwater, whilst Arthur used his axe from the topside. Each downward hit carried more purpose, but the ice was not breaking. He could see Hosah's face underneath and the two dead flesh eaters closing in.

Arthur had to stop momentarily as a flesh-eater, hissing and gnarling, was almost upon him. He took aim and shot an arrow at its head; this flesh-eater had been turned a while; the only indication it was a female in a previous life was what was left of her dress. The rest of her was rotten and partially frozen as she made her way towards him. The arrow sailed past her head; the sheer panic of Hosah drowning beneath him and the dead coming to eat him was clouding his senses. He drew another arrow and took aim; he felt the ice underneath him still being hit, which gave him the urge to fire quickly; the relief as it struck her in the head and brought her crashing down spurred him even more. Her weight was enough to cause a crack in the ice under Arthur's feet, but before he could look down, he was knocked back by the second flesh-eater. It was thin and gangly, not as rotten, maybe a teenager prior to the war. The flesh-eater was hard to hold off; he had dropped his bow and could not reach for his knife. There were still two more flesh-eaters making their way to feed on Arthur. Carl had killed three of his and only had one to finish off.

Arthur felt he was losing his strength; its biting teeth began to come closer and closer to his face; suddenly, on his left-hand side, the ice burst up; coming through it was Hosah. He was spluttering and coughing, but focused quickly; he pulled himself out of the ice and, in one blow, stuck his knife into the flesh-eater's head. He was cold and shook himself as the snow started to fall. Arthur had a deer pelt wrapped around his shoulders and quickly handed it over to Hosah. He then picked up his bow, took an arrow from the pouch on his back, and took aim. He let it fly into one of the flesh-eaters' heads, killing them on impact. The other slowly came forward but slipped into the broken ice and sank with the rest of the dead into the dark waters below.

"Thank you, Hosah, you saved my life."

He smiled, though cold, "You saved mine."

"We must get the elks off the ice and back to the camp; there may be more rebels or priests in the area."

Chapter 43

The months passed, and winter rolled into spring. The leaves returned to the trees, and life began to return in abundance to the great plains and the steppes. The winter had been a struggle to survive, but Charles was happy to see the gathering of the American and European forces. The size of the force was spread across many miles. The forces were mixed and would be under the command of the officers for their area. The battle plans were still being drawn up and debated.

Arthur had turned sixteen and was happy to get nearer to Naomi, who had turned seventeen. They had time to ride onto the plains as hundreds of patrols guarded each camp. Tom and Florence would sometimes come with them and, other times, stay back at the camp. The prairie grass swayed from side to side as the wind picked up, and the rolling hills stretched for miles.

Charles was in his tent, looking over a map of the area and digesting where the main forces would be. He was pleasantly interrupted by a deep voice.

"You need to get your tactics spot on with this."

He immediately knew who it was and went over to embrace Sergeant Thomas Butcher.

"Dear god, man, it's so good to see you again."

Thomas thanked Charles for visiting him in the spring and sending letters updating him on what was happening at the front. He explained how they had just managed to survive the winter, but many perished in the attacks. The campaign they fought was effective; many of the soldiers had taken a while to recover from fatigue. The fear of a spring attack had worried the high command, but it didn't materialise, which made them concerned in another way.

"Has your family moved to Canada?"

Thomas nodded his head.

"It was good to spend time with them, especially with what's coming. I found it hard to let go." Thomas was sensitive to the fact that Charles's family was now separated from him and in grave danger.

"We must make this final battle count, Charles; there is nowhere else to run?"

Charles agreed.

"Nazar will sense he has forced us into his plan, back to the Rocky Mountains; he wants to destroy the resistance once and for all. We have to hope the tactics of drawing them into the chosen area will help. We know what they did to us in Europe, and we know how they overcame one of the best armies in the world in Great Britain, and slowly but surely, they have pushed America back to the Rockies."

Thomas looked at the map.

"Would you agree with this battlefield location?"

"We have hills to base the cannons and good topography, but the battle will be fought over a large area, and lines of communication will be essential."

Thomas asked where they would be based for the pending fight.

"Rattlesnake Butte."

He smiled, "It sounds like an imposing place?"

"Well, maybe we can throw rattlesnakes at them?" Charles laughed after saying that and found himself thinking about the fact that he hadn't laughed for a long time.

"The full debriefing will take place over the next few weeks, but the plan is to split their forces where possible. The fight will be across a large area, so we will rely on our mobile units to help counterattack and separate them."

"Do we know what numbers they will have, Charles?"

He looked at the map and then at his old friend.

"I would imagine over a million; they have drone soldiers, rebels, the dead. It will be more than he had in France all those years ago."

Thomas sat down on a chair in the corner of the tent.

"Have you written your final words down?"

"I have. I hope you have, too."

He nodded.

"Where will Arthur be?"

"I've asked him to be with the supply wagons at the foot of the Rockies."

"Will the other teenagers be there?"

Charles tilted his head. "I don't think they will leave each other's side. If we lose this battle, they will need to flee into the Rockies and live under the rule of Nazar."

Standing and moving just outside the tent, Thomas reminisced about the journey from the Carpathian Mountains to the American Rockies over the past several years.

"I never thought I would see the world, not like this anyway. If I had worked as a fisherman or farmer, it would have just been stories of far-off lands, but now I have seen so many of these lands and their beauty, it would be a great shame if they were to fall into his rule forever."

Charles joined him outside the tent. "The journey has been emotionally hard, and I'm grateful to have had my close family and friends with me on it; also, I cannot forget the great soldiers who served by my side."

"We have a chance to go out with a bang," Thomas said.

He added that he would ride out to the butte and examine what they would need to do.

Charles returned to his tent and took out the picture of his family. He thought about Rebecca and Emily in Nazar's camp. Perversely, he was happy Nazar was getting closer. As he prayed, he could see them alive one more time. He didn't let his mind go too deep into whether this was impossible anymore.

The following week saw them camp closer to Rattlesnake Butte. Charles took his officers and kept leaders to the top of the butte; from there, they looked towards the open plains. Captain Kiesl was there with a small contingent of Austrian soldiers. Corporal Heinz and Sergeant Butcher moved around at the top of the Butte. Hosah was talking with Little Bear and Mad Dog. He grabbed the soil beneath his feet and let it fall out of his hand; a gentle breeze took the small granules a little further from where he tipped the remaining soil. The Arapaho walked around, pointing out the various key locations to the officers; they advised of the topography and where they thought the battle defences would give the allied forces a chance. They had all witnessed the great numbers of the dead, and the elders had spoken with other fleeing tribes from the east that his army was second to none.

Hagen went to a rock protruding from the ground. Standing on top of it, he looked at the layout of the land.

"Major, will the artillery be based on the top here?"

Charles walked over towards him. "We will be protecting an artillery battery during the battle."

Pvt Chamberlin joined Hagen on the rock.

"This would give me a good shooting spot,"

Hagen smiled. "Snipers are not going to be needed; even I couldn't miss when there's over a million of them."

Alexander saw the funny side as they looked out across the grasslands.

Pvt Brown was talking to Dai Evans. "Is Heidi going to be with the reserves in the Rockies?"

"No, she will be with a handful of frontline nurses that will treat the soldiers on top of the butte."

Dai looked surprised.

Pvt Brown raised his shoulders. "If we're going to die in this battle, we might as well be close to each other."

"Fair point, John."

"I hope the defences stop those long limbs from climbing up this hill."

John shook his head. "Unfortunately, not much can stop them, apart from the bayonet at the end of your rifle or the bullets in its magazine."

They both laughed.

Captain Somersett's men would hold the south part of Rattlesnake Butte, tasked with keeping the enemy from flanking from that side. He spoke to Charles about where the munitions would be stationed. The general plan was to keep them centralised so everyone could access them.

Charles used his binoculars to look across to the other planned locations, and the main thing he could see was the figures moving about. There were concerns over whether they should show their hand by building such defences, but with the vast advancing army, time was against them.

Chapter 44

The day of the battle plan debriefing came around fast. The officers representing all of the forces gathered around a small hill. The senior officers would be at the front, and the officers' presence would reinforce the battle plan itself. After many meetings and debates, the idea was to entice Nazar's forces past Corner Mountain and Nemrick Butte on both sides. Charles's forces and an artillery battery to help pound the enemy are sitting behind that. The other sites would also have artillery to inflict as much damage as possible. There would be forces stationed on Larkspur Butte and Raspberry Butte.

They spoke about previous battles where a massive amount of ammunition was wasted on the dead, thus allowing the drone soldiers to gain the upper hand eventually. The flesh-eaters had always been a driving force in Nazar's attacks, as they were expendable. The plan this time was to lure them through and towards Butler Canyon and across Cook Creek. The terrain would allow firing from the ridge behind it, and they would dig pits to trap thousands. It would never suffice to deal with all of them, but the idea was simple: draw them through and keep the main body moving. Then, the forward positions would concentrate fire on his soldiers and rebels.

Some familiar faces were speaking from the top of the hill. Brigadier Baker and Major General Green stood alongside allied generals, giving their views on the forthcoming battle. Charles got a nod from General Baxter Washington; he had turned out not to be the buffoon Charles thought he would be.

Standing close by was the new British Field Marshal Bartholomew Humes. He had seen action in Africa and the battle for Great Britain. He was liked by the officers and the soldiers under him and was known for not making rash moves or sacrificing his men.

Marshal Humes was a reserved character. He was relatively young to hold such a powerful position in his mid-fifties, but he had proven himself a leader, and it was time for him to unite the British forces for what lay ahead.

In turn, the senior officers discussed how they saw the battle unfolding, stressing that this was the end of the line. If things did go bottom up, a plan had been put together: retreating into the Rockies and sending small sortie attacks into Nazar-held territories.

The general consensus also saw many of the civilians who had fled to Canada being allowed back under some sort of deal. The politicians wanted to strike that deal immediately, even forgoing the final battle and the foot of the Rockies. The army did not agree with that idea and felt they should make an attempt to stop him once and for all.

The cavalry would be heavily favoured if the battle were there for the taking. They would come around from the hills behind the mountain and Buttes to swing the battle.

Once the briefing had finished, the officers would carry the message to their units and help it spread amongst the soldiers under their command; from that moment, preparations began in earnest, fortifying the locations mentioned to the men. The scene for miles reflected worker ants streaming out of their nest, busy carrying supplies to each location. The work was being carried out at haste, as scouts saw a dust cloud stretching on for miles, moving towards Colorado.

Some generals asked whether he would wait a few more winters, slowly pillage farms, and hit the small resources they had left, forcing them to surrender or face starvation.

Major Hayward had spoken about how he thought Nazar would not be patient. He was a man who feared nothing and could not stop himself from grabbing it all. If he knew the Allied army was gathered in one place, he would not be able to resist attacking, considering the size of his force and that he had never been defeated in all these years. They may have lost small battles, but the decisive ones—no, they always prevailed.

Two more weeks passed, and the defences were in place, the days were growing warmer, which meant water supplies were needed up on the defensive locations. Charles looked down from the Rattlesnake Butte. They had cleared some plains cottonwood trees, which would have acted as cover from the south side. Some bushes had been left in parts to help form a natural defence alongside the man-made ditches and stakes which layered the Buttes. The artillery pieces were in place and fell under the command of Captain Benjamin Brice; he was not overly experienced in warfare but was skilled at getting his weaponry to hit targets when needed. He lost his family in the invasion of Great Britain and felt compelled to fight to the bitter end. A young corporal had confided in Major Hayward that, since landing in America, understandably, Captain Brice was not the same man anymore. He treated his soldiers respectfully but rarely joined them for a beer or sing-along. He would often retreat to his tent; sometimes, he could be heard weeping, but he channelled that sorrow into perfecting his craft with the cannons.

The soldiers were camping further down the hill and would only fully commit to the defences once the enemy was advancing. Riding out onto the Great Plains was the 7th Cavalry. They had been given orders to lead the enemy to the American and Allied forces. The braves with them would send smoke signals to help speed up the message of the impending army.

Arthur was allowed to stay with his father until the message came that Nazar was close. Charles took great solace in having him close. He enjoyed seeing Arthur laugh and joke with Naomi; they were close, and he hoped they would have more time together after the war. Tom was already with the reserves with Florence; Charles said it would be better to know they were already safe, leaving only Naomi and Arthur to join them in the mountains.

Chapter 45

At the beginning of July, while Charles was having coffee with Arthur, he saw smoke across the Great Plains.

The buglers sounded the call to arms, and the whole area had an air of tension and contemplation about what was coming. Charles walked into his tent, tightened his kaki tunic, and looked into a small shaving mirror; he then tightened his collar. Arthur came running into the tent and hugged him.

"They're here, Father."

Naomi was waiting outside.

"You know where to go, son, keep them safe; you have been a rock by my side; I couldn't have asked for a better son." Charles had tears falling down his cheeks.

"I love you, Dad."

"I love you, too, son."

They both hugged each other. Arthur didn't want to overthink about what lay ahead, as he was scared to think he might never see his dad again. When they broke their embrace, Charles checked his Enfield revolver, reached down to the side of his bed where his Lee-Metford rifle stood, and put it over his shoulder.

"You must leave now, Arthur." He stepped outside the tent and saw Naomi; she couldn't help herself and hugged Charles. "You both must stick to the plan and stay safe."

Naomi kissed Arthur on the cheek and took his hand. She knew he did not want to leave. A Pvt came over to the major, leading his horse towards him. Charles mounted his horse and put on his helmet. He smiled at Arthur and Naomi. He then turned his horse and rode to join his men and officers at the top of Rattlesnake Butte. He looked back once to see Arthur and Naomi riding off; Arthur must have sensed he was looking and looked back and raised his fist in the air. Charles replied by raising his hand.

At the top of Rattlesnake Butte was a frenzied scene of soldiers moving into position; even if most of the legwork had already been done, they still had to settle themselves into the defensives. Towers on all of the buttes gave the soldiers viewing points so they could look across the open plains. Charles dismounted from his horse, and it was taken to where they had built a decent-sized paddock for a number of horses. He was joined at the top of one of the towers by some of his trusted men, Sergeant Butcher, Corporal Heinz, Captain Somersett and Captain Kiesl. They all looked through their binoculars at this enormous dust cloud stretching for miles. There was a distant drumming, almost a constant hum, as this wall of dust moved towards them.

The 7th Calvary had engaged a small enemy scouting group but fell back quickly rather than be outnumbered. They had joined the American units on Corner Mountain and would act as a rapid counterattack force if they had the opportunity. The drums slowly grew louder, and the dust settled, revealing a force as far as the eyes could see.

They were too far away for the naked eye to see in detail, but with binoculars, it helped reveal what they had all dreaded: an army to end all resistance in America.

"It's what we were expecting", Sergeant Butcher said softly.

"It is, we knew they would try and end this now." Charles continued to look along the front of the enemy line; it did not look like they had any of the dead in their ranks or long limbs or other animals. Charles concluded quickly that it could mean they would not attack straight away. It might be an evening attack or an early morning. He kept his thoughts to himself and continued looking along the line. It looked like rebels and drone soldiers were in the forward ranks; in front of them, there seemed to be priests, maybe half a mile apart. The ranks of soldiers blurred into the distance. It sent a shiver down all of their spines at what was ahead. The enemy stood there for an hour, not moving; then horns sounded out all along their front line. In unison, they turned and started marching away from the frontline.

"Mark the time, please, Corporal." Charles then walked down the steps to the primary defences. He wanted the men to see him and feel he was there with them. The soldiers were told to stand down for now; a man-made ramp leading to the butte was not destroyed; this would only happen when the attack reached them. The other locations had the same access points. Scouts would be sent out from all areas to watch Nazar's forces; the tension was now felt amongst everyone. He showed how big his force was, which was unnerving for everyone to witness.

"We must be ready for an attack this evening; he may send a probing force to test our firepower." Charles walked with Sergeant Butcher as he gave out his orders for what lay ahead.

Chapter 46

Nazar brought his horse high up on a hill for all to see. He felt unbeatable and ready to claim another piece of the world map. The orders had been given for units to test them all along the front; then, in the early hours, they would attack.

Oksana joined him at the top of the hill. Her horse was as dark as the night. She was dressed in light black body armour and had two swords strapped across her back. She also had daggers tucked into either side of her horse's saddle.

"This will be a great few days, my love." Nazar marvelled at it, all of his forces moving around like ants.

He did not want to wait long before sending out a small force to test their defences. He had chosen soldiers who had been sick or officers who had not carried out his orders to the letter; they would be involved in this fight. He then set up an open tent and told his armies to feast before battle. He had given orders for beer and wine to be made abundant to his forces.

General Georgiy sat on his left-hand side with Queen Oksana on the other; next to her were Priestess Eveline Arnoult and Priestess Jane Llewellyn. Arriving late were Lev with Priestess Catherine Bonnaire and his right-hand man, Captain Rimmel.

"Nice of you to join us, brother." Nazar raised a glass of wine.

"This is one of our most important battles in recent times, and yet you are late." Oksana's tone quieted the gentle conversation around the table when she questioned Lev.

"I am the commander of the northern armies and have assisted my brother in every campaign since the beginning of this war. Do not lecture me on my timing." He paused to tip wine down his throat; with it still spilling out of his mouth, he stood up. "I raise my glass to Nazar," he said sarcastically, adding "Oksana" at the end of the toast.

"Soon America will fall, and he will be Emperor of the world."

Nazar stood up.

"You have served me well, my brother! But do not treat me like anything other than your emperor. As my queen has stated, no one defies my orders." He looked around the table. Wars can be won on attrition and good planning." He then focused on Lev. But battles are about timing. Do not fail me, brother."

Lev stood there; his face gave away his aggravation at what had been said.

"Have I ever failed you, my brother?"

The tension was rising with Nazar getting more irritated with his stance towards him. He would allow nobody to question or challenge his authority,

Lev sensed his anger and went and sat down.

Nazar took this as a backdown and sat down himself. They drank and ate; the conversation was about the battle ahead. There was a boastful chat from all of the generals about how their forces would dominate the battlefield. Nazar just drank and ate whilst letting them discuss this.

Soon, the initial attack wave was marching by the tent. Nazar stood and raised his fist to the small army.

A selection of Priests would travel with the reconnaissance force to monitor the firepower of the Allied defences. Apart from them, the whole force was dispensable. Seeing them leave made him feel empowered. He took Oksana's hand and led her to their tent. She knew he wanted to make love to her before the battle.

Chapter 47

A young American cavalryman was the first to notice movement by Antelope Creek. He was meant to ride with another soldier but had to return to the main group after feeling unwell. The young soldier thought it was down to nerves, which he understood as he was hanging by a thread. He brushed the side of his horse's mane and steered it towards the creek. The closer he got, the more the horse became agitated. Underneath the horse's hooves, the grass swayed in the wind, which whistled along the creek. The moment he saw several figures moving in the shadows was enough to get him to reach for his rifle.

"Ya'll all with the allies." He said this in a low voice as he reached to unclip the rifle from his holder.

The bullet that whizzed past his horse was enough to signal that an attack was coming. He turned and galloped at full speed towards Corner Mountain. The war cry that erupted behind him made his heart beat even faster.

As he got closer to his unit, he looked over his shoulder; coming behind him were hundreds of horses spread out in a long line. He did not check again; he just started shouting the closer he got to the first outpost. The soldiers there were sitting around a campfire drinking coffee, but their horses were tethered nearby. They threw down their mugs and rushed to get mounted as quickly as possible. The speed of the enemy attack gave them no choice but to ride towards Corner Mountain. The second outpost saw the cavalrymen coming at speed and mounted up without asking a question,

Soon, they were riding around the mountain and towards the track leading up to the defences; the roar of the attacking force forewarned all of the other defences. Allied soldiers had moved from their camps on the grasslands in the evening, resting in the fortified buttes and mountains. The charging enemy was brutal to see in the darkness, but the oil fires dug around the defences were quickly lit. This gave some light to the dark landscape. Some of the cannons and mortars began to fire; their thunderous shots shook the valley and ground around them. The explosions lit up the sky, earth and rock were thrown hundreds of meters into the air. When a shell landed amongst the attacking force, the carnage that followed was as destructive as ever. Flesh was ripped from man and beast, and screams of terror were lost in the instant explosion that engulfed them.

Charles watched from his lookout post at the top of the butte. Captain Somersett stood next to him, watching the shells land on the grasslands below.

"Do you think this is the main attack?"

Charles shook his head. "They will test our defences first. Then, more than likely, come in the early morning."

"I will ready my men." He put his hand out to shake the Major's.

Charles embraced it with both his. "You have helped us survive this long, and I'm grateful to have you and your men with us."

As he walked down the steps, Sergeant Butcher accompanied Charles at the top.

"They're coming around the west and east sides of Rattlesnake Butte." Sergeant Butcher bent down in the lookout and noted the time under candlelight.

"Let's see how they fare against the spikes and volley fire."

Most of the soldiers were crouched in the trenches, holding their Lee-Metford or Martini-Henry rifles tight and listening to the unfolding events. There was a sombre mood amongst the men. Some had not been involved in a battle of this scale before. They were buoyed by the sheer number of Allied soldiers but grounded by the veterans' tales of fighting across Europe and Great Britain. The night guarded the anxious expressions on many of their faces.

The order was not given to open fire on the attackers as they rode around the butte. Gunfire could be heard along the defensive line. The east and west soldiers opened fire as their targets circled. They fired at the movement, and as the shells landed, they lit up the area where they hit.

The British engineers had success in knocking riders off their horses and causing heavy casualties. Once they had dismounted, they began to try and make their way up the sides; this was always going to be hard with the numbers they had available. The American soldiers had supplied barbed wire to go all around the butte. Originally, the wire was used for the cattle ranches, but these same men had suggested its potential to help stop the enemy from surging up the slopes. The wooden stakes of various sizes would still be there to prevent humans and beasts alike.

The probing force was met with an incredible onslaught of bullets, causing the enemy not to make much headway; they began to be bogged down on the lower slopes. There was no need to use the Maxim machine guns; this was about the soldiers at the top picking their shots. Charles knew Nazar would test their defences, which also helped the Allied forces pinpoint any weak spots. The attacks broke off after around twenty minutes or more, and the enemy sustained heavy losses, but this meant nothing to them. The enemy soldiers who made it back to the priests would pass on the information.

No losses had been confirmed on Rattlesnake Butte; some men had been wounded, but the defences had held firm. Charles walked around checking on his men. The heavy artillery pieces did not open fire and were still covered. This had been the plan not to use all the heavy pieces, there were also a few other hidden traps awaiting the main battle. Corporal Heinz would lead a small group of soldiers to check on the dead or wounded. All had been warned that some of the dead could come back to life as flesh-eaters.

Corporal Heinz led his men down to the fallen enemy. There were groans and pleas for help. Some had already changed and were now feeding on the poor souls who were not infected. He gave the order to finish off those who had changed or were changing. The other wounded enemy soldiers would be assisted the best they could, but the looming threat meant not too many resources would be spent on them. Corporal Heinz looked at the attacking force strewn around the bottom defences; they looked old or poorly, which he concluded meant expendable to Nazar. He knew how his army model worked, and it was a dangerous machine that would take some stopping.

An old rebel raised his hand towards Corporal Heinz. He started talking to him, but his voice was quiet; blood was all over his jacket and around his head. The corporal leant in but had his revolver ready at his side.

"This was not what I wanted."

The corporal came in closer.

"Rest, soldier, you will be treated soon."

The old man's face grimaced in pain. "You cannot stop his army; it's too big. You might as well flee."

The corporal raised his shoulders. "There is nowhere left to run. We have been doing that for years. Rest now." He turned and continued checking on the soldiers around him. Once this was complete, he returned with his men to report on his findings.

In the daytime, the Arapaho communicated with the other tribes using smoke signals, but in the evening, they used dispatch riders. This was a dangerous role, as enemy riders would look to intercept them. As soon as the attack had broken off, these riders were sent out to gather information and report to each other.

The orderlies were spread out around the Rattlesnake Butte. The ammunition would be brought around as quickly as possible to keep the rate of fire up during the battle. Pvt Brown had asked permission to check on Heidi, which Sergeant Butcher allowed. When he reached Heidi, she was busy dressing a wound on a British Engineer; the medical area she was working in was near the centre of the Butte and had lanterns laid out in a reasonable circle; she looked up and smiled when she saw him. He felt instantly calmer seeing her and was glad she would be close to him. After treating the soldier, she came over to him.

"Nice to see you, John." She rubbed the side of his arm. She wanted to kiss him, but it would be inappropriate.

He touched her hand gently and waited for her to finish her rounds. John grabbed a cup of tea and sat on a log near a small campfire. It felt good to let the hot tea flow down his throat whilst he looked at the stars. He couldn't let his mind wander too far from the current situation as he knew what lay ahead and realised that his days and Heidi's could be numbered. Once she had finished helping the wounded, the other nurses said she could spend some time with him.

"I always get a bit nervous when the wounded come to us. I worry that one of them is going to be you." She looked a bit teary-eyed.

John brushed her cheek. "I can understand, but try not to think that, whatever happens, we will be close to each other, even if I were to pass." She reached over and pulled him in tight. John looked around and then kissed her on the lips. "I'm sorry this war ever happened, but I'm not sorry I met you. I love you, Heidi." She wiped away her tears and just held him tight. A call to return to their posts broke up their embrace.

"Stay as safe as you can, John."

"You too, Heidi."

Charles had finished walking around the defences; there was some time for them to rest; he took this time by resting against a post. He awoke with a dry mouth, removed his helmet, and swept back his hair. He cleared some dust from his eyes and asked a passing soldier on watch what time it was. He was told it was four am; Charles took out his water carton and took a swig. He thought about how the sun was slowly starting to rise. Hosah was walking towards him, covered in war paint.

"They're coming."

Charles nodded his head. He felt he needed to pause for a second to take in what was about to happen. He reached into his tunic and took out the picture of his family, kissed it and tucked it back in. Hosah spoke to around fifteen braves; there were more on Rattlesnake Butte, but they were spread out and ready to help with the hand-to-hand fighting. Charles kept walking to the nearest lookout post; he climbed to the top and took out his binoculars; it was still too dark to make out any true definition, so he lowered them to allow his eyes to see into the vast grasslands.

The noise sweeping towards them was that of the dead; no drums or rousing voices were calling for victory. This was a known, dreaded sound. A thing whose only purpose was now to consume everything that was living. Selected riders went out with lit torches; there was a good number of them to create enough presence for the flesh-eaters to follow. The chatting, gasping, groaning noise was suffocating in volume; the army of dead moved past at a slow pace. The soldiers held off firing as instructed and awaited the first wave.

Some of the Nazar priests were amongst the dead and tried to lead them towards the defences, but the masses were already in motion and could not be deterred. American soldiers with Native American Scouts were there to disrupt communication about what was happening at the front; if they intercepted a messenger, they would try and kill them before the message got back.

Emerging from the darkness came the second wave. They expected to hear the roar of enemy machine guns and artillery, but the silence had not altered Nazar's attack plans. He was so assured by previous victories and his armies' more significant numbers that the orders were to press on.

The time had moved on and was soon approaching 5 am. The sun would be coming up around 6 am, which would mean better artillery accuracy. Nazar's oncoming second wave was quiet at first, but this didn't last; as a slow rumbling filled the early morning darkness, a persistent rhythm of beating drums followed it. Voices started to chant a war song, which could be heard for miles in each direction. It was intimidating because of the sheer numbers singing it, and it had the desired effect of causing concern and questioning amongst the soldiers awaiting the start of the battle.

The cannons were prepared for the first volley, and the machine guns aimed towards the noise. Pvt Chamberlin had gone to a high position and was scoping the landscape; he could come into his own with better light. A cry went out, and the drums stopped. This was followed by silence from the singing voices. You could almost hear a pin drop. It was so quiet; the breeze whistled around the defences, but even that did not disturb the eerie silence; what broke it felt like a wall of noise. The war cry was so vast and long that it engulfed everything; it was more than anything Charles had heard in the many battles he had experienced with Nazar.

"Fire"

The large artillery pieces began letting go of the shells sitting inside their chambers. The sheer power in each shot was frightening. When the shells landed, the area around the explosion lit up. The advancing enemy soldiers found themselves at the mercy of each shell that crashed into the ground. The screams of the men and women who were hit by the impact of the shell could be heard all along the valley. This did not stop their steady advance; the darkness was still their friend.

The second wave broke onto Nemrick Butte first, as it was ahead of Corner Mountain and Rattlesnake Butte. This was where the sound of machine gun and rifle fire came from initially, and then Corner Mountain followed suit. The soldiers and machine gunners on Rattlesnake Butte almost held their breath while waiting for the enemy to reach their defences. A second roar helped indicate they had reached the barbed wire; there were a lot of soldiers stuck at the defences trying to shoot up at the British and American positions. Charles had instructed his officers to take control of their own areas unless ordered otherwise. The Maxim guns began to open fire; the rattle of constant fire was ruthless all along the frontline. The bullets ripped into the soldiers who were bunched at the foot of the butte. Their groans could be heard at the top of the butte as the guns went to work in devastating fashion.

The bullets smacked into wooden stakes which had been dug into the soil all around the butte, rocks and soil flung into the air as the hail of bullets landed amongst the onrushing enemy rebels and drone soldiers. Priests amongst the soldiers and rebels kept them from turning back; anybody who did so was shot or stabbed to death. There was no retreating unless the order was given.

The British and Allied soldiers built parapets with a fire step around the defences. They listened for the bugler to sound the permission to fire, and when it rang out, they advanced to the fire step. The younger soldiers followed the veterans, hearts beating fast and eager to get involved. They had range markers to help gauge the distance, but it was to fire at the base of the butte in the darkness. Each soldier had been told to fire at will; they began to unload into the noise below. Bullets hit the sandbags around them, the enemy returned fire and inevitably hit the defenders at the top. Charles had ordered all soldiers down from the watch towers whilst the initial attack was underway; there was no point during this attack. He was firing at the hordes down below with Sergeant Butcher on the northeast trench.

Wiping sweat from his brow, he loaded another bullet into his Lee-Metford rifle, then brought the rifle butt into his shoulder, took a breath, and squeezed the trigger. There was no time to think; just keep firing; the machine guns would fire more sporadically now. They also used slightly modified Ketchum grenades, first used in the American Civil War. They were not the most reliable weapon; when they did explode, they helped light up the area where they landed. Nazar's forces struggled to make headway as the sun rose, exposing them to more accurate fire. The casualties could be seen stretching on for miles. This second enemy wave was still strong, but it could not break through yet. The smaller artillery pieces could target the tighter-knit groups, leading to cries for this attack to break off. The drums began to beat loudly further back on the battlefield. Rebels and drones began to fall back under mortar and artillery fire.

Once they had moved out of sight, the complete carnage was exposed; dead bodies lay strewn across the battlefield. Plumes of smoke rose from the Arapaho fire; the smoke signalling was to check on the other locations, and the different tribes responded by sending back that they were okay.

Charles climbed the post steps; he glanced around at the defences and could see soldiers being treated for their wounds or the dead ones being carried out on stretchers. He had to steady himself for a moment; he took a moment and then carried on walking up the steps to the top. Charles looked around at the devastation; the groans of the fallen wounded could be heard everywhere. Some of the enemy were changing into flesh-eaters and attacking their dying comrades. A sombre sight made him reach for a small hip flask in his inner tunic pocket. A quick swig of whisky helped him ease his feelings. Then he took his binoculars and searched the distance for the next attack.

"Major, what shall we do with their wounded?"

"Let them retreat if they can, otherwise ease their passing."

The young officer nodded his head. Charles knew they could not keep any prisoners with them or even spare soldiers to escort them to prison camps, as they didn't have enough resources. It was the dark side of war; they were now facing a battle for survival, and decisions like this would not be easy.

Hosah spoke to Charles and said Mad Dog and Little Bear had ridden out to follow the retreating army. Charles said they should prepare quickly, as he expected Nazar to attack again shortly. Sergeant Butcher came and joined them on the lookout post.

"Sixteen dead, forty-five wounded, sir. You know where to place them."

The dead would be taken below ground in tunnels which had been dug out, and then, if there was time, the bodies burnt.

Corporal Heinz went over to Pvt Alexander Chamberlin and shook his hand. "The daylight will not fair them well, but now you can see them."

Alexander smiled, "God willing, I'll kill as many as I can."

"I'm counting on it." Corporal Heinz said with a smile.

Chapter 48

Nazar was sitting on his horse, surveying the returning units.

"There seem to be a lot more casualties, General Georgiy."

The general nodded his head. "We have reports of the first wave of dead not doing the damage we expected sire."

Nazar pulled his reins towards him, bringing the horse's head up. "Bring up the long limbs, the bears and wolves".

"Sire."

Nazar looked over to his general, but it was not the look the general wanted.

"Where are my forces, Georgiy? Where are my fucking forces, Georgiy?"

"My lord, most are with Oksana and the mobile units; remember, she will sweep in behind the enemy and break them from the rear."

The silence that followed was enough for the general to stay still.

"Fine, muster what mobile creatures we have. Have General Conway report to me straight away."

"Yes, my lord."

Within minutes, General Richard Conway had arrived. Standing alongside him was General Eltsina. She looked up at Nazar and quickly lowered her head.

"I have fond memories, General Eltsina. This will benefit both of you if you succeed and if you don't. Well, there is no failure, is there?"

Both of them lowered their heads.

"No, my lord."

"Oksana has most of the cavalry and mobile creatures, and the frontal attack from the dead did not go according to plan. You will be tasked with breaking through their defences."

General Conway nodded his head, and General Eltsina gulped.

"We will use prisoners at the frontline; mixed in between will be our creatures. Let's see if they will fire their artillery on their own civilians and soldiers."

"This is an excellent plan, my lord." General Conway was very enthusiastic.

"Is it!"

Nazar's response was enough to have both of them keep quiet unless asked to speak.

"You will have a division of Riders of the North accompanying you and all of the rebels and drones that fought earlier; if they fail to breach the enemy this time, they might as well die on the slopes."

Nazar had an awkward smile on his face, which they interpreted as don't ask any more questions.

Both of them lowered their heads and turned to join the next attack.

"We cannot fail," Eltsina said quietly.

She glanced at Richard with a slight look of concern.

"I believe we have a chance to break their defences; it might not mean outright victory, but Nazar could then join the attack with his main force."

"Yes, but we are the third wave, and if we do not make a good impression, he will take out his wrath on us."

Richard looked at her. "We have no choice; we know what riches await us."

She brushed his leg surreptitiously. "We would rule our own country as king and queen. All the riches I never had as a little girl would be mine."

"That is what we need to drive us to victory. Europe has gone, the British Empire has fallen, and now America must yield."

Two horses were brought forward. Both had been groomed and looked in prime condition. Once mounted, the generals rode to the front of the next advancing wave.

Chapter 49

There was not much they could do to repair all of the damage around Rattlesnake Butte. Charles had told his officers to get the men to repair what they could and to rest.

The temperature rose as the day progressed, meaning extra water runs were needed to quench the soldiers' thirst. Hosah reported that Mad Dog and Little Bear had seen Nazar's forces moving their way for another attack. He pointed out they were coming with the long limbs and other beasts from Nazar's array of demons. Charles thanked Hosah and asked if he could prepare his braves for when they breached the defences. He knew their hand-to-hand skills would be invaluable and wanted them in groups around the butte to help reinforce the frontlines.

Hagen was standing next to Pvt Brown whilst he checked on his boot.

"I'm glad to have you near me, Hagen; I'll look after you?" Which he followed with a cheesy grin.

"I may need your wit to help keep me going."

Before John could answer, the bulgers blasted out a call to arms.

"Oh bugger, they're coming again." He felt Hagen's hand squeeze his shoulder.

Hagen raised his rifle and checked it one more time.

Pvt Chamberlin could see the dust cloud forming in the south, away from Nemrick Butte, which was in the distance in front of them and to the northeast of Corner Mountain.

"They're going to hit us from the south!"

Smoke clouds indicated a full-on attack was coming to Corner Mountain and Nemrick Butte. The next moment was the sound of the heavy artillery opening fire. The ground shook, sending chills down each soldier's spine; many of them said prayers as a distant rumble carried on.

"Look, riders"

Charles brought his binoculars to his eyes; it was Captain Kingsbury with a handful of lancers.

A young soldier called out, "What's he doing?"

Charles rushed down the steps of the lookout post, climbed on top of the parapets, and raised his helmet. Waving it in the air as they passed Rattlesnake Butte, other soldiers saw what the major had done and did the same. They began to cheer and roar with this show of defiance.

Captain Kingsbury and his lancers raised them higher in the air as a sign of respect to the men and women in the defences.

"They are with us, lads; they are waiting for the moment."

The cheers and cries continued as the lancers swung around the north of the butte and disappeared into the distance. The attention was soon refocused on the army approaching from the south. General Eltsina oversaw the forces attacking Corner Mountain and Nemrick Butte.

At the front of the army from the south were wolves, long-limbs, flesh-eaters, and further behind, rebel soldiers and drones who had fought earlier that day. The creatures had not been fed for days and nipped and bit at each other. General Conway rode up onto a slope with the Riders of the North around him. The priests amongst the creatures and soldiers awaited his order. He raised his arm and let it fall to his side. A scream went out, and the whole force began to move forward.

The Allied forces did not have all their heavy artillery pointing south, as they needed to be pointed in many directions. Captain Brice had two more heavy guns winched to face the south side of the butte.

The prisoners, being forced to the front of the advancing force, tried to break free from the ropes they were tied to. This made the priests at the front of this force order drones to start shooting at them; it happened all along the battlefield. It was an orchestrated sign of defiance, meaning they knew their fate was already sealed. The allied officers on Rattlesnake Butte watched in vain as they saw the prisoners being overpowered and executed.

They did not wait long after this before opening fire on the advancing army; as soon as the shells started to land amongst the creatures and soldiers, the shriek went up, which was followed by a roar of charging soldiers. The long limbs raced ahead of the attacking force, with the wolves amongst them. The British and American soldiers and small artillery pieces fired upon them. The long limbs were quick and clambered onto the stakes and barbed wire.

The British engineers with Captain Somersett's men had the job of keeping them at bay. The 303 rounds rained down on the creatures coming their way. One struck the head of such a beast; the impact sent its brains onto the stake it had just climbed over. The wolves used the dead bodies of the long limbs to help jump over the barbed wire and rush up the slopes. On the east side of the butte, the horde of creatures was like a wave breaking on a beach. The machine guns opened fire furiously, cutting into the animals below; soon, this was repeated on the north side and west. They had encircled them.

Priests led Razor and Roughback Razor teeth to help break through the British and Allied defences. Their giant claws wrapped around the stakes; they bit into them and tried to clear them out of the way. Captain Brice received notice of what was happening and was asked by Charles to use the smaller cannons to help prevent this. The soldiers were up on the parapets, raining down fire on the enemy below; soon, though, the rebel and drone soldiers closed in behind the attack and started firing on their positions. This kept them pinned down, making it harder to target the troublesome areas.

A small field cannon was directed towards a razor tooth, and the moment it fired, I saw it literary blown to pieces; there was no time to celebrate as a rough back razor tooth broke through barbed wire and started to reach another level of the defensive stakes. One of the gunners who was helping move the cannon into place was shot in the shoulder; slowing down the process, he carried on helping turn it with blood gushing from his wound. Three American 10th Cavalrymen came over to assist. As they lifted themselves over four layers of sandbags, a wolf came up behind the last man just as he pulled himself over. It lunged at his legs and dragged him back onto the ground. His rifle was strapped across his back, but he tried to reach for his revolver. The wolf bit into his shoulder and spun him around. His two comrades turned to see what was happening and tried to push it away with their bayonets; one of them rammed it in the wolf's side, causing it to twist and try and nip at the blade sticking into its side. The second soldier put his rifle down and withdrew his sabre, striking its head before finishing it off.

The wounded soldier was pulled over the sandbags and lent against them whilst the other two helped turn the artillery pieces.

All around Rattlesnake Butte, the third wave was starting to make progress. The wolves were breaking through, and the long limbs were not far behind. This was creating pockets for the rebels and drones to advance through. The allied soldiers were laying down as much fire as they could. Charles had Sergeant Butcher and Corporal Heinz close by. Hosah and several braves were further down the trench. Charles fixed his bayonet as the rebels began to break into the first trench; the fighting was brutal. The hand-to-hand melees broke out all along the trench. Charles pushed two rebels back, a man and a woman, both looking like they were malnourished and had missing teeth. They screamed at him that he deserved to die as they swung an axe and billhook his way; Charles parried the first swipe by the male rebel and used his rifle butt to drive back the woman. They snarled at him and came again. He used the side of the trench to lean against and lunged at the male rebel, bringing the bayonet into his chest; before he could withdraw it, the female rebel was lashing at him. Charles felt the blade hit his helmet and come across his tunic.

She did not stop there and bit into his shoulder whilst he tried to hurl off. Charles could not shake her off his body; her teeth could not bite through the cloth, but they pinched at his shoulder blade. A gargling sound was followed by blood coming out of her mouth, and then a loosening of her grip.

Hosah was behind Charles, fighting another rebel; Charles let her fall to the ground and picked up his rifle.

"Thank you."

"The large riders are here!"

Coming up the south slope were the Riders of the North. They were armed with an array of weapons and were prepared to fight hand-to-hand. Corporal Heinz moved into a good firing position and began to open up on them.

Pvt Chamberlin saw the giant men and women moving up the slope; their power was frightening, and they charged into soldiers who came across their path. He followed a group of five of them, moving towards the firing cannons. One of them had a shaved head and war paint across his face. Alexander brought his rifle up to his shoulder and looked down the sights; the crosshair followed the rider's head, and within seconds, he pulled the trigger, causing the large man to fall backwards as the bullet impacted his skull. Alexander loaded his rifle and took aim again; his second bullet took down a female Rider of the North as she tried to climb over a sandbag wall.

Another one was shot by the 10th Cavalrymen, who faced the other three; more soldiers were sent to support the artillery pieces.

Sergeant Butcher told Charles that long limbs had breached their trench. Whilst the sergeant reloaded his rifle, Charles looked down the trench, which veered off to the right. British soldiers behind him moved to fall back down the trench, whilst his eyes caught the corner of the crumbling earth as the trench swung to the right. The first sight of a claw coming around the corner was enough for him to raise his rifle. The long limb that revealed itself was missing half its jaw, but still had jagged teeth sticking out. Looking down at the sights, he waited as it started to make its way towards him.

Bang

He shot it in the head, causing it to stumble and collapse in front of him.

"Move", Charles turned as more long limbs appeared around the corner and along the top of the trench. The others had already fallen back further along the trench, so he moved as fast as possible. The deep, throaty calls from the long limbs filled the trench as Charles tried to focus on not falling over. The trenches had wooden boards along the ground, which helped with his speed. What he didn't see was an ammunition box jutting out from a corner; it was enough to cause him to lose his balance and fall against the side of the trench. At that moment, they were on to him. Charles turned out of instinct to have his rifle and bayonet pointing their way. Instantly, a long limb knocked him backwards, its head trying to reach his body, mouth snapping away at anything it could. He put the rifle on its side to stop this, but was being pushed backwards. Another long limb pushed in at the other side to try and get in some meat.

A groan was followed by a long-limb body falling into the trench. Charles was using all his strength to keep a set of jaws from biting into him, and did not see this.

A cry from above saw Hagen come down on one of the long limbs with his axe, striking it in the back; the creature let out almost a human-like yelp as the one next to it tried to wriggle backwards and to bite at Hagen. They were tightly crammed together, meaning Hagen could withdraw his axe and bring it down on the other beast. Blood flew over both of them; there wasn't time to wipe it off. Hagen reached down and pulled Charles out from the dead creature. He thanked him, and they continued to move along the trench.

Captain Somersett was fighting hand-to-hand with his men. The long limbs and wolves were amongst them, soon followed by Riders of the North, rebels and drones. Their Winchester rifles were helping contain some of the fighting from spreading further into the centre of the defensive fortifications.

Alexander continued to rain terror from above; his sniper skills picked off beast and man alike. Hosah and the Braves were leading the British into another trench. The drone soldiers were targeting the guns; once they had broken through, they rushed them with explosives. One of these disappeared as a bullet from Alexander's rifle hit the dynamite he was carrying. The blast sent the others around him backwards, but more were approaching the guns.

John was carrying ammunition to one of the Maxim guns; he had two Engineers with him. They joined the soldiers who were firing down upon the attackers below. John's eyes were turned to the long limbs approaching the wounded soldiers and nurses. The two soldiers with him were helping distribute the ammunition, and he could not get their attention, so he took his rifle and went after them. There were trenches leading off in different directions, but instead of climbing down into them, he kept above them and moved towards the medical station.

When he reached the medical area, two flesh-eaters were feeding on a wounded soldier. John pulled out his revolver and shot both of them in the head. The injured soldier had died from the attack, and John moved in and used his bayonet to make sure he would not come back as one of the dead. He heard muffled screams as the medical hospital was underground, laying the rifle on the ground. John reloaded his revolver and held his bayonet in his left hand. There were many heavy doors leading below ground; some were still shut and had side hatches for defenders to look out of. John called into one of these, but there was no response.

He found an open door and pressed forward. The dim light inside was because only a few oil lanterns were burning periodically along the passageways. A growl and a hiss echoed around him, but he couldn't see any long limbs in his vicinity. Rooms were all along the passageway. Some were large and used for operating, and others were more for the wounded soldiers to rest.

"Help"

"Help me."

He followed the voice, and when he turned a corner, he could see a long limb pressing up against a door, using its weight and head to try and gain access. It let out a call to bring others to help it; fortunately for John, it had not seen him. They were big, powerful creatures, and he had a split second to decide how to attack them. Its erratic movement meant it would be hard to shoot it in the head, so he opted to aim for the body; raising his rifle, he aimed at the creature's midriff and squeezed the trigger. A groan was followed by it, looking for what caused the pain; John didn't waste any time and ran at it with his bayonet attached, sticking it close to where he had shot the long limb. The beast recoiled from the bayonet, sticking into its side, and shifted its weight from pressing against the door to focus on John. He was quick to react, letting go of his rifle and pulling out his revolver, letting off several rounds into its head. It did the trick, causing the creature to fall and slump to the ground. Wasting no time, John picked up his rifle and re-holstered his revolver before moving through the door, which was left half ajar. Inside were nurses holding a chair and perched behind a makeshift operating table.

"Where are the rest of the doctors and nurses?"

"We're all spread out. When the long limbs started to break inside, we retreated into some of the rooms. A small detachment of guards was trying to clear the animals from the tunnels, but we got separated from them."

John led both nurses out of the room. He scrambled around to find them some sort of weapon to use in case they encountered another long-limb or wolf.

Moving along the passageway, they looked for more soldiers and nurses. They came to a larger area with overturned tables. Suddenly, two British soldiers appeared. Both almost jumped as they saw Pvt Brown and the two nurses.

"British" was the first thing to come out of his mouth.

They quickly nodded and asked them to follow them down another passage. After a few minutes, they came to a door guarded by two Burley Black watch soldiers. Seeing the returning soldiers and nurses, they were ushered in. John was instantly relieved to see Heidi helping a wounded soldier. She looked over at him and reciprocated his smile. A surgeon came over to him and asked how it was up top.

"Overrun, sir."

As they spoke, the two Black watch soldiers shouted that wolves and long limbs were approaching fast. Leaning their rifles against the walls, they grabbed what they could to barricade the door as others rushed forward to assist them. Heidi stepped forward and kissed John on the cheek. He handed her his revolver and turned to face the door. The noise coming from the passageway filled the room they were in. The sound of screeching, snapping teeth and throaty calls followed the beasts as they piled into the door. Bits of wood started to crack and splinter off, and long-limb arms began to protrude through the disintegrating door. The two Black Watch soldiers began to fire at the door; two other British engineers joined them behind a turned-over table.

John moved backwards into the room with Heidi. Some of the doctors and nurses were still trying to help the wounded soldiers. Once the door collapsed, wolves and long limbs came bursting through. The room broke into a melee of fighting, and bayonets were needed to push them back. Heidi picked her shots, hitting wolves in the body and legs.

One long limb knocked back a British engineer, sending him flying into the corner of the room. Shouts and cries blurred the noise inside.

Outside, Charles was tucked into a corner of the trench network with several soldiers firing at the numerous targets moving along the trench and over the top of it. A messenger almost fell on top of them; he was wounded in the leg from a bayonet but wanted to convey the message that the 10th was holding firm and managed to push back the enemy. As he delivered his message, shells began to land around the butte.

"They're firing on their own soldiers." The young soldier who said this took cover as earth and rock landed on top of them.

Charles had experienced this before with Nazar; he would sacrifice his own men. The artillery shelling and mortar fire were impacting all over the butte. General Conway was annoyed that his men were under fire from his own side; he felt they were starting to get a foothold in the battle for Rattlesnake Butte. General Eltsina had a group of drones with her, taking cover in a trench. The shelling started easing up, followed by horns, signalling the retreat.

As General Eltsina began to move with her drone soldiers, she came across a small group of Arapaho braves; they were prepared. She told her soldiers to move down the butte and began fighting a rear-guard action as they fell back. The Arapaho were geared towards picking off the retreating enemy, beast or man. They headed towards gaps in the defences and barbed wire. She looked across to Richard coming her way; he had riders of the north with him; he was happy to see her and brought his soldiers closer to hers. He then ordered his men and women to fire on the approaching Arapaho. Smoke was rising from the smouldering crater holes from the recent shelling. Richard led them into the largest one to take cover; as he descended into the warm soil, a cry behind him made him turn instantly. General Eltsina staggered forward; sticking out of her back was an arrow; she looked up at him and fell into his arms. "We nearly did it," her voice grew weary,

"Stay with me, please." He held her tight, picked her up, and carried on moving down the butte. They came under fire as they drove down that side. Once down at the bottom, he sent riders of the north to get a wagon. She could barely open her eyes but mustered what little strength she had left to look at him. "It's no use, leave me here." Richard shook with anger; he wanted to carry on the attack and was livid. The retreat had been ordered; in his head, this was the reason she had been struck with an arrow. As the wagon was brought closer with a stretcher, he kissed her on the lips and forehead. She passed in his arms.

The British mortars and artillery opened fire on the retreating enemy. The fleeing rebels and soldiers took a lot of casualties as they pulled back. The priests managed to bring as many wolves and long limbs with them as they could. The dead that had made it up were left behind to cause as much trouble as possible.

Richard was given a horse to ride alongside his lover's body. They rode across the plains to Nazar's makeshift camp. Sitting on his horse, on top of a small mount, was Nazar himself.

He briefly looked at Richard Conway before turning to bark out orders to General Georgiy. Richard continued to ride alongside the cart. Nazar then rode down from the mount and brought his horse close to Richard's.

"You did well at Rattlesnake Butte."

Richard looked at him and then at the cart.

Nazar looked at the body of General Eltsina. "She died fighting for the cause. Is there a better death?"

Richard found it hard not to answer.

"Why did we retreat? We were starting to win at Rattlesnake."

Nazar stopped his horse.

"I did not ask you what you thought about why we retreated."

Richard looked at her body lying there.

"I could have beaten them."

"I will let this insubordination slide this once; if the General were not lying there, you would be."

He turned and led his horse towards his other officers. Richard felt resentment and despair, but knew he could not push this any further; it was not the time or place to let his emotions get away with him. Instead, he told the soldier steering the cart to leave it by his tent. He instructed them to build a fire to burn her body. Richard then went to join Nazar's gathering.

Lev was coming up the hill as Nazar started to speak.

"This is not the time to be late!"

He said nothing and joined the others.

"We have failed to get a foothold on Corner Mountain and Nemrick Butte, but progress was made at Rattlesnake Butte." Priestess Llewellyn was giving the briefing, and she made sure she did not show too much emotion about the gains or failures.

Nazar was pondering over a rough map with his index finger, "I will pay a visit to Rattlesnake Butte."

This drew a look from those around him, but no one dared question his logic or reason for going to Rattlesnake Butte. Nazar had been informed that the British engineers were part of the force holding that location, and he wanted to meet his old adversary. He asked General Georgiy to fetch Rebecca and make sure she was ready to ride out with a small party to Rattlesnake Butte.

The Priestess continued to discuss the next planned attack, how the previous assaults had weakened the defences, and how this was the moment to seize.

Nazar had mounted up whilst she was still debriefing the others. Several destroyer drones were alongside him, mixed in with riders of the north. Tied to her horse was Rebecca; she had blood dripping from her lip and onto her ripped trousers.

"If I do not return, General Georgiy will carry out the battle plans as laid down by me."

Priestess Arnoult was riding next to Rebecca, with a rope tied to her horse in case she tried to break free, but they knew keeping Emily in the camp would make this unlikely.

With that, he rode off.

The priestess leaned into Rebecca. "I hope my hand did not hurt too much." She said this with a smile.

"If you didn't have your guards, I would show you hurt." Rebecca stared at her after she had spoken.

"You are very feisty; I will enjoy watching you suffer when they kill your husband."

Rebecca turned her head.

Nazar led from the front, sitting proudly on his horse as he rode past his soldiers and beasts of different shapes and sizes. His light armour did not disguise his powerful, muscular physique. Nazar had not even changed his shape in earnest for the forthcoming battle. He was relishing meeting his old adversary in a perverse way. He wanted him alive to the bitter end so he could see the fall of the Allied forces.

They rode for thirty minutes or more before closing in on Rattlesnake Butte. The smoke rising from Corner Mountain and Nemrick Butte made him laugh. He was particularly happy to see the devastation around Rattlesnake Butte.

"General Arnoult, this is a glorious day."

She looked at Rebecca before answering.

"It certainly is, my lord."

"Send several riders with white flags, and make sure they reference Hayward's wife." He said this with a smug smile beaming across his face.

Four riders rode off to the foot of the defences.

Alexander scoped them with his rifle but was told by Sergeant Butcher to hold fire. Charles surveyed the riders and the small group sitting further back. He let his binoculars fall out of his hands as he steadied himself against the parapet.

"Are you okay, sir?" Corporal Heinz helped keep upright.

"It's Rebecca; she's down there with that group of riders."

Corporal Heinz stood there in silence.

"You must keep calm, Charles; it could be a trap."

"Maybe, but I must speak to her."

Charles felt his Enfield revolver, which was tucked into his holster on the right-hand side, and his sword on the left. He would not be taking a rifle; if something was going to happen, it would unfold without him being able to use it. Corporate Heinz and Sergeant Butcher said they would come with him, but he said he would only take one soldier. Pvt Brown saluted him. "I've been with you, sir, from the start. I will come with you now."

Charles nodded his head and put his arm on his shoulder. "Let's go."

They both walked through the network of trenches and past the wounded and bloodied soldiers. "Good luck, sir, good luck, lads," were the calls that went out. They passed over the last trench and on towards the crater-ridden track leading down to the foot of the butte. The closer they got to the riders, they could see them smirking and looking victorious in their saddles.

Pvt Brown had his rifle across his back and followed Major Hayward towards the other riders situated a little further back from the Rattlesnake butte. Horses would have been an option, but Charles had chosen to walk on foot.

The escort flanked either side of them as they walked towards the other riders. Coming down the butte but staying at its base were several Sharpshooters. They took each of the riders in scope, and whilst it wasn't the most assured defence, it gave a bit of cover to Charles and Pvt Brown.

The closer Charles got to Rebecca, the faster his heart started to beat. His hand naturally started to slide towards his revolver. Her eyes began to focus on his. He did not even see Nazar watching him from his horse.

"Captain Hayward."

Charles's gaze was suddenly broken upon hearing that voice. Hope and love had become hate. His eyes were averted straight to Nazar.

"Nazar."

"It's been a long time, Captain."

Charles took off his helmet.

"You have my wife and hopefully my daughter?"

Nazar lifted himself in his saddle.

"I seem to have a lot of things of yours."

Charles felt his revolver again. "Why, why, why?"

Nazar looked directly into Charles' eyes.

"You took it upon yourself to go to my place of worship and destroy something very precious to me. Did you not think there would be repercussions?"

"You have started a world war? Did you not think that there would be no repercussions?" Charles's voice had a more substantial, aggressive undertone.

"You make it sound like none of these nations have engaged in war? It is part of an empire, and so it should be."

Charles shook his head. "Nazar, you are destroying the world, not improving it. You've unleashed death upon us, creatures that never existed until you and your priests created them. Now you want to destroy America and the people who inhabit it."

"We could discuss this at your execution, but, for now, I'm offering the chance for your men and women on this defensive mount to surrender, and they will be spared; the officers will not be. There has to be some compensation for my soldiers who died. Also, I will spare your wife and daughter."

Charles looked at this formidable foe in front of him.

"I do not trust you to keep your word. I do not trust you in any shape or form. You are the closest thing to the devil I have ever met, and I'm sure you burn in hell."

Nazar let a big smile creep across his face. "Captain, you have fought a long campaign against me, but you still do not understand what I will achieve. Humans are expendable; do not think you are anything more than a moment in time."

Nazar kicked his horse to turn around. "You have ten minutes to decide and raise a white flag from your defensives; otherwise, the next time we meet, I will collect my debt in blood."

Charles just stared at him.

Rebecca sat in her saddle while Priestess Arnoult held the rope tight. She looked at him with loving eyes.

"Speak to her now; maybe she will help you decide?"

Pvt Brown looked at Charles. He told him to wait there while he walked over to her. Moving close to her horse, he put his hand on her leg. As she looked down, tears fell onto Charles below. His eyes welled up. "I," he struggled to continue. "Is Arthur alive?" Rebecca softly asked.

"He is." "Is Emily?"

"She is"

She swung herself down from her saddle and stood in front of him. The priestess narrowed her eyes in disapproval, but she was given no order to stop it from happening.

Rebecca leaned into Charles and kissed him on the lips. "I love you."

"And I you."

He pulled her in close, with her head resting against his.

"Charles, don't offer yourself for us; he will kill us all either way."

He held her tight, saying, "I wish I could just take you and our children away and keep running."

"You have to fight and lead your soldiers, and he has to be stopped at all costs, even us."

Charles put his head against hers. "I pray to god we all meet again."

A whistle went up.

Two drones rode next to him, and Priestess Arnoult came in close behind Rebecca.

"Get on the fucking horse bitch."

Rebecca looked up at her with raging eyes, but Charles refocused her by kissing her one last time before the drones moved him back.

Nazar turned his horse and slowly drew it past him.

"I'm happy you chose to die a warrior's death" His smirk was enough to make Charles feel uncontrollable anger.

"I hope we get to meet one more time," Charles said with gritted teeth.

This brought a raucous laugh from Nazar. "You can fantasize about killing me all you like, but as you have seen over the years, you will lose. You've lost your wife to me, your daughter, your country, and I'll take your life."

He then kicked on his horse.

Rebecca had tears rolling down her cheeks as her horse was turned and led away. Charles continued to watch her as they disappeared in the distance. Pvt Brown put his hand on the Major's shoulder.

"I'm sure you'll see your wife and daughter again, sir."

Charles looked at him.

"I'm not so sure, John."

Pvt Brown noticed his major's eyes had gone cold as if a light had gone out. They both turned and moved back to Rattlesnake Butte.

"Please gather as many officers as possible when we return."

"Yes, sir."

Chapter 50

Charles finished talking to his officers and then addressed his men. He spoke to them about the final push by the enemy, as they aim to finish the allies off once and for all. Charles said it would come down to hand-to-hand fighting, with the will of our spirit and the grace of God. Charles said this would be the most challenging battle the Allied forces had ever faced, as the enemy sensed victory for the continent. Despite what lay ahead, he said it had been an honour and a privilege to lead and fight alongside such brave men and women over the past several years. He felt his emotions running high, especially as he could see Rebecca and Emily in the back of his mind. He brought his speech to an end with a quote from Napoleon.

"The battlefield is a scene of constant chaos. The winner will be the one who controls that chaos, both his own and the enemies. Gods Speed, men."

A soldier shouted out 'hurrah' and was soon joined by his fellow soldiers from different regiments and nations. Charles acknowledged all of them as he walked to his watch tower. The rousing cheers slowly damped as the sound of banging drums began to gently float over to them on the wind. The soldiers began to disperse to their fighting positions. Charles had Sergeant Butcher and Corporal Heinz next to him as they made their way up to the watchtower. They would move from that position once the battle for Rattlesnake Butte commenced again.

"Do you think our plans will work?" Corporal Heinz asked with a hesitant voice.

Charles looked at him. "It's all we have!"

Private Johnson arrived with news that a rider had taken a message to Captain Kingsbury and General Baxter Washington. He stood for a moment, taking in the moving horizon. "I've never seen the land move like this before."

"This is Nazar's army coming to finish off what's left of ours," Charles said under his breath, but they all heard it.

The ground trembled the closer this mass of bodies got. Horns began to play, and the drums momentarily stopped and began again. The noise filled the valley, making the hairs rise on the men and women waiting patiently in the defensive trenches or with the wounded soldiers.

Even in the distance, the giant Lagorians looked ominous. The rough-back razor teeth moved alongside the Riders of the North. The dead were being kept in rows; they were not going to make the same mistake of allowing the dead en masse to be moved away from the battlefield. The swathes of rebels and drones dressed in black looked fearsome.

The sheer numbers dwarfed what they had faced in France and previous battles. This was an army made of man and beast. The fact it was spread across the valley was soul-crushing. Charles knew Nazar would not spare anyone from the Allied forces, as total annihilation would help send the message to the rest of the world that resistance was futile.

The mass-advancing army came to a sudden halt on the blood-soaked battlefield. Horns played in unison, a sharp, chilling sound that danced over rocks and stones alike. The heavy artillery, pulled by large, shyer horses, emerged from their ranks.

Charles gave the order for everyone to take cover; the first shell hit one of the northern slopes, and the others started to land around Rattlesnake Butte. In the darkness of the underground shelters, eyes looked around for courage and hope. Charles sat there with his rifle, looking at the closed makeshift door. Soil fell onto his helmet, and the fine dust could be tasted on his lips. His grip on his Lee-Metford tightened, and he thought of seeing Rebecca; it gave him solace and hope, but also despair that his daughter and wife were at the mercy of Nazar.

The shelling stopped as abruptly as it started. Then, officers' whistles brought the soldiers out of the underground holes and into the heavily hit defensive lines. Not all made it out. Teams of soldiers and nurses dug frantically at any underground shelters that had collapsed to free those trapped underneath. As this unfolded, the horns sounded again, initiating a full-frontal attack. Charles moved with his men to the front trench; Sergeant Butcher stood next to him.

"Corporal Heinz, it's time. Hosah looked at Charles and said he was a great warrior; whether they met again in this life or the next, he would be remembered in the stars.

"Hosah, you have saved us all on so many occasions; you and your tribe have shown immeasurable bravery, and if fate allows us, you will dance on the great plains once more."

Hosah turned and left with Mad Dog, Little Bear and a collection of braves.

Captain Benjamin Brice was ordered to prepare the artillery. As Charles looked along the trench, he saw young and old soldiers bracing themselves for the battle of their lives.

The onrushing screams and roar meant all eyes were on the sea of bodies coming their way. Captain Brice directed the heavy guns to open fire, and the mortars waited anxiously to add their voices to the battle.

Charles looked at Pt Brown, "Take two soldiers and help guard the nurses." Pt Brown knew this was the major's way of making sure he would be close to Heidi,

As the mortar shells landed amongst the on-rushing enemy ranks, it did little to stop the sheer volume from pouring forward. The cannons continued to fire, inflicting devastating damage wherever the shell landed, but the inevitable surge brought them ever closer to Rattlesnake Butte.

The soldiers prepared as the noise intensified. Sergeant Butcher called out to fix bayonets as the first wave of enemy soldiers hit the slopes. The twisted barbed wire and broken stakes did little to stop the sprawling army from quickly reaching the lower trench. The volley fire was released before Nazar's soldiers threw themselves into the trench. They came in with axes, knives, swords and spears. The British soldiers in that trench tried to stay close to each other, jabbing and using the rifle butts to beat back the attack. Charles had two rebels come at him; one had a homemade mace, iron wrapped with broken glass. This mace was swung at Charles, forcing him to move backwards to avoid being hit; as he did so, he stumbled back and knocked his head against the side of the trench. Soil fell off his helmet and onto his face, his mouth filled with dry sandy soil, causing him to spit it out. They came at him in this moment, sensing an opportunity to finish him.

Charles did not pick up his rifle; instead, he used his bowie knife, given to him by Texas, to stab the rebel with the mace in the shoulder as he came forward. The other rebel lurched towards him, but his plight was ended by Corporal Heinz sticking his bayonet into the rebel's back. Charles retrieved his knife and picked up his rifle, knocking back further rebels and drones as they piled into their trench.

Across the front, Nazar's forces were engaged in hand-to-hand fighting. Nazar had stayed back to soak up the fighting; he wanted to ensure his battle instructions were being carried out. He had held back a lot of the long limbs and dead; he wanted those to help overpower any defensive fornications that were holding out.

Pvt John Brown was backed into a corner with Heidi; they had the wounded on stretchers around them; Heidi and some of the other nurses that could fire a rifle were helping shoot at the enemy as they moved around them, amongst the soldiers and rebels were long-limbs and wolves, they were so good at getting into trenches and occupying defenders to deal with them. Little Bear landed on the back of a long limb, which was biting into a British soldier who lay strewn underneath it. Using his two axes, he swung them deep into the neck of the long limb, cutting and slicing lumps of flesh out of it. The creature tried to roll on its side to get him off its back, but Little Bear had already done the damage; the soldiers around the dying long-limb pulled the wounded private clear.

Giant bears with two heads bullied their way to the top of Rattlesnake butte; their roars carried through the battlefield mayhem. Soil trembled as a logarithm came close to the defences; it began to use its head to clear a path through the barbed wire and wooden stakes.

"Tell Captain Brice to focus his fire on that beast now, Corporal."

Cpl Heinz moved at speed to get to the gun batteries. He used his sabre to force back a rebel and take the head off a flesh-eater blocking his way; arriving at Captain Brice's batteries, he saw the fight unfolding around him. He could make out the captain fighting back; he had blood streaming from his shoulder and a large gash across his face. His men were knee-deep in bodies, assisted by American cavalrymen from the 10th. It was a precarious situation, with them just about holding onto the position. He made his way to Captain Brice. "We need to take done that creature, Captain."

Blood dripping from his chin, he nodded; the gunners with him followed his orders to swing one of the cannons in place; taking aim, they unleashed a shot into the lower part of its body. It did catastrophic damage to the logarithm's hind legs, making it groan and sit back. Bullets ricocheted off the cannon; two gunners were hit, one in the shoulder and one in the leg. A bear with two heads moved into the battery section; it had drones following behind it; they flung themselves at the allied soldiers, hacking, bayoneting and killing indiscriminately. A crunching noise made Corporal Heinz look around; his eyes witnessed one of the heads of the bear tearing at a dead allied soldier, and the other head tried to pull the beast towards the Corporal.

"We must fall back!"

Captain Brice looked at Corporal Heinz as he shouted at them to retreat, but he did not intend to leave wounded men around him. Using his sword, he dispatched two rebels who were in close proximity. The bear lifted onto its hind legs and swiped at anything near it, knocking over a drone soldier while coming at the captain. Bleeding from his nose and mouth, Captain Brice stood his ground; the bear moved over a situated cannon and lunged at him; as it came down, he used the cannon as a shield and stuck his sword into the neck of the bear; it thrashed around, knocking him back. He gingerly staggered to his feet but was shot by more drones moving into the gun battery section.

Corporal Heinz tried to press forward to get him, but the melee around him forced the small group of men around him to fall back. They fought a rear-guard action into a trench near one of the supply redoubts; several orderlies were opening ammunition boxes.

"We'll hold here before moving to join the others."

Major Hayward was fighting with his men on a lower slope. They formed a square and repelled wave after wave of the enemy force coming at them.

Nazar was sitting on his horse, enjoying what he was witnessing. He was being updated on how the other battle lines were unfolding. Whilst a drone officer informed him of the allied forces retreating off Corner Mountain, a call went up from his left flank. "The British have field guns and Maxim machine guns on the ridge." A young priest cautiously said.

"Well, deal with it then."

General Georgiy looked at his emperor and then at the priest. He ushered him to go without muttering a word, and then he focused his attention back on Nazar.

"Should we move further back from the action, sire?"

Nazar laughed. "You've lost your battle nerve, Georgiy?" He paused. "The younger you loved to fight, especially when the fight was coming to an end.

"My lord, I will stand by you to the very end, but I think you have become too personally involved with fighting Major Hayward." General Georgiy steadied his horse as the cannons on the ridge began to fire on their left flank.

"I respect your wisdom, but do not try and stop me from taking what is mine."

"Yes, my lord." The general looked up at the artillery firing down on his soldiers and a division of drone soldiers being led by the young priest to stop the bombardment.

Nazar did not even bother to look in that direction.

"Send orders to have Oksana and her force attack Captain Hayward's position."

He paused.

"Have Lev use his force to push the Americans from Corner Mountain and reinforce us here."

The general looked at Nazar. "Shall you wait here, lord?"

"Bring up the destroyer drones and Major Hayward's wife?"

"And his daughter?"

Nazar smiled, "Why not? It would be good for her to witness the end of her father before she turns."

Chapter 51

Wave after wave came at the giant square; they had placed several small field cannons within the square with limited shells. Rows of British and Allied soldiers stood in firing ranks. The volley fire worked well to stem the flow of dead and rebels mixed with drone soldiers. This momentum was now thrown into question with the trembling of the sandy soil beneath their boots. Screechy war cries came from behind the onrushing horde. They began to fall away and were trampled as cavalry units from Oksana's regiment pushed onto the square, regardless of what was in the way. These units were a mixture of long-limbs, wolves, riders of the North, drone cavalrymen and priests.

"Brace yourselves, men." Was the cry from Major Hayward as he brought his rifle and bayonet facing upwards? You could feel the tension amongst the soldiers as Oksana's cavalry units smashed into their ranks. The volley of bullets brought horses with men and women drones crashing to the ground. Clambering over their dying bodies came long limbs amongst the other riders, their oversized bodies ploughing into the tight ranks of the allied forces. Captain Somersett drew his sword and revolver, slashing and shooting every creature that came his way; his soldiers were pushed into hand-to-hand combat.

Sergeant Butcher looked at Charles as they moved back-to-back, fighting everything coming their way. Oksana had changed her size and was moving amongst the soldiers, using her sword to swipe at anything in her way. She was flanked by male and female priests, who used spears to puncture a wedge into the formation. Once inside, they were causing a lot of trouble behind the lines. They used their power to break the square and attack soldiers as they tried to form smaller groups to repel the riders.

The allied cavalry was sweeping around the back of the Nazar army; they came at his forces hard with the British 17th Lancers and US cavalrymen, Native American Indians and 14th Bengal Lancers. It was a large, deadly, mobile army that took the commanders at the back by surprise—lancers charged into the loose ranks, picking them off before they could close ranks. Nazar could hear a commotion towards the rear of his reserve regiments, but was still buoyed by his superior numbers. General Conway arrived next to him; he was still upset with the loss of General Eltsina but did not want to show this to Nazar.

"I need you to take a small division and deal with the rear of our army."

"Yes, my lord." General Conway said in a lowered voice.

"Do not fail me again, General, or you will join Eltsina in the next life."

Disgruntled and slightly disillusioned with his leaders' comments regarding his lover, he rode off to gather some rebels to challenge the rear-guard action.

A young priest who was leading the attack on the batteries to the side of the butte was failing to get his soldiers up the hill. Grapeshot and machine gunfire were cutting through his ranks as they advanced up the hill. This meant other field guns continued to rain down shells on the tightly packed units advancing towards Rattlesnake Butte.

General Conway moved his force in the direction of the rear attack. When a shell landed next to a group of his men, bits of their bodies covered him. He looked to the hill where the artillery was still firing and decided to change his attack plans. Moving with his mounted units, they swept towards the cannons. This meant Captain Kingsbury and his lancers could continue to cause havoc at the back of Nazar's army.

Lev's army had pushed the Allied forces off Corner Mountain, but Nemrick Butte was still holding firm. It was being attacked on all sides, and the longer it held out, the more Nazar could not bring his whole force down on the remaining British and American forces.

General Conway used his mounted soldiers to come around the side of the cannons; the Maxim machine guns had run out of ammunition and could not stop his men from coming into the gunners and the soldiers protecting them. They fought bravely, but General Richard Conway took out his anger on his fellow countrymen, cutting down anyone who stood in his way. He did not, however, see the swathes of allied cavalrymen pour towards their position as they came in hard on his mounted troops; the effect was to scatter them amongst the cannons. The general changed his shape and size as he let his anger flow through his body. He charged into the Bengal lancers, knocking several to the side; he brutally dispatched three more riders coming at him. Richard could see that most of his soldiers were engaged in a futile fight against superior numbers and decided to return to the main Nazar army. Hot on his heels were British lancers led by Captain Kingsbury. His helmet covered his shaved head, and with a long beard, he led his men after General Conway; he had seen the shape-changing before and knew the sheer power and danger of these types of human beasts.

Four soldiers from the 17th British lancers joined their Captain, charging down General Conway; as the lance tips closed in on their victim, Richard turned his horse as the first lance crashed into his side. He managed to stay mounted and brought his sword around, cutting the lancer from his saddle. The second lance that pierced his skin and midriff caused him to fall from his horse. The General got to his feet and used his strength to take on a charging horse and rider, knocking the horse onto its side, then using his dagger, he rammed it into the fallen British soldier. Two more came at him, and somehow, he managed to dismount them before finishing them off.

With smoke floating across the battlefield and great plains, General Richard Conway stood there, feeling like a warrior; only one rider was left. Unfortunately for Richard, it was Captain Kingsbury; his wife and daughter had been killed by Nazar's army many years ago. In his blue war-torn uniform, he came at him. His speed did not deter the general; he wanted to do the same as he had done to the other soldiers and maybe even make this Captain suffer more.

As Captain Kingsbury brought his lance up, he thought of his wife and young daughter. Richard Conway had blood seeping from his wounds and splattered across his face. He waited for his moment as Captain came in fast with the lance; he let go of it just as Richard tried to grab the lance; strapped across his back was his sword; swiftly pulling this out in one motion, he swung it around, taking the generals head off in a clean strike, the body fell effortlessly to the ground, and the head rolled only a few meters away.

Captain Kingsbury brought his horse around to check on his fallen men. As he did so, a small detachment of his lancers joined him. They helped take the wounded off the battlefield before joining Captain Kingsbury as he went back to lead the rest of the regiment deeper into the battle.

Chapter 52

Lev leaned forward to speak to Captain Rimmel. "We have pushed the Americans back."

"I sense their blood and despair!" He laughed and rubbed his blood-soaked beard.

"Should we reinforce the rear of your brother's army, sire? We have reports of a large cavalry attack from the enemy?"

"Captain Rimmel, should we not bask in our glories for a moment or two?"

The captain reluctantly nodded his head as Priestess Bonnaire joined them. She had a woven sack hanging from the back of her horse; blood had accumulated at the bottom of the sack and was seeping through onto the back of her horse.

"You have rich pickings, I see?"

"I did, my love; they all suffered for their cause." She laughed as she tied her hair back and brought her horse close to Lev's.

She leaned forward and kissed Lev passionately.

"You stir my emotions; I must have you," Lev ordered Captain Rimmel to set up a tent. The battle was still raging, but his lust was more important to him.

Once it was set up, the priestess dumped the sack outside the tent and joined Lev inside.

Chapter 53

Nazar was receiving reports of the death of General Conway.

"Where are my reinforcements? Where is Lev?"

Oksana returned to report on the progress being made at Rattlesnake Butte. Priestess Eveline Arnoult and Priestess Jane Llewellyn joined her.

"We must finish the British force on the slopes and take out this cavalry force."

Nazar looked over to see Rebecca tied to a horse, with Emily sitting behind her. She had spoken to Emily before they were taken to the battlefield. During that moment, Emily had given her mother a pocket picture frame necklace. Rebecca subsequently hung it on her neck, which made Emily smile.

He spoke to Priestess Arnoult to keep an eye on them as he wanted to finish the British himself.

"Georgiy, bring up my Destroyer drones." He looked around the sprawling battle, "This is our time." He felt his sword strapped to his back and the dagger tucked inside his belt.

He led his sizable force towards Major Hayward's men. They marched towards the broken square and prepared to engage the enemy. Coming through a cluster of flesh-eaters was General Baxter with his US 7th cavalrymen. They cut and sliced into the marauding dead before charging into the destroyer drones; this moment of surprise meant they could plough into them before they could regain their shape. Whilst the attacking cavalry unit would never break Nazar's attack, the distraction gave Major Hayward time to form a better defensive line. Nazar's anger at seeing his destroyer drones being cut down enraged him. His human form changed as he became the monster that had terrorised the battlefield across the world.

The US cavalrymen ploughed into Nazar's soldiers until they came across him. He brought his shyer horse around and charged into the onrushing US soldiers. His first action was to decapitate a cavalryman, sending blood on the fighting soldiers around him; another came alongside him and swung his sabre at Nazar; it slashed into his arm. Nazar reached over and pulled the soldier in close and bit him in the face, then pushed him off his horse. Two more came in close, but Nazar used his terrifying seize to swing his sword across the face of one and the mid-riff of the other. General Baxter tried to charge in to save them, but Nazar was too quick, bringing his sword into the on-rushing General's horse, causing it to fall forward onto its knees. Dismounting quickly, Nazar pulled out his dagger as the General reached for his revolver. The first shot clipped Nazar's shoulder, the second his side. Nazar smiled as he moved at speed and grabbed the general. Crushing his hand holding the revolver, he moved in close to his face. "You fought well, but your war ends here." He brought his knife straight into his chest and withdrew it as quickly as it went in. The general fell back on the soil next to his dying horse. His eyes slowly shut with the battle raging around him.

Nazar re-mounted and continued to lead his men forward. Barking out orders like a rabid dog, General Georgiy told the priests riding close to bring their forces to attack Major Hayward's line.

Coming up the southern flank was Priestess Jane Llewellyn, with a small unit of drones and rebels. She pushed her soldiers up that side of the slope as quickly as she could. The opposition to this attack had been reduced, as most allied forces were now fighting on the northwestern side of Rattlesnake Butte. She ordered her drones and rebels to kill the wounded and any stragglers.

As they reached the top, there were bodies strewn around the defences, dead long limbs with limbs hacked off, wolves with smouldering fur from cannon fire. The battle had been fierce, and the dead walked amongst the carnage. The Priestess ordered her soldiers to search the trenches as quickly as possible, as she wanted to rejoin the battle. They were unaware that Pvt Alexander Chamberlain was located in one of the watch towers. A drone soldier thought he had spotted several nurses looking after the wounded allied soldiers; as he turned to call this out, a bullet entered the front of his neck and out the other side. The others instantly ducked and tried to find cover; the priestess was anxious that they should find the sharpshooter. The wounded soldier lay there groaning for a moment or two whilst holding his neck before passing.

"Find the sniper, you fools."

A rebel moved towards two of her fellow compatriots. This was the last thing she did as a bullet smacked her in the chest. This sent panic amongst the rest who were at the top. The priestess ordered those cowering in the trenches or behind sandbags to move to the high points. She then moved on down a trench with six drones. They came across several wounded British and allied soldiers and killed them on the spot.

"There must be more", she proclaimed with spit coming out of her mouth.

Her eyes lit up on seeing a collection of nurses helping wounded British soldiers. "Kill them"

They began to move over the smouldering soil and broken trenches towards this group. The first two rebels took aim, but both missed as the nurses tried to pull the wounded soldiers into cover. A soldier with a crutch got himself to a rifle, which was leaning against a broken ladder. He managed to squeeze off a shot before being hit in the stomach by the advancing drone soldiers.

A female rebel lurched forward with a knife and revolver; she shot a wounded soldier who was being dragged to safety as the nurse was pulling him. The nurse tried to fend her off, but the rebel slashed her across her waist; as the rebel went in to finish her off, a bullet hit her between the shoulder blades. Pvt Brown moved over several grain bags as he tried to get closer to Heidi. The drones around the Priestess lunged at anything they could, like a fox in a chicken's coop; they tried to kill everything. One of them went to bayonet a soldier who was lying strewn on a stretcher; Pvt Brown shot the drone in the back, causing him to fall on the injured soldier's legs. They kept on trying to reach the wounded around them, but Alexander had already claimed another victim from his lofty perch. Priestess Llewellyn told the rebels to charge Pvt Brown; he dodged the first one who tried to bayonet him and brought his bayonet through the midriff of this rebel. The other one came at John and used his rifle to knock him back over a sandbag wall before bringing the bayonet round as he prepared to finish him; a bullet through his left eye socket ended that attack.

Alexander looked below. Two of the Priestess soldiers had found him and were now climbing the steps with knives drawn.

John pulled himself back up, only to be pushed down by a boot. "You should have stayed down." The Priestess lunged her sword into John's side as he turned. He let out a yelp and tried to grab something to fight her off; she stood on his arm and smiled. She suddenly lurched forward as she brought her sword up to deliver the final blow. A bayonet stuck through her chest and was withdrawn and thrust through again. She was then knocked aside with a hefty boot.

"John, are you ok?" Heidi's words were loaded with fear.

"Just about Heidi, I think you saved me again." He winced as he smiled. Heidi bent down to check his wound.

Alexander let one of the soldiers reach the top of the steps before he shot him three times with his revolver. The second one sprang at him, pushing his revolver out of his hand. This man had a thick beard and yellow teeth; he was stocky and fast; he punched Alexander in the face and body and threw him back. Blood ran from his mouth and nose onto his tunic. The drone soldier smiled and swapped his knife into his right hand, then came at him. Alexander braced for the impact and was flung back onto the wooden beams. The drone then pushed himself into a dangerous position and began to use both of his hands to lower his knife into the chest of Alexander. He could not reach his dagger, which was still sheathed on his belt. The drone spat on his victim's face and pushed harder. The blade began to pierce the tunic fabric into the shirt underneath before entering his skin. He used all his strength to keep the man from plunging it deeper, but the attacker was too strong. He knew it was futile, but utilised every last drop to keep it out.

In a split second, the body above him lost its power; an axe had come down on the drone's head, and he was rolled off with ease. Mad Dog stood there. "I have a message from the Major; he needs to cover fire on Oksana's mobile cavalry units. Alexander nodded his head; he was still in the moment of near death, but thanked Mad Dog for saving his life. Before he could add more words, Mad Dog said he must check on the nurses and wounded. With that, he moved off with speed and stealth.

Alexander took a minute to collect himself before gathering more ammunition and moving down from the lookout post. The shelling created plenty of craters, so he placed himself in one with the best viewpoint. Further down, the broken British and Allied square had fragmented into smaller groups as the battle for survival raged. Oksana's mobile units were moving swiftly around the broken squares; wolves, bears with two heads, long limbs, Razor-tooths, Riders of the North, drones, and rebel cavalry covered that part of the battlefield.

Mad Dog arrived with Heidi and the other nurses. They had done well helping the wounded stay alive during the Priestess' attack. Pvt Brown looked up, and Mad Dog and several braves in war paint appeared next to him.

"How is the battle going?"

Mad Dog looked to the skies and back at him. "It is in the hands of the spirits now; we must rejoin it." He then spoke in his native tongue to the braves around him, and they moved.

Heidi patched up John, and he then began to help them move the rest of the wounded into an underground shelter next to a trench section. Heidi kept the rifles over her shoulder; she wanted them to be ready should the drones or the dead return.

Charles was fighting hand-to-hand with his men. Heinz on one side and Sergeant Butcher on the other, waves of wolves broke into their ranks, but volley fire killed many of these beasts, leaving their blood-soaked bodies piling up around the slopes. Using their bayonets and rifles butts as the melee fighting intensified.

On their right flank was drone captain Pavel Grengo. He led his mounted unit towards the broken ranks, but as he did so, Hosah came into their side with his braves, letting out war cries as they smashed into them. Hosah swung his tomahawk across the neck of Captain Grengo, severing an artery; the wound sprayed blood over Hosah, giving his warrior appearance even more menace. Pavel held his hand over the cut and tried to steer his horse away from the attack. He did not get far before being knocked off and lost in the sea of fighting bodies. The other tribes had been swooping around, breaking up the enemy lines.

The dead were still entwined on the battlefield, even with the main herd being led off. The various creatures could no longer be focused on specific positions, the allied forces had spread the battlefield over a large area. Charles tried to keep his men close as they fought. The screams and shouts were engulfed in the bedlam of the chaotic battlefield.

Further across from Corner Mountain, Lev and Priestess Bonnaire brought their forces to join Nazar, but their progress was suddenly halted. Blocking their path was a large array of British cavalries; their numbers did not seem too deep.

Captain Rimmel looked at Lev and then at this impressive force in front of them. "Should we divert from charging them head-on, sire?"

"Are you a fucking coward? He looked at his Priestess. Then, he raised his sword and kicked on his horse. The horde of drones and other mounted Lev soldiers poured forward. As they bore down on the British forces, Lev was shocked to see a wall of Lancers coming from his left-hand side; they ranged from the 17th through to the Bengal lancers, so many regiments. Leading from the front was Captain Kingsbury. The tip of their lances caught the late morning sun. The sheer power of this force and its energy crashed into Lev's cavalry, sending soldiers and horses tumbling to the side. The lancer's impact was huge, swinging the pendulum of Lev's attack. They reached the British cavalry, but their charge had already broken in the direction of the assault.

Lev fought hard, changing in size; he was an imposing sight; using his sword, he smashed riders from their saddles, keeping a close eye on Bonnaire; she had grown in size and was fighting like a processed demon. They were slowly cut off from their main fighting force as they became encircled; her fighting was ferocious, like a wounded animal. Lev tried to steer his horse closer to her, but was caught in a melee of fighting as household cavalry surrounded him, causing him to block several blows.

She let out a wounded scream as a lance pierced through her back. She struggled to stay mounted and fell to the ground; still using her extra human strength, she pulled a British cavalryman off his horse and struck him down with her axe, but this small victory was short-lived, as the other cavalrymen and lancers closed in and unleashed blow after blow. Her eyes looked for Lev as blood came from her mouth and torso. He pushed hard to get to her, knocking over horse and man to clear a path. Two of his mounted drone soldiers helped cover him as he took her in his arms. She looked at him for a moment before her eyes closed. Those two soldiers were soon overwhelmed; as this happened, the British cavalrymen moved aside to reveal Captain Kingsbury.

Lev was broken, but he ran towards Captain Kingsbury, letting rage engulf him. The captain brought his lance up and charged at Lev. He was deadly with a lance, ramming into Lev's chest. Lev still managed to pull Captain Kingsbury off his horse. Lev had lost his sword in the fighting, but was still able to take the axe from the holder on his back. He snapped off the lance sticking out of his chest.

"You will all pay for her death."

Captain Kingsbury rose to his feet. "Your cousin killed my wife and daughter, and I'm going to kill you." This brought a blood-soaked smile from Lev. Arghhhhhh !!

He grabbed the captain and flung him around; as Lev swung his axe towards the captain's face, it was blocked by his sword. The lancers around began to move towards them, but he shouted at them to shield the fight. The dry soil kicked up as they wrestled back and forth, occasionally landing blows, but none were decisive. Lev managed to land a blow in Kingsbury's shoulder whilst feeling the impact of the broken lance; this strike encouraged Lev. He leaned in, "You can now join your wife and daughter." Captain Kingsbury had other ideas, as Lev pressed the axe in harder, he did not see the hand of his foe bring around a knife, which was struck into his neck. It's the blow that ended the Lev's onslaught. Robert Kingsbury lowered Lev to the ground; he kept eye contact; he was feeling his wound, but wanted to see Lev pass. When his eyes finally closed, Robert collapsed onto Lev. The fighting was still raging around them, but the captain was lifted onto a horse with a rider and moved off the battlefield.

Chapter 54

The drones that had seen the fall of Lev and his Priestess rode on to inform Nazar. When they caught up to him, Nazar was standing next to his horse, dripping in blood. He drank from a Bota bag, letting the wine fall out of his mouth and onto his blood-soaked clothes.

"You better tell me he is close."

The two drone soldiers felt sick. Neither could answer.

One of them finally spoke up: "He's been killed, sire."
Those were his last words. Nazar had withdrawn his sword and decapitated both of them as they stood there. With their heads lying freshly on the ground, Nazar turned to General Georgiy.
"The battle has spread because of his incompetence".

Nazar was muttering to himself with gritted teeth as he mounted his horse.

"He deserved his death for stupidity."

General Georgiy chose his words carefully, as he knew the wrong tone or wording would see his head next to the drone soldiers.
"Should we re-group and gather information on our fighting armies?"

"There is no time. We have the numbers, but our forces are spread across the battlefield."

He paused and drank again out of his bota.

"Ride back to the camp and make sure we have everything at the front. Also, ask Priestess Arnoult to ensure Major Hayward's wife and daughter are right up at the front. Nazar had his destroyer drones clear an area around him.

Captain Somersett had moved his unit closer to the destroyer drones as they pushed closer to Major Hayward's unit. He saw his chance to advance with a handful of men; by his side were Sergeant Jackson and Private Johnson. They fought past rebels, wolves, cavalry, and bayonets, saving them from the dead. Mason Somersett led from the front. A bullet nicked his thigh, causing him to pause; with his men in close attention, he pressed forward. The destroyer drones were a different story; their size and fighting skills more than matched Mason Somersett and his men, but they eventually broke through Nazar's lines. They were weary and battered but determined. Nazar looked over at them; he almost smiled, then charged.

He was fuelled by his brother's death and eager to unleash his pent-up hate; the first couple of soldiers felt the power from Nazar. Their efforts to stop him were wasted; he pushed through, killing and maiming as he went along. He came to Sergeant Jackson, blood-soaked and full of rage. The Sergeant lunged at him, catching his side; Nazar let out a roar but swung around with his left hand, which, in his changed shape, was more like a claw.

Grabbing at the sergeant's neck and holding him aloft, he almost wanted to show what lay ahead for those who stood in his way. Captain Somerset jabbed at a destroyer drone as he tried to get to his sergeant. Private Johnson was fighting a flesh-eater and a wolf; the dead drone tried to bite his arm and kept moving closer despite the blows to the body. The wolf kept its eyes on Pvt Johnson; it lowered its head, bringing its ears back, just waiting for that moment. As the flesh-eater came in at his side, he spun and rammed his bayonet into the dead soldier's head; at that moment, the teeth of the beast sank into his leg. The sharp pain was nauseating; it shook its head violently. It only eased when a soldier next to him shot the wolf in the head.

Nazar brought his hunting knife around and into Sergeant Jackson. He watched his eyes slowly close before tossing him aside. Captain Somersett was a second too late; Nazar looked down at the dead sergeant and smiled at Captain Somersett. They charged into each other, slashing and cutting what they could. Mason Somersett was a strong man and used that strength to push Nazar backwards, but in his half-human, half-creature form, you would need much more than just strength to beat him. Pvt Johnson tried to move forward with the remaining men around him, but the destroyer drones were tough and fought vigorously.

As the battle evolved, the pockets of fighting groups tried to get closer to each other. Charles Hayward could see Captain Somersett fighting against this formidable foe, punching and kicking, biting where he could. He felt a lump in his throat at the bravery around him as he fought to keep those around him and himself alive.

Captain Somersett managed to get his bayonet into Nazar and swiftly brought the butt of his rifle around to knock this devil back. Nazar had felt the sharpness of his bayonet in his stomach, wiped the blood from his mouth, and licked his hand. "You have fought excellently, but it is not enough". Nazar moved forward with his sword, swinging it high and bringing it down hard on Mason Somersett's rifle, splitting it in two and allowing the blade to come down on his head. His eyes looked at Nazar, and he tried to reach for him one last time before being cast aside.

Nazar did not focus any more energy on the remaining fighting soldiers under Captain Somersett. Pvt Johnson used his strength and skill to guide those around him to keep close ranks and beat off those attacking them. The destroyer drones moved more with Nazar as he ventured back towards several priests carrying flags. He knew what they were bringing him. Amongst them was Priestess Arnoult, and alongside her on a horse was Rebecca, with Emily sitting behind her.

He was happy to see them arrive, as the destroyer drones formed a protective square around them. Nazar wiped some of the blood from his face before moving closer to Rebecca and laughing, "This is war."

She turned her head away from him.

"Priestess Arnoult, bring them down from the horse. Major Hayward will pay the ultimate price today."

Rebecca screamed at her not to touch Emily; she begged Nazar to spare at least her daughter. At that moment, he was distracted, and Oksana and her close guard were moving through a mass of fighting bodies. They were under heavy attack from the Arapaho Indians and the Comanche. Sioux and Apache came in from the other side. Many more tribes were attacking the dead, drones, and long limbs. It was causing havoc amongst the priests trying to lead a uniformed attack.

Nazar shouted for his horse, wanting to be closer to Oksana as her fighting units came under heavy attack. Just as he began to steer his horse away, Priestess Arnoult asked what she should do with the prisoners.

"Kill them, kill them both." He then moved his horse and elite guard towards Oksana.

Eveline brought herself closer to Rebecca. "I'm going to make you watch".

She dismounted and handed the reins to a drone soldier. The fighting around them started to break into pockets as the majority of the destroyer drones went with Nazar. They were on slightly higher ground. Rebecca looked in the distance to see if she could see Charles or his men, but alas, the mixture of bodies was too dense.

Eveline snatched at Emily, who clung to her mother for dear life, her hands dug into the fabric of Rebecca's top she was wearing. It was not enough; Eveline dragged her through the soil, and as she did so, Rebecca rolled herself onto the ground below. The thud made the priestess look up; her instinct was to laugh at the predicament of Rebecca crumpled in an unceremonious heap.

"At least get to your fucking feet to watch her die."

Rebecca was in tears as she did so. "Please, Eveline, you do not have to do this. You will have children one day. Please do not do this."

Eveline looked at Rebecca before reaching to her belt to bring out a dagger.

"This world is not meant for your kind anymore. I am helping you."

"No, Eveline, you are destroying everything in this world."

Eveline could see Rebecca moving towards her and ordered two drones to hold her. Kicking and fighting like a wounded animal, they managed to pin her down and raise her head towards Emily. She looked up and stopped fighting. At that moment, she wanted to support her daughter in the only way she could. "I love you, Emily."

Emily cried out her love for her mother as Eveline brought the blade up to her throat and began to cut. Eveline looked at Rebecca with darkness in her eyes, but this was the last thing she saw. An arrow pierced her left eye socket; she stood for a moment and then fell to the side. The drones holding Rebecca let go of her to assist the prestress. Rebecca moved forward on her knees. "Emily, please stay with me, sweet child." Blood was coming down her neck, but the wound hadn't struck an artery, as it had been stopped just in time.

Breaking through the ranks was a mixture of braves; amongst them was Arthur. He tried to reach them, but a large pocket of the dead moved across his path. He began to fight with all his might to clear a way to them. Rebecca saw the dead moving their way. With her hands still tied, she moved closer to Emily to protect her. "Whatever happens, we will be together; you're so brave." They put their heads together; Rebecca kissed her on the forehead and tried frantically to pull at the rope which tied her hands. "Mother, lie down, and I will crawl on top of you; the dead do not like me."

Having no choice, Rebecca laid down and let Emily lie on top of her; sure enough, the dead moved past them and focused on the 10th Cavalrymen who had been under the command of Captain Somersett.

This surge of extra youthful fighters on horseback was turning the battle alongside the different tribes; their skill and effectiveness from the saddle had split Nazar forces, his officers had tried to push for decisive victories against the allied forces, the defensive high points had cost them many soldiers, and now they were split across a large area, the communication was struggling to get to the officers who were left, allowing the cavalry and mounted Indians to cause havoc.

Nazar reached Oksana and helped protect her right flank. She rode over close to him, saying, "My lord, should we regroup? The battle is swinging in the enemy's favour."

He was not thinking straight, muttering under his breath and cursing everything. "Hayward and his family are to blame for this; he destroyed my source of power." Oksana sensed he was lost in his thoughts. "There is another rock, remember!! We can locate it and rebuild our armies before finishing America."

A message arrived that Priestess Arnoult had been killed, and Hayward's wife was still alive. Nazar struggled to sit in his saddle, lifting himself up and down. "Oksana, bring me her head."

She looked at him anxiously. He was no longer thinking straight; he was letting his rage take over him. She also knew it would not be the time to question his judgement. She took half the cavalry units near her and set off to where the flags were.

As she rode to kill Rebecca, her forces came under attack from the different Indian tribes around them. They fought like wild animals and were such a formidable foe. The rebels and drone cavalry started to break ranks; some even fled the battlefield. A female priest next to her fell from her horse, holding an arrow in her neck. Two braves came at Oksana; she fought them back, wounded one and knocked the other off their horse. She did not try to engage anymore. Instead, she carried on to where the flags had been placed in the ground. The dead had been killed or moved onto another target. Oksana clamped her eyes on Rebecca; she was getting to her feet, and her hands were no longer tied.

"Rebecca!"

She looked around and saw Oksana coming through the fighting figures.

"Emily hid by the fallen horses." She scuttled off to do as her mother said.

Oksana dismounted from her horse.

"I need your pretty head." She unclipped her robe and moved forward, taking out her sword. Rebecca did not have a weapon and realised she needed to arm herself quickly. A spear was sticking out of a dead flesh-eater's head. This was the first thing nearest her, so she grabbed it and pulled it out.

"Nice, a spear from these primitive people."

"They are turning the tide of this battle, Oksana; why don't you take your emperor and leave America whilst you can?"

Rebecca raised the spear towards Oksana. Several of her guards fought to keep a circle around them.

"I could order them to kill you, but the pleasure should be mine."

Oksana was larger in her beast form; she was powerful and would be difficult to beat.

She came at Rebecca, bringing the sword towards her head. Rebecca used the spear to block the blow, which split the wood. Oksana laughed, "I like your courage. I would have kept you as my personal slave, but I must bring your head to the emperor."

Rebecca dropped the lower, broken part of the wooden spear. It now resembled a Zulu spear. Close to where she had pulled the spear from the flesh-eater, Rebecca saw an Arapaho shield. She quickly bent down and placed it onto her left arm. She even bashed her spear against the shield. Charles had talked about the fearsome Zulu warriors and how they would intimidate their foes.

"Ha, do you think that works with me?"

She came at her again, moving at ease and swinging the sword skillfully. When she did land blows, it was slightly rebuffed with the shield, and Rebecca even managed to cut Oksana's arm, causing her to look a little shocked. She retaliated by pushing her sword through the shield, which consisted mainly of animal skins; they grappled around, with Oksana kicking Rebecca in her side and leg. She brought the sword handle around, hitting the side of Rebeca's head. Blood instantly flowed down from the wound. This encouraged Oksana to increase the attack, breaking the shield and knocking her to the ground. Oksana plunged the sword forward into Rebecca; it was partially blocked before finding its way into the side of her ribs. Rebecca had turned her body, meaning the sword had gone through the skin to the side of her ribs. She let out a cry of pain; Emily raised herself from the fallen horses as Oksana looked over at her and pulled the sword out.

"I will have her head alongside yours, mother and daughter. This makes me happy."

Oksana leaned into Rebecca, "I thought you would have fought harder for your daughter; still, the outcome would have been the same." She let herself become more human as she stood over her. The Priestess' beautiful features and piercing eyes were more apparent as she leaned in and kissed Rebecca on the lips before stepping back and raising her sword. "You should have joined us."

Rebecca did not wait any longer and brought the spear off the ground and into Oksana's chest. Oksana still managed to bring the sword down, but not with the same accuracy and power, meaning it came into Rebecca's shoulder. Oksana staggered backwards before sitting back and pulling out the sword. The guards around her were struggling to contain the braves who were breaking their lines. A drone soldier near Oksana bent down to aid her. She muttered something to him, and he raised his rifle towards Rebecca, who was still half perched on the ground. She could only look in their direction before a bullet hit her in the chest. Emily screamed and raced to be with her mother. Oksana had collapsed back onto the ground; the soldiers around her picked her up and placed her on a horse before setting off to Nazar.

Emily hugged her mother and cried over her still body, but she felt a hand rub her arm. "Keep low, Emily; they might shoot again." "Oksana has been carried off by her soldiers." Emily could see her mother was wounded in her ribs and shoulder, but she could not understand how the bullet that hit her in the chest had not killed her. Rebecca raised herself slowly, then put her hand inside her top. "I kept this close; it was the picture of their family, and the closed case had a bullet dent." Emily was crying with joy, and so was Rebecca.

"We must move from the battlefield. The fighting still happened around them, but it had cleared in pockets. Several riders veered their way, and Emily reached for a revolver on the ground to give to her weary mother. "It's okay, they're Arapaho. Riding amongst them were Arthur and Hosah. He could not hide his happiness at seeing them both alive. He came alongside them and was joined by several braves with an extra horse. They could see that Rebecca was wounded. Mad Dog quickly slid off his horse and helped Arthur lift her up. A large Indian brave held Rebecca in place as Emily was hoisted up to sit before her brother. Hosah said they would send riders with them to Naomi and the others, where Rebecca and Emily could be helped. Arthur spoke to Hosah and promised to return to the battle. They then set off at speed.

The news arrived to Nazar via the personal guard of Oksana. He gave orders to the officers who were left and the priests who gathered by his side. On seeing her body come back slumped in the arms of a destroyer drone, he stopped giving his battle plans and dismounted; his legs went weary at what his eyes were seeing. He staggered over to the soldier and let him lower her body into his arms. She was holding on to life as he sat back on the ground. "Did she do this? How could she beat you?" His voice was trembling with rage and sadness. Her voice was soft, and her skin was almost grey; Oksana had lost a lot of blood. "We shot her!" This brought a smile to his face.

"My time is not long for this world." She mustered the strength to pull him in close to kiss him. "I love you, my king." Nazar felt a tear roll off his cheek and onto her face. "I love you, Oksana; I will avenge you and destroy them all." Oksana's grip began to loosen, and her eyes slowly closed.

"Please stay with me. We can conquer the world. Please stay with me." She passed away in his arms.

Instead of an instant rage, he lowered her to the grass below his feet. The officers and priests around him stayed still. No one dared move or say a word. He then raised himself to his feet. "Where is General Georgiy? His counsel is desperately needed in my moment of despair."

A young officer stepped forward. "My lord, Major Hayward's engineers have been separated from the main regiment on the slope."

"Good, bring me my horse. Also, sound the advance on the slopes of Rattlesnake Butte."

Once mounted, he moved his units with him to confront Major Hayward and his men.

Chapter 55

Major Hayward moved as many of his men into a circle. There were some stragglers from other regiments; even Pvt Johnson and several of the 10th cavalrymen had made it to them. They were holding their own as the British lancers continued to raid the enemy ranks; the American Indians were turning the tide of the battle.

Nazar had lost so many soldiers while attacking the mountains and other defensive locations; he had also lost most of the flesh-eaters. While they were still out there, he did not know if he could bring them back into the battle. The surge of soldiers coming their way indicated to Charles that Nazar was coming. They managed to get four to five ammunition boxes to them, and as the dead, long-limbs, drone soldiers, and rebels advanced on them, those extra bullets would prove invaluable.

Sergeant Butcher and Corporal Heinz stood by his side, bayonets in the air. They glanced at each other. "He's coming," Charles said under his breath. The moving wave of different creatures and humans flooded towards them. Sergeant Butcher told them to close ranks and hold firm. When it hit, men were flung in the air like ragdolls. A razor-back came snapping in from one of the sides; its weight and ferocity were hard to stop; behind him was a long limb; it lurched at Major Hayward but felt the cold steel on Sergeant Butcher's bayonet through its neck. Corporal Heinz was picking his shots, trying to kill as many of the enemy as they came on mass at them. When the main surge pushed into the circle of kaki-dressed British Engineers, they split even further away from each other. Sergeant Butcher was still close to Major Hayward, but a sea of fighting bodies surrounded him. He did not see Nazar coming at first, but as the allied soldiers in his path were dispatched with clinical precision, it indicated a powerful force was heading his way. Charles bashed and knocked back the enemy soldiers as they came at him. His rifle and bayonet were his lifeline. Then his eyes fell upon Nazar; there was a split second where Nazar almost stopped; the battle had cost him his brother and his Queen, and it was almost a moment for him to reflect on it before charging at Charles.

Sergeant Butcher rushed in, getting a strong lunge with his bayonet, catching Nazar across his side, but he had anticipated it and swung his sword, pushing it away before bringing it across. Sergeant Butcher wounded him and kicked him to the ground; Nazar didn't stop coming forward. An Engineer shot him in the shoulder, but was run through by Nazar's sword. Two more came at him and were dispatched with ease. Charles steadied himself; his sword was still not drawn as he lowered his rifle towards Nazar.

Nazar drew closer to Charles, smashing through his own soldiers to get to him; he ran directly towards him. Charles waited until it was the right moment before thrusting his bayonet into his chest. Nazar did not try to avoid this. Instead, he placed his right hand on the rifle and pulled Charles in close.

"I've waited so long to meet you on the battlefield." He did not bring his sword around to strike Charles. Charles stood back as the fighting continued around them. Nazar stood there for a second, holding the rifle, which he then let fall to the soil below.

"Draw your sword."

Charles did just that. "You can still end this war, Nazar."

He smiled, "You know your wife killed Oksana." He paused, "That is why she had to die."

Charles felt an instant loss of control and charged at him. He swung his sword at Nazar's head and body, but both were blocked and parried away. "You'll have to do better than that, Major."

Nazar then swung his sword, pushing back Charles, who had to be alert and defensive as each blow arrived with malice. Nazar's size and power were dominant. Using his left fist, he punched Charles in the face before bringing his left knee into his body. Blood flowed from his nose and mouth, but Charles held onto his sword despite the beating he was getting. He momentarily wanted to let him finish him, and he could then join Rebecca, whether she was.

"Even if I lose this battle, it is not over; I will re-group and come again."

Charles gingerly got to his feet.

"Your fixation with me has cost you everything! I'm glad it helped you lose so much." Wiping blood from his mouth. Nazar swiftly moved closer again, this time bringing the sword across Charles's mid-riff, slicing through his tunic. He had tried to block it, but he was too quick. He waited again for Charles to get to his feet. This time, Charles tried a different manoeuvre, which succeeded in slicing the legs of Nazar, causing him to let out a yelp in pain.

"Bravo, at least you had something." He did not see Corporal Heinz come from behind and dig his bayonet into his shoulder. This caused an instant reaction from Nazar, plunging his sword into Cpl Heinz. He then kicked him off it and let him fall to the ground. Charles let out a roar and came at him with all his strength; the sword fight was furious; Nazar was more skillful, but the attack from Cpl Heinz had distracted him. Charles kicked Nazar back and managed to bring his sword up into his ribcage before pushing it up and through whilst maintaining eye contact. Nazar lowered his head towards Charles, "Now that was worthy." He then brought his dagger into Charles's side; the impact was enough to cause him to lose grip of his sword and stagger backwards.

Nazar then slowly withdrew the sword from his chest whilst looking at his foe, half slumped against the bloodied dirt and grass below. "It's time, Major." He brought up his sword into the air. Charles looked at Corporal Heinz, who was lying close to him. Sergeant Butcher was struggling against two destroyer drones, as were the Engineers around him. He knew if Nazar escaped, he would rebuild; he felt all was lost.

He closed his eyes and waited.

At that moment, war cries surrounded that area of the battlefield. Hosah, leading the Arapaho, unleashed arrows into Nazar and his destroyer drones around him. It was enough to stop the final blow from being struck. With arrows sticking out of him, he caught a brave as he rode past, pulling him from his horse and biting into his neck before tossing him aside. Another threw a spear, but missed as Nazar ducked this projectile.

Mad Dog hurled himself into the destroyer drones around the wounded Sergeant Butcher. He had two tomahawks and lived up to his name with a frenzied attack on those around him. Little Bear brought his horse across Nazar's path before Nazar chopped at the horse's legs, causing it to fall. Little Bear engaged in an attack with his spear but was shot in the back by a drone and then stabbed in the chest by Nazar.

Hosah steered his horse around to get closer to Nazar. His horse reared up onto its hind legs, and Hosah fired an arrow into Nazar's cheek; this increased his anger, and Nazar came under the horse and lifted it over, pinning Hosah underneath.

The fighting was manic; two braves pushed back into Nazar, stopping him from finishing off Hosah with his sword. He struck down one of the braves before knocking the other onto destroyer drones who were by his side; he then moved with purpose to finish Hosah. Putting his foot onto the horse, he did not get time to raise his sword as Charles came in at his side. Nazar picked up Charles and hurled him over to Hosah; he landed close by and was winded by the action. Hosah tried to pull his leg from under the horse, but it seemed in vain, as he was stuck fast.

There was a deep, bellowing laugh as Nazar picked up an axe from a fallen Rider of the North. "You lost Major Hayward." Charles looked over at his sword and gathered what energy he had left to reach towards it. A white horse flashed before them as he closed in with his axe. An arrow flung into this fearsome warrior's chest, and then another into his side. He looked around for the rider, and as he clocked his eyes on the young warrior, he found himself falling back with Arthur on top of him. Arthur managed to stab him once before easily turned over. He started to squeeze his neck; Arthur's eyes began to close.

A sharp pain stopped Nazar; he looked around with blood coming from his mouth as the sword was withdrawn from his throat. Charles was standing over him. "It ends." With that, he brought the sword down and decapitated Nazar's head. The huge frame took a few seconds before it fell to the side; the fighting was still ongoing around them. A bloodied, weak Charles pulled Arthur up; there wasn't time to say more than thank you for his bravery as the battle raged on. Charles moved over to Hosah, and with Arthur's help, they pulled him free.

Charles tried to gather those around him, but he did not have time to celebrate the death of this dark lord; he did not feel a great relief which he thought he would.

"Father, mother, and Emily are still alive." Which brought a look of hope to his eyes.

"We must fall back up the slopes."

The news broke that Nazar was dead, and it had a demoralising effect on the enemy force. There was no Oksana or Lev to rally them. The allied cavalry harassed the enemy soldiers, and the beasts amongst them started to be picked off. His vast army had taken such heavy casualties and, without leadership, started to split up. As they started to leave the battlefield, the allied cannons began to pound them. Some of the rebels surrendered, whilst the other drones ran.

The priests who were left continued to fight. Hagen was there with a mixture of soldiers, taking the fight to them. One of them was James Smith, Tom's brother, who had fought across Europe and ended up fighting in this battle. He was handy with a sword and revolver, which meant they could tackle the male and female priests who were left. Captain Kingsbury's lancers surrounded the last of this group and asked if they wished to surrender. They chose to fight on and were quickly dispatched.

Hosah and Arthur helped Charles as they stretchered Cpl Heinz up the slopes; Mad Dog guided along Sergeant Butcher. Little Bear had not survived his wounds in the fight with Nazar. There wasn't much time to re-group as the fighting was still ongoing; even with the battlefield thinning, news being brought to Major Hayward, the flesh-eater horde was returning to the battlefield. Priests were not leading them; this was the herd following the sound of the battle and the hunger for food. This army of dead would not turn the battle now, but it meant the remaining allied forces would have to leave the lower slopes and save as many of the wounded as possible before the dead came to feast on them.

The Lancers and Native American Indians were doing exceptionally well at picking off the retreating enemy; it meant the other soldiers could help those around them. Some had been sent to slow down the advancing dead, but they did not have great numbers of artillery shells left after the remaining shells had been used to target the retreating Nazar forces.

Charles reached the top of Rattlesnake Butte. He looked at Arthur and saw a boy who had become a warrior and helped save his life. Heidi was there with the other army surgeons and nurses to help the wounded. On the other side of the butte, wagons were brought behind it to help move the injured soldiers to the mountains, where camps were set up. The casualties had been high; fighting a large army dictated it that way.

Hagen was gathering a few more soldiers to help slow the herd. Pvt Johnson stepped forward, battered and bruised. Hagen thanked him for his courage and the others who volunteered to help those already on the frontline. Arthur said he would come. Charles looked over at him, but Hagen was the one to speak up.

"Take your father to your mother and sister; we will meet you there."

The next hour was spent moving as many of the wounded as possible. The dust cloud gave away the impending threat from the dead.

It took a while before they reached the base camp. Charles was helped down from the wagon, and so were Sergeant Butcher and Cpl Heinz. They were taken to make-shift tents and had their wounds treated. Arthur said he would be back shortly. He walked over to where his mother and Emily were. Naomi was helping treat her wounds; Arthur came forward and kissed Naomi on the lips. She hugged and let tears of joy fall down her cheeks. Crying behind her was Rebecca. "Is he alive?" Arthur nodded his head. She beckoned him in and winced as she hugged him. Emily also hugged him.

Rebecca was helped to her feet, and Arthur and Naomi helped her walk over to Charles' tent. Her eyes fell upon her husband, and she couldn't help but smile. Charles slowly brought himself up.

"You had that sparkle in your eyes when we first met," Rebecca said as she leaned in to kiss him on his lips. They continued to kiss passionately until Arthur cleared his throat. Emily lurched forward and hugged her dad, which allowed Arthur to do the same. It was a feeling of relief and happiness.

"I love you all." Pulling them all together with his arms.

Tom came in with Florence, and seeing them all together made him smile. They spent time talking, and news circulated around the camp that Nazar was dead. The enemy was broken; it would be hard for them to reform now. The real problem was the flesh-eaters and other creatures that Nazar had brought with him.

On the battlefield, the thin line repeated volley fire and moved slowly backwards. The Walking Dead moved forward in a line over a mile or so. The depth was unknown as it carried on to the distance. Some of the drone soldiers, who had been infected and died in the fighting, were coming to life behind them. Hagen had two axes and tied his hair back. He took on these with Pvt Johnson. They fought hard to stop the dead, cutting off the retreating line. Hagen swung his axe into two dead rebels as they moved to bite him. He brought the axe into each of their heads, in and out. Soon, though, they were seeing an increase in the dead coming from the battlefield. "You're a good man, Matthew, now run. There are too many now."

Pvt John looked at him." I've been running all my life. I'm not leaving you today." Hagen nodded and then started banging his axes together; this meant the dead that were slowly getting up came their way. The other line had to retreat off the battlefield as the dead now moved in on Hagen and Pvt Johnson.

Pvt Johnson used his rifle to push back the dead. He picked up a Winchester off a dead US cavalryman and began unleashing shot after shot on the dead. The smell of the thousands of decaying bodies was overpowering.

The numbers were now causing a problem; Hagen was kicking and punching, and every punch was for the family he had lost and his homeland. Pvt Johnson was almost knocked to the ground by three flesh-eaters, but Hagen threw them off and kept swinging his axe. He let out a cry and shouted to Valhalla for a good death.

They stood back-to-back, and with a last bullet in Matthew's rifle, he faced the dead.

A shout went up; Elin was coming through the ever-increasing dead from the battlefield. She rode to them with horses tied to her saddle. There were two British soldiers with her, James and Isac, Tom's brothers. They were in full British uniform. Both had Martini-Henry rifles, and the thunderous shots smacked through the dead. Elin rode around and told Pvt Johnson and Hagen to mount up quickly. They did just that and managed to flee the battlefield as the horde started to engulf the whole area; as they rode higher, they could see the sheer extent of the flesh-eaters' numbers. It was mind-numbing and hard to take in.

Elin brought her horse in close to Hagen. "I'll decide if it's your time to leave me." She said with a smile and kissed Hagen. They met with the other soldiers and made their way back to the camp.

When they arrived, they were greeted with helmets lifted in the air. In the hills around them and rising to the mountains were tepees. The great tribes of America would play a massive part in their survival now; they would have to move in the same way as the nomadic life of the American Indians did. Avoiding the enormous herds of dead and other creatures roaming different parts of America.

Rebecca went to Elin and Hagen. She was happy to see him alive, as he had helped save her children all those years ago. They were joined by John and Heidi, who kissed each other out of sheer happiness to be alive.

"Pvt Brown," a voice rang out. Sergeant Butcher was standing there with a ready-made crutch. His family joined him. "You did well today, soldier." John went to thank him and speak to his family.

Hosah came over to them with Mad Dog and Little Feet. They were to Charles to check on him.

"I cannot begin to thank you for what you have done for us and your people. You have saved the world from a darkness that would have destroyed it."

Hosah smiled. "We must all work them together. The great plains have changed, and one day, that darkness may return." Hosah whispered something in Charles's ear. He looked hopeful, even tearful. The plan was to ride to a medicine man in the Black Mountains. There had been stories of him helping those who had been partially infected and not changed. There was hope that Emily could be saved from turning into a flesh-eater.

Charles called Rebecca over. Rebecca could not hide her emotions, letting tears run down her face. Emily went to comfort her and held her hand. Rebecca rubbed the side of her cheek. "I love you, Emily," she said, bringing a wide grin to her face.

Arthur looked for Hosah; he had just mounted up. "How can we thank you for all that you have done?"

"There are many more battles to be fought; you can thank me when this ends."

Arthur nodded and cleared his throat. "You gave me the courage and skills to save my family. I will never forget that."

Hosah smiled. "Young warrior, it was always there."

He spoke to some of the other braves before riding to Rebecca and Charles and told them they would leave in a few days for the Black Mountains.

Tom was sitting next to Florence on a rock; their view in front of them was the sprawling great plains, and smoke was rising from the battle that had taken place. The giant dust cloud was moving east, giving the survivors time to heal and move to their next safe haven. Tom saw two soldiers riding into the camp wearing British khaki uniforms. He did not recognise either of them at first glance, but when it dawned on him that it was his brothers, he leapt from the rock and ran towards them. Their eyes lit up on seeing their little brother, and they dismounted as quickly as possible. Both brothers engaged him, taking turns lifting and hugging him tight. There were tears of laughter and joy. Tom took them to meet Florence and then led them to meet their mother.

Reunions were happening all over the camp, but as with any battle, there was also despair over loved ones lost. Heidi was tending to Cpl Heinz, whom Sergeant Butcher and Charles visited. He looked perkier, but he knew it would be a while before he was moving around freely. John Brown joined Heidi and the others.

"We did it. After all those years of running and fighting, we finally did it." Heidi stepped forward and kissed him on the lips.

John bent to one knee and looked up at Heidi with tears in his eyes. "You have saved my life on many occasions. Would you do me the honour of becoming my wife?" She burst into tears and rushed forward to hug and kiss him repeatedly. The others around them cheered and clapped.

Emily stroked some of the horses that had returned from battle, and Charles saw Rebecca sitting, looking at her. He made his way over to his wife slowly and helped her stand. Charles held Rebecca in his arms. "I did not think we would see this day." She brought her hands over his. "If the medicine man can help Emily, I." She could not say anything more. Charles kissed the back of the head. "I will pray to god he can."

The next day saw pockets of rebels surrendering to the Allied forces. Nazar's remaining priests and generals were reportedly retreating. Spies said they were bound for Europe. A rumour was only whispered around the camps that there was another meteor somewhere in Asia that the priests wanted to use to build another army. Charles did not concern himself with this. There were enough problems to deal with in America. Canada was struggling with the refugees from America, and those who went south to Mexico saw the same problems. The dead had infected people in South America, and it was causing problems across the South.

For now, they would live the same way as the Native American Indians and learn to be at peace with the land.

The weeks passed, and only time would tell if the herbs, spiritual dances, and rituals would work for Emily. A telling point for Rebecca was when they were out gathering food, and a flesh-eater appeared, a dishevelled drone who had turned and wandered towards them. The fact that he went for Emily before Little Feet hit it with an arrow made Rebecca smile joyfully. Emily was looking better each day and was learning how to fire an arrow and build a tepee.

When she returned to their winter camp, she broke the news to Charles about what had happened with Emily. He brought her in close.

"Our prayers have been answered."

"For now, my love, but our children will have to face that darkness again one day."

Charles kissed her. "We'll make sure they'll be ready."

Printed in Dunstable, United Kingdom